I STEPPED FORWARD, WATCHING THE CREATURE climb to its feet as it loosed a low, dangerous-sounding growl.

I held both of my arms out and willed weapons into my open palms. The twin Khopesh swords appeared out of nothing in a flash of shimmering light. The curving silver blades glinted brightly. I glanced over at Will. I could now see intricate black tattoos twisting out from beneath his shirt all the way down his right arm to his knuckles. I remembered the beautiful symbols woven into the spiraling design, because I'd seen them before with different eyes, in another time.

COURTNEY ALLISON MOULTON

Angelfire

 KATHERINE TEGEN BOOKS
An Imprint of HarperCollinsPublishers

Katherine Tegen Books is an imprint of HarperCollins Publishers.

Angelfire

Library of Congress Cataloging-in-Publication Data

Moulton, Courtney Allison, date

Angelfire / Courtney Allison Moulton. — 1st ed.

p. cm.

Summary: A seventeen-year-old girl discovers she has the reincarnated soul of an ancient warrior destined to battle the reapers— monstrous creatures who devour humans and send their souls to Hell.

ISBN 978-0-06-200235-8

[1. Reincarnation—Fiction. 2. Soul—Fiction. 3. Angels—Fiction.] I. Title.

PZ7.M85899An 2011   2010012821

[Fic]—dc22   CIP

                                                                AC

Typography by Joel Tippie

14 15 LP/RRDC 10 9 8 7 6 5 4

❖

First paperback edition, 2012

For my mother,
who never for a single instant
stopped believing in me

Angelfire

1

I STARED OUT THE CLASSROOM WINDOW AND longed for freedom, wanting to be anywhere in the world other than gaping up at my economics teacher like the rest of my classmates. The last time I had listened to him, Mr. Meyer had been lecturing about fiscal policy, and that was when he'd lost me. My eyes rolled over to my best friend, Kate Green, who was doodling intricate flowers all over her notes and looked like she was thoroughly entertaining herself. Meanwhile, I was reduced to staring at the wiry, gray chest hair puffing out at the collar of Mr. Meyer's polo shirt like overgrown steel wool and wondering whether he'd ever considered waxing.

Finally, after another tedious twenty minutes, the bell rang at two thirty and I leaped to my feet, instantly energized. Kate stuffed her papers into her notebook and followed me up the aisle between the desks. The other seniors and a handful of juniors all filed out swiftly, as if they'd only been given a five-second window to escape or they would never get out alive.

"Miss Monroe?" Mr. Meyer called after me just before I left the room.

I turned to Kate. "Your locker in five?"

She nodded and left the room with the rest of the students until I was left alone with our teacher. Mr. Meyer smiled from behind his thick eyeglasses and beckoned me over to his desk.

I took a deep breath, having a pretty good idea of what this discussion might be about. "Yes, sir?"

His smile was warm and friendly, his coarse, gray beard wrinkling around his thin lips. He pushed his glasses back up his nose. "So last week's quiz didn't go very well, did it?"

I braced myself. "No, sir."

He tilted his head up at me. "Last year in my civics class you were doing very well, but the last few months of class, your grades began to slip. Since school began this year, they're worsening. I want to see you succeed, Ellie."

"I know, Mr. Meyer," I said. Excuses ran through my head. In truth, I was distracted. Distracted by college applications. Distracted by my parents' constant fighting. Distracted by the nightmares I experienced every single night. Of course, I wasn't going to talk to my economics teacher about my issues. They weren't any of his business. So I gave him a vague response in return. "I'm sorry. I've been distracted. There's a lot that's happened in the last year."

He leaned forward, digging his elbows into the cluttered desk. "I understand the senioritis thing. College, friends, Homecoming, boys . . . There are countless things grabbing your attention from every angle. You've got to stay focused on what's really important."

"I know," I said glumly. "Thank you."

"And I don't mean just schoolwork," he continued. "Life is going to test you in ways it never has before. Don't let your future change the good person you are or make you forget who you are. You're a nice girl, Ellie. I've enjoyed having you in my classes."

"Thanks, Mr. Meyer," I said with an honest smile.

He sat back in his chair. "This class isn't so hard. I know if you just apply yourself a little more, you'll get through it. My class is nothing compared to what's out there in the real world. I know you can do this."

I nodded, assuming he saved this speech for everyone who got a D on a twenty-question quiz, but he spoke with such sincerity that I wanted to fall for it. "Thanks for believing in me."

"I don't say this to everyone whose grades start to fall," he said, as if reading my mind. "I mean it. I believe in you. Just don't forget to believe in yourself, okay?"

I smiled wider. "Thanks. See you tomorrow?"

"I'll be here," he said, rising weakly to his feet. "Your

birthday is coming up, right?"

I gave him a puzzled look. "Yeah, how'd you know? Do you want me to bring cupcakes to pass around or something?"

He laughed. "No, no. Unless you really want to, I mean, be my guest. But, happy birthday, Miss Monroe."

"Thanks, sir." I smiled and gave him a polite wave before turning away. As I left the classroom, I couldn't help thinking that speech was a little heavy for an economics teacher about to retire to Arizona.

I found Kate by her locker. She frowned at me as I walked up to her.

"What did Meyer want?"

I shrugged. "He wants me to apply myself more."

She smiled. "Well, I think you're perfect."

"Thanks," I said, laughing. "Are you coming straight over to study for Thursday's math test?"

She shook her head and pulled her blond hair over one shoulder as she dug her backpack out of her locker. "I'm going tanning first," she said.

"Why? It's September and you still look like you hang out at the beach all day." I bumped her shoulder with mine and grinned. Her skin was a glorious golden tone, but I still teased her that she'd end up looking like the other orange Barbie dolls at school if she kept going.

"I'm determined not to get pasty this winter like you always do." Kate was very pretty, and even when she scowled she looked glamorous. She was also almost a head taller than me, but that wasn't a huge feat. I was a couple of inches shorter than most of the girls my age.

"I'm not pasty." I glanced down at my arm sneakily so she wouldn't notice. I wasn't *that* pasty.

"This dazzling skin isn't easy to achieve, you know." She stroked her collarbone for effect and laughed.

I stuck my tongue out at her before we moved on to my own locker. I dumped my bio book inside and stuffed my lit materials into my bag to take home. My paper on *Hamlet* was due the next week, so I needed to get started on it. A thud against the locker next to mine made me look up.

Landon Brooks leaned his shoulder against the locker and ran a hand through his professionally highlighted caramel-colored hair. He was one of those guys who thought surfer hair was the only way to go, even here in Michigan, where there is nowhere to surf. In fact, that was how most of the soccer team felt. Landon was my school's star forward, so of course whatever he thought was awesome everyone else agreed was awesome too. "So what's up with this party Saturday? Is it still happening?"

My seventeenth birthday was on Thursday, the twenty-second, and I planned to have a party Saturday night. For some reason, the entire school had picked up on it and the general consensus was that it was going to rock. I wasn't wildly popular or known for amazing parties, but usually any party at my school stirred up a fair amount of buzz. That was what happened in a suburban Detroit high school like Bloomfield Hills, I supposed.

"Yeah," I said tiredly. "We just need to keep the number of guests down. My parents are going to kill me if a hundred people show up."

"Too late," Kate chimed in. "This is the first party of our senior year, so of course everyone is going to be pumped about it. And Homecoming is next weekend, so we need a good party to start the semester off right. The masses are growing restless. It's not like you're Leper Girl or anything. People *do* like you."

"And you invited Josie, remember?" Landon nudged.

Oh, yeah. Josie Newport. Our moms had been close in high school and they still talked sometimes. Josie and I had played together a lot when we were little, but things change. She was very popular at school, but outside our moms' engagements, we rarely spoke and never hung out together. I had invited her to my party when we ran into each other at the salon a couple of weeks back. I never understood the stereotype that all the popular, gorgeous girls were complete bitches. Josie was a really nice girl. She was perhaps a little clueless, but she'd never be cruel to anyone on purpose. I had to admit, though, she had some friends I couldn't say the same thing about.

"*And* Josie has to take her posse with her everywhere she goes, right?" Kate added. "That includes half the school, Ell."

I made yet another face and shut my locker. "I'll figure

it out." Of course, I wasn't actually going to do anything. I wasn't going to walk up to Josie Newport and say, "Oh, by the way, when I invited you, I meant just you and maybe a friend or two. Not *everybody* and their cross-eyed cousins."

"Maybe she thought she was doing you a favor?" Landon offered. "Boost your popularity or something?"

While that sounded cool, I didn't suspect that it was probable. Josie wasn't going to do me any favors. Most likely, if the party sucked, Josie would simply move her entourage elsewhere. They would be like a party within a party. If mine sucked, then Josie would just make a new one. She'd already have enough people to do it.

"All right, I'm out," I said, happy to end the conversation and get out of school and go home, even if it was just to study.

"Okay, I'll see you in an hour," Kate said.

"*Adios*, ladies," Landon said, mock saluting us. "Why don't you study for me, too, so I don't have to?"

Kate gave him a sarcastic thumbs-up before turning and making her way to the student parking lot. She'd had her license and her car since she was sixteen, like most of the kids I knew. I had my license too, but not a car yet. Kate's daddy had bought her a red BMW for her birthday. I found it to be an absolute miracle of God that Kate hadn't pancaked it yet. She drove like a blind person going into diabetic shock.

I waved good-bye to Landon, scooped my long, dark red

hair out from under my backpack strap, and headed out through the school's front doors to meet my mom.

As I crossed the front lawn, I spotted a boy I'd never seen before lounging against a tree. He wore a brown shirt and jeans, and his hair, which waved around his face in the breeze, looked black until the sun caught the walnut shine. He actually looked a little too old to be in high school, maybe twenty or twenty-one years old. As I looked at him, I felt a certain fondness deep in my heart, but I shook the feeling off. I didn't know who he was. Maybe he had graduated a year or two ago and I'd seen him in the halls at some point? My school was pretty big. There was no way for me to know everyone who went here. I watched him for several more seconds until I noticed that he was watching me back. I blushed fiercely and looked back to the roundabout ahead, where the parents' cars were idling. It was strange how he was just hanging out there, but I had to assume that he was waiting for a younger sibling.

My mom's Mercedes was nearly indistinguishable from every other silver Mercedes lining the roundabout. I peered through windshields until I spotted my mom. She and my dad looked nothing like me. Mom's hair was more of a light brunette compared to my rich chocolate red. People asked me all the time if I had my hair colored this way, as if it were hot pink or some other unnatural shade. No, my hair just came this way. Also, she didn't have any freckles. A lot of people think all redheads are completely covered in freckles. Not true. I only have six on the bridge of my nose. You can poke at my face and count them. There are *six*.

I climbed in and we exchanged our typical after-school conversation.

"How was your day, Ellie Bean?" my mom asked, like she did every single time.

"I didn't die," I answered, as usual.

"Well, that's good news" was always her reply.

I looked back out the passenger window to the tree where I'd seen the boy, but he was gone. My eyes scanned the lawn, but I couldn't see him anywhere.

"What are you looking at?" Mom asked as we pulled away.

"Nothing," I replied distantly.

My mom shouted an obscenity at the driver in front of her, who was taking too long to turn at the light. Wiping her expression clean of anger the next moment, she smiled at me. "I'm so happy this is the last week I will ever have to pick your butt up from school."

"Good for you."

Mom was a web designer and worked from home—she had always been able to drive me to and from school, thankfully sparing me from ever having to attend daycare. My dad, on the other hand, was rarely home. He worked in medical research, and there were many nights when I would go to bed without seeing him. Sometimes I wouldn't see him for a week. Lately, that was a good thing.

"So you never told me what you want for your birthday," my mom said.

"Lambo."

She laughed. "Yeah, sure, let's just sell the house and get you a Lamborghini for your birthday."

We finally pulled out of the school's drive onto the main road and headed home.

"Really, what *do* you want? I know we talked about a car, and your dad says yes."

"I don't really know."

"Don't make me choose," my mom warned. "I'll get you a moped to drive to school on."

"I'll bet." I rolled my eyes. "I don't know—just get me something cute, safe, and that has an MP3 adapter. I'll be set for life with that."

I woke to music blasting into my left eardrum. I grappled for my cell phone and hit the reject button without opening my eyes. A few seconds later it rang again. I opened a single eye to check the clock. It was a quarter to six in the morning. Uttering a half-mumbled curse, I dragged the phone off my nightstand and looked at the caller ID. It was Kate.

I rubbed my hand against my forehead, forcing myself out of that groggy post-nightmare haze. In the past few months, I'd been having the strangest dreams that were like period horror films, like the Dracula movie with Gary Oldman.

Creepy stuff. They'd kept me from sleeping well for the first few weeks, but I'd started to get used to them, and now they didn't bother me so much. Up until a month before, I'd woken up screaming every single night.

Too lazy to press the phone to my ear, I turned it on speaker mode and thunked it back onto my nightstand. "What is your damage? My alarm hasn't even gone off yet."

"Jesus, Ellie, turn on your TV." Kate's voice was low and frantic. "It's Mr. Meyer. Channel four."

I reached for my remote, flipped on the television, and went to channel four as instructed. I bolted upright.

"He's dead, Ellie," Kate whispered. "They found him behind that bar, Lane's."

My eyes were glued to the chaos live on-screen.

". . . the lack of blood at the scene indicates to investigators that Frank Meyer may have been murdered at another location and dumped here behind Lane's Pub along with the possible murder weapon: a very long hunting knife with a gut hook. The reason for that can only be a matter of speculation at the moment, as authorities have revealed very little about this gruesome discovery. In case you are only just tuning in, this is Debra Michaels reporting from Commerce Township, where the severely mutilated body of one of the community's most beloved educators, Frank Meyer of West Bloomfield, was found early this morning. . . ." I felt like vomiting. I saw the location behind the reporter, swarming with police, the fire department, and ambulances. Mr. Meyer? He was one of the nicest teachers I'd ever had. I had seen him less than twenty-four hours before. How could he be dead? He was *murdered*? And *severely mutilated*?

"Do you think school is canceled?" Kate asked.

I had forgotten she was on the phone. "I'm going to talk to my mom. Meet me here." I hung up.

An hour later I was sitting on a stool at the island bar in the kitchen, staring at an untouched plate of pancakes. Mom only ever made pancakes when I was sick or had a horrible day, or when it was a special day like Christmas. I supposed this was one of those days when pancakes were warranted, but I couldn't bring myself to take a bite. The too-rich smell nauseated me.

Mom walked up behind me and wrapped an arm around my shoulder. "You need to eat, honey. Please? Get some food in your stomach and you'll feel better."

"I'll just puke it all up," I grumbled dismally.

"One bite," she ordered. "Then I won't feel so bad about having to throw away this uneaten breakfast."

I scowled and stabbed begrudgingly at the stack before scooping up a bite with my fork, but it toppled over and plopped into my lap. I groaned and banged my head on the counter.

Mom frowned. "You have to be smarter than the pancakes, Ellie."

I glared up at her. Weren't teenagers supposed to be the smartasses, and not their parents?

She ignored my reproachful look and handed me a paper

towel to clean up my pajama pants. "Well, I finally was able to reach someone at the school. They've been trying to deal with this tragedy all morning, so their lines have been all tied up. I'm sure every single parent in the district has been calling them. Anyway, school is closed today, but I suspect it'll reopen tomorrow. I know you really liked Mr. Meyer, and the assistant principle let me know that grief counselors are being assigned, so if you need to talk to anyone—"

"I'm fine, Mom," I said. "I'm not freaking out or anything. I don't feel well, that's all." She was always so on top of things. She had a plan for everything.

She looked at me fondly. "You're my little miracle. I want you to be okay."

I rolled my eyes. "You always say that."

"I'm worried about your nightmares," she said sadly.

"I barely have them anymore," I lied. I thought it would be better for her to worry less about me than she did. I still had nightmares almost every night, but I was learning to deal with them, since the medication I'd been on was useless.

"What if this tragedy starts them back up again? I can get you an appointment with Dr. Niles next week."

"Bye, Mom," I said, dismissing her. I hated when she brought up the shrink she and my dad had sent me to for three months. All that guy did was tell me a bunch of crap I already knew and give me drugs that didn't work. Of course, they thought I'd been fixed. What they didn't know couldn't hurt them.

"I didn't mean to make you angry, Ellie Bean."

I exhaled, letting the tension wash from my face, and I looked back up at her. "I know. You just have to trust me when I say I'm going to be fine."

She paused a moment before she said anything. "I'll tell your father to say good-bye to you before he leaves." Mom disappeared from the kitchen.

I picked up my cell phone and texted Kate, asking where she was. A few moments later, I received a reply: "B therr so5on! mayb." I immediately regretted texting Kate while she was driving—for obvious reasons.

I poked at my breakfast a few more times. My dad walked into the kitchen, adjusting the front of his suit jacket. I looked up at him briefly and gave a small smile. He patted the top of my head awkwardly as he passed by.

"Sorry about your teacher," he said. The lines in his face told me that he was sad, but his eyes didn't match. They were calm and unaffected, his mind elsewhere.

I was sure he meant what he said, but he never really knew how to show it. I assumed he had learned how to comfort others by imitating someone else—like he saw it on TV somewhere. It never felt natural, never felt as if he really cared.

"Thanks, Dad," I said sincerely. "Kate's on her way over."

"Oh," he said.

"I don't think we'll do much," I said.

"Okay, then. Good-bye."

"Later." He probably should have said something like

how he hoped I'd be all right and that he loved me, but it would shock me to death if I heard those words come out of him these days. I watched my dad head to the garage and listened to him drive away.

When Kate arrived, she let herself in the front door. She sat down quietly on a stool next to me, picked up my fork, and took a bite of my pancakes.

"I can't believe Mr. Meyer's dead," Kate said through a mouthful.

Thinking about never seeing his kind, smiling face in class again made me really sad. "I can't believe he's dead either. Did the news say anything else about it?"

"They just said he was 'severely mutilated.' I have no idea what they mean by that, though. Could be anything. It was probably some psychopath. Detroit *is* like five minutes away."

I took a bite of my breakfast. Immediately, I felt ill. "I think I might sleep a little more. Come with?"

"Best idea I've heard since Landon and Chris decided they'd steal a zebra from the zoo and turn it loose during commencement for our senior prank," she said. "Do you think they're really going to do it?"

"Doubt it."

2

I WAS SMOOTHING MY HAND OVER THE WIDE CLAW marks that ran down the length of the metal door when I heard the roars from somewhere deep within the cavernous textile plant. The angry wails shook the dusty floor beneath my shoes in desolate echoes, announcing the reaper's presence below. I conjured both my swords out of thin air and stepped silently through the door and into the darkened hall. The air smelled like smoke and brimstone, the unmistakable stench left behind by the demonic and the only thing that linked the mortal world to the Grim. The floor was littered with yellowing paper, and nothing remained of the small industrial windows dotting the walls but jagged broken glass. Sickly pale light from the streetlamps lining the darkened streets outside streaked in through the shattered windows. Trash was piled up against the walls, which were covered with strips of peeling, decomposing paint. I stepped around everything, making no noise, but I knew the reaper could feel me. My silence could not mask the energy rolling from me. Nothing could, and the reaper was hungry for me.

I stepped into the Grim, passing through the smoky veil and into the world that most humans could not see. Here the reapers dwelled. The remnants of the mortal plane tugged at my arms and clothes like viscous tendrils. A passing police cruiser lit up the ground floor of the factory like blood-red fireworks, the wail of its siren deafening me for a moment. I took a deep breath to regain my composure and stalked toward the closest emergency stairwell. I kicked the door open, and the heavy clunk of steel gave my position away. I held the helves of both my silver sickle-shaped Khopesh swords tightly as I peered over the edge of the metal railing down the shaft to the basement level.

A dark, massive shape flashed across the floor below. The reaper roared again, making the stairwell shudder.

I descended quickly, whipping my body around the steel spiral staircase at every turn, determined not to let him escape. My footsteps were light, barely brushing the floor beneath me. With one story to go, I jumped over the railing and landed safely with nothing more than a bend of my knees and a thud of my shoes. I kicked open the stairwell door and froze to peer carefully into the darkness. Unseen claws raked the concrete. He wanted me to know he was there.

Behind me came a low, throaty rumble. I spun around

and caught a glimpse of the reaper, but he vanished deeper into the blackness. I clenched my teeth bitterly, and angelfire erupted from my swords, readying for battle. The flames were the only thing that could truly kill a reaper, and I was the only one who could wield them. They lit up the cavernous basement in white light, but the reaper evaded the glow and stuck to the shadows.

He was toying with me, luring me. I held the swords ready and followed him anyway.

The reaper's power was all around me now, washing over me like a flash flood of smoke from an extinguished flame, heavy, inky, merciless, and without warning. I wheeled around and slashed with both swords. The firelight illuminated the colossal, bearlike shape of the reaper as he reared up, his front legs outstretched, waving paws the size of dinner plates. His eyes were black and empty like a shark's, and his Goliath jaws dropped to release a roar like an oncoming train straight into my face.

I ducked into a roll as the reaper swiped his foot-long claws at my head. I jumped to my feet and bounded backward. The reaper heaved toward me and took only a half stride to reach me. He spread his mouth again, revealing a set of enormous teeth that could have belonged to a saber-toothed cat, each fang easily as long as my forearm. He reared over me and his roar thundered once again through the factory. I dropped to my knees and slashed at the reaper's chest and across his hind legs. He collapsed in a spray of

*blood but righted himself quickly and leaped into the air,
landing thirty feet away from me. His flesh sizzled where the
silver blades had sliced and the fire had burned. He wheeled
and charged.*

*I stepped back onto my right heel and prepared for impact.
Instead, the reaper slipped to my left just before he would
have collided with me, and he disappeared for a moment.
Claws slashed down my back, shredding my body like ham-
burger meat. I screeched and fell forward. I shuddered and
dropped my swords. The pain I expected never came; I felt
nothing at all.*

*The reaper was distracted by my pooling blood for a
moment as I lay unmoving. He paused to taste it and growled
a guttural noise of approval with his inhuman mouth before
descending on me to finish the job.*

I couldn't finish my last breath before I died.

I sat straight up with an enormous gasp of air, feeling as
if the life had been taken right out of me. I reached around
my back and felt smooth, undamaged skin there and let out
a sigh of relief. My nightmares were getting more and more
real every time I slept, and I began to worry that I really
needed to go back to therapy.

Beside me, Kate stirred. She sat up with me and frowned.
"You okay? Bad dream?"

I tucked my knees up to my chest and rested my cheek
against them. "Yeah."

She touched my hair soothingly. "Want to watch a movie?"

I nodded. Kate never judged me for my nightmares, never treated me like a psycho, and she understood better than anyone else that the meds and therapy didn't help. She was the only one who listened to me instead of trying to constantly diagnose me. I folded over and curled into a ball while Kate fumbled through the DVD binder on the floor in front of my TV. We went through three fun movies, including one of my favorites, *Sixteen Candles*, to remind myself that it was my birthday the next day. That movie always made me feel better. Happy movie marathons—and pancakes—had been our bad-day cure since we wore pigtails, and I figured the ritual would follow us to college the next fall. But attempting to make today seem less crappy was useless.

"What next?" Kate asked, dragging the binder onto my bed. "*Clueless?*"

I shook my head. It was after four now, and I was beginning to feel restless. "I don't feel like watching another movie. Do you want to go do something?"

"Like what? The mall? We should investigate before Gucci's fall stuff is picked clean."

I scrunched my face. "No, I don't want to have to straighten my hair and look decent. We could just go get ice cream."

Kate brightened a little. "Sounds good. I'm game."

I pulled on jeans and a lightweight zip-up hoodie over my tank top. "Should we call Landon to meet us there?"

Kate gave a quick nod and dialed him up. We let my

mom know where we were going, headed outside to Kate's BMW, and drove to Cold Stone. Landon was waiting for us in the parking lot, talking to a few other people in our circle of friends: Chris, Evan, and Rachel. Chris was on the soccer team with Landon, and they'd been best friends for as long as I could remember. They all stopped talking when Kate and I climbed out of the car.

"Today's been so crazy," Landon said. "How are you guys doing?"

"Fine, just vegging out," Kate said, taking my hand and leading me past him.

We ordered and sat down at the metal tables outside. Landon and the three others joined us. I poked around at my cup of Cookie Doughn't You Want Some before taking a small bite. In spite of how little I had eaten that day, I wasn't very hungry. Mr. Meyer's murder bothered me more than I'd expected it to. I had never known anyone who'd died before, besides my grandfather. He had died peacefully. Something very bad had happened to my teacher.

The others were rambling away at one another about Mr. Meyer.

"I heard it was a bear attack," Evan said through a mouthful. "And Meyer tried to defend himself with a knife."

"There aren't any bears on this side of the state," Rachel said.

"Maybe it was someone's pet cougar," Landon offered. "I know a guy with an ocelot."

"You do not," Chris scoffed.

"Yeah I *do*."

Rachel scratched the top of Evan's head with her fingernails. "What's an ocelot?"

"Was it that awful?" Kate asked.

Chris nodded. "A buddy of mine is doing community service at the morgue for a DUI, and he heard it was messy. Like he was in *pieces*, man. I don't think a bar fight would have gotten that far unless the chick it was over was *smoking* hot. I'd tear a guy up if he got between me and Angelina Jolie."

I didn't like the way they were talking about Mr. Meyer, so I tried to block them and the disturbing mental images out. Cold Stone was busy; since it was past four, the elementary school nearby had let out and now the place was beginning to swarm with screaming, squabbling little kids. I tried my best to ignore them, since fifth-grade boys tended to hit on high school girls. My eyes scanned the area, distantly watching their faces, until I spotted the strange boy from outside school the day before.

Today he wore a black long-sleeved tee and dark-washed jeans. He was sitting alone at a table about twenty feet away and staring off into space. I knew him. I had to know him from somewhere. When I looked at him, brief images of his face, his eyes, and his smile flashed in my mind. A warm scent struck me that I knew was his, but

I wasn't close enough to catch it. The tenderness overtaking my heart both frightened me and brought me peace. When he noticed that I was staring at him, he looked back and didn't look away. I tried to block him out, too, but I realized I couldn't ignore everybody. I turned back to my friends.

"School should be open tomorrow," Rachel said.

Kate licked up a glob of whipped cream. "That sucks."

"Do you think we'll still have to finish this week's economics paper?" Landon asked.

Chris shrugged. "Why wouldn't we? We're just going to have a sub until they find a full-time replacement."

I finished my ice cream quickly, without joining the conversation, and then got up to walk to the trash can on the side of the building to throw my cup away. When I turned around, I nearly bumped into a tall form, and I jumped, startled. Looking up, I found myself standing face-to-face with the boy I'd seen the day before. He was tall, maybe six feet, and broad shouldered—and he was standing much, much too close. His presence wrapped around me—not suffocating, as I would have expected, but peaceful. I didn't pull away from him. He looked down at me with bright green eyes, saying nothing. Around the collar of his shirt were strange black markings like tattoos. His dark hair was tousled just a little by the September breeze.

"Um, *hi*," I said, drawling in my uneasiness. "Do you . . .

need the trash can?" I felt like an idiot as soon as I said it.

"Hi," he said, and gave me a quiet smile, one that amplified the gentle contours of his face, the curve of his lips, the little line beside his right eye that appeared when he smiled—a smile I felt I'd seen a million times before. "No, I don't need the trash can."

"Okay . . ." I started to walk around him back to my friends.

"Do you remember me?" he asked.

Other than having a distinct sense of déjà vu, I was very sure I didn't know him. "I think I might have seen you yesterday at school."

"That's it?" His expression showed that he felt hurt.

Yeah, he was really weird. "I'm pretty sure. Are you looking for someone?"

"No," he mused. "You're Elisabeth Monroe, right?"

"Ellie, yeah. Do you go to my school?"

"No, sorry. You're having a party Saturday, aren't you?"

Good grief, did the whole world know? "Yeah. How'd you hear about it if you don't go to my school?"

"A friend." He smiled.

"You okay, Ellie?" Landon had joined us. He looked annoyed, almost hostile. "Who's this guy?" He stared at the boy up and down.

The stranger's smile faded. "Just call me Will."

His words triggered something in the back of my mind,

just as his smile felt familiar to me. I felt as if I'd heard him say that before.

"Don't talk to her, man," Landon said, taking a step toward Will.

I put a gentle hand on Landon's chest. "Landon, chill, he's not bothering me. I was just throwing my cup away. Let's go. Nice meeting you, Will."

I nodded to Will and led Landon away. "What's your problem?" I asked him once we were out of earshot.

"Nothing—don't worry about it. He shouldn't be talking to you."

"I thought you were going to punch that guy."

"If he touched you, I would've."

I blinked in surprise. "Well, he didn't."

He huffed. "Good."

I tried not to laugh. Landon had been my friend since the sixth grade, but he was a boy, and boys made no sense to me.

My dad actually made it home in time for dinner, to my astonishment, but as soon as we all sat down at the table, I wanted him gone. Dinners recently had mostly been spent with my parents trying to get me to talk. I didn't need to talk about Mr. Meyer. I wasn't ten years old and I wasn't traumatized. I was just sad. That was natural and to be expected. I didn't need to be babied about it.

I dreaded school the next morning. It was going to be today all over again times a thousand. Not to mention I still had that math test on my schedule. What a way to spend my birthday.

My dad's fist slamming on the table jarred me brutally from my thoughts. I sat up like a shot.

"That's not the point." His voice was frigid and harsh, as if he were holding back an angry yell.

"It's not?" my mom asked. "This is the first night you've been home all week. It wouldn't surprise me to find out her nightmares are a result of her lacking a father figure."

"That is ridiculous. Don't give me that psychobabble, Diane."

"I'm just trying to find a solution," Mom said tiredly. "Her teacher was murdered. If anything, that will start the nightmares again. We should take her back to Dr. Niles."

It was as if she'd totally forgotten what I had told her that morning. I wanted to chuck my spaghetti into both their faces and scream, *Hello! I'm right here!* It was almost more comical than enraging when they argued about me as I sat right next to them. When they totally forgot about my presence in a room, they made it obvious that they cared more about fighting with each other than about my mental health.

My dad huffed. "If you feel that's necessary."

"There are a lot of things that I feel are necessary."

"What's that supposed to mean?"

She stared at him. "You know exactly what it means."

"Don't play mind games with me."

It was nights like these that made me wish I had a dog. I needed an excuse to get out of my house and go for a walk. Anything to get the hell out of there.

"You're never home, and when you are, all you do is yell," Mom accused him. "I'm afraid of you when—and if—you come home at night. So is Elisabeth. It wouldn't shock me if her nightmares are a result of all these years of you screaming at her for every little thing. This isn't about you and me, Rick—this is about the way you treat your daughter."

That was all I could stomach. I stood up from the table and took my plate into the kitchen, mentally blocking out my dad's enraged response. Everyone's parents argue—that just happens in any relationship—but parents shouldn't fight in front of their kids. My mom and dad were focused on blaming each other for my nightmares, when both of them were probably the cause.

I went up to my bedroom and sat on my bed, staring into the mirror over my dresser. The pink music box my dad had given me when I was seven sat between a pair of scented candles and a birthday card my grandmother had sent me earlier in the week. I got up, walked to my dresser, and lifted the top of the music box. The little plastic ballerina inside unfolded and stood. I lifted the box and turned the key on the bottom. Delicate music began to play, and the ballerina turned slowly. I watched her dance for a few moments, wondering how my life had gotten this way, how my dad had turned into such a hateful person. I loved that music box, now mostly because it reminded me of the wonderful father the man downstairs used to be. I'd have given anything to turn back the clock on the last ten years of my life—and that wasn't something someone my age should have to feel.

3

REFUSING TO LET MY DEPRESSION SINK DEEPER, I popped in a movie. I settled on *13 Going on 30*, since that was how old my parents made me feel. At least the happy, funny moments might be able to restore my cheer. On and off I could hear the yelling. When my clock rolled past midnight, my parents had begun arguing again.

"Happy birthday to me," I said dismally. Within the next minute, I received eight text messages containing variations of "happy birthday!" involving excessive punctuation and two texts including "luv u bitch!"

I decided to spend my first few minutes as a seventeen-year-old by sneaking out the front door to sit on the porch. I leaned against one of the columns and took in a deep breath. Night had settled and the air was a little chilly, but I was comfortable in my T-shirt.

After a little while of sitting on my porch and picking at my nails, I stood up and started down my driveway to the sidewalk. Once around the block should be enough, I decided. I *really* needed a dog. I considered for a moment: a car or a dog for my birthday. . . . Yeah, car. I didn't think I'd get it exactly the next day, but more likely over the weekend. I knew a lot of kids didn't get cars for their birthdays, or even cars at all, let alone the chance to go pick one out, so I shouldn't complain. But then again, a lot of kids got to have parents who didn't scream at each other. Everyone made their sacrifices.

I heard a low rumble in front of me and stopped walking. It didn't sound mechanical like a car engine, and I definitely didn't see any headlights ahead, either. I strained my eyes to peer into the darkness. The streetlamp above me buzzed and went out. Past the sidewalk corner and deep into my neighbor's wide lawn, I could see nothing. For an instant I thought of Mr. Meyer's murderer. Maybe it wasn't such a good idea to go walking around outside after midnight?

"What are you looking at?"

I let out a small cry and spun around as my heart leaped into my throat.

It was Will, as if he'd appeared out of nowhere. He looked worried and determined, but he was obviously trying to hide those feelings.

"What are you doing out here?" I whispered harshly.

"What are *you* doing here?" he countered.

I threw my hand up. "I live here!"

Suddenly, I had a terrible thought. I had first seen Will the day before, the night Mr. Meyer died. No, no, no. That was ridiculous. Will was just some hot, weird guy I happened to be seeing everywhere I went. That didn't make him a murderer. Hadn't my mom given me a can of mace for Christmas? What had I done with that?

"So why are you out for a walk this late at night?" he asked, distracting me from my thoughts. "Even if you live here, it's pretty late to be wandering around at night."

"Well, *you're* out here too. I like being outside at night. It's relaxing."

That smile widened. It was like he thought this was funny. "Most people would feel nervous."

My hands rested on my hips. "Why? Should I be?"

"What?"

"Nervous."

"Probably."

"You don't seem like *you're* nervous."

"I can take care of myself." His smile turned dark, knowing.

"You're the weirdest boy I've ever met—and believe me, every single one of them is weird, so that's saying a lot." Once I realized what I'd just said, I wanted to smack my face into a brick wall. My mouth sure liked to run when it should have been my feet running.

He laughed. "At least you're honest about your feelings."

"They say it's a virtue." I turned around to walk back to

my house. It was time to leave. "Do me a favor and leave me alone. I just know you're going to go all Ted Bundy on my ass any second." I looked around me, hoping one of the neighbors would flick their porch lights on and burst out holding a shotgun. I felt pretty sure I wasn't that lucky.

"Are you afraid of me?" Will asked, jogging to catch up to me.

"Are you passive-aggressively trying to tell me that I should be *afraid* of you, too? Not just 'nervous'?" I was only four houses away from home now.

"No, but have you ever heard the saying 'The brave may not live forever, but the cautious never live at all'?"

"No, I haven't heard that, but I'll keep it in mind. Thanks for the proverbial insight, my stalker friend."

He threw an arm across my chest to stop me and looked ahead, staring coldly into the dark. His body stiffened, but something in my gut told me that it wasn't because of the chilly air.

I turned my head to follow his gaze, but I saw nothing in the street ahead. A breeze scattered a handful of already fallen leaves. I smelled something strange, like eggs and black smoke. "Do you smell that? What's wrong?"

He stepped around me to put himself between me and wherever he was staring. "You can't see into the Grim yet."

"See what? The grim what?" I peeked over his shoulder. I thought I saw a shadow cross my path, but when I blinked, nothing was there. It was too dark.

His gaze was fixed on something in the blackness. "It's not time! Stand down. I don't care if it's after midnight— she cannot be touched, unless you're prepared for the consequences."

He was clearly not talking to me. I was suddenly very aware that though I knew his name, I had no idea who he was. He could have been some junkie. I had never seen any-one on anything other than pot or alcohol, not even shrooms, let alone anything worse, so I had no idea what to expect. My body tensed with fear. "What are you *on?* I've had enough. I'm leaving now."

I started to turn back to my house.

"No, wait," Will said.

I heard the rumble again, only this time it was louder. That was not a car engine. Was it a growl? Was there a dog— a *big* dog—out there in the dark? My mind raced with thoughts of a rabid-dog attack. If the dog was close enough for me to hear it, then I should have been able to see it.

Another growl came, and then very heavy footsteps— like *T. rex*–shaking-the-water-cup *Jurassic Park*–style heavy footsteps.

"What is that?" I asked, trembling, my eyes searching the dark. I felt like I'd fallen right into a real-life version of one of my nightmares. My head whirled dizzily, and fear made my stomach churn.

Hot breath, reeking like roadkill, blasted my face from an unseen source, and I spun around, gagging. "Oh, my

God!" I groaned, covering my mouth.

"Come here," Will said slowly, reaching back for me without taking a step. The look of worry on his face that I'd noticed earlier had deepened. Now he looked afraid, and that scared me a thousand times more.

"No way!" I cried, reeling away from him.

His fear spun into frustration as I pulled away. "Don't scream. You'll make him attack."

Panic set in. "Get away!" I shrieked, and tried to run, but Will grabbed my arm. I twisted and pulled, but his grip was amazingly strong. It was like trying to drag an eighteen-wheeler; I couldn't get him to give even an inch. How could anyone be that strong? I started to pry at his fingers, but they were like solid rock.

"It's time to end this game," he said, sending stabs of ice down my spine. He yanked me to his chest effortlessly and pressed his palm to my forehead.

Bright white light flashed, blinding me. Every inch of my skull felt as if it would explode from the pressure. The ground felt as if it were rocking and rolling at my feet, and a cruel wind—I didn't even know where it came from—punished me violently, beating at me from all directions. My knees began to sway, unable to hold my weight, but Will held me up so I wouldn't fall. The light vanished just as abruptly as it had appeared as he took his hand away and released me. I staggered back and fell on my tailbone, my vision blurring— but through the haze I could have sworn I saw shadowy wings towering over me, spreading wide. I blinked and saw only Will's blurry form where I thought wings had just been. Every muscle in my body ached as if I'd just run a mile, but I was energized. There was a rushing sensation through the air, through the ground, and every inch of my body tingled with tiny prickles of electricity, as if I were moving a hundred miles an hour, even though I hadn't moved an inch. The air around me was sticky for a moment, sticky and smoky, and I squeezed my eyes shut and opened them again to clear my vision. After a heartbeat, the haziness faded. I stared confusedly at the pavement, rubbing my forehead.

"Ellie!"

My eyes suddenly focused and I saw Will again. My vision was crisp and the world had brightened. I looked past Will, marveling at how easily I could see through the darkness, distinguishing every leaf on my neighbors' bushes, every groove in every shingle on their roofs.

And then I saw the monster: something vaguely resembling a huge dog covered in thick, black fur loomed over us, standing easily five feet tall at the shoulder. It lumbered over on all fours with a snout full of gnarled, vicious-looking teeth in the jaws of a heavy, oversize head. Its paws were the size of elephant's feet and ended in talons that looked like they could tear a man in half.

But I wasn't afraid. A calmness washed over me, and my mind analyzed at a lightning pace. Strange memories and thoughts that didn't belong to me flooded into my mind: faces and violence I'd seen long ago in different times. I looked up at Will, whose face sparked the clearest and fondest memory. I knew I had to fight now, but I needed my weapons.

The beast leaped toward me, claws outstretched, and took a swipe with one of its front paws, but Will appeared between us. He grabbed the beast's forelimb and kicked full force into its chest, sending it flying back, shattering my neighbor's mailbox into countless little chunks of wood and brick.

It happened so fast that I knew I shouldn't have been able to see it, but I did. I stepped forward, watching the creature climb to its feet as it loosed a low, dangerous-sounding growl.

I held both of my arms out and willed weapons into my open palms. The twin Khopesh swords appeared out of nothing in a flash of shimmering light. The curving silver blades glinted brightly. I glanced over at Will. I could now see intricate black tattoos twisting out from beneath his shirt all the way down his right arm to his knuckles. I remembered the beautiful symbols woven into the spiraling design, because I'd seen them before with different eyes, in another time.

My thoughts were calm and unnervingly clear. The blades exploded into white flames at my command. Blinding light devoured the silver, and the power coursed through me. My fingers squeezed the cool, familiar helves as the scents of silver and old blood flooded my heightened senses. The swords felt right in my grasp, like hugging an old friend.

The monster began to circle me, growling low and releasing an unearthly hiss. Its eyes were bottomless pits of blackness set deep into its deformed, terrible skull. I stared right back into those eyes without fear or hesitation.

I moved with the creature so that it was never at my back, and in a voice that did not seem my own I challenged the beast: "Come for me."

The wolflike monster charged, paws and talons outstretched, massive jaws gaping. I spun out of the way just as teeth clamped down on the hood of my sweatshirt instead of my throat. The beast yanked the cotton flap, wrenching me around awkwardly, twisting, growling. Its paws clawed at my body, pulling me closer to its mouth so it could take a bite out of my face. I smashed my elbow into its nose, and it slumped back onto its haunches with a groan. Then my elbow slammed down on top of its skull and something crunched, but the monster only bit harder on my hoodie, shredding the fabric. Abruptly, it threw me to the ground, and I looked up. Will had it by the throat, his arm buried elbow deep in its thick fur, forcing the beast backward.

"Now!" he roared.

It thrashed like a giant pit bull and broke free.

My eyes locked on my target and my mind cleared to seize the opportunity. Quicker than my heart could pound, I was on my feet and shoving my fiery sword into its soft throat and straight through the top of its skull. The creature's legs buckled as its fur shimmered oddly before exploding in flames. It happened very quickly. Fire devoured the reaper, swallowing it in white light, consuming it until finally the head disappeared, leaving nothing but empty space and falling ashes where a monster had just been.

Then the shadows closed in around me.

4

THE NEXT MORNING, MY HEAD AND EVERY MUSCLE in my body hurt as if I'd run a marathon through six feet of snow in stilettos. Fragmented chunks of the nightmare I'd had the night before spun through my head. As much as it annoyed me to have dreamed about Will, I was more unsettled because it had been way more vivid and scary than my usual nightmares. Why was I still in my jeans and shirt? My hoodie, however, was AWOL. I dug through my dirty-clothes hamper and the blankets on my bed, but it was nowhere to be found. How had it just disappeared?

What if what happened last night wasn't a dream?

There was a knock on my door. "Is the birthday girl awake yet?" It was my mom. "Come on, Ellie! Get up!"

I headed to the bathroom to shower, straightened the obnoxious waves in my hair with the flatiron, and tugged on fresh jeans and a T-shirt. I hopped downstairs to meet my mom in the kitchen.

"I made you pancakes, since it's your birthday," Mom said cheerfully, and smiling brightly, she presented a platter stacked high. "I know you didn't eat the ones I made you yesterday, so I hope you're feeling well enough to appreciate them more this morning."

"Thanks, Mom," I said, sitting down at the counter to eat.

"Happy birthday, honey." She kissed the top of my head. "Love you."

"Love you, too. Where's Dad?"

Her smile vanished. "He had to leave early. He's got a meeting in Lansing. He told me to tell you happy birthday and that he loves you."

I forced a smile, pretty certain that she had made the last part up. More likely he had just left for his meeting without saying a thing.

Mom's face brightened. "So I thought we would go get your present after school. I know today is going to be very difficult with everything that happened yesterday, but hopefully this will make today a little less awful. Sound good?"

My heart lifted. "Yeah."

"Okay, then. I'm going to get some work done before we take off for school." She turned to go back to her office. "Make sure you eat. We'll go by the dealership after school and see what they have."

Awesome. "Hey, Mom?"

She turned back around. "Yeah, sweetie?"

"Did you hear anything last night?" I wasn't sure what I expected her to answer with.

She frowned. "Oh, honey, I'm so sorry your father and I were arguing. I'm so sorry you heard that."

"I mean like growling, like a huge dog or a bear."

Mom gave me an odd look, gauging what I had just said. Heat rushed into my cheeks as I realized how stupid I'd just sounded. "It wasn't another nightmare?"

"No, I was awake."

She sighed and her lips tightened. "Maybe it was a couple of dogs outside fighting? I didn't hear anything. You wouldn't hear strange noises if you shut your window at night."

"I guess you're right." The consensus was official: It was just a dream and I was a lunatic.

As soon as I got to my locker, I was greeted by Landon, who carried a vase of roses. My jaw dropped to the floor.

"Are you serious?" I asked, my gaze spilling over the lush bouquet.

"Happy birthday, Ellie." He kissed my cheek. Any second I would implode from the sweetness.

He handed me the vase. "I don't want your birthday to suck, even though it's a sad day and all. I hope this makes it better."

I wrapped my free arm around his shoulders and hugged

him. "Thank you so much, Landon! You are too good to me. This will definitely make my day rock."

His smile widened. "I have to run to class, but I'm really glad you're happy. See you later."

"Bye!" I had to remove a pile of old papers from the bottom of my locker to safely make room for the vase. I'd known Landon for a long time, but he had never given me flowers before. What a doll. I was practically dancing on my way to homeroom.

Classes went just as I'd predicted they would. During morning announcements the principal gave a long speech about Mr. Meyer over the intercom, and then my homeroom teacher, Mrs. Wright, gave another. The first four periods of the day were very much the same. Teachers said their bit, did very little lecturing, and gave no homework. My math test had been postponed until the following Monday, which was fine with me since I had no desire to take a test on my birthday. During third-period shop class, which I swear I was taking only to boost my GPA, we did nothing but sit at our tables and discuss the sanding projects for the following week. I assumed getting mushy would be too much for poor Mr. Gray to handle. Even an idiot could see how loved Mr. Meyer had been. When lunchtime came around, I met up with my friends. We all made an effort to have a decently normal lunch.

Kate, Landon, and I sat in our usual place in the right-hand corner by the windows looking out into the courtyard.

Evan, Rachel, and Chris joined us, and to my surprise and happiness, everyone avoided the subject of Mr. Meyer's murder. When I finished my lunch, I headed to the bathroom for a quick break.

As I washed my hands in the sink, something made me stop and take a second look in the mirror. My throat squeezed with fear as I stared at the right side of my face. Black things—spidery, threadlike lines—were creeping from my scalp and across my cheek and around my right eye, interlacing with one another. Fear spun into revulsion as I rubbed my cheek hard, trying to smear the blackness away. The lines kept coming, getting longer and covering more and more of my face. I rubbed, but I couldn't feel them on my skin. Were they *in* my skin?

Half crying, half scared out of my mind, I grabbed a handful of paper towels and wet them under the running water. I rubbed my face vigorously with the wet towels, but when I lowered them, the lines were still there and my eyes had turned solid white like cue balls. I dropped the towels and backed away from the mirror until my back hit the solid frame of the toilet stalls. I covered my face with both of my hands, my fingers weaving through my hair, pulling it in desperation.

When I looked back up, I saw nothing on my face in the mirror but the streaks of tears. No black things. No darkness. They were gone. My eyes were normal again.

I splashed my face with cold water to dull the redness

there and took several long, slow breaths to steady my nerves. When I felt confident enough to return to the cafeteria, I burst through the bathroom door, determined to forget what had just happened to me. As I rounded the corner, I turned right into Will.

"Oh, God!" I cried out, fighting the urge to smack him. "You scared the crap out of me! What are you doing at my school? I thought you didn't go here." I nervously tugged my bag higher on my shoulder and took a deep breath. That was when I noticed that the black, spiraling tattoos all up and down his muscled arm were plainly visible— the exact same tattoos he'd worn in my dream. I stared at the strange symbols, and the winding blackness reminded me of the blackness spreading on my face moments before. But this was different. His tattoos were beautiful, frighteningly so, and unearthly. They wound and danced across his skin as if they were proud and defiant. I couldn't take my eyes off them.

He ignored my question. "Are you all right?"

Had he heard my crying? How did he know? Wresting my gaze away from his tattoos, I dismissed my thoughts and sternly asserted, "I'm fine."

"I need to talk to you." He wasn't smiling. In fact he didn't look cheerful at all, and his questioning gaze fell on my still-red cheek. I self-consciously covered it with my palm.

"About what? I have to get back to lunch." I started to

walk around him, but he sidestepped in front of me, blocking my path. After what had just happened in the bathroom, I was not in the mood to deal with any more craziness.

"We need to talk about last night."

My stomach clenched, and the fear I had felt moments before came raging back into my body. "I don't know what you're talking about. I was home last night. There's nothing we need to—"

"Don't you remember?" He leaned into me, his green eyes wide and tearing into my hazel ones. He was so close that he was all I could feel, see, and smell. My senses were drowning in him.

"Remember what?" It was just a dream—it *had* to be. What happened could *not* have been real. I'd imagined it, just like I'd imagined the black spiderwebs on my face.

He took my arm and pulled me gently against the lockers when a couple students walked by. "The reaper? The one you killed?" he asked in a harsh whisper.

"The *what*? What the hell are you on, Will?" I tried to pull myself away, but he held me tighter. "Look, I'm not into that stuff, whatever it is, so—"

"Enough of this," he growled, leaning closer to me. "You need to accept what happened last night and what you are, no matter how much you don't want to. Pretending that it was just a dream or that I'm insane isn't going to help you. It'll only make things worse."

"I don't know what you're talking about!" I snarled through

gritted teeth. I was desperate to keep my anger from causing more tears.

Will took a breath and spoke his next words slowly. "Look, I feel awful and I don't want to scare you—"

"Well, you're doing a damn good job of it!"

"Just listen to me for a minute and I'll leave. Okay?"

I studied his face. He was really serious about this. I might as well humor him. "Fine."

He took another deep breath. He spoke slowly, but with an intensity that frightened me even more. "What you saw—what you *fought*—last night was a reaper. Forget the scythe-wielding skeletons in long robes. This is real. Most don't need scythes, because they have teeth and claws for weapons. They *eat* you. They eat your flesh and your blood, and then they drag your soul to Hell. Your teacher, Frank Meyer, was killed and eaten by the same one you killed last night. You are the Preliator, the only mortal in the world with the power to fight them. And I am your Guardian, your bodyguard, sworn to protect and defend you. And *you* are making my job *excruciatingly* difficult."

I stared at him for a few moments, unable to decide how to respond. I settled for the easy thing. "You're completely out of your mind."

"Damn it!" Will threw his hands up. "This is ridiculous. I don't understand why you don't remember. I triggered your power last night. You woke and entered the Grim on your own and killed the reaper. Why don't you remember now?"

He stepped away from me and clamped his hand over the top of his head. His voice was rapid and worried. "Maybe because it's been so long. Before, it was always only eighteen years between cycles. Your soul has been asleep too long."

I backed away, my hand crawling along the wall, unable to make sense of anything he said. Then I noticed the metal chain around his neck, tucked into his shirt. An image flashed across my mind of something gleaming, dangling—a plus sign. It was like déjà vu, a memory I didn't remember ever having, if that made any sense at all.

"And if you're wondering where your hoodie went, check your wastebasket. Sorry it was ruined."

"Ruined?"

"Is there a problem, Miss Monroe?"

I turned around to see one of the assistant principals, Mr. Abbot, standing behind me, looking from me to Will.

"Who is this young man?" Mr. Abbot asked, clearly seeing that Will was not a high school student. His accusing gaze lingered on the tattoos covering Will's arm. To him, the tattoos must have been a sure sign of delinquency.

"A friend," Will said. "I stopped by to bring some of Ellie's homework she had forgotten at my house."

Mr. Abbot looked questioningly at me. "Is this true?"

I nodded. "Yes, sir. It's okay." I didn't know why I was covering for him. Maybe his craziness had rubbed off on me like a bad cold, or something worse.

He turned to Will. "Young man, I'm going to have to ask

you to leave campus. You've done Ellie a good service by bringing her homework. However, as you are not a student and have not signed for a visitor's pass, you'll need to be on your way."

Will nodded. "That's fine. I'll say my good-byes and go." He stared intently at Mr. Abbot, refusing to budge. Strangely, my assistant principal made a peculiar face before he turned and left. "Ellie, will you talk to me after school?" Will asked me.

"No way," I said, turning my back to him.

He stepped around me so that we were face-to-face. "If you don't, then you won't know how to call your swords and you won't be able to defend yourself."

I felt a shiver crawl up my spine as his eyes bored into mine, locking our gazes, his voice low and downright invasive. "Was that a threat?" I asked cautiously.

His expression gave nothing away. "They'll come for you."

That shiver turned into a brutal stab of fear straight into my gut. My pulse quickened and I pursed my lips together when I felt heat rushing into my face.

"Now that I've woken your powers, you're fair game to the reapers. You're at your most vulnerable, and this is when they'll strike."

I took a deep breath. "If you don't leave me alone, I'm going to scream for security and they're going to call the cops."

He watched me for a few moments. His jaw was clenched

tightly and he sucked in his upper lip in frustration. "It takes a while for your memory to return sometimes, but it's never been this bad before. I know you're having the nightmares. You've always had them when you're ready to face who you are. Of course, the last time I saw you—the *real* you—well, that was more than forty years ago. You were gone for twenty-eight years."

My throat tightened.

He flashed me that astonishing smile, only this time it held something different, something secretive. "Happy birthday, by the way. I'm sorry I didn't say that last night, but I have a gift for you. You passed out before I could give it to you."

Will pulled something out of his pocket and held out his hand. On his palm lay a pendant shaped like a pair of white wings hanging on a gold chain. The necklace was gorgeous, ethereal, the wings so brightly white that they shimmered and appeared to glow in the light. When I blinked, the glow was gone.

"What is this?" I asked, marveling at the winged pendant.

"It's always been yours," he said, lifting my hand and placing the necklace on my palm. "Since before I knew you. It never tarnishes or fades. Always the same. Always permanent even when fate takes so much away." He gently closed my fingers around the pendant, his warm hands lingering a moment too long. "I'll talk to you soon."

Will turned and left. I opened my hand to stare at the

beautiful necklace. Brushing my fingers across the wings, I couldn't decide what it was made of. The pendant's surface was smooth and luminous, as if it were made of mother-of-pearl but something more precious than that. Its beauty lulled me, and I slipped into a strange, nostalgic trance; and the whispers of memories that couldn't have belonged to me surfaced in my mind. Distant images of Will's face, of reapers lurking in the dark, of me running through alleys and forests, of the necklace in my hands. Things I shouldn't have remembered but did.

I shook my head and stuffed the necklace into my purse.

More than forty years? I fell back against the lockers tiredly and rubbed my face with both hands. Why wouldn't Will just leave me alone? He seemed to firmly believe that I was some kind of superhero, and that had to be the craziest thing I'd ever heard. As if that wasn't enough, he said he'd talk to me soon. Although I knew little about Will, I knew for a fact that was a promise.

I went back to lunch with my friends and tried to forget about him, but I couldn't. Fourth period came and went without incident other than Kate distracting me from the discussion of the week's assignment. Something about dress-shopping plans for Saturday's party outfits. Thankfully, that was the only other class I had with Kate, so I was able to concentrate a little more during my other classes. Fifth-period European history was mildly more interesting because I actually liked history. It was something I got easily, unlike economics.

As I sat at my table, ignoring my tablemate, who absently picked at his face, I found myself thinking about the night before. I tried to remember the horrible creature Will had called a reaper. The snarling, dead-eyed monster stared out at me from my memories, its enormous talons digging into the earth, ready to leap. Why would I dream about such awful things? I rubbed my arms, recalling the sensation of its fur brushing against my skin. Never had any nightmare felt so real, in my mind, on my skin, and in my heart.

I decided to imagine for a moment that Will had been telling the truth. If I was indeed what he claimed, the Preliator, then those monsters, the reapers, were real. What did he mean when he said I'd been gone for twenty-eight years?

I was so confused. Just trying to make sense of Will's claims was enough to drive me crazy.

I couldn't get past Will's surprise that I couldn't remember anything. Of course, nothing happened—it was just a bad dream, and Will was nuts. But how could he know so many details from my nightmare? He had even mentioned the "grim" again, whatever that was. And his tattoos . . . I had not seen those when I'd met him the previous afternoon. The first time I saw them was in my dream.

Will had touched me and I suddenly had become

someone different, someone powerful, someone very frightening. That scared me, but I was still drawn to the idea. I pulled the winged necklace out of my purse and studied the delicate edges and intricate etchings.

Remember. I thought hard, shutting my eyes tightly and closing my fingers around my pendant. Remember, remember. *What* was I supposed to remember? I stared down at my history notes. If only my own history were written on those pages instead of Charlemagne's.

The events from the night before replayed over and over in my mind like a horror movie: the reaper stalking through the dark, charging at me as I swung those strange, flaming, sickle-shaped swords. So much blood . . .

And then my eyes went out of focus. I squeezed them shut and opened them again, turning my face away from the harsh light of the classroom to stare at the floor. The temperature plummeted, and I shivered and rubbed my arms. The floor blurred and my desk and all the faces around me vanished, leaving me alone in the dark and kneeling on a snowy ground. I stood and looked around me, and I saw the dense, shadowed forest closing in on me and felt the icy, unyielding wind on my face.

My eyes fell to the trail of blood dotting the snow in front of me as I moved through the Grim. I knew the reaper couldn't be far. He had taken nearly a hundred lives already in the poor region of Le Gévaudan in southern France. The dragoons sent by the French king had found nothing and left an endless trail of innocent wolf carcasses in their wake. The lupine reaper was smarter and hungrier than any of them, and that made him far more dangerous. They couldn't hunt something that they couldn't see and that was smarter than them.

I could suddenly feel it—the tingle of the darkest power crawling across my flesh, rolling through the earth beneath the snow.

Something dark flashed to my right. Then it flashed to my left. He was circling me.

I hated when they hunted me back. I held my swords closely. The flames didn't melt the snow around me. Angelfire only ever burned evil and left everything else untouched.

Footsteps crunched the snow in front of me. The reaper had finally decided to show himself. He stepped closer, allowing me to get a better look at him. He gnashed his teeth with the promise of death, and his black fur glistened with a dark, lurid liquid. Blood. I didn't know what, or who, it belonged to.

"You are a fool for hunting me, Preliator," he growled through wolflike jaws, jaws that should never have been able to speak human words. "This is my territory. The souls in this land will be mine. You will meet your end in this forest."

I scoffed and tightened my grip on both helves. "I may, but before I die, I'll make sure you don't leave this forest alive either. That is the price you pay for taking so much blood."

The reaper lifted his head, his black eyes watching me

curiously. *"And what price do you pay? For all the blood you've spilt?"*

"This is my duty."

He ignored me. "Loneliness, I suspect." His voice was so deep, it hurt my ears trying to hear him.

"Stop trying to get into my mind and just fight me, Holger."

He lowered his head, and his muzzle formed a strange wolfish smile. His eyes were nearly invisible against his black fur, revealed only by the angelfire cast across their glossy surfaces. "You know my name."

"I know a lot more about you than that."

"Does that knowledge make you fear me?" he asked, frighteningly hopeful. He was old—older and more powerful than most of the reapers I had fought in recent years. Three hundred years was certainly something to boast about.

"That would make you happy, wouldn't it?"

"Yes, yes it would," Holger said, the words rolling over his giant tongue. "Where is your Guardian, Preliator?"

"Not far behind." It didn't matter. I had to destroy the reaper on my own or he would send more innocent souls to Hell.

"Well, that is quite fortunate for me."

He launched, jaws and claws spread wide. I bolted and he landed to the side of me, sliding through the snow and spraying glittery white powder. He leaped for me again, and I dived behind a tree. He collided with it, shaking half the tree free of snow and gouging a massive hole in the bark with his body. He roared in fury, and every tree near him shook with the force of his energy. His power exploded and he bashed a tree trunk with his paw, his talons ripping the trunk nearly in half. The tree groaned, and I stared up as it came crashing down; but I fell back before it pinned me to the ground. Though it missed me, the log had trapped one of my swords beneath it and the flames went out. I grabbed the handle and tugged, but the blade didn't slide free.

Holger climbed over the trunk, and then his snarling muzzle was inches from my face. He snapped his jaws, lashed his thick tail in anger, and lunged at me, but a powerful blow to his skull knocked him off the tree.

My heart leaped when I saw Will. He pounded the reaper's head again, crushing Holger to the ground. Will snapped back around to face me and bellowed, "Your sword!"

I nodded and gave the Khopesh another strong tug, grinding my boot into the trunk for leverage, and finally the blade slipped out. Angelfire burst from it. I turned my head just in time to see Holger charge at me where I lay. His jaws snapped at me, but I twisted away, and his teeth clamped down on earth and snow instead of flesh. With a desperate cry, I swung my sword as hard as I could. The blade cut deep through his neck, and his body burst into flames. Holger's head toppled off his body and onto my face.

I cried out and my chair slipped out from under me. The racket echoed through the classroom as my butt hit the tile floor and the chair crashed.

Everyone around me was silent, too shocked to laugh, but I didn't dare look up. My entire body flushed with heat.

Oh God, oh God . . . Both my hands covered my face as I sat on the floor, absolutely mortified.

"Holy *crap*, Ellie, are you okay?" asked my table partner.

I looked up to see his face peering down at me. "The chair . . . it slipped."

5

THE REST OF THE DAY WENT BY WITHOUT ANY MORE incidents. No more daydreams, I told myself firmly. My nightmares were scary enough and I had no desire to have them while awake. The memory of what I had experienced during history was fresh in my mind and stung like a paper cut; the episode fluttered around school, so by last period I was already known as that chick who fell on her ass during class. I'd have to move away. Probably to Alaska.

At last, school ended and I hurried to my locker. My interlude there with Kate and Landon was brief—I had other things on my mind. Like getting my car. And my nightmares coming to life.

I halfheartedly agreed to meet Kate at the mall on Saturday to get our outfits for my party, as we had discussed during math earlier. After saying a hasty good-bye and thanking Landon once again for the roses, I headed outside with the vase in my arms to meet my mom.

She seemed as excited as I was. "Honey, who are the flowers from?"

"Landon," I said, smelling them again.

"Well, that was very sweet of him," she offered.

"I suppose he's making up for all the snowballs he's thrown in my face and shoved down my shirt over the years."

She nodded slowly and her brow flickered. "If you say so."

We drove to the dealership a few miles from school and inspected nearly every single car there. I was set on a sedan, so we decided to test drive a couple of different cars, with the busty saleswoman tagging gleefully along. I fell in love with a little white Audi with a black interior. It was sportier than the others and definitely felt perfect to me.

After my mom had organized the purchase and we were ready to head home, I hopped into the driver's seat of my birthday present. The interior was wrapped in smooth, cool leather and I let myself sink into it.

Mom dipped her head to smile at me through the driver's-side window.

"I'm going to name him Marshmallow," I announced.

My mom raised an eyebrow. "Marshmallow?"

"Yes, and he loves it." I tenderly ran my fingers along the leather-covered steering wheel.

"So what do you say to driving home in your new car?"

"Yes!" I almost shouted.

"Be sure to tell your dad thank you when you get home."

I nodded, smiling widely. I was almost ecstatic enough to forget my frightening daydream from earlier. Almost.

I followed my mom home. The Audi glided along the hilly roads like a dream. Up and down, left and right, the vehicle handled effortlessly and I felt in complete control, otherworldly. I didn't know what had come over me, whether it was the thrill of having my first car or my party coming up, but I felt energized. *Different.* I felt *good.* None of the soreness I had woken up with that morning remained.

As I pulled into the driveway behind my mom's car, I happened to glance at my neighbor's mailbox, which lay in a pile of splinters. My neighbor, Mr. Ashton, was picking up the wooden fragments and chunks of brick scattered across his lawn. A very clear memory from the night before crept into my head, and the blood drained from my face. A cold rush flooded through me as I stepped out of my car, dizzying me so much that I had to lean against the door for support. I noticed a jagged crater in the street not too far off.

"That happened last night," my mom said with a frown on her face. "It appears a sinkhole may have caused a driver to hit the curb and then Mr. Ashton's mailbox. The neighborhood association is having someone come by to fill the hole in tomorrow. It's strange, since these things don't usually happen until spring."

I leaned back against my car for support, my breaths

long but dizzyingly shallow.

"Maybe that's what you heard last night?" Mom offered. "The loud noise you mentioned."

I watched Mr. Ashton dump the remains of his mailbox into a wheelbarrow and haul it into his backyard. "Maybe."

I ran up to my bedroom and dumped the contents of my wastebasket onto the carpet. Will had to be wrong. My missing hoodie couldn't be in there. But right in front of me, in the midst of crumpled notebook paper, wadded tissues, and a candy wrapper, was my hoodie. I lifted it, gingerly plucking the hood up with two fingers. The cotton was shredded, stiff from something wet and thick that had dried all over it, and splattered across the sleeves and chest were dark dried droplets. The whole thing had a sour dog-drool smell laced with the faint tang of old blood.

Scrambling into the bathroom, I threw up into the toilet.

Kate called me that evening at seven to meet her at Starbucks. Any reason was good enough to get me out of the house and driving. As I left, I took a whiff of the roses on my dresser and tried not to think about the shredded discovery in my wastebasket. I let my mom know where I was going and she gave her permission without much resistance. When I arrived, Kate was standing by her car in the parking lot with Landon and Chris. She let out a high-pitched squeal when she saw my new car.

"Ah!" she shrieked. "It is *so* cute! I approve."

"Thank you!" I said, beaming. "I named him Marshmallow. Isn't it perfect?"

"Oh my God, yes," Kate said, peeking in the driver's-side window. "Ruby wants him to be her boyfriend." She was referring to the name of her red BMW.

"You rich girls and your stupid names for your cars," Chris said, sighing as he checked it out. "A4, nice. I'll race you with my 370Z."

I laughed. "No way. I'm not going to kill myself, thanks, and why would you even bother? I'm pretty sure you'd destroy me in that thing anyway."

"Fine," he said, and turned to Kate. "Let me take on the E90."

She eyed him, grinning. "Keep dreaming."

"You ladies are wasting your cars," Landon said, examining my tires.

"It's really going to suck when we're freshmen at Michigan State and have to leave our cars at home," Kate said, pouting.

"Did you send your application in?" I asked.

She nodded. "Yeah. Haven't you?"

I grimaced. My grades hadn't exactly been awesome, but I was still treading water. "Not yet."

"Well, do it quick," she said. "Spots fill up fast."

I made a mental note to start my application next week. Neither of us wanted to go anywhere else. Well, of course I had wanted to go to Harvard when I was six, but my goals had gotten more realistic since then.

After the boys inspected the Audi from grill to tailpipe, we went into Starbucks to order. Kate bought me a cappuccino for my birthday, and I sipped on it while we talked and laughed. I was happy not to have to worry about the strange events of the past couple of days. At the moment, all I had to worry about was not spilling my coffee on myself and not letting Landon get too close. He seemed to shift himself closer and closer to me as I watched him out of the corner of my eye. I wasn't claustrophobic by any means—but I soon would be if he got any closer.

"So what are we seeing tomorrow?" Chris asked, licking the whipped cream topping his cup.

Friday night was Movie Night for our group of friends. It was pretty much a religious event for us. I shrugged. "I don't know. What's out?"

"There's that ghost movie that opened last week," Kate offered.

"Eh," I said. I had had enough of scary situations in the last twenty-four hours.

"Action movie, then?" Landon asked.

We settled on a movie about an existential hit man. Movie Night wasn't about seeing Oscar-worthy films. It was about spending a sweet night out. Clichés be damned.

Suddenly, I remembered my lit paper. I snarled at the ground. "I really need to get started on my paper."

Kate frowned. "Already?"

"Really, Ell," Landon said, flashing a stupid grin. "What's the point of drinking coffee at night if you're just going to go fall asleep?"

I shoved his shoulder playfully. "While your logic is flawless, it doesn't help me get my paper done. This cappuccino will, on the other hand."

"Fine, fine," Kate said, waving her hand in a shooing motion. "You suck. Leave."

"You shouldn't tell me I suck on my birthday," I said with a grin.

"Happy birthday!" She beamed.

"Thanks, lover." I gathered my purse and cup. I said good-bye and headed back out to my car. When I got home, I went up to my room and immediately realized I had left my lit book and notes in my locker that afternoon. I swore loudly and plopped heavily down on my bed.

"Damn it, what am I going to do?" I said aloud to no one. I stared at my backpack, angry at it for not containing the things I needed. If I didn't start my paper tonight, I would never get it done. I'd be too busy with my party. I had to go back to school to get it.

I glanced at my clock. It was almost nine, but the school should definitely still be open for the adult-education night classes. If it wasn't open, then at least I had a pretty good excuse to drive again. I could be optimistic when needed.

I grabbed my backpack, purse, cappuccino, and cell

phone and headed back to school to retrieve my forgotten homework. The grounds were weakly lit, and I found only two other cars parked in the student lot behind the building. The faint illumination was provided by the orangeish blotches beneath the parking lot lights, so I parked under one of them instead of in a dark patch. I figured I was less likely to get jumped there.

I found that the doors I usually entered through every morning were locked, so I rounded the building until I found an unlocked one. Inside, I nodded to a janitor I recognized, who smiled kindly at me as he swept the floor, listening to the MP3 player plugged into his ears. The halls were dimly lit, and my footsteps echoed solemnly. It was amazing how creepy this school got at night. I raced to my locker, yanked out what I needed, and stuffed it into my bag before jogging back out of the building. For some reason, outside it now seemed darker to me.

The light on the pole beside my car flickered and hummed. Something tugged on my body, and a hazy veil covered my vision. I had trouble stepping forward, and I looked down at my arms to see what was holding me back. The world—not just the air, but everything solid— stretched and melted away as if I were moving through a gelatinous wall. One more step, and I was suddenly free as a burst of black smoke wound around my limbs and cleared away, leaving the world normal again.

Halfway across the lot, I heard a distinct—and all too familiar—rumble.

"Oh God," I whispered, halting in fear. After two excruciatingly long seconds I heard another growl rolling through the darkness.

I bolted, digging my hands frantically into my pockets for my keys. Something heavy pounded the pavement behind me, but I was too terrified to look back. I pressed Unlock fifty times before I crashed into my car door. A giant, dark shape flashed in the corner of my vision, and I screamed and ducked just as an enormous paw raked its talons across the front fender of my brand-new car.

I hit the ground, spilled my coffee and my bags, and looked up to face my attacker: a reaper, as big as the Audi, loomed over me with one paw on the hood of my car. It looked down on me, covering me completely in its shadow, blocking out the streetlight, its chest heaving with every breath. Its shaggy, dark fur gleamed an ugly charcoal color in the yellow light. The reaper was wolf shaped, just like the ones from my daydream and my nightmare the night before.

"I have found you, Preliator," the reaper said in a deep, husky, but oddly feminine voice. "And now you are *mine*." She grinned a mouthful of fangs and snapped at me. I screamed and threw my arms over my head. The reaper laughed, her hot breath strangling me.

A shadow zipped behind the reaper and suddenly she

was sent flying over the Audi. She landed and skidded across the pavement, digging her claws into the pavement and leaving white streaks behind.

I lowered my arms and looked up to find Will standing over me. His skin beneath the tattoos on his right arm glowed brightly in the streetlight.

"Are you hurt?" he asked, offering his free hand.

I took it, staring at him dazedly, and he helped me up. "The cappuccino . . . It must be the caffeine. . . ."

Will grabbed my shoulder suddenly, threw me back against my car, and looked fiercely into my face. "Snap out of it, Ellie! Denial isn't going to make the reaper go away!"

"I can't! I—"

"Stop saying you can't! You *can*! You must fight!"

I wheeled around, bumping into Will as I searched for the reaper, who had vanished. I grabbed at Will's shirt in terror, shuddering closer to him, my head whipping around wildly, desperate to find the reaper.

"Release her, Guardian!" Her voice rang out from somewhere unseen.

Letting out a hoarse cry, I snapped my gaze up to see the reaper crouched on the roof of the Audi. Thick saliva dripped from her jaws, hitting the roof and sliding down the driver's-side window.

"Oh, poor child," the thing half cooed, half snarled. "She's shaking. What's the matter, girl? You were supposed to be a nightmare, but all I see is a whimpering little lamb.

We don't even need the Enshi. I'll kill you myself."

Horrified, I scrambled away, but Will caught my arm.

"Again!" he cried out, slamming his palm into my forehead for the second time in as many days. The blast hit me, stronger this time, and the white light blinded me once more. The world shook and roiled, and I felt like I was trapped in the center of a tornado again. An eerie gust of wind spiraled around me, pulling my hair and body toward the sky. I squeezed my eyes shut, bracing myself. Will released me and I fell back, but his arm wound around my waist and pulled me to his chest. After a woozy moment I had the strength to stand on my own, and he let me go.

When I opened my eyes, I called my blades and they appeared in my hands, growing magically from the pommel at the bottom of each of the helves to the tips of the blades. The simplest tug in my chest sent flames bursting from the swords, as if they came alight by my will alone. My power surged through me, and the creepy, spiderlike energy of the reaper heated my face like crackling fire. I could feel—and see—Will's power as he stood beside me. He looked dark and beautiful.

"I'm ready now," I said.

The reaper snarled and leaped off the car, landing with an earthshaking thud. I didn't wait for her to charge. I crouched to the pavement, tightened my grip on each sword, and let out a terrible cry. My power erupted, deafening me momentarily, bursting forth from my body as an explosion of inky, wispy white smoke, its strength rocking the ground like an earthquake. The pressure slammed into the reaper and my car with enough force to shove it several feet to one side. My ears rang as I watched the reaper brace herself and hold her ground. Her empty eyes stared back at me like pieces of twisted volcanic glass.

I shot at the reaper, swords high over my head. I summoned my power and leaped up, spinning through the air and crushing my foot into the reaper's jaw. As I came down, I slashed my flaming blades across her body, slicing both her shoulders. She ducked her head and chomped at me as I landed, her fangs nicking my arm and tearing the skin. She swung her neck and her head into my body, smashing me into a light pole. The light went dark as the glass rained down, shattering all around me.

I lay there, my eyes fogging over for a moment, and looked down at my arm. Cuts lined my skin from the lamp's glass and the reaper's teeth. I wiped away the blood and watched my skin heal right before my eyes. The torn flesh wove in and out as though it were being sewn back together with invisible needle and thread until my skin was smooth and flawless except for smears of blood. My gaze snapped back up to see the reaper stomping toward me. Her jaw clicked and contorted grotesquely as the bones I'd smashed with my foot healed back into place.

"You taste good, Preliator," she snarled, giving her jaws a stretch. "I think I'll have another bite."

I grabbed one of my swords and charged. The reaper saw me coming and threw her paw into my face, snapping my head to the side. I ground my teeth bitterly, reeled my arm back, and pounded my fist into her jaw as hard as I could. Instead of just breaking again, her jaw flung free from her skull and skidded across the pavement in a spray of blood.

Another reaper came out of nowhere. It sprang from the shadows at my left, its fangs a flash of white in the dark, but Will swept his own sword through the air between us, stopping my breath. His giant blade sliced through the reaper's neck, sending its head spiraling high over me as it hardened to stone. The head and body hit the pavement and smashed into a thousand stony pieces.

I spun back around as the first reaper reared onto her hind legs, swinging her head in a rage, and I slammed my sword through her ribcage. As the fiery blade struck her heart, she crumpled to all fours. She wheezed and gagged just before her shuddering body erupted into flames and she was gone forever.

6

I PICKED UP THE BLADE AND WIPED IT CLEAN ON my jeans. Will watched me with careful, darkened eyes.

"Thank you," I said.

"Are you going to black out on me again?" he asked, hoisting his sword over his shoulders as if it weighed nothing. Now I got a better look at it. The blade was wide and almost as long as my whole body, and the hilt was incredibly beautiful, with its sleek silver and gold curves molded into what looked like a wing.

"No, I'm okay," I said. "Sort of. So then—I did black out last night?"

"Yeah. You hit the ground pretty hard afterward."

Heat crept into my cheeks. "Thank you for getting me back to my room."

"I wasn't going to just leave you there," he said. "So,

you're remembering then?"

I shrugged. "The fighting part has come back to me and my swords appeared when I called them. I felt like I knew what I was doing." What freaked me out the most was that I didn't really need to think when I fought. My body just kind of knew what it was doing, and I was only along for the ride.

"You've had a lot of practice."

"But everything else," I said distractedly, looking down at the vicious swords in my hands. "It's so fuzzy, still. It's strange, because I know it's all there, but I just can't dig it out. I don't know what I am."

"You are the Preliator," Will declared with an edge of authority to his voice.

"I know *who* I am," I said. "I can remember that, but I don't know *what* I am. And I don't know who *you* are."

Hurt crushed his stony resolve, surprising me. "I am your Guardian, your servant. I'm here to protect and guide you. That is my duty, and that is all that I am."

"How old are you?" I asked, studying his face.

"Six hundred."

My head grew foggy. "How old am *I*?"

"I don't know exactly. A few thousand years, maybe. We have records of you predating ancient Rome."

I crumpled to the ground next to my car. I looked up at the enormous gashes and the dent in the Audi's fender. My parents were going to kill me.

"This is all real, isn't it?"

"Yes." Will crouched down in front of me. He wiped at my cheek. The touch was soft, kind, *familiar.* His gaze was firm but gentle. "You had blood on your face."

I nodded toward my weapons. "Those swords are so strange looking. Why am I able to just make them appear out of thin air? Why do they light on fire? *How?*"

"They are Khopesh, an ancient weapon," he explained. I recognized the name from my nightmares. "They are exceptional blades—meant for slashing, not stabbing, but they get the job done. We are both able to call our swords through our power with angelic magic, but once they appear, they are here. We can't conjure new ones, so you had better not lose either of them. We can will them away also, when we are holding them in our hands, or when we die. They disappear until we call them again."

He held his sword out straight, and it vanished right before my eyes with that same shimmering light. He opened his palm and conjured the sword once more to show me how simple it was, and then he willed it away once more.

"The fire around your swords is angelfire, the only thing effective enough to destroy reapers besides decapitation. Or destruction of the heart—that's what those hooks on the backs of your blades are for."

I examined my swords. Sure enough, the tip of the blunt edge of each blade curved back into a hook that I imagined could do an extreme amount of damage if lodged in soft flesh. I swallowed hard, picturing what had happened to the first reaper's heart when the hook had grabbed it.

"If a reaper dies by means other than angelfire," Will continued, "its body turns to stone instead of burning up. Silver also burns, which is why our blades are made of it, but it doesn't have the permanent effects of angelfire."

I nodded. "That's what happened to the second reaper. Can you make the angelfire appear?"

"No. Only you can, because you are the Preliator."

I held both swords and wondered how I'd made them light up before. They had done it just because I'd wanted them to. Could I do it again, outside of battle? I watched the blades. Was it like an on-off switch? I let one word cross my mind and concentrated. *On.* Flames erupted around the blades, leaving the handles and my hands unscorched. They didn't feel warm and they didn't burn anything. I touched the fiery swords to my pant legs and felt no heat. I touched the flat side of a blade to Will's arm. He looked at me oddly but otherwise did not react. *Off.* The flames vanished. "Cool."

I studied one of the blades closely. Etched in the silver, just above the helve, was a series of strange, whirling, beautiful markings. "What does this mean?"

I looked up at him, and his gaze met mine.

"It's Enochian," he explained, his attention flickering to the sword. "The language of the divine, angelic magic. You once told me that it's a prayer of power, but I can't read it myself. We've tried re-creating the writings on other weapons in order to make them as powerful as your Khopesh swords, but so far they are the only weapons able to light with angelfire."

"That's pretty cool," I said. "Who engraved the prayer onto my swords?"

He sat down on the ground next to me, his back up against my car. "You did."

I blinked in surprise. My fingers brushed the strange words, the edges of the markings scraping my skin softly. I felt a sense of nostalgia, but it was distant, like the memory of a wonderful dream. The more I admired them, the more I remembered. "Just like the tattoos on your arm. I put them there a long time ago."

"Yes."

I traced the spiraling symbols of the tattoo with my finger. His arm tensed under my touch and his breaths became slower and steadier. "It's so strange," I said. "I can't believe that what I'm saying out loud isn't something I made up. I remember tattooing this into your arm. I meant for it to protect you."

"It's an Enochian spell, like the one on your swords."

I noticed he was watching my fingers on his skin, and I pulled back shyly. "Well, you're still here, so it must work. Why don't I have one?"

"The spell is ineffective on human skin."

How inconvenient. "How did you find me? Do you always know where I am?"

"Yes. I can sense you above all others. I always know

where you are, and I try never to be far away. I found you again a few years ago, and the reapers found you more recently."

"Are they hunting me now?"

"Most don't. They're too afraid. But yes, some will hunt you. Be glad it's only a few. Most of them try to stay under the radar, and the weakest ones wouldn't even know you until they saw those swords light up."

"Will, I'm so confused," I began. "How can I be that old when I know exactly where and when I born? I have baby pictures. I'm only seventeen."

"When you die, you are reincarnated," he explained. "Your body and soul are reborn over and over in the same human form. I find you again, usually when you're just a small child, and guard you as you grow up. When you're seventeen and ready to face your true identity, I wake you."

"When you find me as a little girl, how do you know it's me?"

I caught the slightest glimmer of a smile. "I've known you for a very long time. I can always tell when it's you."

I let my head fall back against the car. "Then I'm not immortal."

"Not in the way that I am."

"Does that mean you can't die?"

"I have never died, but I am not invincible. I just don't age."

"You're so strong," I noted. "You punched that reaper so hard and you picked her up just by her neck. She was as big as my car. How can *anyone* be that strong?"

Will's expression turned very serious. "You're stronger than I am, Ellie."

I shook my head tiredly. "I don't understand how it's possible—how *any* of this is possible. What are they? The reapers?"

"They are monsters in this world," he said with an edge to his voice that forced shivers through my body. "They hunt humans for their flesh and their souls, which they harvest in order to restore the armies of Hell for the Second War between Lucifer and God—the Apocalypse. The reapers are immortal and come in many forms; they are most effective killing machines."

"I don't understand how there can be creatures that big and no one knows about them. How come I've never seen any of them until last night?"

"The reapers don't like to be seen," Will explained. "They spend most of their time in the Grim, where they hide from human sight. Powerful psychics, however, can sense them like the ground rumbling as a train passes by and can enter the Grim at will. Beings within the Grim can see and even interact with objects and people still in the mortal world, but they cannot be seen or heard through the veil. The reapers have had many thousands of years to perfect their hunting. They've been seen a few times by ordinary humans, but these sightings are rare and usually happen only because the reaper is being careless. It's even rarer for reapers to intentionally allow a human to see them and not kill them, but some like to do that for sport. There are legends about them in virtually every religion, with all the legends identifying them as harbingers of death. But instead of guiding people to the afterlife, the reapers eat them, and their souls get one-way tickets to Hell."

"So there are no studies of them, even though there have been sightings?" I asked. "Never? People believe in Bigfoot and the Loch Ness monster, and I see documentaries about expeditions to find them on the History Channel all the time—not that I watch that channel much or anything. There's no proof that either of those exist. Yet the reapers leave bodies behind like Mr. Meyer's and no one ever stops to wonder?"

"Reaper attacks are usually blamed on animals or psychotic humans. Bigfoot and the Loch Ness monster aren't real."

"The reapers obviously are! Why hasn't there been some hysteria over sightings?"

Will took a breath and spoke slowly. "There've been many reported sightings of reapers. The most famous are the ones that resemble humans, hence the legend of the Grim Reaper."

My eyes shot wide. "There are human reapers?"

He nodded, watching the ground. "Yes, there are

human-shaped reapers, called the vir, and they are the most powerful. They're also the cockiest and the most likely to show their faces to humans. The other forms, like the ursid, the lupine, the nycterid, and others, have been mistaken for other monsters, because the humans don't know what they're seeing. Like your Bigfoot, dragons, or even werewolves. The reaper you just fought was lupine."

I remembered my daydream about the snowy forest in France. I remembered that I'd been in the Le Gévaudan region, a place where the villagers were ravaged by a wolf-like monster. Historians blamed the hysteria on moldy bread, but I knew better. I felt like I had really been there.

"You keep talking about the Grim," I said. "What is it?"

"The Grim is a dimension parallel to the mortal plane," he explained. "Supernatural creatures live there unseen by mortals and are able to cross over into this dimension. Most humans cannot enter the Grim, unless they are true psychics or creatures like you and me. Last night, you entered the Grim unwittingly so you could see the reaper hunting you, but you did that by pure instinct."

"How was I created?"

"We don't know what you really are. Your body is human, but your power . . . it's something very different. There are a lot of things about you that we still don't understand."

"By we, do you mean you and me? Does anyone else know about me? Is there another Preliator?"

"No, you are the only one."

"Are you my only Guardian?"

"Yes, but before me, there were others who protected you."

"Why don't I have any others?"

"Now it is my duty alone."

"How long have you been my Guardian?"

"Five hundred years."

I blushed and looked away from him. "You've been following me around for five hundred years?"

"I'm your soldier, your protector. And I don't follow you around all the time."

"So I'm not human, am I?"

"Not entirely."

"Am I a psychic, like the ones who can see the reapers?"

"No."

"Then how can I see them?"

"I don't know. You're the Preliator."

I remembered my torn arm. "How was I able to heal so quickly?"

"Your power regenerates your body when you're injured," he explained.

"Then how do I die, if my body just fixes itself right away?"

"Some injuries are too traumatic for your body to heal. I am the same way, and so were your previous Guardians."

"Are *you* human? Or a psychic?"

He paused before he answered me. "No."

"Then what are you?"

"Your Guardian."

"That's not a straight answer," I said, frowning. "Is Will your real name?"

"Of course."

"So, what are you?"

"Your Guardian."

I frowned. I had a million more questions, and I had a feeling he'd dodge as many of the good ones as possible. It should all come in time, right? There were flashes of images, of terrible things, battles and blood, scattered across my memory in distorted fragments. I looked down at the reaper's blood on my hands and I felt very sad. How could I adapt to this? I wasn't dreaming anymore. My skin felt raw from when I had hit the ground. My arm ached where it was cut. Dreams never hurt you. This was real. My nightmares had become real. I was frightened, and I didn't want to have to deal with this. Wasn't it enough worrying about getting into college?

"Why can't I remember?" I asked. "This isn't normal, is it?"

Will shook his head. "No, this has never happened before, but it's been a very long time since you were last alive. Usually your reincarnation is almost immediate and you are reborn somewhere in the world, but this time, instead of eighteen years you took four decades to become the Preliator again. I don't know why."

"My memory should return in time, right?"

"It will."

"When you touched my face, everything became so clear. My strength, my purpose . . . How did you do that?"

Will leaned forward, resting his arms on his knees. "Because I'm your Guardian, I have the ability to awaken your power. You were a normal girl until the moment you turned seventeen, and it's my duty to restore your power and memories and defend you in battle from that moment on."

I suddenly remembered my lit paper and scrambled to my feet, looking around for my purse. I spotted it lying beside my backpack, right where I'd dropped them. My car had been moved two parking spots away from where I had left it. I paused, realizing the impossibility of what I had done.

"I did that, didn't I?"

"You can do a lot more than that with your power."

"Is it telekinesis?"

"No, your power can only push things, not pull them. It's like an immensely strong gust of wind made of pure energy, of life force."

"That is insane," I mumbled, retrieving my lost items. I dug my cell out and checked the time, then shoved my phone back into my bag. It was after ten. Fantastic. I'd never be able to get anything written on my paper and wake up with a working brain in the morning. Strangely, my homework seemed quite insignificant.

"I need to get home. My parents are going to flip when they see what that thing did to my car. What do I tell them?" I stroked the deep claw marks in the Audi's fender. It would have to be repainted, possibly replaced. How would I explain it, though?

"Tell them someone hit your car and drove off. Your insurance should cover the damages."

"They'll never buy that."

"You don't have another option."

I made an ugly noise and scowled. My dad was going to slaughter me no matter what. Distracting my thoughts from my likely fate, I remembered something the first reaper had said. "Did you hear the reaper say something about an Enshi?"

He stared at me. "Enshi? What exactly did she say?"

"She said, 'We don't need the Enshi,' because she'd just kill me herself. Do you know what that word means? And who are 'we'?"

"It's Sumerian," he said thoughtfully. "Lord of . . . something. I'll need to check exactly what -shi means."

"You speak Sumerian? Who speaks that? Seriously."

"Can you meet me at the library after school? We should look into it."

"I have too much homework," I said. "How about Saturday afternoon? Three o'clock?"

"That will work. Tomorrow night we need to train. Your

skills need to come back to you faster than they are."

"But it's Friday night. That's our Movie Night."

"Otherwise you won't last."

"You mean I'll die." It wasn't a question.

"Yes."

I shrugged. "Well, we don't want that, but my friends and I always go to the movies Friday night, so it'll have to be later."

"I can wait. The night is long."

"I'll give you a call when we're done. What's your number?" I started to get my phone back out to punch in his information.

"I don't have a phone. You won't need to call me."

I looked at him quizzically. "No one can survive without a cell phone. Are you going to be stalking me at the movies, too?"

He seemed unaffected. "I've been your companion for five hundred years as your Guardian, your bodyguard. During the day, while you're at school, you're safe, so I'm usually home until dusk. I need to rest too. I'm not following you around constantly, but I can sense if you're distressed or frightened. If you're attacked, I'll know. It's part of the bond we share."

I wondered if he had sensed my fear during my hallucination in the bathroom earlier at school, and if that was why he had come to find me. "So while I'm at school, how do you keep yourself busy? Got any hobbies?"

He smiled. "You're enjoying all these questions, aren't you?"

"I'm just trying to figure you out."

His eyes met mine challengingly, but I was too tired to keep interrogating him.

I sighed. "I really need to get home. I'm so exhausted."

He nodded. "I will see you tomorrow after your movie."

"Yeah," I said, not particularly ecstatic about it. I understood what was happening to my life, but I wasn't entirely sure I wanted to accept it. At this point, there could be no denying that my life would never be normal again.

7

SCHOOL FLEW BY LIKE A BREEZE. FRIDAYS WERE
often that way. Everyone, including teachers and staff, just
wanted to get the hell out of there and enjoy the weekend.
The night before, I had fallen asleep almost upon impact
with the pillow, and obviously I hadn't gotten any work
done on my paper. Luckily, neither of my parents had
looked closely enough at my car that morning to notice the
giant claw marks in the paint. I knew it was only a matter
of time and bad luck before they did, however. Kate, on
the other hand, had noticed them right away. I went with
Will's story and explained that someone had hit my car
in a parking lot, but I wasn't sure Kate was convinced. I
would still need to figure out how to fix those the cheapest
way possible and without getting caught by my parents. I

drove home right after school to squeeze out three of the five pages needed for my lit paper.

That night I wore the winged necklace Will had given me. It felt right wearing it, like reattaching a lost fifth limb. The feeling was comforting, and the necklace was beautiful. I loved it.

I met Kate and Landon at the theater, and we were soon joined by Rachel and Chris. As soon as I arrived, Kate noticed my necklace.

"Where did you get that?" she asked, gaping at the pendant and examining it closely. "It looks antique. So gorgeous."

"Yeah, it's pretty old." I didn't want to tell her Will had given it to me, or that it was mine to begin with.

"I'm going to steal it," Kate said, and walked away.

I smiled and followed her inside. It was chilly outside, so I was glad I was wearing a hoodie over my tank top. We wouldn't have many more seventy-degree days in September.

The movie was all right, with some pretty good special effects, but I couldn't focus enough to enjoy it as much as my friends seemed to. I had already forgotten most of the plot by the time we all left the theater, with my friends chattering about how sweetly some random henchman had taken a knife to the head and how the hero had escaped the burning train. The boys were pretty stuck on recalling how hot the love interest was. All I could think about was meeting Will afterward and about how God only knew what other horrors

I'd have to witness. I found myself looking in the darkest places around me, fearful of what might leap out from the shadows. I wondered if I would pass someone on the sidewalk who might be killed by a reaper that very night and lose his soul to Hell, no matter what kind of good life he had lived. If I was to be some kind of hero, how many people would I be unable to save? I couldn't even eat fries without dripping ketchup on myself. How could I be responsible for someone else's life when I couldn't even be responsible for my own shirt?

"You okay, Ell?" Kate asked, lowering her head to whisper into my ear. "You seem so distant and quiet."

I nodded. "Yeah, I'm fine. I've just got to get going."

"Huh?" Kate asked, surprised. "Are you ditching us early again?"

Landon overheard and jogged up beside me, throwing an arm over my shoulder. "You'd better not be thinking about bailing. It's only ten and your party is tomorrow. There's got to be a preparty and then an after party. And a *day-after* party. Stay out later. Your paper can wait. I haven't even started mine."

"No, it's not my paper." I didn't want to lie, but I couldn't exactly tell the truth, either. A partial truth would do. "I'm meeting Will in a little bit." Landon's arm became stiff around my shoulder.

Kate's eyes bulged. "You mean that weird guy from Cold Stone? You're going on a date with him?"

I put my hands up defensively, not wanting them to get the wrong idea. "No, no, no. It's not a date, we're just hanging out."

"Honey, it's Friday night, and when it's just you and him hanging out, that's a date. He's hot as hell, so have fun, okay?" Kate winked.

Rachel nodded. "*Yeah*, he is. Let me know if you don't want him! I will gladly take him off your hands." She laughed and playfully pinched me in the side. I twisted away uncomfortably.

Landon's expression turned dark and he withdrew his arm. "Are you serious? You're going somewhere with that guy? You don't even know him!"

"Yeah, do you think that's such a good idea?" Chris asked. "He's got to be, like, twenty."

"He's just fine," I said, scowling. "Yeah, he's a little strange, but he's actually a really nice guy. And so what if he's a little older than me?" On second thought, neither of us was sure how old I actually was.

Kate shrugged. "Okay, well, let me know how it goes."

"I can't *believe* this!" Landon said, the volume of his voice causing people to turn their heads and stare. He stomped off toward the parking lot.

I ran a hand through my hair. "Seriously! What is wrong with him?"

Kate laughed. "Ellie, are you really that blind? He likes you."

I gaped at her. "Excuse me?"

"Yeah," Chris said, the look on his face telling me that he found this far too amusing. "We thought you knew."

Just what I needed. I had thought his newfound extreme interest in my well-being was something more benign—I must have been mistaken. I remembered my birthday roses and the kiss on the cheek. Was I *really* that stupid? Landon was cute and a nice guy and all, but this was *Landon.* Just . . . no way. I put a hand to my forehead. "I have to go. Now."

"See you later, Ell," Rachel said.

"Be safe," Kate said. "Just call me if you want me to bail you out."

I nodded. "See you bright and early? We'll get to Somerset around eleven? Maybe lunch while we're there?"

"Sounds great!" She smiled, and then her expression wiped clean.

"Ellie," said Will's voice behind me.

I turned around and was shocked to see him. "Will! What are you doing here?"

His eyes flickered to the necklace around my neck and a warm smile shaped his lips. "We were going to meet, remember?"

"Right," I said, glancing back at my friends. I waved good-bye and headed to where I had parked. "I didn't know you were going to surprise me right outside the theater."

"Well, you said we could meet right after, so here I am."

"Where's your car?" I asked, as we climbed in and buckled up.

"I didn't drive."

Taxi, I guessed. "Where are we going?"

"I've found a good location in Pontiac," he said.

"Pontiac? All the way there? Why?" That wasn't exactly the safest area around here to hang out in at night. I panicked a little inside.

"Would you like me to drive?"

"No, it's *my* car," I said possessively.

"Then don't complain about where we're going."

It took longer than usual to travel the thirty-five miles to Pontiac because of heavy traffic. Will didn't say much during the drive, and the awkward silence was beginning to take its toll on my psyche.

"You're tense," Will observed, staring out the windshield.

"I have a ninja sitting shotgun. Of course I'm tense."

The smallest smile formed in the corner of his mouth.

"So where are you living?" I asked him, trying to make conversation during the back-up.

"Don't worry about it."

I waited for him to elaborate, but he didn't. "Don't you have an apartment or something? How do you pay for it? Do you have a job?"

"Don't worry about it."

"Why all the secrets?"

"You haven't asked the right questions." He glanced at me and smiled.

I huffed, annoyed. "You have a place to live, right?"

"Yes, but I'm only there for essentials."

"What is that supposed to mean?"

"I need to sleep, shower, and eat, of course. I'm not a robot."

I sat there seething for a moment. He obviously wasn't going to give me a straight answer, so I changed my question. "Why are you my Guardian?"

"I am very proficient at fighting. We made a good team."

I glanced at him. "Are we still?"

"I hope so. You ask a lot of questions. I am not what's important right now. We need to focus on your waking up and becoming strong again."

"Well, it would be nice if I could remember it all, since I'm supposed to know this already." It all sounded so covert. I was having a difficult time believing that I could be part of something so much bigger than myself. I stared out the windshield at the cars zooming by on the opposite side of the highway.

"Do you mind?" Will asked.

"What?" I blinked at him. He had his hand on the stereo knob.

"It's a bit of a drive," he said. "I don't like sitting in silence."

"Yeah, I guess."

He turned on the radio and flipped over to the classic

rock station. Satisfied, he leaned back against the seat.

"Pink Floyd?" I probed, unable to keep the smile from creeping to the corners of my lips.

"I've had a lot of time to myself, waiting for your rebirth," he confessed. "You were gone for so long. I had to think of something to do, and I found rock music." He grinned. "I've gotten pretty good at the guitar. I'll play some Rolling Stones tabs for you someday, if you're lucky."

I laughed. "If I'm lucky, huh?"

His grin widened brilliantly. "Oh, yeah. Only if you're lucky."

When we finally got to Pontiac, Will gave me specific directions and we drove into an area that looked pretty rough. We turned onto a very dark street with no streetlights, and the only buildings I could see were a boarded-up gas station and a warehouse that looked as if it hadn't been in business in twenty years.

"Are we seriously parking my car out here?" I asked nervously, my eyes flitting everywhere.

"No one's around," he said. "Pull up into the alley. It's secluded. If anyone comes by, I'll hear them. No worries. I found this building last week, and it should be a great place to train."

"Whatever you say, chief." I drove into the alley he'd pointed out, barely squeezing my chubby little sedan through. The tires rolled over rocks, garbage, and massive weeds that were beginning to look like trees. I reached the end and shut off the engine. "What now?"

He smiled. "We go inside."

"I'm going to get tetanus in there," I grumbled.

"Don't go rolling in piles of dirt and rusty nails and you'll be fine."

"You're an ass."

8

WILL SHOWED ME TO THE DOOR, BUT IT WAS BOARDED up. He plucked the sheets of plywood off with no effort at all and tossed them aside. The interior of the warehouse was surprisingly clean. Junk had been moved off to the side, and there wasn't any broken glass lying around. Tires were stacked in a corner by a pile of rusting hubcaps and wooden crates. Moonlight streamed in through high, mostly intact windows. Steel columns stretched from the concrete floor to the ceiling.

"I've even cleaned it up for you," Will said, obviously trying to suppress laughter. Laughter that, I was sure, was directed at me.

I glared at him. "Why was it boarded up if you've gotten in already? Did you nail the boards over the door when you left?"

"I didn't come in through the door," he said, and pointed up.

My gaze lifted to the windows. "Nuh-uh."

"Once you figure out what you can really do, you won't be surprised at how I got in. That's why we're here."

"So you can murder me and steal Marshmallow?" I mumbled absently as I picked at the peeling paint on the door.

He blinked. "Steal what?"

"Never mind."

"You are a very strange girl," he said, stepping very close to me.

His closeness alarmed me for a moment, and then I felt my unease melt away. It was really odd, my reaction to his presence. Perhaps it was because he was the only one I knew in the world who had the power to protect me. That should have made anyone feel pretty safe, right? Perhaps it was the "bond" he said we shared.

"What are you doing?" I asked, my eyes wide.

His fingers traced the curve of my shoulder softly, as his gaze fell. I gasped sharply. If he tried to kiss me, I'd slap the crap out of him. Bond or no bond.

He slipped my purse off my shoulder and tossed it. "You won't need this." He turned and stepped away.

I let out a long breath. "You're weird, you know that? Way weirder than you think I am."

He laughed. "I believe you've told me that a few times."

"Do I need to be in the Grim in order to fight or do those crazy acrobatics?"

"No," he said. "The only time you need to enter the Grim is when a reaper is hiding there. When they're hiding, that's the only way we can see them."

"So what can I really do? If you can jump through a two-story window, then what can I do?"

"You can do that too. You don't even need wings to do it, either."

I ignored his smartass remark, which made no sense at all anyway. I unzipped my hoodie, shrugged it off, and tossed it over by my purse. Wearing just my tank top, I folded my arms across my chest. "Yeah, right. Show me something, then."

"You can bring this whole building down."

I huffed in disbelief. "Show me."

"I'm not going to destroy the warehouse with us in it," he said. "We'll need this place for a while, so I'll give you a taste."

He stepped farther away from me, his eyes locked on mine, and stood next to one of the steel columns. For a moment—I had to blink several times—it looked as if the air around him moved, like heat waves swaying just above the pavement on a hot day, only they radiated off his *body*. The green of his eyes seemed to intensify until they almost glowed, even though I knew that wasn't possible. Then a blast hit me like a truck, knocking me flat on my back. I struggled back to my feet, gaping at Will in awe. I could see the energy rolling from him. I could feel it on my skin and lapping up my legs.

With a quick swing of his torso, Will smashed his forearm into the column, and the steel gave with a piercing whine until it bent at an angle, ripping almost fully free from the beam high above it. Dust blasted free and settled to the floor.

I staggered back, tripping and nearly falling. I stared at him, fearful, confused, and completely stunned. "H—how?"

"I could take it down if I wanted to," he said, relaxing his power, letting it wash away like the tide. "You're stronger than me, Ellie. I need to prove it to you."

"Oh God" was all I could say.

"You try it," he said. "I know you remember how. I've seen you do it since you awakened. By summoning your power, you will have the strength to kill a reaper. They can do the same thing, though, so you have to be cautious, and that is why you have the angelfire. If you come across a vir, you may not know what he is until it's too late. The weaker ones seem the most human. The powerful ones don't bother to hide what they are. They don't usually like to be compared to humans, but they'll shape-shift to take the form of a particular human in order to infiltrate."

"Do you have to touch my face again to trigger me, in order to bring my power out?" I asked.

"No, I don't think I'll have to do that again." He held out his arm and conjured his sword. The enormous silver blade glinted into being. "Call your swords now."

"Why?" I asked, uncertain of his motives.

"We're going to bring out your power so you will learn to do it on your own. I am your soldier, but I am not your crutch."

"But I—"

In a flash he sliced his sword at my throat, but I instinctively ducked, shocked by my own quickness. Without my consciously calling them, my swords appeared in my hands. Will swiped his blade down again, but I swung my swords up, catching Will's blow with a *shing!* of metal against metal. He pushed down, hard, but I held my position, refusing to let him overpower me, and angelfire ignited on my blades. Will's foot suddenly connected with my chest and slammed me into one of the columns behind me, my back crunching against the steel. The wind rushed from my lungs, but Will was coming at me too fast for me to catch my breath. He swiped again and I rolled away. His blade clanged off the column, and I looked back, eyes wide.

"Stop running!" Will shouted. "Fight me!"

"You're going to *kill* me!" I shrieked.

"Only if you let me!" He leaped into the air and came down at me, his sword held high. He slashed, but the Khopesh caught his blade and deflected it away from my face. I swung my other sword and slashed—Will recoiled as the blade cut neatly down his cheek. His face snapped to the side and he groaned in pain. He looked back at me, his green eyes brighter than I had ever seen, and the gash on his cheek melted together again, leaving only a thin line of blood. The angelfire didn't harm him.

"Keep fighting and don't stop!" he thundered. "If you stop, you're dead!"

He vanished suddenly and reappeared behind me. I reeled around to face him, swinging one sword up, and it collided with his. I slashed the other sword at his belly, but he jumped back, spun around, and kicked my wrist. The Khopesh went flying. I gaped at it in fright, and when I looked back at Will, he had already lowered his sword and was reaching for me. He clamped his hand around my throat, threw my back against a column, and grabbed the wrist that held my remaining Khopesh. He had me pinned. I struggled against his grip, but he was just so, *so* strong.

"Let me go!" My free hand clawed at his hand around my neck.

"I'm not releasing you," he said. "You've lost. You stopped fighting and took your eye off me."

"Please, *please*, Will." I gasped, my windpipe closing. Panic grabbed at me and my eyes welled with tears. "You're going to kill me."

"Then do something about it!" he roared into my face.

"You have that strength! If you want me to let you go, then *force me to*!"

I screamed, filled half with fear and half with fury, and my power exploded, my hair whipping around my face so wildly I couldn't see. The column behind me crunched, and the floor rolled and sank beneath my strength. Will was blown away from me and landed sliding across the concrete floor. I bolted forward and my sword burst into flames as I swung it at Will's throat where he lay. I poised the tip at his jugular, my lungs heaving, my heart pounding, and my power swirling like a hurricane all around me, swallowing me in diamond light.

My eyes darkened as I stared Will down. He put his hands up slowly.

"You lose," I said cruelly. My power receded and my body relaxed. I collected my fallen sword and willed them both away.

Will smiled and rose to his feet.

I promptly punched him in the face hard enough to make him drop back to his knees. "You're a bastard!" I shrieked down at him, my voice cracking.

He laughed and rubbed his jaw firmly. "And you're frightening." He stood back up.

I hit him again, making his head snap around. "Why'd you scare me like that?"

As I swung a third time, he grabbed my wrist. "That's

enough hitting," he growled. "You don't exactly hit like a girl, you know."

I wrenched free and walked away from him, breathing heavily. "Good God, that felt amazing."

"Hitting me?"

"Yes," I said, glaring back at him briefly. "And the power. I felt like I could punch through walls." My gaze found the crater I had made in the concrete floor. The column was twisted and mangled, barely connecting to the ceiling any longer. It groaned, as if just a gentle nudge would send it crashing to the ground.

"You can," he said.

"I'm afraid, Will," I confessed. "I scare myself. If I'm capable of doing that, what's preventing me from doing it to someone who doesn't deserve it? What if I hurt someone?"

"I'll help you avoid that," he assured me. "When you're faced with a reaper, you can't worry about anything else. That's *my* job. You have to use everything you've got to defeat it. If you hesitate, you will die. You hesitated just a moment ago, and that's how I was able to overpower you. You can't stop for any reason. Trust me always to guard your back in battle. I will protect you."

He walked past me, but I grabbed his shoulder. "Wait." I guided him around to face me, my hand sliding to his collar. I was picturing that shiny plus sign I thought I'd seen before, and I slipped the chain out from beneath his shirt. Dangling from the end of the chain was a silver crucifix, not a plus sign. As soon as I saw it, I remembered what it was and my heart warmed. It felt good to see it again.

I looked up and saw that his gaze was glued to mine. "I remember it."

His body was stiff and his jaw tightened. Suddenly his reaction was as fascinating as my remembering the crucifix around his neck. "It was a gift," he said. "From my mother."

"Does it protect against the reapers?"

"No."

"Then why do you wear it?"

"My mother gave it to me."

I nodded, angry at myself for asking such a stupid question. Despite his stone-hard expression, I could sense that I'd hurt him. The crucifix had sentimental value to him. Maybe it meant as much to him as my winged necklace did to me— if only I could remember where my own pendant had come from. His crucifix was centuries old. If he'd held on to it for so long, it had to mean a great deal to him, and so must his mother. "I'm sorry."

"Don't worry about it." He tucked the crucifix back into his shirt. "It's nothing, really. It's stupid."

I stared at him for a few moments. It didn't seem right to me that he was so evasive. The object obviously wasn't *nothing* to him, but I didn't feel it was my place to probe him about it.

"Training tomorrow evening?" he asked, interrupting my thoughts.

I frowned. "No," I said. "It's my birthday party."

"Oh, yes. I forgot." He sounded not disappointed but neutral, as if simply observing a fact. "Are we still on for the library at three then?"

"Sure, but there's no way I'm missing my own birthday party."

"I'll stick around close by for that."

"I'd like it if you were there," I said. "As a guest."

"Nonsense. I'll guard on the roof."

"You don't have to be a creeper *all* the time, you know. Come to my party and have a little fun for once in your life."

"I have fun."

I scoffed. "I'm pretty sure our ideas of fun vary drastically."

He flashed me a grin. "I'll show you someday."

I smiled back. "Now you've got me all intrigued."

"And you'll have to stay that way until the day I decide to divulge my secrets to you."

I laughed. "So will you come? Indoors, too, and enjoy the party?"

His smile was sly. "Don't you think Landon will have a problem with that?"

"How did you—? Oh, right."

"I've seen the way he looks at you," he said. "What

shocks me is that you *don't*."

"Well, now that it's been pointed out to me, I just may."

He drew his face close to mine. "You don't read people very well, do you?"

I playfully shoved his shoulder away. "I read people just fine. I just don't have a thousand years of practice like you."

He stepped back and laughed. "All right, I'll come by, as a guest. I'll allow you to see me there."

I blinked. "Oh, you *allow* me to see you, is that it?"

He nodded, failing to stop a smirk from forming. "Oh yes. You have only ever seen me when I will it. I'm spectacular at hiding."

"You're sure of yourself, aren't you?"

"You have no idea."

I narrowed my eyes. "We'll see about that." I turned away from him and left the warehouse. I climbed into my car, but when I looked for Will, he was standing at my window instead of getting in the passenger seat. "Aren't you getting in?"

He bent over to look at me through the window. "No."

"You're going to walk all the way back home to Bloomfield Hills?"

He nodded. "I can travel easily."

"That's a load of bull. Get in."

"Just go," he said. "Don't worry about me."

"I'm not stranding you out in the middle of Pontiac. Get in."

"I can obviously take care of myself. I'm not driving with you."

"Yeah, you are. Don't lie to me and say you're going to walk."

"Good-bye, Ellie," he said, turning away from the window.

"Will!" I cried out, opening my door and jumping out.

He was gone.

I spun around, looking for him, but he was nowhere to be seen.

"Will?"

The street was dark, and the wind blew leaves and old papers down the sidewalk—the only movement I could see. "I am so sick of you pulling this Batman shit on me!" Exhausted and angry, I got back in my car and drove home.

9

I WOKE AT NINE, AND AS SOON AS I CLIMBED OUT OF
bed, I felt the effects of my training with Will the night before.
My back and shoulders ached, and the anti-inflammatory
pills I had taken did pretty much nothing to ease them. After
a shower I made myself some coffee to try to wake up. Kate
called at ten, confirming she'd be there at eleven to pick me
up, but I told her we had to be done by two so I would have
time to get to the library. It was already warm enough outside
for me to feel comfortable wearing a denim skirt and flip-flops.
Despite being sleepy, I felt good. I felt different and I liked
it. Taming my wavy hair, I pulled half of it up and pinned it
behind my head. Straightening sounded like too much work
today. Back in my room, I pulled on a favorite knit top and was
ready to go.

There was a knock on my door. "Yep?" I called.

The door opened and my mom came through. I didn't like the look on her face. "Ellie, is there something you want to tell me about?"

Panicked lists streaked through my head. What had I done? Did I get back too late? "Uh, don't think so," I replied, trying to sound calm as my heart picked up its pace.

"About your car, maybe?"

Lightbulb. "Oh yeah," I groaned. "Somebody must have hit my car at school and driven off. I couldn't believe it."

She watched me disapprovingly. "I'm surprised you forgot to mention it. You didn't hit a sign or something, did you? Be honest, Ellie."

I would have much preferred to have just hit a sign instead of what had actually happened. "I found my car like that yesterday," I explained. "I swear I didn't hit anything, Mom. It made me so angry and I didn't want it to ruin my day, so I tried not to think about it. I was so busy with homework and then going out for Movie Night, I totally forgot. I'm sorry."

She frowned. "I guess we'll have to take care of that. I hope the dealership's repair shop will fix it up, since you've only had the thing for *two days*." She stressed those last two words uncomfortably. "Whoever you've pissed off at school . . . you should try to make nice before that someone slashes your tires and breaks your windows."

"Yeah, for sure," I added. If she ended up having to pay for it, I'd feel really crappy.

"I'll give them a call." She sighed. "Try parking in the back of the lot, Ellie."

"Mom, it's almost winter," I protested. "I don't want to park out in the middle of nowhere and freeze to death walking inside. Not to mention, my car is white. He'll camouflage in the snow and I'll never find him."

"You're wearing a skirt," she observed. "It's perfectly warm outside."

I huffed. "Not for long."

She frowned again. "Well, I don't know what to tell you. Have fun with Kate today." She handed me a credit card. "Be reasonable. *One* dress. And get yourself lunch while you're out. You look tired, and I don't want your blood sugar to get too low. You know what a grouch you become when you don't eat."

I smiled. "Thanks, Mom."

She turned but did a double take. "Where did that necklace come from?"

I touched the pendant. "A friend."

"A boy?"

Yikes. "He's a friend who's a boy."

Her mouth twitched in amusement and her gaze left the necklace. "First roses, and now a necklace? Are you sure Landon isn't your boyfriend?"

"This wasn't from him, Mom."

"So you have two boyfriends?"

"No, Mom!" I almost shouted. "Neither of them is my

boyfriend. Trust me. They're just boys who are friends. No connecting of words going on . . . or connecting of anything else, for that matter."

She stared at me. "Hmm." Then she left my room. She was so weird sometimes.

A few minutes later Kate burst into my bedroom, almost obnoxiously cheerful.

"So!" she chirped, flopping onto my bed, blond hair flying. "How did it go?"

"How did what go?" I asked, pulling a bit of the front of my hair out of my eyes and pinning it down with a bobby pin as I stared into the mirror over my dresser.

Kate chucked a pillow at my butt, knocking me into my dresser and making me rattle a couple of perfume bottles. "You know what I mean! How was your date with Will?"

"It *wasn't* a date," I said, scowling at her through the mirror, steadying the vase of Landon's roses. "I promise you."

"Then enlighten me. What exactly was it?"

"He's been helping me with . . . homework. Econ has been kicking my ass." And so had *Will*, I thought.

Kate laughed aloud. "He's your tutor? Oh, Ellie, that is the biggest load of crap I have ever heard."

"Well, it's the truth," I lied. I hated lying to my best friend, but it wasn't like I could tell her what was really going on. "I don't *like* him or anything, trust me. He's kind of a jerk, actually. He's not as nice as I thought."

"I wish I had a hot tutor."

"Don't be so smart then."

"Whatever," Kate said, sitting up. "You're a big, fat liar. Let's go shopping."

We drove in Kate's BMW to the mall and pulled up to the Saks Fifth Avenue entrance. Kate gave her keys to a really cute valet guy and tucked her ticket into her purse before we went inside. Glamorous counters gleaming gold and ivory lined the main floor with just hints of frosty hues announcing the fall and winter arrivals. Kate stopped to ogle a table topped with shoes by Chanel and slowed us down again to fondle a particular bag in the Valentino collection as I dragged her up the escalator to the dress boutique.

I decided on a cute, strapless, cream Badgley Mischka cocktail dress. The bodice fit comfortably and the poufy chiffon layers of the skirt fell to just above my knees. I knew I had the perfect matching black Marc Jacobs satin shoes to complement it. I wasn't surprised when Kate chose a rather adventurous black mesh-front Dolce&Gabbana bustier sheath dress. If anyone could pull it off, Kate could. She had legs that went on for miles, and if all she wore was a handful of raggedy old washcloths pieced together with duct tape, she'd still look ready for the red carpet.

I paid with the card my mom gave me, and then we walked around for another hour before we went to eat lunch at P. F. Chang's. Kate knew a manager there who helped us skip the two-hour wait and seated us immediately.

As I ate my Szechuan chicken and listened to Kate run her mouth about spotting Josie Newport leaving the Louis Vuitton boutique with a new bag, I found myself thinking about Will. I wondered if he was in the Grim at that moment. I felt comforted, safe, knowing that if something decided to attack, he'd be there in an instant. Even though I'd righteously kicked his ass the night before, I still didn't want to fight on my own. To be honest, it probably would have felt very weird if he had decided to accompany us where we could see him. I imagined him wandering around the mall, following us on our shopping trip with our bags in his hands, helping us choose dresses, and I couldn't help letting out a little laugh.

"I know, right?" Kate asked with a nod, mistaking my laugh as a reaction to something she'd said about Josie.

I looked around me, hoping to maybe spot him and disprove his claim that I could never see him unless he let me, but I failed. The restaurant was too crowded, too noisy, and too dark. Disappointed, I turned my attention back to my meal and Kate's colorful conversation.

"So when are you seeing Will again?" Kate asked, as if reading my mind.

"He's coming to my party tonight," I said.

Her face lit up. "He is? Is he bringing any of his friends? He's got to be in college. Where does he go? University of Michigan? Oakland University?"

I nodded. "Uh, yeah. U of M. I don't think he'll bring any of his friends, though."

"Oh, come on! No hot college boys coming? Why do you get to hog the only one?"

I prodded my rice. "Guess I'm just lucky." For a brief moment I imagined myself dancing with Will, and the next moment I felt like spitting up my chicken.

On our way out of the mall, Kate stopped by Valentino and bought the bag she had had her eye on earlier. Surprise, surprise.

When we got home from shopping, I told my parents that I would be at the library for a few hours. That wasn't a lie, but I wouldn't be there to study for Monday's math test, as they'd assume. I'd be reading up on something else. I didn't know why there would be books that had anything on reapers, or whatever the Enshi was, at an ordinary library, but I suspected Will would know better than me.

When I arrived at the library, I parked, and immediately I saw Will sitting on the front steps. He wore his usual serious expression.

"I can't believe you're making me study on my birthday," I grumbled. "You aren't my real tutor, you know."

"Today isn't your birthday."

"My birthday *party* is today and that's as good as it actually being my birthday."

He stood. "Let's go inside. I want you to meet someone.

He's been a friend of mine—of both of ours—for a very long time."

That got my interest. "Who is this guy?"

"You'll see," Will said. "I think he might have an idea of where we should start looking to find out what this Enshi is."

I followed him inside and spoke quietly. "Why do you think that? What information about reapers could we possibly find at a library? It doesn't seem a likely place."

"You need to trust me more."

He led me past the front desk and waved at a plump woman in glasses who sat there shuffling through a stack of papers. "Hey, Louise."

The woman nodded and smiled at us as I followed Will through a set of doors on her right and down a flight of stairs to another set of doors. We entered a long hallway whose scuffed white walls were lined with wooden doors. I heard nothing except for the hum of the air-conditioning system and our footsteps echoing off the linoleum floor.

Will finally stopped at a door indistinguishable from the others, opened it, and stepped aside so that I could walk through. The room within was dull and smelled thickly of musty, old books. All four walls were lined with large, leather-bound volumes, and double-sided bookcases stood tall on either side of an aisle that led to the back of the room. A young man was sitting at a desk against the wall, reading a book that I was sure was thicker than my upper body. A girl who looked about Will's age sat in a chair across from him.

She turned her head to look at us, her long, black-brown hair swinging. She was a beautiful Asian girl, and she smiled sweetly as we approached.

The young man—he looked maybe the same age as Will—was unnaturally pale, as if he didn't get out much, and he watched us as we approached his desk. He looked kind of nerdy, but the adorable kind, with a silly, lopsided grin. His maple brown hair was untidy, but I got the impression that he was one of those guys who didn't really care how presentable he appeared.

"Hey, Nathaniel," Will said. He nodded to the girl. "Lauren."

Nathaniel looked only at me, smiling the type of smile that reminded me of Mr. Meyer, even though he looked barely any older than Will. I smiled back, instantly liking him. His eyes were vivid and coppery, like iridescent pennies. With every movement of his gaze, they glinted.

"Hello again." Nathaniel smiled brightly. "It's been a while."

"I'm sorry, but have we met?" I asked, unable to recall his face.

"Oh, yes," he said. "We've known each other for many ages. Will told me that your memory is having a little trouble coming back to you, but that's all right. You will remember in time."

"I hope so," I said honestly.

"You're as lovely as ever," he offered.

"Thank you," I said.

The Asian girl stood and held a hand out for me to shake it. "You must be Ellie."

I smiled. "That's me."

"Lauren Tsukino," she said. "Nice to meet you. I'll get out of your hair now. Nathaniel, you'll look into that for me, won't you?"

He nodded. "Of course, my dear. You'll be hearing from me shortly."

Lauren squeezed by us and disappeared out the door.

Nathaniel turned back to me. "Lauren is a very powerful psychic," he explained. "She sensed something arriving in the area recently that gave her quite a shock. It would be nice if she could see the future—then we'd have this one in the bag. Alas, she is only clairvoyant, but she knows a nasty reaper when she feels it!" He beamed as if he had just told an incredible joke, but I failed to find it amusing. I could see the punch line—I wasn't stupid—but it just wasn't *funny*.

"I didn't know psychics were real until Will told me about them," I remarked, looking around at Nathaniel's collection of books.

"Oh, yes," he said. "If they don't go bad, they are invaluable allies to us. Lauren's been most helpful since I met her. Your teacher, too. Frank Meyer."

My jaw dropped. "*Mr. Meyer?* You're joking."

"He was recently killed on a hunt," Nathaniel explained, "as you know, of course. He was good for a human, but his age slowed him down. The reaper got the better of him."

"You're telling me that my economics teacher was a reaper-hunting psychic? That's kind of too badass for a high school teacher."

"Frank was one of the best," Will said.

"Nuh-uh." My head spun. "I had no idea he was that cool."

Will gave a small laugh. "He was wild in his teens. Worse in his twenties."

"You knew him then?"

His laughter died. "So did you."

I stared at him. "I knew him in a past life?"

He shot Nathaniel a quick glance. "Yes, in Chicago. Around forty-five years ago. He was a good friend to us. I spoke to him recently, and he told me he recognized you on your first day of high school as a freshman. He never forgot you. He told me it was quite an experience seeing you again."

"I knew him?" I repeated, my mind juggling a thousand questions and thoughts. "He must have been about twenty, right? Why didn't he ever say anything to me? He went on pretending like I was just another student. He fought with us once? Of all the people in the world to run into in another life—Mr. Meyer?" I wished I could remember his younger self, but I couldn't, and it broke my heart a little.

"True psychics are rare," Nathaniel explained. "Especially ones who *want* to find reapers. And kill them. But these mortals who hunt reapers want to stop this as much as we do. It's an amazing loss we've suffered, losing Frank."

He and Will were quiet for a moment. Nathaniel seemed lost in thought. I wondered what Kate would think of Mr. Meyer's being so cool, but I could never tell her anything about my new life. She could never know. Dragging her or any of my friends and family into this would get them killed. Just like Mr. Meyer.

"I had no idea," I said. Things that I should have said and done haunted me.

Will's hand covered mine. "It's all right. He always said the only thing that would ever take him out in the end was a reaper. He never regretted any of it."

The warmth of his hand on mine made me jarringly aware of how cold I'd become since learning of Mr. Meyer's true identity. I thought back to the news reporter's description of his murder, and it made me sick to my stomach. I'd died that way countless times, but Mr. Meyer would never come back the way I did.

Desperate to talk about something else, I looked down at the book Nathaniel had out on the desk. "What is this place? These books look ancient."

"They are," he said.

"Nathaniel is in charge of the rare books here," Will explained.

"Correct," Nathaniel added. "I can basically bring in any books I want and keep them here. I have a few volumes documenting reapers throughout history. I'm also a collector of antiquities, and that's how I make my money, since I only volunteer here. I like old things, probably because I am very old myself. You'd be surprised how lucrative it is to buy a few ugly paintings and sell them to billionaires a hundred years later. Tens of millions of dollars for an original Picasso are nothing to sneeze at."

I nodded, imagining what I'd do with tens of millions of dollars. Oh, God—the *shoes* I could get with that. "So you've known us for a long time? Then you're immortal like Will? He told me there were no other Guardians. Not now, at least. Didn't I have other Guardians before him?"

Nathaniel gave Will an odd look. Will only stared intently back and said nothing. "Yes . . . I am an immortal, and you have had other Guardians before. They have protected you until their deaths. The duty is for life."

He left me speechless. I stared at Will, who avoided my gaze, and had to force myself to look away from him. Those people had died for me? How many?

Will spoke suddenly, but I didn't hate him for changing the subject. "We fought a reaper who mentioned something about the Enshi. Does that ring a bell?"

Nathaniel pursed his lips tight. "An Enshi? Lord of life—of what *makes* life, to be more correct; of souls."

"*The* Enshi," I corrected. "The reaper made it sound like there was only one."

"Only one, you say? Perhaps that's what Lauren sensed."

"Sounds likely," Will said. "This might be big, Nathaniel. Do you think Bastian might have something to do with this?"

"Who is Bastian?" I asked.

When Will didn't answer, Nathaniel spoke, flashing him another strange look. "Bastian is a very, very powerful vir, a humanlike reaper. A vir may appear as an ordinary man or woman, but they possess the shape-shifting power of reapers and often have strange eyes, claws, scales, tails, horns, wings . . . you name it. They can choose to hide these aspects or to reveal them at any moment. Some of them can shape-shift their entire bodies to look like someone completely different. The vir are also more powerful than any other reapers, and they will often choose to control reapers like the one you killed at the school, as Bastian does. He is cruel and cunning and has been trying to figure out a way to destroy you for the better part of a millennium, Ellie. He and his reapers have killed and taken the souls of more humans than can be counted."

Nathaniel's expression let me know he was serious. "That's why it's our job to help you protect human souls from them. Bastian and his followers may very well be on the hunt for this Enshi."

"We need to borrow a few books and see if we can find anything out about it," Will said.

"Go ahead," Nathaniel said, standing. "The good stuff is behind my desk."

Will examined each book on the shelf Nathaniel had

pointed to, running his fingers down each spine, reading the inscriptions, and finally choosing three books. He laid them across the desk, and I tried to read the titles. Nathaniel chose a clean but old leather-bound volume and began thumbing through it.

"This is in Latin," I said, taking a seat next to him. "I can't read Latin."

Will sat and flipped the pages to skim over something I could only guess was an index of sorts.

"Can *you*?" I asked when he didn't respond.

"Of course."

I looked at the two others books. One was also in Latin and the other was in a language I didn't immediately recognize. "What is this language?"

"Hebrew," he answered without looking at me.

"You can read Latin *and* Hebrew?"

"As can you."

"Ah," I said. "Another one of my mystery skills I can't seem to remember. I really hope cooking is on that list, because I'd like to be able to make cupcakes without turning them into cement."

He rewarded me with a little smile. "Cooking well was never something you worried about in the past."

10

AN HOUR LATER WILL AND NATHANIEL HAD VERY little to show for their efforts. I amused myself by watching the two of them, particularly fascinated with the intensity in Will's eyes as he read the ancient languages, and with the fine muscles as his forearms tensed with each page he turned. He finally closed the first Latin book and took up the one about ancient Sumerian lore. After a little while, he slapped the open page he was reading, making me jump.

"I found it!" Will chirped. He stared at me with an excited expression, but I only shrugged. He frowned and continued. "Enshi, the Lord of Souls. The giver and taker of the breath of life."

"Breath of life?" I mumbled. "That sounds a little too philosophical for a Saturday."

"Whatever this Enshi is, it's as big as we thought," he said as he read further.

Nathaniel peeked over his shoulder. "What is it?"

"It says the Enshi is a dormant being who is the god of life under the command of Enki, the supreme god of Earth, according to Sumerian mythology. Many ancient civilizations mistook powerful reapers for their gods, so that's one possibility for its origin. It's associated with this symbol."

He flipped the book around to show the page to Nathaniel and me. The image was of three open circles arranged like a dartboard, with four small solid dots arranged horizontally across the center and two crescents facing each other vertically.

"This is the seal of Azrael," Nathaniel explained. "Could the text mean that the Enshi serves the Destroyer?"

"That's definitely the impression I'm getting," Will said in a dark voice. "Azrael is the angel of death, but not an archangel—at least not anymore. Archangels are the highest ranking and most powerful of the angels. If the Enshi is a reaper, then this has to mean that the Enshi is actually an angelic reaper. There's no way a demonic reaper would serve an angel. It goes against the nature of reapers and everything they are taught to believe."

My head spun trying to make sense of what they were saying. "Angelic reaper? The Destroyer? Angels? What are you talking about?"

Will glanced at Nathaniel, who stared back intently, as

if he didn't want to answer the question. I hated it when they exchanged glances. It made me feel like I was a naughty child listening in on the grownups' conversation.

"Yes, angels," Will explained. "The counterpart to the Fallen."

I studied his face, shocked by what he was telling me. "Do you mean that real angels exist? The Fallen are demons, aren't they? Does that mean that God exists? Satan, too?"

He took a breath. "Yes. Lucifer rebelled against God and lost the First War, as you have probably learned at some point in your life. God banished Lucifer from Heaven, and he fell into Hell, but his war fell to Earth. The angels who joined Lucifer's cause fell with him and became demons— the Fallen. Two of the Fallen bore horrible children, whose descendents are the creatures we know today as the demonic reapers. In desperation for more soldiers to fuel his army of the damned, Lucifer uses the reapers to collect human souls."

I was thoroughly fascinated. "And the angelic reapers? What are they?"

"The descendents of the Grigori," Will explained. "Not all the Fallen who fought for Lucifer were truly wicked. God believed the Grigori could be rehabilitated, and so they were imprisoned in the mortal world. In order to make amends for their betrayal, they were ordered to watch over humanity. They're the keepers of angelic magic and medicine and the gateways into Heaven and Hell. They bore children between them, but these children weren't created out of wicked spirit and savagery. They became the angelic reapers, the earth-bound soldiers of God who destroy the demonic reapers and stop them from taking human souls. The Grigori have four lords, the Elemental Watchers, who rule over the quadrant points of Earth. They are Fomalhaut of the northern winter, Regulus of the southern summer, Aldebaran of the eastern spring, and Antares of the western autumn. They represent the spirit of their quadrant's element."

"Have you ever met one of the Grigori?" I asked. "Do they fight the demonic reapers too?"

"No, sightings of them are very rare," he said. "But Antares, Watcher of the West, does live in America. Colorado, I think. And I don't think any of them fight. They are peaceful for the most part, but that doesn't mean they're weak."

"So I'm not descended from them, then," I concluded. "Where do I come in?"

"The most powerful of the demonic reapers outnumber the most powerful angelic reapers, and God needed help," Will said. "You and the angelic reapers are fated to prevent Lucifer's Second War, the Apocalypse. If this war happens, that's the End of Days. Your job is to stop as many of the demonic reapers as you can. The best way to kill a demonic reaper is with angelfire, but the angelic reapers can't wield that power, because their ancestors are fallen angels. We don't know *what* you are. You aren't a reaper and your body is human. You just kind of appeared, and we all accepted you. But when a reaper kills you, it can't do anything to your soul. You're reincarnated and you fight again, as if your soul is immune."

I chewed on my lip, forcing myself to believe him, but the what-if? still lurked in the back of my mind. I remembered Friday, in the bathroom, when the strange black things were crawling on my face and suddenly disappeared. I couldn't forget my horrible nightmares. Was I one of the Fallen? No. Not if I could use angelfire. But I couldn't escape the fear that something dark lurked inside me, something more frightening than the thought of Lucifer's Second War and the end of the world.

"What if you're wrong?" I asked. "What if I'm a reaper?"

"You're not," Will assured me. "You're something different. Trust me."

I looked back at the strange symbol of Azrael. "So there are good reapers and bad reapers? The good serve the angels and the bad serve the Fallen?"

Nathaniel nodded. "Simply put, yes."

"I kill the bad ones, right?" I asked. "The demonic reapers." What if I killed the good ones? A heavy pit grew in the bottom of my stomach.

Will's firm gaze locked on mine. "We fight only the demonic reapers."

"You are like the angels' secret weapon," Nathaniel added. "Your presence in this war makes things balanced."

"Don't I make things *un*balanced, then?" I hated playing

the devil's advocate—no pun intended—but I needed to fully understand who and what I was.

Nathaniel said, "No, because there are too many demonic reapers for the angels to destroy them all on their own."

"Do the Fallen have a Preliator?"

"No," he said with a twitch of his nose.

"Could the Enshi be another Preliator?" I asked. "Maybe a demonic one?"

Will exchanged a look with Nathaniel. "While it's unlikely, it is something to think about. We can't rule it out."

"Will," I began, "the night of my birthday, you told that reaper he couldn't touch me until you woke me or he'd have to face the consequences. Were you talking about the angels?"

"Yes," Will said. "The demonic reapers strive for chaos, but there are rules very few of them will dare to break, especially if it means they will have to face a soldier angel as a result—a kind of angel below the rank of archangel, Heaven's law enforcement officers, if you will. You can't be touched until you've regained your powers, and the soldier angels enforce that law."

I frowned. "So the demonic reapers are just *made* to be evil? It sounds so Disney villain–ish. Can't they choose to be good? It feels like genocide or something to me, just wiping them out the way I'm supposed to do."

Will's eyes drilled into mine intently. "If a human is devoured by a demonic reaper, it's a one-way ticket to Hell.

The reapers gain complete control over the soul. It's much like the way the people of some cultures eat the flesh of their enemies or powerful predators to gain their strength through magic. The angelic reapers protect human souls but can't manipulate them. Only God should have the right to decide if a soul should end up in Heaven or Hell."

"They can't all be that way," I said. "There must be some of them who have chosen not to steal souls for the Fallen."

He shook his head. "The only demonic reapers you have ever fought have also tried to kill you. They've only ever been monsters. They're *demon* spawn. I've never heard of one changing his ways. Every single person they have ever killed will burn in Hell for eternity. They kill innocent people, they kill you, and *we* kill them."

"I don't know," I said sadly. "It seems like there should be more to it."

"What do you mean?"

My shoulders sank. I didn't like being put on the spot like that. "I don't know. I just don't believe in absolute evil . . . or absolute *good*. No one's perfectly one or the other. Why can't some demonic reapers turn good or some angelic reapers turn bad? If the Enshi is an angelic reaper, then why would it help the demonic reapers? Maybe it went bad."

"Ellie, we aren't—" Will's mouth snapped shut and his expression filled with pain. His gaze fell away.

"What's wrong?" I asked.

He waved a hand dismissively, but he didn't look at me. "Never mind."

I watched him for a moment, wondering about whatever it was that he wouldn't say.

"We should get back to the Enshi," Nathaniel said.

I didn't object. "So, the Enshi serves an angel?" I asked. "The one whose seal is in that book. Azrael. The angel of death."

"Well, one of them," Nathaniel said.

"There's more than one?" For the first time in my life I wished I'd gone to at least one day of Sunday school just so I could get the basic gist of what they were trying to explain.

He nodded. "The other true angel of death is Sammael, but he fell."

"Why did he fall?" I asked.

"Sammael committed an unforgivable disobedience to God when he became the lover of Lilith, queen of the Fallen. Together in Hell, they are Lucifer's left and right hand, though Sammael is sometimes misidentified as Lucifer. Sammael and Lilith are the forebears of the demonic reapers."

I gaped in surprise. "*Their* children are the demonic reapers?"

"Yes."

"So these demonic reapers want a creature that serves Azrael," I said.

Nathaniel shrugged. "If the Enshi does indeed serve Azrael, then I don't know why Bastian would want it, or why the demonic reapers think it will help them."

That made me feel a little hopeful. "If it's on our side, can't we get it to help us? Who says it has to be evil?"

"The reaper sounded pretty clear that they would use the Enshi against you," Will said. "That's not something that I'm willing to risk."

"I apologize in advance for being so blunt in your presence, Ellie," Nathaniel said. "But it's a fact that no matter how many times they kill the Preliator, she will be reborn and kill a hundred more of them for every one of her deaths."

I cringed. He was a little more blunt than I had been prepared for.

"Exactly," Will said, leaning forward. "So what does it matter if this Enshi wakes up? Maybe it has the strength to kill Ellie, but she'll just be back a few years later. The cycle will never end."

Nathaniel sighed. "I don't know. Maybe they know something we don't."

"I don't like this," Will confessed. "Could this have anything to do with how long it took Ellie to be reborn?"

"I hope not."

"Nathaniel," said a tinny voice from an intercom above our heads.

"Yes, Louise?" he replied.

"We have another shipment in if you'd like to come up and sign for it."

"Be there in a minute." He stood. "I'll be back in a little

bit. If you need to leave, feel free to go. Swing by upstairs and say good-bye if you do." He left the room quickly, leaving Will and me alone.

After a brief, awkward silence, I spoke. "It's getting really late and I still have to set up for tonight. Is it okay if we call it quits with the researching for now?"

"Yeah," he said with a nod. "Let's go."

We found Nathaniel in a room on the second floor of the library, examining delicate documents inside protective sleeves. We said good-bye, and he promised to keep an eye out for anything that could lead us to more information about the Enshi. Outside, I paused before getting into my car.

"What are your plans after this?" I asked.

He looked up at the sky. "It'll be dark soon."

I nodded knowingly. That was when his watchdog duties began. "Well, if you'd rather not sit on my roof like a wallflower, you're very welcome to help us set up for the party. Or at least hang out. You don't have to be by yourself all the time."

"No, thank you," he said. "That's not the best idea."

"Okay, Batman," I said with a smile. "But if you're going to claim to be my bodyguard, you might as well hang out with me."

His expression was thoughtful. "It's better this way."

"Why?"

"Because when I'm around you, instead of looking out

for you, I let down my guard."

"Well, don't do that."

He smiled brilliantly, his first genuine smile of the day, and my gut did a flip. "I can't help it."

"You said it yourself—the reapers don't come out during broad daylight."

"That doesn't mean they *can't*. They're still opportunistic. An easy kill is an easy kill."

"But don't you think they'd be less inclined to attack me if you're standing next to me than if you aren't?"

"It doesn't matter."

"Why not?"

"They know that I can sense if you're distressed, and I'll be with you whether I'm close by or not."

"You always have to disprove my logic, don't you?"

"And you always ask too many questions."

I narrowed my eyes. "And *you* never answer enough of them. You're obnoxious. I'll see you later. You're still coming to the party, right?"

"Yes," he said. "Because you wish me to, I will."

"Great. I'm counting on you."

"You always can."

11

BY SEVEN O'CLOCK, MY MOM, KATE, AND I HAD MOST of the decorations up. Landon and Chris had taped streamers and dangly stars to the ceiling and columns in the living room. I tried not to let things get awkward with Landon, but he seemed to be over what had happened the night before. He helped reach the higher places for decorations and strung up paper lanterns outside on the patio.

I jogged upstairs to the bathroom to shower and put on my dress. My winged necklace was the perfect accessory. Kate and I did each other's hair, and when we were ready, we met the boys out on the patio to show off our outfits. Landon and Chris seemed very pleased with the dresses.

"You look great, Ellie," Landon said.

"Thank you!" I replied, beaming.

"Kate, don't you think that is a little revealing?" my

mom asked, shooting her an odd look.

Kate shrugged. "My boobs aren't showing."

"That is such a shame," Chris said as he passed her, and she promptly smacked him on the shoulder.

Night had fallen, the paper lanterns were lit, and my backyard was a glittering stage. The lantern light gleamed and sparkled off the surface of the pool. Beyond the back-yard was a stretch of woods that led to a small lake behind our neighborhood, and moonlight streaked in between the trees, making the lawn glow. I couldn't be happier. Burning with excitement, I hugged and thanked everyone. When my dad got home, I dragged him outside to see everything, but his expression made me clam up.

"Do we really need all of this?" he said, scowling.

"It's my birthday," I insisted. "Doesn't the yard look nice?"

"This is absurd."

"We just put up paper lanterns."

Something in his gaze flickered, dark and deeper than anger, like shadows passing behind his eyes. I blinked in surprise.

He gave his head a shake and the look vanished. "I have no idea why you'd make such a big deal out of this."

I would have laughed at the ridiculousness of his state-ment if I hadn't been so close to tears. "It's my birthday."

"Aren't you getting a little old for birthday parties?"

He held my gaze for another agonizing few moments, his upper lip twitching. Then he made an unintelligible noise and eased across the patio to inspect the burgers Mom had cooking on the grill. He inhaled the grilling meat deeply, acting as if he hadn't just practically broken my heart. Why would he say something so dismissive and hurtful? Didn't he understand how important my birthday party was to me? Wasn't I important to him?

I bit hard on my tongue to keep myself from crying and making my mascara run, and I stomped inside the house. Mom had set a beautiful two-tiered cake on the bar in the kitchen and moved the stools out into the dining room so people wouldn't have to scramble around them to get to the cake. Chris had brought some speakers; he plugged in his laptop, and soon the house was filled with thumping music. Everything was almost enough for me to forget how cruel my dad had just been to me. Almost.

At eight the guests began arriving. Kate enjoyed playing hostess, letting everyone in the front door and leading them through the foyer into the living room. My friends told me how great I looked and, one by one, hugged me before going off to enjoy the cake and music. Evan and Rachel had arrived just as the house was beginning to get crowded. I was happy to see that Josie Newport showed up—with her entourage trailing behind her. She wore a sunny yellow cocktail dress and her walnut-colored hair hung in loose curls around her tanned shoulders. She smiled at me and gave me a hug that felt authentic and wished me happy birthday.

My house and backyard were filled with high school students by nine thirty. Mom and Dad had retreated upstairs when the place started to get too busy for them, and I was glad. No one wants their parents hanging around their party. I moved from group to group, chatting and dancing, and when I spotted Will, I stopped dead in my tracks.

He had *actually* come. I was even more shocked to see him wearing a nice pair of black slacks and a well-fitted garnet-colored silk shirt with the top few buttons left undone and no tie. Only a small portion of his tattoos was visible above his shirt collar. Before I could get his attention, one of Josie's friends, Harper—or Harpy, as we all liked to call her behind her back—was there in front of him introducing herself. I stifled a laugh when I saw the apathy on his face. Harper wrapped an arm around his and proceeded to guide him farther into the party. Behind them, Kate made a comical face and an equally appropriate hand gesture that made me laugh. When Will's gaze caught mine, he pulled free of Harper's grip without a word to her and walked up to me. She deflated and gaped in disbelief, while I couldn't stifle the victorious smirk on my face. That would teach Harpy to think she owned the place—*and* Will! Not that I was territorial or anything. Okay, maybe a *smidge*.

Kate brushed by me and stopped to make a gagging noise into my ear. "I can't believe Josie brought Harpy Knight," she said in a low, annoyed voice. "She's such a termagant."

I laughed and nodded even though I had no idea what that meant. Kate grinned, flashing her bright white teeth, and moved on.

Will stepped close to me and bent his head down to speak into my ear. "You look beautiful."

"Thank you," I said, biting my lip when I felt myself blushing. "You look very sharp yourself. Where'd you get the shirt?"

"A friend."

"*You* have friends?"

"Don't be so shocked. I've lived a long time. I was bound to find someone who likes me. It was just Nathaniel, anyway."

"Oh, that's so cute," I said, pinching his cheek. "He shopped for you. You're, like, biffles."

He brushed me off and looked around the living room. "That's enough of that."

I grinned at him, resting my hands on my hips. "You look so tense."

"It felt weird coming in the front door."

"Oh, yes," I replied with a small laugh. "You should have just climbed in through the window, since you're so good at that."

He smiled crookedly and turned to face me. "I thought about it."

"Or you could have just hopped off the roof and dropped in on the patio."

"I'm not really one for an entrance that dramatic. I don't

like drawing attention to myself."

I laughed. "You fail miserably at that, in case you haven't noticed."

He seemed to ignore the observation and lifted my pendant with his hand. He turned it over in his palm, looking at it fondly. "I'm glad you're wearing this."

"It matches my dress."

He smiled softly. "That it does."

I glanced behind him and spotted Harper staring at us with a look of derision on her face as she talked to another girl. I looked back to Will. "Do you want some cake?"

"No, thanks."

"Come and eat some cake. It's really, really good." Ignoring his response, I grabbed his arm and led him into the kitchen. I smiled at a couple of girls grabbing their slices as they stared at Will. He seemed unfazed, as if he truly didn't care about the attention and was not just oblivious.

"I really don't want any cake," he said, eyeballing the sugary masterpiece laid out on the bar counter.

"Are you sure?" I asked, disappointed. "Well, I'm having a piece." I cut myself a slice and started eating it. "You're really boring, you know that?"

"I'm anything but boring. You're the one prancing around in your little dress pretending to be a normal human girl. *That* is boring."

I stuck my tongue out at him. "I *am* a normal human girl, despite what you'd like to believe, and I'm going to enjoy my birthday. You only turn seventeen once."

"*I* might have turned seventeen only once," he said. "But *you* are a pro at it."

My heart sank. "Well, this is the only time I remember, so don't ruin it for me."

"Forgive me," he said, surprising me. "I don't mean to upset you." He studied my face for a moment before taking my hand. "Let's go enjoy your party."

"Wait, wait," I said, pulling away from him to finish my cake before dumping the plastic plate and fork in the trash. I wiped at a little bit of frosting on my lip and allowed him to lead me from the kitchen, but in the archway opening up into the living room, we came face-to-face with Landon. He looked from my face to Will's, to Will's hand holding mine, and back again to my face, his expression quickly filling with contempt. He said nothing and pushed past us into the kitchen.

Back out in the living room, Will turned to me. "Your friend was right."

"About what?" I asked dreamily as he leaned into me and I took in his scent.

"He is very jealous."

"Oh." Landon. "How do you know what Kate said?"

"I have very good ears."

"So you were eavesdropping?" I asked playfully.

"I might have been," he said with a wide smile.

I rolled my eyes. "You should meet Kate officially. Then

she might not think you're so weird."

"I'm afraid that might have the opposite effect," he said dejectedly.

I rolled my eyes and led him out onto the patio.

Kate was standing in a group of other guests, laughing in a high and gracious voice. When she spotted Will and me, she waved us over. Everyone wished me happy birthday for the billionth time and Kate held out a hand for Will to shake.

"I don't think we've formally met yet," she said. "I'm Kate."

"Will," he replied. "Nice to meet you."

The others introduced themselves, and we engaged in tedious small talk I knew I'd forget in five minutes. Will continued to surprise me, as he seemed to slip comfortably into the role of attentive guest. He cracked jokes, chatted amiably, all the while keeping a close eye on me. I didn't think anyone thought he was too weird, much to my joy.

Josie appeared with Harper on her heels, and she placed a hand around my arm and kissed me on the cheek. "Hi, Ellie, how are you?"

"I'm really good, Josie," I replied happily. "I'm so glad you could make it. Are you having a good time?"

"Yes," she said. "The party is great and the decorations are so pretty. I love your dress!"

"Thank you so much! We got the boys to do most of the work."

Josie laughed. "Well, that's what they're for, right?" She

smiled at Will, tilting her head and bouncing her circus-shiny curls. "Who's your friend?"

"This is Will," I said. "Will, this is Josie."

"Are you new at our school? I've never seen you before." She examined him much too thoroughly, her eyes moving up and down, her lips curving delicately. "Are you on the football team?"

"No," he said. "I graduated. I'm actually at Michigan."

Her eyes perked. "Oh, really? What's your major?"

"Economics."

"Well, that's interesting," she said, lighting up a bit more, toying flirtatiously with her curls. "So you're going to be, like, a top CEO someday?"

"Probably not," he said honestly.

Josie frowned.

"I have your birthday present," Kate said suddenly and excitedly, grabbing my arm. She pulled out bottles of Goldschläger and Dr Pepper and waggled them both enthusiastically—much to my delight, as I was sick of watching Josie flirt with Will. "Time for this party to get started."

12

BY ONE IN THE MORNING THE PARTY HAD CLEARED
out, leaving only my closest friends and Josie's group. Chris
and Landon had made an excellent DJ team all night, and
I was still feeling the shots a little bit. After another dance
with Kate, I bounced up to Will, who was leaning against the
wall in the archway to the kitchen.

I grabbed his hand, smiling. "Dance with me!"

Will laughed and shook his head. "No, I don't think so."

"Why not?"

"Because you're drunk," he said carefully.

I glared at him. "Am not. I just feel good." Which was
true. I might have been tipsy, but I wouldn't have called
myself drunk. My body didn't feel warm anymore, but I
was still a little giddy and I wanted to have a little more
fun before I stopped feeling it altogether. "Come on, it's

just for fun. Please dance with me?"

"Go ask Landon," he said, nodding behind me.

As I turned around, Landon walked up to me, right on cue. He looked dejected. "Ellie, can I talk to you?"

Buzz kill. "Yeah." This couldn't be good.

"Can we go outside?"

"Yeah." I caught Will's eye as I followed Landon.

Out on the patio there were only two other people, who when they saw the unhappy expressions on our faces went back inside the house. We walked across the long lawn toward the trees and the stone bench surrounded by my mom's lilies. When I realized that he'd brought me all the way out here for privacy, my jaw set tightly and my breathing became shallow and nervous. I sat heavily and lost my balance. He caught my shoulder.

He peered into my face and laughed. "No way! Ellie, are you drunk?"

"Not anymore," I grumbled.

"What? If you want more, I've got a few beers left."

"No, whatever. So, what's up?" I knew what this was about and I dreaded every word that was going to come out of his mouth.

His expression washed blank. "I wanted to talk to you about something."

Obviously. Get on with it. "Okay."

"Something has been bugging me lately," he said.

"We've been friends for a pretty long time, and you know I care about you."

"Of course," I said honestly. "I care about you too. You're one of my best friends."

"Yeah, but I feel a little bit differently than *that*." He leaned a little bit closer. "I really like you, Ell. You're funny and smart—"

"Oh, I'm not that funny and especially not that smart. . . ."

"—and beautiful, and I want to be more than friends with you." He brushed my hair behind my shoulder. The gesture was meant to be affectionate, but Landon was practically my brother and the touch just felt invasive.

I sat there, looking down at my knees and pulling at the hem of my dress. I had been expecting this, yet I had never planned my reply. "Oh, Landon, I—"

"Please say you feel the same way," he breathed, getting even closer. "Will you be my girlfriend?"

I struggled to keep a grimace off my face. "Landon, I—"

His hand cupped my cheek and pulled my face toward his; then he tried to kiss me. The idea of kissing Landon was awkward, and frankly kind of gross. I twisted away and felt horrible instantly. When I stood up, he sprang to his feet with me, holding my arm.

"Landon, I just don't feel that way about you—"

He turned angry very suddenly, startling me. "Why? Is it because of that Will guy? You've know him for what, *two days*, and you're already going out with him?"

I blinked at him and pulled away. "No, that's not it, I—"

"Ellie, it's *me*! You've known me since—"

I withdrew my arm from his grasp gently, cutting his words short. "Yes, that's it. It *is* you. You're my *friend*, Landon, one of my best friends. You're like a *brother* to me. I love you like a brother. I—"

Something ominous tugged at my core, stopping me mid-sentence. I knew that feeling.

"Look out!" I shrieked, grabbing Landon's shoulders and throwing him to the ground. I slipped into the Grim just as the biggest reaper I'd ever seen charged out from the darkness. Landon cracked his head on the edge of the bench and lay still on the grass. I spun around and darted toward my house. I screamed Will's name as the footfalls pounded the ground behind me. I turned back to defend myself.

The reaper roared and head butted me square in the chest, knocking me right out of the Grim and rocketing through the air, clear over my pool, and sending me smashing through the picture windows that covered the back of my house. I landed on a sea of broken glass in my living room, surrounded by screams. For the longest two seconds of my life I couldn't breathe or move. My back hurt like hell, and I groaned painfully as I picked myself up, brushing the glass off me. My gashes healed almost instantly and left a few bloody streaks behind on my face and arms.

And my party was ruined. I was so pissed.

"Ellie!" Kate screamed, and rushed toward me. "Are you okay?"

I glanced back at her as she stood with Josie and a couple others gaping at me in shock. I said nothing and jumped back out through the broken window as Kate shrieked my name again.

Back within the Grim and out of my friends' sight, the reaper was standing at the back of my lawn, waiting for me only a few feet away from where Landon lay unconscious. He was the size of a Chevrolet Tahoe, with coal-black eyes set in a face that was short and bulky like a bear's. His wide snout was packed with jagged, serrated teeth, and his nostrils flared as he took in my scent. He dug his claws into the grass, his shoulders rolling luxuriously, like a giant Hellcat kneading a blanket of earth.

"You get away from him," I growled as I called my swords into my hands. The blades exploded in flames of angelfire, and I braced myself.

Will entered the Grim behind me, his heavy blade already drawn. The reaper flashed his giant canines and hissed like a crocodile in response.

"We meet again, Preliator!" the reaper said in a voice that shook the earth beneath me.

"Ellie!" Kate called from across the lawn. "Where are you? Are you hurt?"

"We've got to get out of here," I said to Will as I saw my friends stepping carefully through the broken window.

They couldn't see either of us, or the reaper, while we were in the Grim, but I couldn't risk losing my concentration and slipping back into the mortal dimension where we'd be seen.

Will nodded and I sprang off, running through my neighbors' backyards to the woods at the end of my street. The reaper bounded after us, the thudding footfalls of his massive paws thundering through my skull. As we reached the trees, I could feel the reaper gaining on us. I ducked and spun, swiping a blade low. The reaper leaped into the air and over my head, landing twenty feet deeper in the woods.

I stood with Will right beside me and stared the reaper down.

"He's an ursid, Ellie," Will warned. "Be careful. He's stronger than the lupines."

The reaper laughed, his voice bellowing deep, shaking the branches around him. "Don't you recognize me, Preliator?"

I looked at him carefully. "I've never fought you before. If I had, you'd be dead."

He laughed again, this time even louder. "I'm shocked you are so bold. We battled long ago. You see, I am the one who tasted your blood last."

He smiled a mouthful of saber fangs, his black eyes glistening in the moonlight.

A terrible memory came rushing back to me—memories of a basement, of eyes in the dark, of pain, *excruciating* pain.

I remembered my vision fading to black, and I remembered dying. The reaper's black form lit with angelfire flashed like a movie on an old silver screen in my head and I cried out, staggering back into Will.

"You!" I yelled, pointing the tip of my blade at the reaper.

"Oh, yes," he growled. "You tasted so sweet then, like sugar and blood and child flesh. I wonder if you still taste just as good."

Fear grabbed me by the throat. "Will—"

"I'm here." His voice was firm and kind.

The reaper stepped toward me. "I am Ragnuk, and I am going to eat you now." A glob of yellowed saliva fell from his mouth to the ground.

"You have to fight him, Ellie," Will said.

I was breathless with fright. "I don't—I can't—"

Ragnuk's jaw dropped and he roared, the mountain of muscle on his shoulders shuddering, and he charged forward. I screamed and threw my hands over my face, losing my swords. I looked up and found Will above me, both his hands gripping the reaper's jaws, preventing him from crunching his teeth down on my head. Will turned his face to me, and his eyes were bright as twin beacons.

"Ellie, *move!*"

I obeyed and scrambled back through the dirt until I hit a tree. Releasing the reaper's face, Will let his power explode, spiraling, twisting wisps of shadows. Ragnuk roared as he was sent flying, smashing into trees and ripping them, roots and all, out of the ground. Ragnuk landed on all fours, his talons ripping through the earth to stop his sliding, and then he thundered toward where I lay. He opened his mouth, his hot breath blasting me, and then Will smashed the top of the reaper's head into the ground. The reaper twisted and raked his talons across Will's belly. He cried out as his knees hit the ground.

"Will!" I screamed, watching him fall.

Ragnuk turned his attention back to me. "I don't know why Bastian is so scared of your power," he rumbled. "You're just a trembling little mouse of a thing."

I shrieked, detonating my power, and the light and wind consumed me. The force of it blasted point-blank into the reaper, swallowing him in white smoky light, and sent him soaring away from me and slamming into trees like a pinball until he dropped to the ground. He snarled in rage at having taken a second hit that hard.

I dived for my swords, but he was already in front of me. I looked up and gasped. He swiped, slashing my dress wide open at my belly. I jumped back, lighting my blades, and swung, one blade slicing through his flesh. The reaper ignored the angelfire torching his wound, roared in rage, and smashed his skull into my body. I slammed into the tree next to me and both swords were knocked from my grip. I slid to the ground dizzily as Ragnuk pressed a paw hard into my chest, shoving my back into the tree behind me until I couldn't breathe.

"Bastian wants me to kill you before you stop us from getting the Enshi," the reaper hissed, blasting me with his hot, rancid breath. "With you out of the way for a few years, we won't have to worry about you spoiling our plans. And when you come back, Preliator, the Enshi will be here waiting for you and you'll no longer be a threat. You won't even be a concern. Your destruction will be your home-coming gift."

I gagged and wriggled so I could get enough air to speak. "What is the Enshi?"

"Death," Ragnuk sneered. "The death of everything. The harbinger of the End of Days."

I punched Ragnuk in the face, and his head snapped to the side as he grunted. My fist crunched into his snout again with all my strength, and something cracked. He staggered and lifted his paw from my chest. I cried out and smashed my power into Ragnuk's leg. The thick bone snapped in half and he screamed, reeling back and releasing me. I collapsed, coughing and gasping for breath.

I climbed to my feet and rushed to Will. The front of his shirt was drenched black with blood. I ripped his shirt open to stop the bleeding, but instead I stared at flawless skin.

"I'm okay," he said, looking up at me. "Where is he?"

I spotted Ragnuk struggling to his feet, favoring his broken leg. The reaper spat up a gobbet of blood and hissed at me. "I'll be back for you," he growled, out of breath. His form blurred for a moment, and then he was gone.

I blinked. "He vanished!"

Will sat forward, rubbing his abdomen. "Reapers have the ability to move at ultrahigh speeds through the Grim when they need to make a quick getaway, or when they're in pursuit. He needs some time to heal his leg. Broken bones of that size don't heal instantly, like breaks in smaller bones and cuts."

"I'm so sorry, Will," I cried. "I froze."

He looked up at me, his eyes warm and forgiving. "My job is to protect you, no matter what happens."

"You got hurt because of me," I said sadly.

"Hey, I'm fine," he assured me, pulling the shredded pieces of his shirt apart to show me his healed wounds. "I can take a lot of damage. That's what I'm here for."

I looked down at my dress and at the damage Ragnuk had done to it. "Oh, my dress . . ."

Will laughed. "You are such a girl."

I scowled. "And you're a jerk."

"It's just that—" He cut himself off.

"What?"

"Every time you come back, you're a little more human." The laughter in his voice had faded.

"I don't understand."

"I don't know," he confessed. "It's strange. You act very human sometimes, much more so than you did when we first met. You aren't as dark, I guess, and you consider yourself one of them."

I almost laughed. "I *am* one of them. Just with weird powers now."

There was no amusement on his face. "You didn't always think that."

What did that mean? Had I once thought I was better than humans, been as dark as the reapers? Had I once been as cruel?

Nausea crept over me. "Will, Ragnuk scared the hell out of me. He's killed me before. I remembered it as soon as he said it."

"You can defeat him," he said earnestly. "We'll destroy him and you can move past it."

"Will, I *died*!" I cried, more angry than scared. "I remember *dying*! I remember him tearing me apart!"

"It's okay—" He touched my arm, but I pulled away.

"No, it's not okay," I said. "You can't imagine what that's like."

"You're right," he said. "I can't."

I stepped away from him. I hated myself for throwing a tantrum. Making excuses for my freezing in the middle of the fight wasn't going to help me. So I wiped at my eyes and took a deep breath. Being afraid would get me killed. "Why is Ragnuk so much bigger than the others?" I asked, my voice shaking just a little.

"He's an ursid reaper," Will explained. "They're bigger and more powerful, but slower than the wolflike lupines. Ursids rely on brute strength in battle."

"He was a monster," I whispered, unable to get his face out of my mind.

"But you defeated him this time," he said. "You injured him badly enough for him to take off. You made him retreat. That makes up for the moment you were afraid. Ellie, you need to understand that once you overcome your fear, you can defeat anything."

"But I didn't kill him, and now he'll be back for me with whatever that Enshi is. And I got you hurt and I feel like crap."

"Don't worry about me, Ellie. I'm supposed to take the hits for you. Trust me."

I studied his face, unable to understand why someone would devote himself to me so strongly. I wasn't worth his pain or his blood.

He forced a smile. "We need to get you back to your house. I'm sure your parents aren't going to be too happy about the broken window."

My heart sank. I had forgotten that Ragnuk had thrown me through the glass. How was I going to explain that? "I don't think I want to go back."

He frowned at me. "Yeah, you need to go back."

I nodded and took a deep breath. "You'd better take off. I don't think it would be a good idea to walk back with ripped-up clothes and you with me. It might look bad."

"Good thinking," he said. "I'll be close."

"Thanks, Will."

He touched my shoulder. "You still look beautiful in your dress."

When I turned to face him, he was gone. Again.

13

I EMERGED FROM THE WOODS AND THE GRIM TO see Kate and Landon standing on the patio calling my name. I was dead. I was sure of it. Kate spotted me first and of course made an enormous deal of it.

"Ellie!" she shrieked, taking off at a sudden run. "Oh, my God, are you all right?" She grabbed me and pulled me into a strong hug. "We had no idea where you ran away to! Where were you? Are you hurt? I can't believe you fell through the glass!"

"I—"

"What happened to your dress? What is this on you? You're filthy. Is that *blood*? Do you need to go to the hospital?" Kate was shooting off her mouth. I only pulled away from her with great effort.

"I'm fine," I said, smoothing out my dress, suddenly

feeling very self-conscious about the naked skin showing through the rips.

Landon scooped me up into a hug. "I'm so glad you're okay! What happened? We were talking and you just said to watch out and then—I don't even know."

I thought quickly for a response. It hurt to have to lie to him, but there was no way I could tell him what had really happened. "You tripped on the foot of the bench and hit your head. Are *you* okay?" Maybe directing the attention toward him would save my ass, but that wasn't likely.

He ran a hand through his hair and shrugged. "Yeah, I'm all right. I just . . . We were sitting and talking and I can't remember anything after you shouted."

I nodded firmly. "We were talking and you got up to go back to the party when you tripped on the foot of the bench and fell. You sure you're okay?" As he gave me a puzzled nod, I wondered what else he remembered—if he remembered asking me to be his girlfriend at all. I hoped he did, and remembered my response too, so he'd move on, but the way he held me made me guess otherwise.

"Elisabeth Marie!" my mom shouted as she stomped toward me in her robe and pajamas. "Are you all right? What in the hell happened to you? Where are you hurt?"

I twisted away. "I'm fine—I'm not hurt."

"What?" Mom grabbed my arm, pulled me close, and examined my skin, looking for injuries. She touched my belly, pushing up the flaps of fabric, her eyes brimming and wide as she found no wounds. "How are you not hurt?" She turned to Kate. "She fell through the window, right?"

Kate nodded. "She went *flying* through it."

Saying nothing, I peeked over Kate's shoulders to see my dad marching through the house. My body locked up, preparing for the screaming match that was about to erupt.

"*How*, Ellie?" my mom pressed. "Did someone push you? And did you fall in the woods? You're covered in dirt. Were you drinking?"

I chose that moment to take advantage. "Yeah, I'm sorry, Mom. Landon and I had been drinking and we were joking around. Landon fell, and I tried to go inside when I tripped and went through the window. When I saw what I did, I freaked and ran. I was too scared to come home. I'm so sorry, Mom."

"You damn well better be!" she cried. I could tell from the look on her face that she couldn't believe I'd managed to break the window with anything less than a car, but nothing had gone through that window but my body. She was forced to accept what I told her.

"You were drinking?" my dad demanded angrily as he appeared on the patio. He spoke to me, but his eyes searched the darkness behind me. I hoped he didn't see Will. "No more parties here. That's it. No Homecoming."

"But Dad—"

"He's right." My mom threw her hands in the air. "I am completely shocked that you don't have a scratch on you!

Where did all this blood come from?"

I thought quickly. "I have scratches, just little ones. It's too dark to see, I guess. All my fingers and toes are still here, see?"

"Did you see the mess you made?" my dad hissed. "You are a complete moron!"

"*Richard!*" my mother cried, covering her mouth with her hand and gaping at him.

I stared at him in shock, registering the blatant contempt on his face and the malice in his voice. Kate took a step closer to me, and I felt her fingers on the back of my arm, letting me know she was there for me. My own father had just called me a moron. What I'd done—or what I needed them to believe—might have been stupid, but what he had said was out of line.

"I'm not stupid," I growled under my breath.

My dad's expression froze. "What was that?"

"I said," I reiterated in a louder, stronger voice, "I'm not stupid. I made a mistake. That doesn't mean I'm a moron."

He gave me an icy sidelong look. "You sure about that?"

My hands rolled into tight fists. I didn't want to fight with my dad, but I couldn't let him talk to me that way. "Very."

"Rick, just go back into the house," my mom said. "I'll handle this."

He turned on her. "Why are you defending her?"

"I'm not defending her," she shot back. "I'm just suggesting that you can't handle this properly when you're so upset."

His nostrils flared and the veins in his temple throbbed as if he were about to explode any second. "And you're doing much better? You let her walk all over you and you're always interfering."

She blinked in shock. "Interfering? With what?"

"I can't discipline her with you always running to her side!"

"Discipline?" she cried with a gasp. "This isn't discipline. You're only making things worse!"

He threw a finger into her face. "Maybe one day you'll learn from all this why everything only gets worse."

As I watched the man who was supposed to be my father stomp back into the house, I prayed he'd just file for divorce and get the hell away from me and my mom for good. What was wrong with him? I remembered having a dad who once gave me piggyback rides and finger painted while we watched Saturday-morning cartoons. This man was no longer the father I had once had. Demonic reapers had more compassion than this monster.

"Ellie," Mom said very seriously, jarring me from my thoughts. "Look, I know you guys are teenagers, and you're going to drink regardless of what anyone says, but please just be safe. And don't be afraid to ask for help when you need it. I'd rather you come to me instead of us finding you dead in a ditch. Running away like that wasn't cool."

"Thanks, Mom," I said, forcing a smile. Kate gave me a

knowing look and pursed her lips tightly. Knowing that she and Landon had to witness all that made me feel a thousand times worse.

"We'll talk about this tomorrow," my mom said, putting an exhausted hand to her forehead. "You're going to be grounded."

"Mrs. Monroe," Kate interjected, stepping forward, "it was all my fault. I brought the alcohol."

My mom *tsk*ed. I didn't want Kate to get any of the heat. I wanted to scream that at the top of my lungs and tell everyone what had really happened, but I couldn't, and that made me feel even crazier inside.

"I'm not your mother, Kate," my mom began, "but the same goes for you and Landon. If you need help, call me. I don't want to have to worry about you two, either. Ellie's enough to drive me insane."

Kate smiled weakly. "Thanks, Mrs. Monroe."

"Is there anyone left?" I asked, fearing the walk of shame back into my house.

"Josie and her friends went home," Mom said. "Her mom is very worried about you. I'll have to give her a call before I fall asleep."

I nodded and laid my cheek on Kate's shoulder. "I'm really, *really* tired. I think I'm just going to go to bed."

"Do you want me to stay with you?" Kate asked.

I smiled. "Yeah, that'd be great."

I said good-bye to Landon, who hugged me again, taking a little too long for my comfort. Things would be weird between us.

Kate and I headed upstairs to my bedroom. I took a quick shower and changed into my pajamas while she watched TV in my room. When I came out, I pulled out another pair of pajamas for her and hung up my dress, even though it was destroyed. What a waste.

"I'll hop into the shower really quick and be right out," Kate said. "I feel so gross from dancing all night."

"Okay," I said absently, plopping down on my bed and taking up the remote to flip through channels.

A minute or two after Kate had disappeared from the bedroom, I heard a voice behind me.

"Hey," Will said as he climbed in through my window.

I jumped to my feet, shocked, my eyes popping wide open. "What are you doing in here?" I said in a raspy whisper. "I was *joking* about coming in through the windows! I can't believe you're in my room. My parents are right down the hall, and Kate could be back any minute. Not to mention my dad is crazy. What if you got caught? He has a gun, you know."

He scoffed and leaned back against the wall, crossing his arms over his chest.

"Why are you here, Will?" I asked, watching him carefully.

He stepped forward, sucking in his upper lip for a moment.

The tiny glimpse of his tongue as he did so was very distracting. "I need to tell you something."

"Can't it wait until tomorrow?" I asked as he sat down on the bed and I sat beside him.

"No, it can't. I should've told you before, but you didn't remember, and I wasn't sure when it would've been right to tell you."

"Why?" I asked impatiently. "I'm not sure there could be much else you could say to me that would shock me."

"The night you died," he said, speaking slowly. "I wasn't there."

"I know."

"You do?"

"The day before my birthday, I had a nightmare, or a memory, of my own death," I said. "I remembered looking for you. That night I wasn't really afraid of Ragnuk. I was afraid because I didn't know where you were."

His gaze fell away, his expression pained. "I'm so sorry I couldn't reach you in time."

"Why? Why did you leave me?"

"Bastian."

"Bastian? What does he have to do with it?"

Will looked back at me, his gaze intense and full of agony. "Ragnuk had been ordered to hunt you down, and Bastian's other thugs got me first. They held me and tortured me. I couldn't escape. When . . . when Ragnuk returned, I knew it was all over. He laid you down in front of me, and you were . . . you were gone. I managed to escape then, because I knew I had to live. I had to be there when you came back. You died alone, but I wouldn't let you come back alone."

"Will," I said, not knowing what else to say, "it's not your fault."

"But it is," he said, shaking his head. "You die over and over and over again, and I try to save you, but I always fail. It's never enough."

"Will," I said again, and my heart filled with so much sadness, I could barely take it. My hand cupped his cheek softly. His own hand covered mine and he leaned into my palm, closing his eyes. It was the first real emotion he'd shown to me, like he was letting me see his soul for the first time. The embrace made me wonder what he truly felt beneath the stoic, battle-hardened exterior. He stayed there for so long that I lost track of time. Then swiftly, painfully, he pulled away and stood, leaving me feeling empty and longing.

"I have to go," he said, letting his gaze fall away. "She's coming."

I said nothing back, but only stared at him as he appeared to vanish into thin air.

The next moment Kate came in through my bedroom door, rubbing a towel through her hair. "Who were you talking to?" she asked, giving me a weird look.

"Oh, no one," I said, and leaped to my feet, my heart suddenly pounding as if it had missed a few beats and was trying to make up for it. I sat back down on my bed. Will had left so quickly that I felt unfulfilled; it seemed there was still so much to say, but I'd have to keep it all inside. I had a feeling there was much more he wanted to say to me, too.

"I could have sworn you were talking on your phone or something," Kate said, adding a sly smile. "Was it Will?"

My face flushed red. "No, I was just . . . saying stupid stuff to the TV. I hate reality shows."

"Right," she said, rolling her eyes. Since Kate was taller than me, my pajama pants came down to just above her ankles. "We'll just pretend these were meant to be cropped." She laughed, pointing down, as if someone might accuse her of dressing poorly between then and morning.

"I won't tell anyone the truth," I said, smiling. I wanted to make jokes and have fun with Kate, but I couldn't stop wondering what else Will had wanted to say to me. More than that, I was afraid of the End of Days that Ragnuk had spoken of.

"You okay, Ellie?"

I looked up to see Kate watching me worriedly. "Sorry. I'm just kind of swamped with life right now."

Kate frowned and plunked down on the carpet, resting her elbow on the edge of the bed. "I'm really sorry about your dad."

The corner of my mouth twitched as if it were trying to offer her a smile but couldn't. "Yeah. You and me both."

"He shouldn't have said the things he did."

The pity in her expression made me take a deep breath. I wished my dad could understand that what had happened was an accident and I couldn't avoid it. Yeah, I had drunk a couple of shots, and maybe that wasn't exactly legal at my age, but I didn't drive anywhere and no one was hurt because of the alcohol. Landon could have been hurt a lot worse if I hadn't shoved him out of the way of the reaper and then lured the beast away.

I tried so hard to do the right thing, but I didn't know how. If I had to keep covering up the reaper incidents by trashing my reputation and lying to my friends and family, then I wasn't sure how long I could keep fighting. None of this was fair to me. Or them.

"I'm worried about you," Kate said abruptly. "It just seems like your dad is getting worse every day. And I think it's beginning to affect you."

A fleeting memory of my dad giving me the flyball he caught at my first Detroit Tigers baseball game played in my head like a movie. He smiled so much back then, and now I couldn't even remember the last time he had smiled or looked at me with something other than disdain.

I shrugged at Kate. "Well, I'll graduate in the spring and be off to college, so screw him."

"But he's your father," she insisted. "Do you really want to hate him for the rest of your life?"

"I think he's made up my mind for me, don't you agree?"

She frowned and sighed. "He used to be so cool when we were little. Do you remember when he took us to Crystal Mountain for the weekend and snowboarded with us? That was one of the best weekends of my life."

I smiled at the memory, and it made my eyes sting with tears. My dad had rented a town house at that ski resort for him, my mom, Kate, and me the Christmas before Kate and I had started high school. That was the last year we'd felt like a family. Kate had always been like a sister to me, and my parents treated her like an adopted daughter. Now even she felt my dad's frigidness.

"You can't let all these new bad memories wash away the old good ones," she said, tilting her head at me. "They're too good to be canceled out. You have to concentrate hard on the great things about your childhood, all the great memories with your dad. He's not evil, he's just changed. He can change back."

I smiled at her, wiping at a tear in the corner of my eye. "Thanks, Kate."

She grinned back and tenderly combed my hair back with her fingers. "You know I love you."

"I wish someone else did too." I hated being so angsty and I would never have admitted that I had "daddy issues" to anyone's face, but it felt wrong to hide what was going on in my life from Kate. That included my Preliator duties.

165

Keeping that from her killed me—it hurt almost as much as my relationship with my dad did.

"He loves you," she said. "If he didn't love you, then he would never have been a good dad ever. He was amazing once. He just sucks at it right now. Maybe things will get better."

"I hope you're right."

She sat up and scoffed at me. "Of course I'm right. I'm kind of amazing, FYI."

I laughed and tossed a pillow at her. "Oh, really?"

"Yeah, really." Her smile got a whole lot slyer. "So how about Will? He looked hot tonight."

My cheeks flushed scarlet. "He might have."

Her expression lit up. "I knew it! You like him, don't you?"

My mouth scrunched indecisively and I ran a hand through my hair. "See, I don't know. He's a little different, but not in a really bad way. He just doesn't act like most guys, you know?"

Kate laughed. "Of course, tall, dark, and stoic would be your type. At least it's better than Landon following you around like a lovesick puppy lately. I'm sorry for that, by the way."

I forced a smile. "Thanks. I feel really bad about it."

She giggled and looked at me like I was crazy. "Why?"

I shrugged. "I don't know. It's like, he really likes me and I just don't feel the same way. He's *Landon*, you know?"

"Yeah, I guess so." Her gaze flickered to the ceiling for

a moment. "It's not like he's an ass. He's a little immature, but he's still a good guy, and he's so cute. And *hello*? Soccer star! Maybe it wouldn't be so bad to say yes and see where it goes."

My face scrunched again. "I'm not going out with a guy to see if I *end up* liking him. That seems wrong. I don't want to lead him on."

"Yeah, when you put it like that . . ." She trailed off.

I eyed her with suspicion. "Why are you his champion all of a sudden? Do *you* like him?"

"Oh God, no. Did he ask you out?"

"Sort of. I didn't get a chance to answer him."

She perked up. "What if he asks you again?"

My heart sank. "I don't know. I'll have to tell him no. It's not like I can do anything else."

"True."

"It's just, with Will, I've only known him for a few days, but I feel like I've known him forever. I feel safe around him. It's nice."

She grinned. "Oh, honey, we all want a white knight. It's programmed into us girls."

My smile was genuine this time. "He *is* kind of like a white knight."

"Yeah, a stone-cold fox, too. Do you think he wants to go out with you?"

"I don't know. We're just sort of hanging out right now,

so no 'going' of any kind. I don't think he likes me that way."

Kate rolled her eyes. "Okay, *hanging out* to me means something entirely different from what I know you're used to. Please don't tell me you've hooked up with him already."

"No, no!" I said quickly. "It's not like that."

"Have you kissed him at least?"

"No."

"Do you want to?"

"I don't know." I blushed again, thinking about it.

"Ellie, you know within five seconds of meeting a boy if you want to kiss him or not. Do you, or don't you?"

Did I? It didn't repulse me, but I had no idea how Will even felt about me. We'd had something of a moment only minutes before, but as soon as he opened up to me, he shut me right back out. He could be really charming and then get so moody. He was my Guardian. Saving my ass was probably just like a job to him. He had protected me for hundreds of years, and what I would have given just to remember *any* of that . . . I was beginning to doubt that the entirety of my memory would ever come back to me. It helped to think about Will, but it also drove me crazy. *He* drove me crazy. I just wanted to understand him and I wanted to know his secrets. What *was* Will? What was *I*? My reincarnation, his immortality, our superhuman abilities, the reapers . . . And the Enshi—what could that be? Could Will be one of the angels he had told me about?

"Ell?" Kate cocked an eyebrow at me.

I sighed. "I'm about to fall asleep."

Kate smiled weakly. "Okay."

We both climbed into my bed and found sleep quickly.

14

THE BROKEN WINDOWS IN MY LIVING ROOM LEFT
gaping holes out onto the patio, and they were covered with
a rather unsightly tarp and tape until the window company could deliver and install the replacement glass. I'd be
relieved when I didn't have to look at it again.

At school—the only time over the next three weeks of
my grounding when I was allowed out of the house—Kate
tried not to bring up the window incident, and Landon still
seemed clueless about what exactly had happened to him. I
hoped and prayed he would never remember that I was the
one who had thrown him to the ground, even if it was to save
his life. If he did remember, he kept his mouth shut, which
was probably for the best. I couldn't explain anything to him.
I had hurt him, and I couldn't even apologize for it. It made
me sick to my stomach.

Being grounded, however, didn't stop me from sneaking out the back door of my house at night so that Will and I could patrol for reapers. We either trained or hunted every night, and I was getting better. I learned to strike for the head or the heart to bring the reapers down quickly and avoid getting injured as much as possible. Will worked with me patiently and tirelessly, and my memory was returning little by little. It was a constant comfort to know he was always there somewhere, completely in tune with me. I knew he had the strength to protect me, even if I didn't know I had the strength to protect myself.

The dark new world I suddenly found myself falling into was becoming the norm. Every night or two there was another reaper in my path. I was getting better, more fluid, more precise in fighting them. Techniques that had once been second nature to me in past lives were returning. It wasn't quite like riding a bike, but I was getting there.

I was grateful to be able to give Will a break from his Guardian duties while I was in school. Reapers didn't normally come out during the day, so Will was able to spend the time at Nathaniel's house, where he showered, ate, and did Will things. If I were attacked, as unlikely as that would be while I was in class, he'd know instantly and come to my side. He needed some time to himself, and I needed to have a normal day. Getting out of the world of reapers for just a few hours helped me stay sane. Perhaps he needed that to stay sane also.

However, the deeper I got into that world, the further away my old world of friends, family, and school drifted. The police had a suspect in custody for the murder of Mr. Meyer. Even though I knew the man was innocent of that crime, he was wanted for questioning for two other violent murders in the Detroit area, with evidence stacked heavily against him. I tried to believe that some good would come from Mr. Meyer's brutal death. It didn't, however, make me feel any better, since I knew that every one of the reapers' victims was in Hell, including Mr. Meyer.

When I got my lit paper back, I couldn't believe I'd done so poorly. I couldn't figure out how to balance my focus between school and my duties as the Preliator. My teacher, Mr. Levine, asked to see me after school so we could discuss the paper. I dreaded the meeting, but it was better than failing the class altogether. If I was really lucky, he'd let me redo it. Unfortunately, I wasn't lucky very often.

After the final bell rang that day, I stopped by Mr. Levine's classroom to talk to him about my paper. As I'd suspected, he wouldn't allow me to rewrite it, but he went over some of it with me, and I left with a better sense of what I was supposed to be learning. I wasn't going to be able to get any extra credit either, but Mr. Levine was very willing to help me get a passing grade.

I was pretty sure my friends were more impatient about my ungrounding than I was. During lunch period on the first Friday of my freedom, I found myself daydreaming again, digging deep inside my head, desperate to remember more. But every time I tried, all I could see was Ragnuk's horrible face, gnashing and biting. When that happened, I forced the memory away and pictured Will's gentle face, and I focused on him as hard as I could. Ragnuk frightened me and I wasn't ashamed to admit it. He was the size of a pickup truck and he wanted to eat me. Fear was, at the very least, reasonable.

"Ellie Marie . . ." came a singsong voice beside me.

"Huh," I grumbled, and prodded my lunch. It was turkey-and-gravy day, which was my favorite school lunch, but I had too much on my mind for me to enjoy it.

"What's with you this week?" Kate asked, her voice low.

Landon sat across from us and was deep into a conversation with Chris and Evan about their favorite video game's being optioned for a major movie. None of them heard us.

"I'm sorry," I said. "I've just been really distracted."

"Is it your dad?" Her tone was serious.

"For once, no, not just him. It's him, school crap, thinking about college, dumb boys . . . There's just a lot of stuff going through my head right now."

She frowned. "You seem so tired all the time."

"I am. I don't know. I'm just going through a funk, I guess."

"Well, cheer up! It's Movie Night and you haven't come

with us in like a million years."

I poked at my lunch. "I don't think I feel like going to see a movie."

"Uh, too bad," Kate said. "You don't have a choice. I need to hang out with you, so you're going."

I forced a smile. "I know, I'm so sorry."

"Bring Will."

I laughed for real this time. "Yeah, right."

"Why not?"

"He's not really a movie person." I tried to imagine six-hundred-year-old Will sitting in a crowded movie theater digging through a tub of buttery popcorn. Then I pictured him wearing oversize 3D glasses, and it was very difficult not to laugh out loud.

Kate made an unintelligible noise. "Who doesn't like going to the movies? That's a load of bull."

"He's a pretty serious guy," I admitted. "Very focused on what he's supposed to be doing. He doesn't put having fun very high on his priority list."

"He's *never* taken you on a date?" She seemed appalled.

"He's not my boyfriend, Kate."

"You hang out with him *all* the time. How are you two not dating?"

I took a bite and averted my gaze; I knew how bad a liar I was. "He's my tutor. That's all."

"Don't lie to me. If you're going out with him, just admit it. I won't judge you for it. He seems nice and he's hot. I don't know why you'd be embarrassed to admit he's your boyfriend. Not to mention he's already graduated. College guys are way better than high school boys. They *know* things. They know how to *do* things."

I didn't want to know what she meant by that. "He's just my tutor. He's been helping me with econ. It's really embarrassing to have to admit it, but that's all he is, I swear." It would have felt really, really strange calling Will my boyfriend, because it was very untrue; but thinking about the idea made me realize that I did kind of like him. He probably wouldn't be my parents' first choice, to say the least, but I couldn't help it. My mom wouldn't like it if I dated someone I said was in college. My dad . . . Well, he'd never like me going out with *anyone*—so, whatever. His opinion didn't count. I didn't remember knowing Will forever, but I could feel it. And it was kind of romantic thinking of him as my protector. I liked that. He was like a security blanket . . . only less fluffy. I wondered, for a moment, if he was cuddly. Probably not.

Kate sat back with a crafty smile on her face. "You're a dirty liar."

"Am not."

"Nobody hangs out with their tutor," she challenged. "Tutors suck. Even hot ones."

"He's a cool guy," I insisted. "We're kind of friends now."

"I thought you said he wasn't that nice."

"He can be nice when he wants to, but he's also moody."

"Sounds like a typical boy. Are you bringing him tonight?"

"I really doubt it."

She frowned. "That'd sure piss Landon off, wouldn't it? I feel kind of bad for the guy."

"He'll have to get over it." I sipped on the straw sticking out of my Mountain Dew.

Kate folded her arms over her chest and sighed. "You're being naïvely optimistic."

Landon looked up. "Mmm? What about me?"

"We're talking crap about your ugly roots," Kate sneered, poking the top of his head. "You might want to get those touched up. David Beckham would weep at the sight of you."

He scowled and flipped her off before going back to his conversation. She laughed.

After the final bell, I stayed an hour after school to go over our next lit assignment with Mr. Levine. When our meeting ended, I went to my locker, retrieved what I needed, and headed to the student parking lot. My friends had all left, and the lot wasn't as full as usual. As I walked to my car, I caught a glimpse of Josie Newport standing by her sparkly red Range Rover. Boldly, I changed my path and strolled up to her. She was texting away on her phone.

"Hey, Josie," I said.

She looked up and gave me a genuine smile. "Oh, hey, Ellie. What's up?"

"Just got out of a session with Levine," I said. "I've been

falling behind, so he's been helping me out after class. What are you still doing here?"

She waved her phone dismissively. "Eh, got out of track early for a doctor's appointment. I'm just killing a few minutes before I have to leave. It beats sitting in a waiting room for forty-five minutes. At least I can enjoy the sun out here and get rid of the raccoon tan my sunglasses made on my face."

"Very true," I laughed. "Hey, listen, about my party—"

"Don't worry about it," she said, slipping her phone into her purse. "Shit happens."

I blushed scarlet. "It was really embarrassing."

"I know some people tried to make a big deal out of it." She glowered. "But seriously, I've made an ass out of myself many times. It happens to everyone when they get drunk— well, not quite flying through the window, but you get what I mean. I got sick once and ruined the interior of my ex's car. Everyone messes up sometimes. You just kind of have to laugh it off and be thankful you weren't hurt."

I smiled, feeling a little better. "Thanks, Josie."

"No problem," she said with a sympathetic grin. "I mean it. Sorry about your window."

"I'm sorry about your ex's car."

We smiled at each other for a moment. It was good to know that we were still cool.

She took her cell back out and glanced at it. "I should get going."

"See you later," I said.

She smiled. "Definitely." She got into her car and left the parking lot.

I turned to walk back to my car and suddenly the world began to slip away. I rocked back on my heels, suddenly fearful that the haziness of my vision might mean that I was going blind for some reason, but as soon as that thought had crossed my mind, the world came back into focus. Only it wasn't a world I immediately recognized.

I was in a much darker world, an ancient, golden world lit by torchlight, and a woman's face—a reaper's—appeared inches away from mine, her hand clamped around my chin, her nails digging into my cheeks and jaw. She had me shoved up against a wall that felt cold and hard at my back. The sheer pleated dress she wore was cool against my arms and legs. Her skin was dark brown and her eyes were inhumanly large, the pupils melting into black irises so wide that only slivers of white curled around their sides. Her hair was long and dark and separated into thin braids, I supposed in order to allow her to blend in.

"You shouldn't have come here," the reaper hissed in a language I somehow recognized as ancient Egyptian and knew to be her native tongue. "Those who love God are slaves, and you are a stranger here."

I could barely speak through her grip. "The business of man is of no matter to me. My only concern lies with their souls—free and captive alike."

"You're a fool. Not even the angelic venture here."

"We both know that is a lie."

Her snarl became a sneer. "Do you mean your Guardian? Ah, yes. I tore her throat out myself. Now even the archangels have forgotten this land."

I set my jaw and ground my teeth in churning rage. "If they'd forgotten it, they wouldn't have sent me here to kill the reaper posing as the pharaoh and stop you all from claiming more human souls."

She cracked the back of my skull into the wall. Pain shot down my back, and blackness crept around the edges of my eyes. "They sent you here to die, killer. Just like your Guardian."

Talons like a harpy's grew from her fingertips, but I didn't wait for her to cut me. My power surged and shoved into the reaper in a flash of white light, but she strained against it. Her face twisted with fury, and her own power exploded as her ash-colored wings burst from her back and she shoved me deeper into the wall, shattering the painting of the pharaoh's gods. I slammed my palm into her chest and sent her crashing to the floor. Unable to catch her balance on her feet, she took to the air, filling up the palace throne room with her massive wings, which smashed through the room's stone columns as if they were made of reeds. A section of the ceiling came crashing down around us, and I sprang to avoid the falling debris. The reaper flew backward toward the throne, where she landed, perching on the gilded chair, her wings spread wide. The torchlight gleaming off the golden walls *gave the reaper an unearthly glow.*

I called forth my swords and swept them upward, instantly lighting them with angelfire. I held them tight as the reaper leaped off the pharaoh's throne and took flight again, her dress billowing around her, wings flapping once, talons slashing. She descended on me, but I made my aim true and swung. My fiery blades sliced the reaper's head clean off, and I ducked as her flaming body exploded above me and was gone.

Ash and embers settled around me, and I stood, letting the angelfire die. I took a deep breath to steady my heart and focused on the next task at hand. I ran from the throne room into a far darker hall to find the pharaoh's reaper imposter, but I stopped dead when I turned around the next corner.

One of the bear reapers blocked my path. I spun around to find another at my back; I was surrounded. Angelfire returned to my blades, and I launched myself at the first reaper. I spun and twisted and sliced, but one of them struck. I jutted a blade straight into the gaping jaws of the first bear reaper and its head went up in flames, but talons wrapped around my waist and yanked me back. I cried out and flailed. . . .

The world spun once more, and a pickup truck blared its horn as it blurred by, narrowly missing me. I wheeled around and bumped into a firm, warm body. I looked up to find myself in Will's arms, and I was back in my school parking lot. He'd pulled me out of the truck's path.

"Ellie? Ellie!"

My heart pounded and my eyes whipped around me

wildly. "Where is it?" I asked breathlessly. "Where's the reaper? My swords?"

He held both my shoulders firmly. "There's no reaper. Relax."

My pulse began to slow down and I took long, deep breaths. It must have been another flashback, like the one I had experienced in my history class. As I steadied my nerves, more of the memory came back to me. I'd been surrounded and alone.

"Where was I?" I asked fearfully. "Who was that?"

He studied my face with a puzzled look. "Who? Who are you talking about?"

"The reaper!" I cried. "She was a vir, I think. And there were more. There were ursids everywhere. The pharaoh—"

"Pharaoh?"

"Yes, he'd been killed and a vir reaper had shape-shifted and mimicked his appearance to take his place. They'd killed so many in Egypt already, taken so many souls, and I was fighting them alone. My Guardian then was dead. It was before I knew you, long before. It must have been thousands of years ago."

My thoughts were scattered and incoherent as I tried to make sense of too many details at once. It had been long before Will came into my life, long before I started to feel human, as he had told me I gradually had as the centuries passed. Had I been in direct contact with the archangels? When had I stopped receiving orders from them? With a reaper posing as the pharaoh, the demonic forces were able to kill an immense number of humans, so many in fact that I had been sent to Egypt to intervene.

But who had sent me? An angel?

"They sent you here to die, killer." The reaper's words haunted me.

"Ellie," Will said, laying a hand on my shoulder. "Are you okay?"

I nodded. "Yeah. I'm just . . . thinking."

"Well, let's think out of the way of speeding vehicles." He led me back to my car, and we sat inside for a moment.

"Something else," I said. "The reaper called me a killer. They usually just call me Preliator. What exactly does my name mean?"

"You didn't always go by that name," he explained. "The origin is Latin, so I assume that people began calling you 'Preliator' while that was an important language in the ancient world. It means 'warrior.'"

Warrior. "I guess I have quite the reputation to live up to."

"Don't worry about it. You'll get there. You always do."

"I hope you're right," I said. "What are you doing at my school, anyway?"

"You were distressed. It must have been the flashback. I rushed here as quickly as I could and I saw a reaper about a mile away."

That caught me off guard. "In broad daylight?"

He nodded. "It might have been looking for you or

following your scent. You should get home so there won't be any fight in public."

"It won't attack anyone, will it?"

"No," he assured me. "They don't feed during the day, and it's very rare for one to be out at this hour. The reaper was smoking like a chimney in the sun. Whatever it is out for must be important, which is why we should get you home."

I looked at him in surprise. "You're riding in my car?"

"Yes" was all he said.

"You're not going to be flying back to my house, then?" I asked sarcastically.

He turned to give me a surprised, questioning look. "No."

"That memory really freaked me out, Will."

"What do you mean?"

"I was so cold and just . . . different. I took my job very seriously. *Too* seriously. It was kind of scary. It was like I wasn't even human." I was glad there wasn't a mirror, so I couldn't see my face. The darkness in my expression would have been too much for me to take.

"You can be very intense," he confessed.

"And something else," I continued. "In my memory, I told the reaper that I was sent by the angels. Do they give me orders?"

He blinked at me and I took that as a no before he said anything at all. "Not that I ever remember."

"If they did give me orders before, why not now? Why did they stop? Why don't I remember speaking to them?"

"I don't know when or why they stopped."

But why didn't I remember it? Was I slowly becoming so human that I was forgetting myself? Had I forgotten where I came from? What I truly was? Was my humanity a weakness? Or was it a strength? Was it my own fault that I no longer spoke to the angels? Had I done something wrong?

Will had told me the angelic reapers served the angels in Heaven. What if I was part of their plan? Who was *I* supposed to serve? What if they had created me?

I scoffed at the idea that I might be some twisted science experiment of the divine, but something was obviously bringing me back every time I died.

Was it angels?

15

"GET UP TO YOUR ROOM AND I'LL MEET YOU THERE,"
Will said when we got back to my house.

I shot him a suspicious look. "My mom will—"

"No, she won't know I'm here. Just get upstairs."

I nodded. There was no use fighting him. As soon as I
walked in the front door, I heard my mom call me from her
office.

"Hey, Ellie? Can you come here for a minute?"

I stopped dead. My heart thumped like crazy as I went
into her office. She looked up when I entered.

"Hey, sweetie," she said. "How was school?"

I shrugged. It took effort to behave normally instead
of like a complete lunatic. "It was okay. I'm doing a little
better in econ. I still don't really get it, though. So what did

you want to talk to me about?"

"Oh, yes!" she said. "The dealership finally called. They can take your car in now. I guess they had a really busy few weeks. We can drop it off tonight or Sunday night, if you'd like. Are you going to the movies again?"

That's right. We were taking my car to get the scratches and dents cleaned up and repainted. "Yeah. You know, we might as well just wait until Sunday to drop it off. They won't start working on it until Monday anyway, and I'd like to use my car this weekend."

"Sounds good."

"Okay. Well, I've got to work on some econ homework before I leave. Talk to you later, Mom."

I jogged up the stairs and found Will standing by my desk looking at some photographs of my friends and me. "Are we hunting tonight?" he asked.

I frowned with a twinge of disappointment. "Yeah, I guess so. Tonight's Movie Night, remember?"

He groaned and turned toward me. "I forgot." He paused. "Do you really have to go to that?"

"Yes," I said firmly. "I want to try and stay a normal teenage girl."

"But you're not."

"Well, then I'd like to maintain the facade."

"I'm really sure if that reaper from earlier doesn't track you tonight, another will, like Ragnuk. I don't think you should be going places with your friends without me, especially at night."

I remembered my conversation with Kate from earlier. "You could . . . come with me." My voice lilted hopefully at the end.

He didn't answer at first, and my heart sank. "I can't really think of a better way to keep a close eye on you."

"Then you're coming. Have you ever been to a movie theater before?"

"Of course I have," he said. He sounded offended. "I don't live under a rock."

"Could've fooled me," I said.

Will sat down on the edge of my bed, leaning forward lazily. "What are you seeing?" he asked, looking up at me.

"Kate said something about a comedy."

"Like what?" He seemed nervous.

"Are you saying you don't have any suggestions?" I smiled slyly.

"Just because I've seen a couple movies in the last hundred years doesn't mean I'm savvy about Hollywood these days."

"I was just curious. I didn't think you would be. Are you cool with seeing a movie? I'll pay." I walked over to my vanity to put on some eye shadow and mascara. I peeked at Will's reflection in the mirror.

"I'm not going so I can enjoy myself," he grumbled. "I'm

going to make sure Ragnuk doesn't snap your neck on the way out the door."

"Why are you always so graphic?" I stroked my lashes with the mascara brush.

"I like to get my point across."

"Apparently." I turned back to him and stepped up to where he sat. "Anyway, I think tonight will be good for you. You shouldn't be so moody and brooding."

"I'm not moody or brooding," he insisted.

I looked down at him quizzically. "Oh, you are."

"Are we sparring first?" he asked, choosing to ignore what I had just said. "Maybe we should go for a run."

"No," I said. "I don't want to get all gross and have to shower again. How about after?"

"That's fine," he said, his voice grim. "If you ask me, I don't think you're taking your duty seriously enough."

I offered him my sweetest smile. "Well, I *didn't* ask you, did I?"

He flashed the slightest glimmer of a grin up at me. "But Ellie, I really need you to understand that this is probably a very bad idea."

I narrowed my eyes. "A trip to the movies isn't dangerous. I'll be fine."

"You can't guarantee your safety."

"Neither can you."

He smiled, ever so slightly. Then he reached up and

touched my earlobe, looking at it carefully. "When I saw you last," he said softly, "your ears were pierced with little pearl earrings."

I almost laughed, not because the memory was funny, but because of the sweet fondness in his voice as he recalled it. It surprised me. "You have a really good memory."

"Pretty good." His smile grew a little wider—that dazzling smile I hadn't seen him show all week. It made me happy. "You're the same person, yet you're someone new."

"Is that a good thing?"

He shrugged a little. "It's like a new start for you. I guess it could be a good thing."

"Why do you think it has been so long?" I asked.

His smile faded and I instantly regretted asking the question. "Since you were alive?"

"Yeah," I said. "Why did it take so long for me to be reborn?"

"I don't know." The sad expression on his face made me feel even sadder.

"Is it weird that I'm different every time?" I asked. "Does it bother you that I have a different name?"

"No, of course not. It never has. You're still you, but you have a different childhood every time and your personality is always a little different. You're certainly more high-strung than when I knew you last."

I glared at him, but I couldn't hide the smile that also

appeared. "What was my name last time?"

"Why does it matter?"

"I'm curious."

"It was a long time ago." He stood up and wrapped a hand around the back of my neck gently. "A name is just a name, not who you are. How about we don't worry about that?"

"What do you mean?"

"How about you just be you tonight and I'll be me? Don't worry about anything else." His emerald eyes were soft and kind. I felt he really meant what he said.

"You mean pretend to be human?"

"Why not?"

I smiled slyly at him. "Well, this is quite the turn for you."

"Maybe I'm thinking it would be good for you to relax from time to time."

"Just for the night?"

"Just for the night."

He dipped his head and leaned forward, surprising me. He didn't kiss me, but he was close enough to do it. My body locked up and my lips parted. His body was warm against mine, and I wanted him to do what I thought he was going to do. I really wanted him to kiss me, and I could feel my insides tugging and spinning. I lifted my chin and waited, but he stopped. His look fell away and he turned his face and stepped back slowly. I deflated.

"So when is the movie?" he asked, running a hand through his hair.

I felt like falling to the floor. "Um, seven or eight is usually when we go."

He nodded. "It's only four. What do you want do until then?"

"Well, I should get a couple pages in on my econ assignment," I said, groaning.

"That's fine," he said. "Would you like me to leave so you can do your homework?"

"Where will you go?" I asked. "Will you go all the way back to Nathaniel's like you do during the day?"

"No. Seeing the reaper this afternoon has made me nervous. When I'm guarding your house, I usually sit up on the roof. It's the best lookout."

"If it works for you, I guess." I smiled. "I'll give you a shout when I'm done."

He gave me a quick nod and turned away, disappearing. I shook my head in disbelief. He was like a ninja or something. He had probably disappeared into the Grim, and I considered for a moment following him. But I was afraid of the Grim and what things I might see there. So instead, I sat at my desk and grabbed my backpack to get out my homework. I could still feel Will's presence in my room, smell his scent, as if he hadn't actually left. And he really hadn't. I knew he was close by, and that comforting thought helped me to get through my assignment with ease.

16

MY STOMACH GROWLED. I LET MY FACE HIT THE desk and rolled my head to the side to glance at my clock sideways. It was just after six. I couldn't believe I'd been working on this homework for two hours. I was so sick of this crap.

I lifted my gaze. "Hey, Will?" I felt stupid talking to no one in my room.

"Finished?" answered his voice a moment later.

Startled, I leaped out of my seat, grasping my heart. My pulse pounded in my head. "What's the matter with you? You scared the crap out of me!"

He stood just in front of the window. He had somehow managed to get in without making any noise at all. "Sorry about that."

I smoothed out my shirt. "What *are* you, Will? How

can you move that fast?"

"I'm your Guardian."

"No, I mean, besides Batman, what is your *species*?"

"I'm immortal."

"Never mind," I said impatiently. "I already know what you are: *obnoxious*. I'm going to go change into some fresh clothes."

"Why?"

"Because I don't like wearing the same outfit all day."

He looked at me like I had a third eye. I rolled my eyes and shut myself in my closet. I picked out a pair of jeans and a black sweater and put them on before emerging. "I'm really hungry, and I know how much you like to be invisible and all, but I think you can make an exception. Would you mind if we grabbed a bite to eat before the movie?"

"Not at all," he said. "You need to eat. You get grumpy when you don't eat."

I blinked in surprise. He really did know me well. "Great. How does Coney Island sound?"

"I have no idea what that is."

"Blasphemy."

I drove us to my favorite, Leo's Coney Island. The restaurant was typically crowded for a Friday night. As we wandered to an open table, I noticed a group of girls sitting at a booth near the front door. Two of them were staring at Will, so I gave them the stink eye as we passed.

I chose a booth on the opposite wall, as far away from the girls as possible. Our waitress was a perky girl maybe a year older than me.

"What can I getcha?" she asked with her pencil and notepad in hand.

"Plain cheeseburger and fries with a side salad and water for me," I said, and nodded at Will. "Do you want anything?"

"No, thank you," he said with a dismissive wave of his hand.

The girl gave a quick nod and buzzed away.

"Aren't you hungry?" I asked him.

He shook his head. "Not often. The only time I eat is usually after a fight. The more heavily wounded or weak I am, the more I need to eat in order to heal and replenish my strength. Calories heal my body, so I need a lot of them."

I stared at him. "I am so jealous." I was excited that he felt like revealing things to me. Perhaps this conversation would go somewhere interesting. Our hostess brought my drink and I stuck the straw in to take a gulp.

"Will you ever tell me how you became my Guardian?" I asked hopefully.

He smiled. "You know very well how that happened. I know you don't have access to that memory yet, but I don't think it's something I can just tell you. It means too much to me, I guess. Everything will come back to you. Be patient."

I huffed at his response, because it only made me more

curious. "Are you going to tell me what my name was, or do I have to remember that, too?"

He rolled his eyes. "You need to stop asking questions. Remember what I said earlier? We're pretending to be normal humans today."

"Well, normal humans don't sit at Coney Island and watch others eat. They order a plateful of chili cheese fries. Don't be so weird." I took another gulp.

My food arrived, and just as the waitress was about to leave, Will held up his hand. "I've changed my mind. I'll take a root beer float."

She flashed a quick smile and fluttered away.

"A root beer float?" I asked. "What are you, five?"

"They're my favorite."

"A root beer *float*?" I repeated. "You're six hundred years old and a root beer float is your favorite food?"

He shrugged. "You wanted me to be normal and order something, so I did."

"That is still weird."

"They're delicious."

The waitress returned with his float, and he stirred and dunked the ice cream immediately. Between his sips and bites of ice cream, Will watched me much too closely as I ate.

"What?" I asked, swallowing a mouthful.

"You remind me of me."

"That can't be good." I took another bite.

"It's not necessarily a bad thing. You must be really hungry."

I didn't like the amused look on his face. I felt very self-conscious suddenly. "So?"

He shrugged. "Nothing."

"Screw you."

I ate more slowly after that. When we headed to the register to pay and leave, I reached inside my purse for money, but Will handed the clerk a twenty-dollar bill.

"No, no, no," I said, reaching for his hand. "That wasn't part of the deal."

"Don't worry about it," he assured me, allowing the clerk to take the bill. "I've got this."

"But all you had was that float."

"We're trying to act normal, aren't we? It's not very normal for a young lady to pay for her own dinner."

I scowled. "You must be confusing right now with a hundred years ago. That's a stupid stereotype. We aren't even on a date, so it doesn't count."

"Perhaps, but everyone around us is assuming otherwise." He nodded, his gaze wandering around the restaurant. "We don't want them to become suspicious, do we?"

"Will, they *really* don't care what we're doing," I said. "It's not like we're undercover or something."

When we met up with my friends, Landon spotted Will, and his attitude soured dramatically. I told myself sternly that

I would ignore Landon's attitude tonight, so I focused my efforts on being in a great mood. I hadn't forgotten Will's earlier warning about the wandering reaper, but seeing Will at ease made *me* feel at ease.

"*E-l-l-l-l-lie!*" Kate grabbed me into a huge hug and held me tightly. "I'm so happy to see you!" She practically shoved me away and turned to Will. She yanked him into a hug as well, resulting in a very uncomfortable Will. "I'm so glad you came!" You could count on Kate to be over the top with everything she did.

I forced a bright smile. "So how about this movie?"

"We have twenty minutes before it starts," Chris said, looking at his cell phone. "We should probably get our tickets and get seats. It's opening night."

After buying our tickets—I refused to let Will pay for ours when he tried—we waited in line to enter the theater. Every once in a while I'd see Will stiffen and swivel his gaze around, as if he were listening and watching very carefully. If anything was considering jumping us tonight, I was assured Will would have plenty of warning. When the usher let us in, we found seats a little toward the back, since the middle was filled. Chris, Rachel, and Evan slipped down the aisle first, followed by Landon and Kate, then me and Will.

Landon leaned over Kate and me. "Where did you say you go to school again?" he asked Will.

"I'm a sophomore at U of M," Will replied.

Landon scoffed. "You and Ellie hang out often?"

Kate elbowed him in the ribs, and he shot her an angry glare.

"Yes," Will said.

Wrapping an arm around mine, Kate grinned at Will. "You shouldn't hog her so much. We miss her!"

Will shrugged and smiled. "Sorry. I don't mean to."

Kate laughed and toyed with a lock of my hair. "I guess you'll just have to hang out with us more so we can see her too."

Yeah, right.

The movie finally began, and by halfway through it, Will seemed to be enjoying himself. He chuckled a few times, but he frequently glanced toward the emergency exit as if expecting something to burst through it. I also noticed Landon repeatedly looking at us. What was his problem? He probably expected us to make out during the movie. That was a junior high thing anyway, so his worry was ridiculous.

At nine thirty the movie had finished and the theater began hemorrhaging high school and college students. We stopped on the sidewalk outside to plan our next move.

"Landon and I are going to Cold Stone," Kate said. "Anyone want to join? Ellie?"

I frowned. "I don't really feel like ice cream."

"Oh, come on!" she whined. "Please?"

I laughed. "Why do you want me to go with you to get ice cream so badly?"

"Because it's *good*!" Kate turned to Will. "You want ice cream, don't you, Will?"

Will's eyes flickered to me and back to Kate. "If Ellie isn't interested, then I'm not. I just go where she goes."

Kate groaned. "You guys can't leave us yet! It's not even ten. At least come over to my place and party for a bit. We can hang out in my basement."

That sounded really good. I hadn't been able to relax with my best friend for weeks. Will leaned close to me, his voice soft, his breath warm on my ear. "I think you should go. You'll enjoy yourself."

"But what about—?" I whispered back.

"You'll have fun," he whispered. "I want you to be happy. Remember our agreement for tonight?"

I smiled. "But I want you to pretend you're human *with* me."

"All right," he said.

"Okay, you two," Kate said. "What's the plan?"

I looked up to her. "We're coming."

"Yay!" she chirped, pulling me into another tight Kate hug. "I still want Cold Stone. Sure you don't want to join us?"

I nodded. "Yeah, I ate right before the movie, so I'm still pretty full. I'll pass, but how about we meet you at your house in an hour?"

"Sounds good," she said with a smile.

"Okay, bye," I said, and waved to them all.

Will and I walked back to my car. "Thank you," I said in a low voice.

"I meant it when I said I want you to be happy," he answered. "It has always made this easier on you—when you're happy."

"Is that so?"

"Yes." He smiled.

"What did I use to do for fun?" I unlocked my car and we climbed in.

"You've always loved horses," he said distantly. "Through every lifetime I've known you."

I perked up. "Really? Did I ride a lot?"

"All the time. A hundred years ago there weren't many cars, so that's how we got around. When you were . . . When I knew you last, you competed in horse shows."

I laughed. "That's cool."

"You were really good."

"Do you think I still am?"

He nodded firmly. "Oh yes. You've always been a natural. It's never failed to come back to you."

"Will you take me riding?"

He glanced at me. "Definitely."

"Promise?"

"I have never broken a promise to you."

I eyed him. "Not once?"

"Not once."

I was skeptical. "You're telling me that in five hundred

years, you have never messed up something you've promised me?"

"Ellie, you need to understand," he said softly. "I exist
only to serve you and fight by your side. Whether that fighting is to preserve your life or to make sure you smile, that is
what I am built to do. You're all I have, and I will watch over
you forever."

I stared at him. "You're very intense, you know that?"

"I do now." He smiled.

We headed back toward my town and exited onto a
wooded, hilly back road. The narrow road was quiet, and I
saw only one other pair of headlights for a half mile.

"I hope you enjoyed yourself," I said to Will. "Did you
like the movie?"

He was looking out the window, but he turned to face me
and smiled. "It was interesting. I think Landon and I could
become friends."

I laughed. "Oh yeah. Best friends in the making, right
there. What did you think of the movie, honestly?"

He shrugged. "It was funny. Humans always amaze me
with how drastically their culture evolves every few years.
Imagine witnessing that over tens of generations."

"I wish I could," I said. "I'm still only remembering
snippets of things."

"It'll come back. I know I keep saying that, but it will."

I nodded glumly. "I'm glad that you came tonight, and
that nothing bad happened. Thank you."

"Of course. I think it was good for you."

My smile returned. "It was good for *both* of us to get out and do something besides fighting for a change."

Out of the corner of my eye I saw a dark shape bound across the road toward my window. Then something massive rammed into my car door, and the Audi was sent spinning counterclockwise, whipping my body around in the seat. The wheel was torn from my grip and the car came to a stop so suddenly, my shoulder slammed into the door panel and the window shattered next to my face. The headlights poured out onto the road into blackness.

"Ellie!" Will shouted. "Ellie, are you okay?"

He undid my seat belt and his hands frantically touched my arms, face, and neck. My head spun and I felt like I was going to be sick. I looked around and saw we had smashed up against a tree on Will's side. The jagged edges of glass from my window jutted out in all directions. Oh God, my poor car.

"I'm fine. Are you—?"

The windshield exploded, spraying chunks of glass, and the hideous, deformed head of Ragnuk burst through with a bellowing roar. He was free of the Grim. He was completely in the mortal dimension.

I screamed and thrashed, throwing my arms up. Will pounded on the reaper's snout several times, and the jaws snapped back, biting at his arm.

"Get out of the car!" Will yelled, leaning back, and

he kicked the ursid reaper in the face. Ragnuk roared and reached through the windshield with his giant claws.

I yanked the handle and slammed all my weight into the door, but it wouldn't budge. It was too smashed. I pushed—and pushed, and pushed, and pushed.

Ragnuk forced himself in until half the car was full of gnashing teeth and swinging talons, and I lay on my back and kicked the door with all my strength. My power flared and the door flew open. I dived out and turned back to see Ragnuk halfway inside the car and Will's much smaller shape fighting him off. My legs turned to jelly, and something dark grew in the pit of my gut, but I had to do something fast. I couldn't be afraid of him. I called my swords, and as the silver filled my hands, angelfire burst from the blades.

I leaped up onto the trunk, surprising myself by how easily I could jump that high. I ran up and over the roof until I was above the reaper. I crossed both blades over my chest and slashed Ragnuk across his back. He roared and slammed his head into the roof of the car before wrenching himself back and finally pulling free. His black eyes snapped up to me. With a great deal of effort, he stepped back and shook his body like a dog. Chunks of glass were embedded in his flesh, and I watched the glass fly from his wounds as he shook, hitting the ground like blood-drenched diamonds.

Ragnuk snarled and leaped up at me. I ducked and plunged a sword into his belly, spilling blood. His claws swiped, ripping my upper arm open, and I screamed. He snapped his jaws down at me, but I twisted away, and his snout smashed into the metal roof. I swung my sword, but he slammed the side of his head into my chest, and the brutal force sent me flying through the air. My back hit the pavement and my skull smacked hard. I didn't feel any blood, so I jumped to my feet.

I could do this. I had to lose my fear and defeat him.

Ragnuk hopped off my car and landed with a thud that shook the earth. He stepped forward and arched his back, his power building like a storm surge. I looked up to see Will leap over the Audi with the bloody slashes across his face and chest vanishing before my eyes. He drove his sword down at the reaper's head. Ragnuk reared, and his paw nailed Will's chest midair, slamming his back up against the rear driver's-side door. I saw blood.

Darkness crept into the edges of my sight, as it did when I was about to have a flashback, but instead of remembering something, I lost all sense of time and place. My gaze locked on my target, and all I thought of was killing. Rage pounded through my body, clouding my thoughts, and I could practically taste Ragnuk's blood in my mouth. I let out a terrible cry and charged at him, swords in hands.

Fingers grabbed me around my neck and yanked me backward—*hard*. My body flew across the road and crashed into a tree. When I hit the ground, I looked up. A female creature landed with a soft step as giant, leathery, batlike wings—*wings!*—stretched, flapped once, and folded against her back. Terror clawed the inside of my throat until it was as dry as sandpaper. Her skin was so lucent, she appeared to glow in the moonlight. Ash-colored hair settled around her shoulders and she stared at me with curious, pale eyes. She had to be one of the humanlike vir reapers. Power rolled from her in terrible dark waves.

"Ragnuk," she snarled, her gaze still locked on mine.

The ursid ceased his assault on Will and whipped away from him, claws scraping the pavement in a rage. *"Ivar!"* he roared, his voice thundering inside my skull. "You dare stop me?"

Finally she looked away, releasing me from her viper's stare. Her movement was fluid, like water, as eerie and terrible as a storm swell on the sea. "There's been a development. Bastian needs us." Her voice was low and sensual, smooth as velvet.

A deathly low snarl rolled from deep within Ragnuk's throat. "It can wait."

"No," the vir reaper said sharply. "You don't appear capable of finishing the job."

Ragnuk's temper exploded, and he threw a paw into the fender of my car, crunching it deeper into the tree.

Ivar looked back at me with that same frightening smoothness. "Preliator," she said, "enjoy the days you have left. Drink the sun like wine, for when the Enshi awakens, the darkness will spare nothing in your world—not even your soul. It ends soon." Her wings spread wide and she took to the air, disappearing quickly.

With a nasty hiss, Ragnuk stomped toward me, halting only a few feet away from where I had fallen. "I'll be back for you, girl," he snarled, curling back his black lips and flashing wet, bloody fangs. "You *and* your Guardian. You're *mine.*"

The malice in his voice assured me that he meant every word. He gnashed his jaws at me before disappearing into the night.

17

WHEN HE HAD GONE, I FOUND THE STRENGTH TO
stand and run to Will's side. He was breathing heavily and
leaning up against my battered car. Through his torn shirt, I
watched his wounds seal and fade to nothing. The skin over
his ribs popped and cracked. Something must have been
broken. Bruises faded, and he took a deep breath now that
the pressure of broken bones was off his lungs.

As I opened my mouth to speak, he leaned forward and
turned me around to examine my head.

"I'm fine, Will," I said as he picked through my filthy
hair.

"You have glass in your hair." He smoothed my hair
back down. "I just wanted to make sure there wasn't any
stuck in the skin."

I laughed. "I think I would have noticed glass sticking

out the back of my head."

He gave me a serious look. "It's not funny. Wounds can't heal if there is something blocking the skin from closing."

"Well, there's nothing impaling my head. How are you?"

"I need to eat."

"Looks like it." I wiped at a streak of blood on his cheek. "Who the hell was that bat chick?"

"An agent of Bastian's," he said. "I don't want you to fight her. Not yet. You aren't awake enough yet."

Ivar's face flashed in my mind, her corpse gray eyes coldly staring into mine. "Why? Was she one of the vir you told me about, like from my memory?"

He nodded. "Yes, she is a vir," he explained. "Ivar is a reaper with shape-shifting abilities. She can appear mostly human if she desires to."

"I didn't like her," I said.

"I never have."

"They weren't even in the Grim," I said. "Why did they attack us on this plane?"

He groaned and straightened out his shirt. "They do that sometimes."

He moved to the side so I could get a good look at my car. What was left of my Audi was a gnarled mess of blood-splattered metal and shattered glass. Some of Ragnuk's fur was caught in the frame of my windshield. The driver's-side door was crunched and hung limply on its hinges. The windshield had exploded all over the inside of the car and on the pavement and grass around it. Blood was smeared across the hood and roof. The red was stark and violently apparent on the white paint. Marshmallow had been turned into a freaking war zone.

"My poor car," I groaned. "What am I going to do?"

Will sighed. "You have to call your parents. Tell them it was a deer. If you want your insurance to cover this, you'll probably have to fill out a police report."

"This sucks." My brand-new car was totaled. I *loved* my car. With nerves shaking my hands, I picked up my cell phone. It rang only twice before there was an answer.

"Hey, Ellie," my mom said. "What's up?"

"I had an accident," I said, my voice quaking.

"*What?* Are you hurt? Where are you?"

"I'm fine," I assured her. "Will is with me. We're fine. I drove into a bunch of deer and my car is totaled." I told her where we were.

"Who's Will, honey?"

Whoops. I forgot I hadn't mentioned him yet. I gave him an apologetic glance, but he appeared unaffected. "This guy I know who came to the movies with us. I was giving him a ride home."

Her words were rapid but carefully enunciated as she tried to stay calm. "Okay, are you on the side of the road?"

"I freaked and hit a tree."

"Oh God! Are you sure no one's hurt?"

"We're in a ditch."

"Are your flashers on?"

No. "Yeah." I turned them on.

"Okay, I'll call the police for you and a tow truck. Sure you're okay? Is your friend hurt? He's not going to sue, is he?"

Ugh, the police? "We're *fine*, Mom. He's not going to sue us. Relax."

"I'm on my way."

I shut my phone. "This is just wonderful. The cops are never going to believe deer did this!"

"You'd be surprised." His expression told me he might have used this excuse before. "Deer kill more people on the road than people kill people. Michigan has a lot of deer."

"Yeah," I grumbled.

"See?" He smiled. "Very likely."

"My poor car . . ." I wanted to cry, and I *really* wanted to kill Ragnuk for destroying my car. I was just very thankful that my first accident had been with a reaper and not another person.

My mom arrived in five minutes, and the police followed only a couple of minutes after. She would not stop hugging me. The two cops who arrived did little besides question me and write stuff down.

"What'd you hit?" the officer with the mustache asked,

tapping his pen on his clipboard loudly. He didn't seem happy to be there.

"Deer," I answered.

Officer Mustache eyed me darkly, like I'd committed a crime. "Must've been a huge deer. Big buck?"

"Oh yeah. Big buck. And a bunch of little ones."

"Where are the bodies?" the younger, cuter cop asked.

"Bodies?"

"Yeah," Cute Cop said with a wave of his hand back at my car. "This kind of damage and no dead deer is a little hard to believe. I can't imagine him getting up and running off."

"Well, he didn't," I said. My voice trembled. I was nowhere near as good a liar as Will. "Some random rednecks drove by in a beat-up truck and offered to take the dead buck who went through my window."

"Random rednecks?" Officer Mustache narrowed his eyes.

"I don't know why they wanted it. It had big antlers, but maybe they were thinking about a barbecue tomorrow. How should I know? I don't want to think about what they wanted with roadkill."

Cute Cop grimaced. "Were you or your boyfriend hurt in any way?"

"He's *not* my boyfriend," I said sternly.

"Answer the question, Ellie," Will said.

"No, we're fine." I glared at him.

"That's a lot of blood on you," Cute Cop noted, eyeballing both of us.

"It's not ours," I said. "The deer was cut wide open. Go look at my front seat. It was a massacre."

Officer Mustache nodded to his partner. "There's a tow truck on the way. He should be here soon to get your car home. Drive safely from now on, miss."

We followed the tow truck to the Audi dealership in my mom's Mercedes. The pathetic remains of my car were left by the service building and I said my farewells. I was quite sure Marshmallow was dead.

Mom assured me the insurance company would either take care of the damage or pay for a replacement car. It was an act of nature, she said. Oh, yeah. That had been one *hell* of an act of nature.

Mom was very interested in Will, and until we got into her car, she could barely keep her eyes off his tattoos. She interrogated him all the way to the dealership and back to my house.

"Is there a place I can drop you off, Will?" she asked in a concerned voice, failing to quell the motherly instinct that had been set on high alert since my initial phone call of doom.

"No, that's all right," he said. "I only live a five-minute walk past your neighborhood."

"Are you sure? It won't be any trouble."

"I'll be fine. You've had enough excitement for one night."

My mom laughed. "Well, I can take a little bit more. Where's your house?"

"I see you're very intent on this."

"I am."

He directed my mom a couple minutes past our street. The house was one of the more modest homes in the area, and I knew it didn't belong to him. The lawn was pristine and ornately designed.

"Lovely gardens," my mom said as she pulled into the driveway. It was after midnight and the house was dark. I didn't need to worry about the real owners of the house wondering why some weird guy was getting dropped off there.

"Thank you," Will said as he climbed out of the backseat.

"It was very nice meeting you," Mom said. "You'll have to come around more often."

"I will," he said, smiling beautifully. "Thank you for the ride, Mrs. Monroe. Sorry about your car, again, Ellie. I hope it gets fixed."

"Thanks," I said, and stuck my tongue out at him.

He winked. My mom hadn't noticed.

We backed out of the driveway, and almost immediately I lost sight of Will in the mirror. I needed to call Kate and let her know we weren't coming. In all honesty, I didn't feel like partying anymore. The fight with Ragnuk had taken its toll on me. I was proud of myself for staying brave—at least until Ivar showed up. She was a whole other ball game.

"Is he really an economics major?" Mom asked, breaking into my thoughts.

"Uh, yeah," I said. It was important to keep Will's identity straight.

I spotted the slightest rise of her eyebrows. "I admire you for working with your teacher and getting a tutor for this class," she said. "It sounds like you're in good hands. He seems really smart."

"He is. He knows a lot."

"Is he your boyfriend?"

I almost choked on my tongue. "What? No. He's just a really good friend."

"I'm surprised that you've never mentioned him," she noted. "He's kind of old for you, anyway."

She didn't fool me. "It's the tattoos and you know it," I said.

She laughed. "Your father definitely wouldn't like that about him, but it's more of an age issue. Wait until you're actually in college before you start dating college boys. Maybe if you were eighteen and had already graduated . . . but for right now, I think he's a little too old."

Just a little. I tapped my knuckles on the window as I watched the world blur by in shadows. I shouldn't even have been thinking about Will romantically, especially given the way our nonromantic relationship worked. "So Mom," I said. "Just being hypothetical, of course, but what would you say if I did like him?"

"How old is he again?"

"Like twenty . . . ?" My voice trailed off uncertainly.

She made a noise under her breath. "There's nothing wrong with *liking* him."

"But not dating him."

"Like I said," she explained, "it would be easier for me to accept if you weren't still in high school. You have to remember that you're only seventeen and he's technically an adult, though it's obvious you like him."

I chewed my lip, contemplating how honest I could be with her—and myself. "I do. It's stupid, I know. He's not perfect, but he does a lot of things right."

"It's not stupid. To start, he's a very good-looking boy and he seems driven."

I laughed. That much was very true. "So when you said he should come around more often . . ."

"Well, now . . ." She trailed off but gave a soft laugh.

"I'm not sure if I could really go out with him anyway," I said. "He's my tutor. We've hung out a few times with friends, but that's it. He's an all-business kind of guy."

"That's good that he takes his duties seriously."

How funny she should use that word. "Yeah. He does. Very much so."

"But you're not satisfied with that."

And my mom was a mind reader. "Not exactly. Is it even possible to be with someone you basically work with?"

"It's possible," she said thoughtfully. "But it makes

working together difficult, because then you're focused on him and not your job. And if things go bad between you two . . . It's hard to keep working together. It makes being around them almost unbearable."

I watched her carefully as her gaze stuck straight forward. "You're talking about Dad, aren't you? Being married to him, I mean."

"He would fall under that category, I guess."

"What happened to him?"

She let out a long breath. "I don't know, baby. I really don't."

"And being with him every day," I began slowly, "it's hard."

"It is. He's changed. That happens. He hasn't been the man I married for a long time." She turned to glance at me for a second. "But you know the craziest part? I still love him."

"I guess it's true that loves makes you blind."

"No," my mom said. "It doesn't make you blind. You're very, very aware of everything about the one you truly love, whether you know it from what your eyes tell you or your heart. So no, love doesn't make you blind. It paralyzes you until you can't breathe or run away from it."

And with that, I knew my mom couldn't leave my dad even if she tried. He'd never struck her, but he was verbally and emotionally abusive. Maybe the clock was ticking. Maybe my mom knew that. In any case, she wouldn't help herself and I couldn't help her, either.

But it made me question my relationship with Will. If he became more than just my Guardian, how would it affect our ability to work together? If he ever did kiss me, would we change?

Mom sighed. "You can't even imagine how horrified I was when you told me that you'd been in an accident. I knew it might happen, but I felt like my heart had stopped."

My gut sank. "I'm sorry."

"Did I ever tell you that I was in a bad accident once?"

I looked at her. "No."

We pulled into our driveway and parked in the garage.

"It was late at night and a driver in the other lane drifted into mine. He struck me, and I rolled and my car hit a tree. I was pregnant when it happened and I lost the baby. After that, the doctors said I wouldn't be able to have children. And then you came along." She ran a hand through my hair and touched my face tenderly. "That's why you're my little miracle. I don't ever want to know what life would be like if I lost you."

I watched her for another moment longer. The silence of the garage curled around me, sucking like a void. What my mom confessed had unnerved me. I knew I was already a freak, but this made me feel even more like one. When I was reborn, who decided what family I'd be born to? I feared the idea that someone—or something—had control over my fate. Over my soul.

"I'll see you in the morning," my mom said. "I'm so happy you're all right."

"Thanks for everything," I told her. "That was really scary."

"I just can't believe the rotten luck you've had with your car," she mused. "If all teenagers have this kind of luck, then I don't blame the insurance companies for their rates."

I pursed my lips tightly. Right—*luck*. It wasn't that I was being hunted down by a baby-eating monster-assassin or anything. Just bad luck.

She smiled warmly and kissed my forehead. "It wasn't your fault, and I think you handled it well. Sleep in tomorrow, okay?"

"Can't argue with that." I laughed. "Good night."

"'Night, Ellie Bean."

I headed toward the stairs, but I stopped dead when I heard a voice growl with rage behind me.

"What the hell did you do?"

An awful feeling in my chest plunged deep into my gut when I saw my father stomp toward me, his face beet red and his eyes wild. I staggered back, tripping on the bottom step of the staircase, and I hit the wall as fear whirled through me. "It was an accident," I pleaded, my hand crawling along the wall to try to maintain my balance. "I didn't mean to—"

"*You wrecked your car!*" he snarled through grinding

teeth, spittle flecking my face. He raised a hand, and I didn't know what he was about to do with it. "You've had it for a *month!*"

"Richard!" my mom cried as she ran up to him and grabbed his wrist. "Richard, be glad she's not hurt."

"*She's* not hurt?" he roared, turning toward her. "What about that thirty-thousand-dollar car I bought for her?"

Mom pushed his shoulder, firmly guiding him away from me. "Richard, listen to me. It was a deer. The accident couldn't be helped." I noticed how she reiterated that it had been an accident, but it didn't make any difference.

"Her *carelessness* can't be helped!" he shouted inches from her face. Mom closed her eyes as she was blasted with his breath and spit.

I felt heat rise in me as my anger grew. I stared at my dad as he yelled those awful things into my mom's face. They weren't true. I had done my best. I was only trying to protect others and myself, but I wasn't perfect. It wasn't my fault that things got damaged when I fought the reapers. It wasn't my fault. "It's not my fault," I said aloud, trying to convince my dad and myself.

"You'd better believe it's your fault!" that monster hissed, turning his attention back to me.

"I'm not careless," I said, my voice eerily calm as the rage churned like an undertow within me.

"All you do is break things and fail in school. Can't you do anything besides cause destruction?"

"I'm not failing in school." My grades weren't amazing by any means, but they were certainly fixable. He had no right to bring up school.

"You have no respect for anything or anyone," he growled, ignoring my retort. "You're worthless."

Fury spun through me. "Not as worthless as you."

He certainly didn't ignore *that*. He grabbed me around the jaw in a surprisingly fast move and lifted my face up so that his eyes bored down into mine. He might have meant the hold to hurt, but it didn't. Not for me. Not as much as his words did.

I fought everything in me not to snap each of his fingers like little twigs. My breathing grew longer and steadier as I stared up at my father and said, "I *hate* you."

His gaze didn't flicker for even a heartbeat, but his fingers gripped my chin tighter. "I don't care."

He held me a moment longer before releasing me roughly, knocking me back into the wall. He whirled around and stomped away. My mom started toward me, but I rushed up the steps and ran into my room before she could say a thing, slamming the door behind me. I flipped on the light and threw my purse at my bed, spilling its contents all over the floor. Once I was alone, my composure was gone and I started to hyperventilate as my gaze spun around the room. I couldn't focus on anything. I was dizzy, furious, and exhausted.

Finally, my eyes rested on the music box on my dresser, the music box my dad had given me, which I loved. Instead of opening it and watching the ballerina twirl around to pretty music, I grabbed the box, shoved open my window, and chucked it as hard as I could into the night. I watched the music box fly through the air and shatter when it hit the ground. I never wanted to see that ballerina dance or hear that music ever again.

Spinning away from the window, I covered my face with my hands and let out a muffled scream into my palms. Once it was out, I began to sob. I ran my hands through my hair, pulling the locks away from my face so I could breathe better, but it didn't work. I cried and cried, and my knees started to buckle, but I refused to fall down.

"Ellie."

The soft voice behind me, more familiar than any sound I'd ever heard before, sent a rush of relief through my body. As I turned around, Will wrapped his warm arms around me. He felt as familiar as his voice, firm like the foundation of a skyscraper, and I hugged him tight and buried my face in his chest as I cried. He touched my hair and held me as close as he could and said nothing. I didn't need him to say anything. I just needed him to stand there and hold me.

We stayed like that until I stopped crying and loosened my grip. He smelled so good, so much like home, more than the house I lived in, that I didn't want to pull away, but I knew I had to. I stepped back and let go, unable to look up into his kind green eyes and face him.

"Thank you," I whispered hoarsely, looking at the floor instead of at him, wiping at the tears streaked across my face. "I'm okay now." I was embarrassed by what he knew had happened and by my reaction to it. But I also knew that he wouldn't judge me, even though *I* did.

"Anything for you."

Those words made me look at him at last. His expression was firm with worry and anger, but he tried to appear calmer than he truly was. The kindness of his effort made me terrifically grateful to have him in my life at that moment.

He swallowed hard and his gaze flickered. "If he had struck you," he said slowly, "I would have killed him."

I stared at him, looking him up and down, registering the rigidity in his shoulders. "I know."

Our eyes met again, and neither of us moved or spoke for some time. I was finally lucid after all, as if his presence had washed away all the sadness and anger flooding my heart.

"I have to go," Will said.

He disappeared out my window, leaving me alone, once again putting distance between us as soon as we got close. I stared after him, past the curtains billowing in the icy nighttime breeze and out that black hole of a window.

18

I NEEDED TO CALL KATE. SHE WOULD BE WORRIED about where I was. I grabbed my phone, cleared my throat, and called her.

"Where are you?" she asked as soon as she answered.

"I'm at home," I said, switching on the lamp by my bed and turning off the overhead light. "My car is totaled."

"What?" She shrieked so loud, I had to pull the phone away from my ear.

"We hit a bunch of deer on the way home. My car is seriously trashed."

"Oh my God," she gasped. "Gross. Are you all right?"

"Yeah, we're fine, just really tired and dirty." I didn't tell her about what had happened with my dad as soon as I got home. I didn't need to relive it again.

"Do you still want to come over? I can come and pick you up. Evan got a fifth."

I felt bad turning her down, but I was just not in the mood to drink. A monster had tried to kill me only a few hours before. All I wanted now was to sleep. "How about tomorrow night?" I asked. "I'm still pretty freaked out. Tomorrow night, we should get everyone together at your house."

"All right," she said. "You had better not bail on me *again*. I think we should hang out before the party, too. It feels like I never see you anymore."

I laughed. "I won't bail, I promise. I'll even bring Will." If he was going to stick close to me, he might as well show his face and enjoy himself a little. It was a good excuse to keep him nearby.

No sooner did I think that than I saw Will climb back in through my window.

"Hey, I'll give you a call tomorrow," I offered, trying my best to be cheerful. "We'll party then, I swear. We'll even hang out earlier, too. Laser tag, maybe?"

"Okay-bye-love-you," she said in one breath.

I hung up, tossed my phone on my bed, and turned my attention to Will. "What are you doing back?" I asked. "I thought you'd be gone for good tonight."

"I changed my mind about leaving you alone. I wanted to make sure you were really okay."

"Oh. Thank you."

An awkward silence fell between us. I hated that it had

come to this when only hours ago, everything had felt so right between us. I had to get away.

"I'm going to take a shower," I said at last. "Are you . . . going to stay here?" I felt a little odd about a guy hanging around my room while I was showering. There wasn't really much I had to hide. I supposed the most embarrassing thing I had was my movie collection. Then again, he probably didn't care that I had all the *High School Musical* movies next to *Sailor Moon* on my top shelf. I was such a dork. At least *Gossip Girl* was up there too, so I was sort of redeemed.

He nodded. "I won't get into anything, I promise. I've known you for five hundred years, so I don't think anything you do now could shock me." He stifled a laugh, but I gave him a quizzical look. A fleeting worry about what he might know about me crossed my mind.

I hurried in the shower as fast as I could. When I finished, I stepped out and toweled myself off. My reflection in the mirror was mildly more pleasant considering how my face no longer quite resembled the car wreck I'd been in that night. I looked around for my robe, but I didn't see it. Worried, I wrapped the towel around myself.

"Oh, no," I breathed. My robe was not in the bathroom. There was no way I was going to put my bloody clothes back on. I kicked at the filthy pile of laundry in the middle of the bathroom floor and cringed. "Gross, gross, gross . . ."

I'd have to go back into my room in my towel to get

clean clothes. This was not good. I did not want to walk around practically naked in front of any boy, let alone Will. I trembled as I walked back to my room. I poked the door open a few inches and whispered just loudly enough for only Will, and not my parents, to hear me.

"Will?"

"Yeah?"

"Can you turn around for a sec?"

He paused. "Okay."

I tiptoed in, hugging the towel as tightly as I could. He had turned around and faced the window.

"I need my clothes. Sorry." I shimmied into my closet and shut the door behind me. I blew out a loud sigh and let the towel drop. I put on a lacy tank and flannel pajama pants and left my closet.

"I was hoping you wouldn't have to meet Ivar for a while," Will said. He didn't bring up my embarrassing episode from minutes ago, and I was eternally grateful.

"Yeah," I said, my voice quivering. "I could feel her power, Will. It was so different from Ragnuk's. His energy felt angry to me, like pure violence. But hers . . . Ivar's power was dark. It made me *feel* fear. Not afraid, but it *felt* like *fear*. Does that make sense?"

His lips tightened. "You've said things along those lines before."

"What does it mean?"

"It means that you, the Preliator, are beginning to awaken," he said, picking absently at a rip in his shirt. "As your strength and memory return, your abilities will too. It will take some time for you to reach your full potential."

I sighed. "And here I thought Ragnuk was the scariest thing out there. Ivar beats him by a mile."

"There will be other vir—Bastian's thugs—that you'll meet," he said gravely. "They will only get worse. Bastian is likely to save his best for last."

"Great," I groaned. "So the scary chick and Ragnuk are the weak ones."

"They are not weak," he insisted. "They've earned bragging rights, believe me. Ivar could kill Ragnuk with a single strike. And she is not the weakest of Bastian's vir. She was sent as a messenger, not to kill you, which makes no sense. I feel like Bastian is stalling. Perhaps killing you isn't his ultimate goal, since that would be pointless. You would just be reborn again."

My lips tightened. That wasn't good. How could I possibly defeat any of them when Ragnuk had nearly killed me twice already in this life, and actually succeeded once in a previous one? What was I going to do when I had to face Ivar and the other vir, or even Bastian? And what was this game Bastian was playing with my life—sending an assassin to kill me and then calling him off? Was he trying to keep me occupied while he looked for this Enshi? Was all of this really leading up to the Apocalypse?

Will seemed to read my mind. He tucked my half-dried

hair behind my ear sweetly. "You can do it," he said, his soft voice filled with hope. "You're stronger than any of them."

"Then why do they keep mopping the floor with me?" I demanded.

He let out a breath. "You need to have more confidence in yourself. Believe you can do it."

"I need some proof first," I said with a small laugh. "It's a little hard to believe I can defeat Ragnuk when he keeps kicking my butt." I sat down on the edge of the bed.

"That's the point of believing in something. There's so much doubt and tribulation during your journey that you've got to hang on to something, or else you'll fall."

I rolled my eyes. "Stop being so wise. You make me look bad. What do you think Ivar meant by 'developments'?"

"Most likely something with the Enshi. We need to redouble our research efforts. Maybe Nathaniel has found something." He frowned. "I don't even know where to start looking for information."

"Then I guess we'll have to concentrate on killing Ragnuk and Bastian's vir?" I asked, unable to quell the doubt in my tone.

He nodded. "Ragnuk is hunting you. We caught a lucky break tonight when Ivar called him off, but I don't know how much we may benefit from that in the end."

"What do you mean?" Lightbulb. "Oh God, you don't think they found the Enshi, do you?"

"We can only pray they didn't," he said. "But Bastian called Ragnuk off for a reason. They wanted you dead and now they don't. But there isn't much we can do about it now."

I tried to steady my nerves, but I failed. Uselessness was *not* the feeling I wanted to have. "Well, what are we doing sitting around here? They could have the Enshi in their hands as we speak!"

"Ellie, what are you going to do?" he demanded. "Just waltz in on all of them? For one thing, we don't know if they found the Enshi tonight. It could have just been a lead. And two, we don't even know where they *are*. I have no idea where Bastian would go once he got his claws on the Enshi. We just don't have enough information to play it safe."

"Isn't that what this is all about? A gamble?"

He laid a hand on my shoulder firmly, his green eyes brightening a little. "We've gambled before, and we always lose. I'm not taking any bets where your life is concerned."

"But I'll come back—"

"It's not that easy, Ellie." He closed his eyes for a moment. "It's not like a video game where Mario dies and pops right back into action two seconds later. You *die*. And it takes you almost two decades before you're back in the game. This time, it took you four. You have to start over completely. It's been harder every time. You're in a weakened state right now, and Bastian knows this. He'll want to finish you off before your full power returns to you. If he fails, there is a greater chance that we'll stop him from getting the Enshi. This thing must be able to destroy you if he's going through all this trouble to find it."

"So once they get the Enshi, they're just going to come full force at me?" He was scaring me again.

"I don't think Bastian is that serious about killing you now. Ragnuk is good at what he does, but it seems that if Bastian really wanted you dead, he'd send more than just one assassin, and he wouldn't have called them off the way he did. I hate to be brutally honest, but if he sent someone like Ivar after you right now, there's a good chance that you would not make it out alive. Again, I think he's stalling for something, like he's keeping you busy while he searches for the Enshi. It makes me terrified of what this thing may be capable of."

I grimaced.

"But you have *me*," he said. "I've done everything I could over the last few centuries to keep you safe. I know I've failed you before, and I hate what you must go through, but how I feel about it doesn't matter. Emotion is not relevant. My reason for existing is to protect you."

What he said saddened me. Not the part about Bastian trying to assassinate me, but rather when he said that it didn't matter how he felt. I wasn't worth someone's entire existence— immortal or doomed. "That's not true," I said.

He studied my face carefully. "What isn't? I try my—"

"I care how you feel. Don't say it doesn't matter."

He smiled. "Well, you shouldn't worry about that. My purpose is to keep you safe and fight alongside you."

"But *why*?" I asked impatiently. "Why are you my Guardian? Did you choose this? Did the others before you choose this?"

"Yes," he confessed. "I agreed to become your Guardian, because I believe in your goal. I believe in *you*."

I glowered. "That is not a good answer."

He smiled crookedly. "You'll understand. You know all these things already—they just elude you for the moment."

My fists rolled into tight balls. I couldn't take it anymore. "I'm sick of being told that all the things I don't understand are right in the back of my mind and I can't reach them. I'm going *insane*, Will."

"Don't be so impatient."

"Too bad!"

He sucked in his upper lip, something I was pretty sure he did when he was nervous. "About tomorrow night."

"What about it?"

"Are you going over to Kate's house?"

"Yeah," I said with a tired voice. "I promised her. You should come."

He dipped his head just a little. "If that is what you wish."

"Yes, that's what I wish. I want you to come. I feel better when you're close to me and I can see you."

He stepped forward and sat gracefully down on the edge of my bed next to me. "Then I will let you see me more."

"Thank you," I said, feeling very strange having a boy sit on my bed. It felt so intimate and foreign to me. "I know you'll protect me."

"I will," he promised, his eyes locked on mine.

I believed him.

"There's something I have to tell you," he whispered. "About what I am. You know this already, but you don't remember, and I didn't want to tell you. I wanted you to remember on your own, because it's easier for you that way, but it's taking so long and I hate keeping things from you. It feels wrong to keep pretending that it doesn't exist, but I'm afraid you may hate me after I tell you."

"I could never hate you," I said earnestly. "What is it? Just tell me." I turned and sat cross-legged across from him.

He took a long, deep breath. "I am immortal because I am not human, as I've told you. I live as long as the reapers because I *am* one, Ellie."

I couldn't speak for the longest time. "You're one of them?" My lips went numb as I asked a question that seemed so unreal. Shock fell on me like heavy snow, and I froze. The blood drained from my head as Ivar's ghastly face flashed across my mind. Will couldn't be anything like her. It wasn't possible. "I don't understand."

His expression collapsed. "No, I am not one of *them*. Please don't think of me as evil, because I'm not like that."

I said nothing for several moments to let it sink in.

"You're a reaper." Though I said it aloud, the statement still didn't seem real to me.

"Please don't lose your trust in me because I didn't tell you before. You knew this the day you met me and you know this now. I'm an angelic reaper, but I am also your Guardian. Your Guardians have always been angelic reapers."

"Then you're the good kind," I said, desperate to anchor myself before I freaked out. "Is Nathaniel like you? Is that how he's immortal too?"

"Yes."

I nodded once, slowly, taking it all in. "So that's how you're able to see the reapers. Is that why you're so strong?"

"Yes," he said. "This is why I have survived this long. You're mortal, Ellie. My body can take more damage than yours can. We're nearly indestructible and your body is human, frailer, but you have the power of angelfire, and we don't."

I thought about that for a moment. What he said made sense. My human body was a weakness. But what was his weakness? What could kill him? "Can angelfire kill you?"

"No. Demonfire can kill me or leave scars, but the Enochian protection spell that you tattooed on my arm protects me from that and binds me to you."

"Were you ever wounded by demonfire before you got the tattoos?"

"No, but I know others who have been," he said, "and

a well-placed hit to my heart or decapitation can kill me just as easily. I'm not that different from you. Please don't say you hate me. I wanted you to remember it on your own. I don't want you to be afraid of me. You have no reason to fear me."

"I don't hate you and I'm not afraid of you," I said gently, but for a moment, I wasn't so sure about the fear part. "If you're a reaper, then why would you kill your own kind?"

"The demonic reapers kill humans to build Lucifer's army in Hell. They are preparing for apocalyptic war, and we have to do everything we can to prevent that."

"But if you serve the angels, why can't the demonic reapers do the same? Why can't they be good like you?"

He took in a breath. "I was born angelic and the demonic are born the way they are. The demonic don't understand the value of human life and as a result don't respect it. No reapers—demonic or angelic—have ever been mortal, so we've never had to feel ourselves aging, growing weaker, being forced to accept death as something that's inevitable instead of just possible. We only get stronger with time. Because of this, many of us are forever childish and impulsive. With creatures as powerful as all reapers are, that translates into violence and often cruelty. I do know a few of the angelic who are dangerous because of that, but we are taught to cherish human life from birth, because it's fragile and so important. The demonic don't care. From birth they are rewarded for violence. To them the only value in human life is food and a soul to reap."

"Does this all just come down to human souls?"

"Not exactly," he said. "The demonic are reaping souls for Lucifer's army. If that army gets big enough, the Second War against Heaven will occur. The 'End of Days' Ragnuk mentioned, which I told you about before. That's it. The Apocalypse. Lucifer's army is already countless times more vast than it was originally. If the legions of Hell and Heaven were to clash again, the Earth and the human race wouldn't survive."

Silence fell between us as I weighed his words. "This is bigger than just me and you, isn't it?"

He nodded. "But we're right here on the front lines. You're our best hope to prevent this from happening. That's why you're here. To protect the human world and Heaven. We, the angelic reapers, are here to serve you and defend you against the demonic."

I studied the fervor in his gaze. "So you're born, and not *made* what you are?"

He nodded. "Correct. We grow up like normal humans, but as we get older, we age more and more slowly, until we just stop aging altogether. We reach maturity in our late teens or early twenties and time sort of stops for us."

I eyed him nervously. "Do you . . . eat people too?"

He gave a soft laugh and shook his head. "No. The angelic don't eat humans. We eat normal food. I like cheeseburgers."

"Not peopleburgers?" For a moment I wondered about

the truth behind Manwiches.

"Of course not."

I breathed a sigh of relief. "So you grew up like a normal boy?" I asked, trying to understand. "Where are you from?"

"I was born in Scotland. My mother was English, but that's where she was staying at the time. The year was 1392. There's not really much to tell about how I grew up."

I tried to imagine Will speaking with an accent as hot as James McAvoy's, and it was almost enough to distract me from the seriousness of our conversation. "How can you say that? People who've done nothing at all in ten years can talk for hours about themselves. I can't get more than a sentence out of you."

"Well, you and I met in London at the beginning of the sixteenth century. I was at court just after the young Henry VIII took the throne, and I was hunting demonic reapers who'd been impersonating nobles."

I couldn't stand how grim he seemed, and all I wanted him to do was smile. "Okay, now I want you to say all of that again, only in your old accent."

He laughed and I felt so much better. "What? No, I can't. It's been a long time. It's not natural for me anymore."

"I'm sure if you *tried* . . ."

"I've learned so many languages over the last few centuries that they all sort of blend together after a while."

"But tell me something about your life from back then. I want to know more about you."

He let out a tired breath. "What's there to tell? The food was horrible and our clothes were too thick and hot in the summer. Humans died a lot. People got sick. Every few decades a plague claimed tens of thousands of lives. It wasn't really a fun time."

I hadn't thought about that. "Yuck."

"Yeah. You learn about it in school, but they don't exactly have color photos from those days in your textbooks." His look was very serious. "Be thankful."

I made a face. "Okay, stop telling me depressing stuff from back then."

"You lived then too. And long before. It's not like you missed out."

"I'll tell you what I *am* thankful for. My amnesia has conveniently erased any memories of the Black Plague. God truly works in mysterious ways."

His laugh was soft again and his gaze fell. That quiet pensiveness returned to his eyes. "That He does."

"But I don't want you to tell me about general things from the fourteenth century that I can find in any history book." I looked down at the chain of the crucifix tucked into his shirt. "Tell me about your mom."

He hesitated before answering, and the patch of silence made me feel guilty for probing him.

"What do you want to know?" He spoke slowly, his words forced.

I was very sure he wasn't keen on divulging the secrets of his childhood, but maybe it would help him to talk about his mother. "What was she like?"

"An angelic vir like myself. Female reapers can have a child only once or twice every century, so births are rare occurrences. Whether a vir is angelic or demonic is determined by the mother's heritage."

"Is your mother still alive?"

"I don't think so. I haven't seen her since I was young."

"I'm sorry," I said.

"It's all right. I've had a long time to accept it. I barely remember her face. It happened when I was so young."

If his mother's death didn't bother him much, then he wouldn't still wear the cross she'd given him, and I'd never seen him without it. "What was her name?"

"Madeleine."

I repeated her name in my head. I tried to put a face to her name, and I imagined she had Will's rich dark chocolate hair and emerald eyes. She must have been as beautiful as he was. "Why do you think she's dead?"

"I left home when I got foolish and decided to hunt the demonic. I went home a decade or so after I'd left, and she was gone. Nathaniel took me in. He's always been like a big brother to me. Anyway, there hasn't been a trace of her since.

It's likely she was killed by another reaper."

That struck me deeply. I imagined coming home one day to find my mom gone forever, and I couldn't take it. My eyes grew hot and tight. "I'm so sorry."

"It's fine, really. I've had a long time to get over it. A lot of people I've loved have died over the centuries. That's just the world we live in. It's dark and gritty and dangerous."

"Do you know your father?"

He shook his head. "No. I don't know anything at all about him. My mother never talked about him. I think she loved him, but she wasn't proud of it, or something like that. I don't think their relationship lasted very long."

I leaned back on my hands and stared at nothing. Emotions stirred deep within me—mostly uncertainty and a little bit of fear—as I tried to focus my thoughts. Will was a good reaper who fought alongside me against the bad reapers. If the only thing that made him good was his heritage, then what was enough to make him go bad? What really was the difference between Will and the reapers I hunted? Was there a chance for the demonic reapers to redeem themselves? Was there a chance they could live alongside humans peacefully? The car-size ursids and lupines probably wouldn't be easily accepted into society—I doubted anyone would want to adopt one from the pound—but was it possible for them to coexist without killing people and dragging their souls to Hell?

He reached forward to cup my cheek, the touch surprising me. "Please understand that no matter what I am or what has happened in the past, I am yours. I am devoted to you above all else, including my own life."

I exhaled after holding my breath for what felt like forever. "That's pretty heavy, Will."

His expression was impassioned, and the backs of his fingers brushed the side of my neck. "It is a burden I am glad to carry."

He held his hand there for another moment before he pulled back and looked away. I felt an urge to reach for him but suppressed it. His face was so vulnerable then, and I realized how much I cared about him. I could only remember meeting him recently, but I also knew he'd been my friend for centuries. That was something I couldn't remember, but I felt it in my bones. My eyes might have been unused to his face, but my soul knew him better than it knew anything else in the world.

When our gazes met again, I noticed the slightest flicker of brightness in that terrifying green before the color dulled again. The flash was so quick, I had to blink, but it did not return.

"I'll leave now," he said, and stood up, pulling away from me.

I wanted to jump forward and tug him back to me, but I didn't. "See you tomorrow?"

"Of course," he agreed, smiling. "I'll let you enjoy your

day with Kate until it's time for the party. You'll see me then."

"Okay," I said. "Good night. Thank you for saving my life tonight."

"You saved mine, too. You were brilliant."

"Thanks." My cheeks grew hot.

"You're coming back to me." He smiled widely—that excruciatingly beautiful smile—and then he was gone.

19

AS THE WEEKS WORE ON INTO OCTOBER, WE HEARD very little from the dark side. Bastian's thugs were lying low, but all that did was make me worry about what they might be up to. My car was beyond repair, but I was really happy to get a replacement almost identical to the one I had lost. I decided to name him Marshmallow II in honor of Ragnuk's victim.

The colder the weather got, the more I found myself lying and keeping things from the people I loved. I snuck in and out of my house through the back door easily, but it was hard seeing my mom's face every night and leading her to believe that I was only going to bed. I felt like I was missing out on a great deal with my friends, since I was bailing on our weekend plans more often than ever. I was worried I'd lose them for good. I wished I could just be honest with everyone and go about my life as I normally had, but it wasn't like the world was going to wait for me to learn how to be a superhero. I wasn't sure how much longer I could stand it all, especially since I lied to the faces of my parents and friends every day.

Two weeks before Halloween, Kate, Rachel, and I were in a costume shop trying on various outfits. The boys, of course, planned to wear hideous or vulgar costumes. Will, I suspected, was going as himself. He could be scary enough. With a bloody sword and a little bit of glow to his already electric green eyes, he'd have even the toughest UFC fighter shaking in his spandex.

The party we were all attending was Josie Newport's annual Halloween bash. It was true that we weren't good friends or anything, but since we had all been in seventh grade together, it was understood that my group always went to her Halloween party—and I was *so* pumped.

"Try this on," Kate ordered as she shoved a nurse costume in my face.

I scowled at it. "That might exceed my skank limit."

"You'll look hot in it with your gorgeous hair," she said. "Now try it on."

Grudgingly, I took it from her and stood in line at the dressing room. Rachel was still inside trying on a costume. Kate had chosen a very revealing devil outfit that was mostly a red minidress and hooker boots.

"You're so bossy," I told Kate.

She grinned and adjusted the glittery devil-horns headband

in her hair. "You like it. Anytime you want, I'll bust out my whip and furry handcuffs. Only for you, boo."

I rolled my eyes. "Oh baby, oh baby."

Finally Rachel emerged. The pink and blue in her costume looked really cute with her brown hair, even if the hat was too big on her and sat a bit low. She smiled sweetly and gave a little turn to show off the outfit. The skirt was a tad long and she had had to pull the white petticoat underneath lower over her hips so it could be seen.

"What do you think?" she asked shyly.

"You're so pretty," I said.

Kate reached forward, picked Rachel's hair up off her shoulders and twisted it into an updo, then tugged the fluffy sleeves down so that more skin showed. Kate stepped back to admire her handiwork. "Huge improvement. Get this costume and wear your hair up. Evan will love it."

"Think so?" Rachel looked down and smoothed out her skirt.

"Definitely," I offered. "He won't be able to keep his hands off you."

Kate shoved me toward the dressing room. "Now it's your turn. If you're a sexy nurse, then *Will* won't be able to keep his hands off *you*."

"That is not what I'm going for!" I closed the curtain behind me.

"Liar!" Kate called from outside the dressing room.

I squeezed into the tight dress and wished I were wearing

something fluffier like Rachel's costume so I wouldn't feel so exposed. My boobs were kind of spilling out, but the sheath shape of the dress made my hips and legs look as if I *had* hips and legs. I pulled back the curtain when I was ready, and Kate loosed a long whistle.

"You hot bitch," she said. "Trade costumes with me."

If my sexy nurse outfit made my boobs look a whole cup size bigger, Kate's devil outfit made her look like a porn star. No way could I pull that off. "No, thanks. You keep yours."

"You know I'm right, though," she said slyly. "He won't be able to keep his hands or his eyes off you all night."

I tried to disguise the smile growing, but I failed. Maybe that was exactly what I wanted. I stepped in front of the mirror and looked at myself from different angles. I did look good, after all. If I was lucky, someone else might notice too.

That Saturday Will and I were sparring in our abandoned warehouse, as we usually did on weekend afternoons. When a beam fell and crushed my hand, we were forced to the sidelines while my bones healed. I watched my skin grow back and the bones reshape, but that wasn't the strangest part. My broken hand never really hurt that badly. Sure, it killed for the first few seconds, but the pain dulled quickly, and then there I was, staring at my bones shuddering back into place. It didn't even nauseate me that much anymore. I wasn't sure which was weirder—my broken bones healing in minutes or my not being grossed out by it. A toss-up, really.

"You ought to be used to that by now," Will said.

I looked up to see him watching me, his own scrapes disappearing from his skin. "I just never noticed my body healing like this before," I said. "It's weird that it doesn't hurt. In the fourth grade, Kate fell off the monkey bars and broke her arm. She cried so much. I break my bones and it just feels a little tingly after a moment or two. And now I realize . . . I never really got hurt as a little girl."

"I'm sure you got hurt," he noted. "You just didn't pay a lot of attention to your wounds because they healed almost instantly."

I huffed, a nostalgic little smile forming on my face. "My mom always thought I was just lucky."

"No normal kid is that lucky." He crouched and reached out to touch my hand. He lifted it up and examined it. "Good as new."

"Does it hurt *you*?" I asked, watching him.

"Does what hurt?"

"When something breaks," I said, and took my hand back.

"Every time." His green eyes held mine for a moment longer, irresistibly, before he stood up.

"Do you think the Enshi could be one of the Fallen?" I asked, getting up also.

"I hope not."

"Have you ever seen one of them?"

"No," he said. "And I never, ever want to. They're the incarnation of everything terrible in this world," he explained.

"The manifestation of hate, sickness, greed . . . everything evil you can imagine."

"If they're so strong, then why don't they come and do their own dirty work? Why do they need demonic reapers?"

"The angels and the Fallen can't fully come into the mortal plane in their corporeal forms. They can wander and influence events, but they can't physically interfere. It takes an incredible amount of energy and strength for their kind to survive long here. A powerful magical relic can help, but they're nearly impossible to find."

"What is a relic?" I asked.

"Relics are powerful objects with a connection to either the divine or the damned," he explained. "They are usually cursed or blessed with angelic magic, an Enochian spell. They have a variety of uses during spells, and some have the ability to give corporeal form to an angel or a Fallen in the mortal realm. The most they can do on their own is show up briefly, perhaps to deliver a message, before slipping back into their own realms. If you come up against a Fallen in his corporeal form, then God help us all. I don't know what would happen."

"Then I'll make a mental note to avoid them," I said with a nervous laugh. "You're coming with me to Josie's party, right?"

He sighed. Loudly. "You're not really going, are you?"

"I wouldn't miss it, even if I was ambushed by reapers and killed. I'd be reincarnated and still go. This will be the last one, since I graduate in the spring—if I survive to see myself graduate."

"Don't joke about that."

I frowned. "Well, I'm going and I want you to come with me."

"You should be concentrating on training and on finding the Enshi, not partying."

"You said yourself that I should relax from time to time. This is a perfect opportunity."

"It's a perfect opportunity to get ambushed, and even if nothing happens at the party, you blathering on about preparing for it is distracting you."

"I don't *blather*," I said, scowling. "What the hell does that even mean?"

"There are far more important things to worry about than finding the perfect Halloween costume."

"I already found it, for your information."

"Ellie, seriously. You can't get distracted like this. You need a clear head. It's my job to—"

"Blah, blah, blah, Ellie this, Ellie that." I reached forward and playfully ruffled his hair with my hand. "Yes, *sensei*, I hear you."

He shooed my hand away and stifled a laugh. "See? Distractions."

"I think *you* need a distraction more than anyone," I said. "If you were human, you would so be that guy who randomly brings an Uzi to work one day and just shoots everybody up. You take yourself *way* too seriously. Lighten up."

"That's an exaggeration."

"Admitting that you have a problem is the first step."

"I don't have a problem."

"Now you're in the negative steps. Not a good start, Will."

He sighed. "You drive me crazy sometimes."

"Ooh, I think that happened *long* before I came along."

"No, no, I'm quite sure it was you who drove me over the edge."

"You're so sweet, you're going to give me a cavity, really."

"Then afterward, I'd be doing you a favor by knocking your teeth out."

"Ha!" I laughed. "You knocking my teeth out would never happen."

"Don't be so presumptuous. You seem to have other priorities coming before your training. You can be lazy."

I wanted to knock *his* teeth out for saying that. "I can still kick your ass."

He flashed a dark, delicious smile. "Then let's make a wager. We spar again before we're done for tonight. If you land a hit first and score, then I'll go to that party with you. If I score first, then you spend Halloween night training."

"That's a little brutal, making me train on Halloween," I grumbled.

"So is making me go to that party."

I stared at him, watching for any telltale sign that he'd strike first. He really was hot. *Damn it!* I couldn't get distracted. I really wanted to go to Josie's party.

His smile flickered and I swung. He threw his arm up and knocked my fist away so his own could push through, right at my face. I leaned back, and his fist skimmed over my hair. I dipped my head and righted myself out of the path of his next strike. I grabbed his outstretched arm and shot my knee up at his gut, but his free hand shoved my knee back down. With both his hands occupied, I cracked the front of my skull into his forehead and he staggered back with a grunt.

"That counts!" I cried victoriously.

"Best two out of three," he grumbled, and rubbed his head.

I deflated. "Are you serious?"

"We've got to be fair about this, don't we?"

"I smell desperation."

"Think you can't win a second time?"

"Desperation!" I repeated with a poke to his chest.

He grinned. "Since I picked the first round, you can decide the terms of this round."

I stared him down. "All right. If we find the Enshi before the Halloween party, then you have to come with me. And you *have* to wear a costume."

"Are you sure you want me to take that bet?"

I flicked a brow at him. "Don't doubt me, man."

"Whatever you say."

I gave a swift nod. "That's right. Do we have a deal?"

"I guess so. Deal."

My phone rang. I scrambled for my purse, which I had thrown against the warehouse wall earlier that afternoon. I was surprised to see that the call was from Nathaniel. "Hey," I said.

"Ellie," he answered. "I have very good news. Come over to the library as soon as you can."

I looked up at Will, who was watching me carefully. I knew he could hear our conversation without effort. "How about right now? We're just sparring."

"Perfect. See you soon."

I hung up. "This sounds promising."

I drove us to the library. It was nearly five thirty, and the library would be closing soon. When we got there, it was very empty and the receptionist kindly reminded us that they'd be closing at six. Nathaniel appeared through the doors to the basement and waved us through.

"I have a possible location on the Enshi," he said excitedly as he led us downstairs.

I brightened and laid a hand on Will's shoulder. "How convenient! Best two out of three. Guess where you're going."

He groaned.

"You're not going to break a promise to me, are you?"

I asked, simpering up at him.

Nathaniel glanced from me to Will and back. "Did I miss something?"

"Not at all," Will said. "How did you get this information?"

"A friend of mine in antiques, whom I've worked with on several occasions, informed me that a client of his, a very wealthy local collector, bragged to him about acquiring something with the sign of Azrael on it." Nathaniel led us into his office.

"Couldn't that be anything?" I asked, skeptical that this mystery object could help us.

Nathaniel shook his head. "This guy apparently sounded beyond thrilled and didn't want to give up much information about the acquisition. He said it's ancient—and if it's got Azrael's seal on it, then I think it is definitely worth checking out."

"Did you get an address?" Will asked.

"I did," Nathaniel said, throwing in a sly smile. "Of course, it would have been illegal for my friend to tell me the address, so I just picked it out of his head."

"You did what?" I asked, confused.

"That's his ability," Will explained. "As an angelic reaper."

"She doesn't remember?" Nathaniel asked.

"You have to tell her."

"Oh," Nathaniel said. "Well, I can hear the thoughts of others. I don't like to fight if I can avoid it, but I can really mess with your head if I want to. It's more of a defensive technique than anything. I could even make you see anything I want to, from Paradise to Hades, or fall asleep with a single word."

"That sounds very useful," I said. "And scary."

"Yes," he agreed. "But it doesn't work so well on powerful reapers. Anyway, I also have a plan for you to get a peek at this object. I hope you don't mind getting your hands dirty."

My eyes went wide. "I have to kill this guy?"

"No!" Nathaniel said quickly. "No, no, of course not, as long as he's human. Just a little sneaking in through a window, nothing huge."

"We're breaking into a house?"

"You make it sound so terrible."

"Well, that's because it *is*. It's also illegal." I couldn't believe what he was proposing.

"Just pray it won't get any more complicated than that."

"How could it?"

20

"I CAN'T BELIEVE I'M DOING THIS," I GRUMBLED A few hours later, as Will drove us cross-country through the darkness. We had rented a U-Haul, and I was still trying to understand why Will and Nathaniel thought we'd need something this big. I thought we could just throw whatever it was we found into the trunk of my car.

"It's a very effective plan," Will offered.

"What do we do if it's the Enshi?" I asked.

"Take it."

"So now we're *robbing* this guy?"

"It's not his anyway."

"He *bought* it."

"We were told he *acquired* it. That doesn't necessarily mean he bought it. He might have killed somebody to get it, and he probably did. You don't know."

I glowered at him. "Is that how you plan for us to *acquire* this thing?"

"I plan to avoid going to that extreme."

I shot him an angry look. "I'm not killing anybody. Reapers, yeah, sure, but only because they'll kill me if I don't kill them first."

"Well, what if this guy pulls a gun on you? Are you going to let him shoot you?"

"I'll . . . run away."

"Sure you will."

He was infuriating sometimes. "How'd you even rent this van? I thought you didn't have a job."

"I don't," he explained, smugly imitating my voice in a high-pitched whine that, in fact, sounded nothing like me. "Nathaniel funds just about anything we need. I need to eat and my clothes get torn a lot. I have to replace them. His job at the library is just a hobby."

I huffed, half expecting him to tell me he was a professional thief. When we got close, we pulled out the directions Nathaniel had printed out for us back at the library. We found the gigantic house off a main road that was nearly deserted in the early-morning hours. Will instructed me to pull the truck over a hundred feet or so down the road, and we hopped out.

"If this thing we're looking for is big enough that we need this huge truck, why the heck are we parking so far away?" I asked. "Doesn't that sort of defeat the purpose? We'll just have to carry that big-ass thing all the way over here from the house."

"I can get the artifact out of the house by carrying it, but it won't be quick. The truck is so we can make a fast getaway. If there's one thing I've learned in the last few centuries, it's that it's better to be safe than sorry."

I crossed my arms and laughed. "Why do you always make so much sense?"

He shrugged. "I've had plenty of chances to make no sense at all. It's about time I got things right. Are you ready?"

"Yeah." Or not.

"Aren't you excited? We're about to undertake a heist. That's cool, isn't it?"

"In the *movies*, Will. In real life, it's not such a great idea. I don't want to get shot."

"You won't get shot, I promise," he said. "We need to secure the perimeter first. We'll move through the Grim so we can see any reapers hiding there."

We circled the house carefully, looking for any possible windows to enter through while watching for inhabitants. The mansion spanned the width of at least two lots like the one my house sat on. When we reached the backyard, I was absolutely amazed. Fine flowerbeds and topiaries outlined the lawn, and tall, majestic statues stood in strategically designed areas. The stone figures shone silver beneath the moonlight. There were replicas—or at least I thought they were replicas—of ancient Roman sculptures, medieval stone figures of knights with jousting lances, iridescent orbs, and dazzling fountains. I blinked several times, certain I was imagining things.

Will passed them without a glance and settled on the doors to the walkout basement. He pulled out a kit containing various small tools from inside his coat.

I almost laughed. "Did you pluck that off your utility belt, Batman?"

He put a finger to his lips, presented a thin device that looked like it came from a James Bond movie, and inserted it into the keyhole. A minute later, the door clicked and he opened it slightly. Then he froze, still as a statue. He didn't even blink. He was listening.

He slipped inside, and I followed him into the dark basement, only it resembled no basement I had ever seen. The lower level of this mansion was vast. It was like an entire house down there. There was a fine kitchen, a living room, a dining room, and several hallways leading off to other rooms. We heard voices upstairs and the clinking of glasses.

Once my eyes adjusted to the dim light, I saw that artwork like those outside were also to be found indoors. Priceless-looking paintings decorated the walls, and statues sat atop marble stands around the wide room. And there, just beyond a plush wraparound couch, was a large, dark box placed on a low slab blanketed in red velvet.

Will made a beeline for it. When I reached it, I was surprised at how big the box was. It was about seven feet long and three feet wide and high, excluding the few inches the slab raised it off the floor. Even in the failing light I could see how elaborate the box was. It looked to be made of sandstone, with gold accents and jewels embedded in the surface. I recognized the seal of Azrael on the lid, surrounded by strange markings, scratches, and more inset jewels. Will carefully examined the markings.

"What is this?" I asked, my voice as quiet as I could possibly manage.

"A sarcophagus."

My eyes widened. Could it have been this easy? Was the Enshi contained within?

"Who are you?" shouted an unfamiliar voice. A light flicked on, blinding me for a second.

I cried out and spun around. Will jumped in front of me fearlessly. We were caught. I was going to jail. My mom was going to slaughter me. I was—

"Why are you in my house?" A man in a very nice casual suit stood at the bottom of the stairs. He was clearly the owner of the mansion, and it surprised me that his voice was so aggressive. I would have expected him to have gone running for a phone to call the police.

"We are taking this now," Will said in a deathly cold voice.

It was then that I felt that familiar, frightening energy prickling the hairs on my arm. And I remembered that we were still within the world of the Grim. Could the man be a psychic?

"I don't think so," the man said. "I paid a lot of money for that. There's no way you're taking it."

Will called his sword into his hand and leveled its point at the man.

"Will, no!" I cried.

"Stand aside, vir," he said. "You'll never defeat me. You've got nothing on my power."

I blinked and looked from Will to the man. Was the owner a reaper? He looked so . . . *human*. But then again, so did Will.

"You certainly aren't going to leave my house with that," the reaper warned. "If you don't depart immediately, I will kill you and your little girlfriend. Of course, I may keep her for myself and eat her later."

Will narrowed his gaze. "Try it."

The reaper bared his teeth and hissed like a leopard. He charged; I willed my swords to appear in my hands and light up with angelfire. Will swung his own blade fast as lightning. The reaper grabbed his wrist, but Will drove his knee deep into the reaper's gut. The vir bent over, choking, and I was behind him in a heartbeat, taking both swords, crossing my arms across my chest for maximum force and slashing the blades through the reaper's neck, decapitating him. He burst into flames and was gone. The angelfire vanished from my blades, and the room was dark again.

"That was way too easy," I said, wiping at a warm spot of blood on my forehead, feeling disgusted.

I felt another power nearby, only far, far stronger than the reaper I had just fought. I looked up to see a man—no, a new vir—standing in the door we had entered through moments before. His face was in shadows as he stood silhouetted in the moonlight.

"Yes, that *was* too easy," the reaper said. "You didn't think you'd be that fortunate, did you?"

Will locked his gaze on the reaper with a hate I'd never seen before on his face. His power was growing steadily; I could see it spiraling with his anger like a damned double helix of black Hellfire, his green eyes brightening and intensifying. "Geir," he growled.

I held my swords tightly, the dead reaper's blood trickling down the blades, and I faced Geir. He stepped forward into the room, and I could now see his face under a mop of wild, reddish brown hair. His smile was wide and insane, like some cracked-out Mad Hatter's, flashing a mouthful of sharply pointed shark's teeth, and his eyes were yellow beneath heavy lids and a thick brow.

"What a fool," he said. "Jonathon was correct. He did have something very special in that box, but he had no idea *how* special. Bastian will reward me greatly. Thank you for disposing of my friend here so I won't have to waste my time on him."

He watched me with a hunger in his eyes. "And so I find

myself face-to-face with the Preliator," he said, my title rolling over his tongue like sticky-sweet syrup. "I thought you'd be taller."

I narrowed my eyes. "I think that about myself every day."

"Still, you are prettier than I was told, but Ivar doesn't like other girls."

"Don't even think about it, Geir," Will warned. "Your head will be rolling across this carpet before you lay a claw on her."

Geir's smile curved into a sinister half snarl. "Is that a challenge?"

Will lifted his sword and leveled it at the demonic vir. "Take it as you wish."

With a laugh, Geir held out both his arms. His hands stretched as bone popped and skin bubbled, his biceps and forearms bulging sickeningly until they were twice their original size. His hands lengthened and his nails grew into long talons, leaving the skin on his arms ripped red and raw as if there hadn't been enough room inside for the monster arms to grow and they had just burst through the surface. Wings burst from his shoulder blades, scattering dirty brown feathers, blocking the light from outside. His wings flapped deafeningly. Horror engulfed me, and I could do nothing but stare at him as the vir reaper unfolded his power before me.

He held out a clawed hand and beckoned to me. My swords erupted with angelfire as I lunged forward in a rage, but I was suddenly hit by a brick wall of energy as Geir spread his wings wide and detonated his power. The glass doors and windows behind him shattered with a thunderous roar, and the infinite shards glittered in the moonlight like rain. A tsunami of black power rushed into me, knocking me off my feet, and I hit the floor on my back. As glass showered down on me, I looked up to see Will leaping over me, his sword high. He swung and slashed, but Geir stepped fluidly out of the path of each stroke. I jumped up. Geir grabbed Will's arm, halting the sword in midair, clamped his other hand around Will's throat, and swung. Will smashed through the exterior wall and disappeared. Drywall, wood, and brick exploded.

"Will!" I screamed, and ran forward, but Geir grabbed me by the back of the neck and yanked me toward him, wrapping his arm around me, spinning my body and crushing me into his chest. His monstrous wings cast black shadows over me, and the darkness made my heart pound so loud it was all I could hear. He grabbed both my wrists with one hand and held my blades away from his skin. His Cheshire grin revealed *two* rows of teeth, and shivers crept down my spine. In the blazing light of the angelfire, he truly looked like a demon that had clawed its way through flesh and fire out of Hell. I shuddered in fear.

"Bastian will be so pleased with me," he said. "I will bring him the Preliator *and* the Enshi. He will be pleased to kill you himself."

I thrashed against him, but I couldn't free my arms. I

pounded my knee into his groin. His eyes bulged and he roared in pain, releasing me. It was good to know that when swords failed, simple girl tactics always worked—even on monsters.

I darted away from him and jumped through the gaping hole in the wall Will's body had created. The settling dust choked me, but I made it through and ran to Will. He was struggling to get to his feet, leaning heavily on his sword as the point dug into the cold ground. When I reached him, I dropped my swords and wrapped my arms around his chest.

"I've got you," I said, helping him lift his torso the rest of the way up. I heard a sickening snap in his chest as he groaned, and I knew something was broken. He buried his face in my shoulder and growled in pain.

A powerful hand grabbed a fistful of my hair from behind and yanked me back. I screamed and twisted, but Geir held me too tightly. He squeezed harder, making me cry out in pain.

"That hurt, you little wench!" he hissed against my cheek, blasting my face with his foul, hot breath. "I don't think Bastian would mind if I maimed you before I brought you to him. I'll just cut you up some before I finish dealing with your Guardian."

From the corner of my eye I saw Will chuck something, and it slammed into Geir's chest. I looked down and saw a two-foot-long splinter of wood protruding from him, just inches from his heart. Without releasing me, Geir scowled and pulled the stake out of his chest and chucked it back at Will, nailing him in the shoulder and knocking him back. My heart kicked when I heard something crack in his shoulder.

"Glad we could share, brother," Geir growled.

Will roared in pain and ripped the stake from his body before raising his sword to fight again. He cradled his wounded arm to his chest as the bones and tissue healed.

"Don't even think it," Geir said with a slow shake of his head in warning, pressing the tip of a claw to my throat. "Do you want the little girl to die?"

I jerked, but fighting the reaper's grip was like wrestling with an office building. He pressed his talon deeper, and I gasped when the skin broke. I watched the blood drain from Will's face, and I knew he knew Geir really would kill me.

I shut my eyes tightly and tried to focus my energy, remembering what Will had told me: *Don't stop fighting.*

With a cry, I let my power erupt, lashing into Geir. The impact surprised him and threw him off me. As he flew, I slung my fist back and pounded him in the face. He hit the ground hard, flat on his back. His wings shuddered and curled with pain.

"You little bitch!" he roared, covering his face in his hands.

I grabbed a sword off the ground and raised it to shove it into his heart, but he rolled out of the way and leaped to his feet. He evaded each stroke as I swung left and right, but something raged through me, a fury spinning with madness. As I fought the reaper, I felt my control slipping, and something dark throbbed in my skull until I could barely breathe. The world around me went black, until all I could see was Geir's horrible face as I swung my sword, unable to think coherent thoughts. I wanted to throw my weapon to the ground and grab at his throat with my bare hands.

Will appeared like a flash between us, shoving me back and swinging his arm out and smashing it into Geir's face. Geir growled and spat in rage.

"Ellie, go!" Will shouted, looking back at me. "Get out of here!"

His voice brought my senses back to me. I blinked and the rest of the world came back, but Will blocked my view of the demonic reaper. "I can beat him!" I cried. "Let me try!"

He took a firm hold of my arm. "You're losing yourself. If I let you continue to fight him, it'll get bad. Now run!"

"What about you?" I cried. "I'm not going to leave you here!"

"You are the only thing I care about," he said. "You must survive!"

Even if I had wanted to, I couldn't move. My pulse pounded inside my head like tribal drums, drowning out Will's pleas. I couldn't force myself to turn and run. Not when he was wounded. I couldn't abandon him.

Geir stood up and vanished for a moment, reappearing in the air above Will. He came down hard, fist swinging. Will jumped behind a statue of a woman and Geir's fist pounded through her abdomen, spraying chunks of marble. Will leaped around the statue and hit Geir over and over again. Geir flew straight back and halted abruptly, gagging, blood dribbling from his lips. He looked down at his chest and found himself skewered on the lance of a stone knight. Blood oozed thickly from his wound and ran down the length of the lance. He snarled up at Will, his yellow eyes flashing, his shark's teeth gnashing like a piranha's. He grabbed the stone and started to pull himself free.

"Ellie!" Will shouted, rushing back to me. "We have to go, *now*! I'll grab the sarcophagus."

I nodded, let my swords disappear, and darted back inside the house, Will right behind me. He bent down over the box and lifted it—almost *effortlessly*, to my amazement— and took off at a run.

"*No!*" Geir shrieked. "You can't! Damn you, *no!*"

As I ran after Will, I looked back at Geir, who was still trying to free himself. I saw him pound his fist into the stone lance and snap it in half. His dark wings beat the air violently. He shrieked like some demon bird spawned in Hell and his eyes glowed brightly with rage. In the failing light, his face appeared to change, his teeth growing longer and sharper, his eyes narrowing to slits. I stopped watching and ran faster.

We finally reached the truck, and I threw open the back doors so Will could set the sarcophagus inside. We climbed in front as fast as we could, with Will in the driver's seat, and we sped off.

21

"YOU'RE HURT," I SAID, LIFTING UP WHAT WAS LEFT of his tattered sleeve to examine the deep gouges in his arm. Though we were free of the Grim, Will's attitude sure wasn't.

He shrugged away from me, his good hand maintaining a death grip on the steering wheel while he cradled his wounded arm against his chest. "I'm fine. You worry too much about me."

"What about your shoulder?"

"I'm *fine*."

"You were *impaled*."

"Geir was worse off than I was when we got the hell out of there, and he'll be back to his old self in minutes."

"But you're not Geir."

He glanced at me. His eyes had returned to their normal soft green. "Our powers are not all that different."

"Did you see what he did with his hands?" I asked, holding up my own. "He practically transformed right before our eyes."

"That isn't exactly uncommon among vir," he said. "Shape-shifting is a trait many of us share."

"Can you change your hands into claws like that too?"

"No," he said.

"What can you do, then?"

"I'm nothing like him."

"Oh." I wondered about his strange eyes. The colors of his and Geir's eyes seemed to intensify as they got stronger and angrier. They didn't exactly change color, but the hues grew brighter, almost glowing. Maybe that was Will's ability. At least he didn't transform into a monster.

I nodded and stared ahead. "Are we going back to the library?"

"Of course not," he said, his voice void of worry. "Bastian's vir will expect us to take the sarcophagus to Nathaniel, since he is the only one I know who might be able to read the inscriptions. They'll be trying to locate him next. They'll learn he's working at the library very soon."

"Nathaniel's not there right now, is he?" I asked, my voice quaking. "What if they find him? He'll be killed!"

"He's fine," Will said. "Don't worry. He's at the warehouse."

"*Our* warehouse?"

"Yeah. Bastian can't know about that location yet. We'll

keep the Enshi there too, for now."

"What if Geir follows us?" I had a terrible vision of him blasting through the wall and killing us all.

"He'll try," he said without fear. "But we're too far ahead. The trail will be cold by the time he gets free. The vir may be stronger than other reapers, but our tracking abilities aren't as good. We don't have the nose that a lupine has, for instance."

His words were a small comfort, but I couldn't help thinking about what had happened to me when I'd fought Geir one-on-one. I'd slipped into a state in which I didn't know anything but the fight and nothing else mattered to me. The same thing had threatened to happen during our last fight against Ragnuk. I'd been horribly angry and felt *wrong*. What had happened frightened me more than Geir did, because he was something that could be defeated. The darkness I felt overtaking me wasn't something I could fight. What if I had lost control completely and hurt someone I cared about, like Will? Dark spidery things had appeared on my face on my birthday, after months of awful nightmares, and now this. I didn't know if I was becoming something as demonic as the reapers I battled—if I was becoming one of them.

"Will," I said, my voice small, "what happened to me back there? Why did you stop me? Did you know something?"

"Your purpose is to fight," he said. "It's what you were

born for. Sometimes it gets a little intense and you don't think straight."

"Is that why you stopped me? Because I was going to lose control?"

"You could have. When you reach that level, you aren't able to fight with a clear head, and it makes a battle even more dangerous. We can fight Geir another day."

"Couldn't it be a good thing?" I offered. "I lost all my fear then. You said that makes me stronger."

"It does make you stronger, but you also lost *yourself* along with that fear. It's not safe for you to lose your head like that, no matter what advantage it gives you."

"You mean I can hurt someone I don't mean to."

"Yes."

"Have I hurt you?"

When he didn't answer, a heaviness settled on me and I didn't want to know any more. His silence said everything. I had lost control before and hurt him. That sent an unmatched ache through my heart. How could I have let something like that happen?

Will's hand lay on mine in a comforting gesture as if he sensed my unease. I looked up to meet his eyes. "Hey," he said with a small smile. "It'll be okay."

We reached the warehouse and Will pulled into the over-grown alley. Nathaniel was standing at the end, his arms crossed over his chest. He let out a low breath when we hopped out of the truck and he saw our torn, bloody clothes.

"I figured you'd run into some trouble," he said. "Who ambushed you?"

"Geir," Will said as he pulled open the back of the van. "And a weaker vir, but Ellie took care of him easily. The weaker one must have mentioned his new find to the wrong reaper. Word got back to Bastian, and he sent Geir to retrieve it."

"If only we had gotten there just five minutes sooner," I said, frowning. "We could have missed Geir completely."

"It's fine," Will said. "We both made it out alive, and we have the Enshi. That was the original plan, wasn't it?"

I looked at him sadly. I'd already told him what was bothering me, so it was meaningless to repeat myself to him. I hated how badly he got hurt every time we ran into a reaper, and I hated anyone to shed any blood for me. It made knowing that all my previous Guardians were dead all too real.

"Let's get the sarcophagus inside before anyone sees us," Nathaniel said.

He and Will lifted the box and carried it inside, setting it gently down in the middle of the main room. They had some trouble finding a spot free of the rubble our training had created.

"What do we have here?" Nathaniel asked no one in particular as he ran his fingers down the top of the box. "The seal of Azrael, as I'd thought. There's something in Enochian around the seal. But I can't read the divine language. No one can. What else do we have? Cuneiform."

"Can you read that?" I asked, looking at the strange markings. "Cuneiform is Sumerian, right?"

"They developed it, yes," he answered, picking a bit of dirt off a glyph. "But cuneiform evolved greatly over thousands of years, and this is different from the Old Assyrian script I know best."

"So you can't read it?" I asked, disappointed.

"Not accurately right now, but I will. I just need some time. I'm guessing that it's from the nineteenth century B.C., based on some of the most frequently occurring glyphs."

My jaw dropped. "That old?"

"How long do you think it will take you to translate the glyphs?" Will asked.

"Couple days," Nathaniel answered with a shrug. "I have an idea of where to start. I'll let you know."

I looked at the sarcophagus. Something ancient and evil was sleeping within. I almost didn't want to speak too loud, lest it wake up. It needed to be destroyed before that happened.

Something prickled along my skin like tiny spiderlings. I could feel the Enshi's presence beneath the stone lid, its power rolling across the floor like a thick fog, clouding my vision and my thoughts. A voice whispered to me, the echoes of some phantom whispering from deep inside my mind, drowning my senses. I lifted my hand and my fingers traced the lid.

Will grabbed my wrist, and I snapped my eyes up to his.

The concentration with which he studied my face made me wonder if he was trying to see through my skin straight to the bone.

"Are you all right?"

"Yeah," I said. "I can feel it in there."

"I know," Will said, his expression dark. "I can sense your fear." He pulled me close to him in a move that felt utterly natural. "I don't think you should touch it."

I didn't object. Whatever was inside that box wanted me. I could feel its lulling voice still creeping inside my skull, so hard to resist. There was a frightening urge inside me to lie across the top, to climb in, to get as close as possible. I shuddered and forced myself to look away. I held my winged necklace in my hand, concentrating on the warmth of the pendant as if it would protect me.

"How do we open it?" Will asked.

Nathaniel knelt to examine the lid more closely. He scratched at the seal before standing. He pushed the lid as hard as he could, but it didn't budge. He shoved again, even harder. Still, nothing.

"We should just burn it," Will said.

"We can't burn it." Nathaniel sighed. "It's made of stone. Let me figure out what the inscriptions say before we do anything. Sit tight. I'll figure this out."

I wanted to believe him, I wanted to trust him, but as I gazed upon the sarcophagus, I watched the beautiful Enochian symbols vibrate and sway while nothing else moved. Between my fingers my necklace pulsed. I didn't think the others could see what I saw or hear the humming inside my head. The gentle voice became more insistent by the second, until I could just make out the alien, childlike voice in the back of my mind.

"Pre-e-eliator . . ."

22

I FILLED MY HANDS WITH COLD, SLIMY INNARDS and dumped them into the kitchen sink. My unfortunate pumpkin had finally been gutted and now sat waiting for me to carve him some eyes. Kate was already carving her own pumpkin's fangs, and Rachel was even slower than I was, still scraping away at the gooey guts. I watched with unease as Landon scooped as much of the pumpkin mess out of the sink as he could and put it in a popcorn bowl.

"What are you planning to do with that?" I asked warily. If he threw them at me, I'd kill him.

"You'll see." He took up the serrated knife and began carving a squinty-eyed face with a large O-shaped mouth on his own pumpkin. He took a handful of guts and let them glop through the top of the pumpkin, positioning the mass until a good amount spilled out of the mouth and onto the counter.

He stepped back, beaming and grinning wide. "Look! He is *hammered* drunk."

I looked at the mess in disgust. Now that he spelled it out for me, I could see the sickened expression of the pumpkin and the "vomit" ejected onto my countertop. "Brilliant. Really, Landon."

Kate glanced over and laughed. "Yes! That is awesome!"

"Oh, hell," Rachel groaned. "That's so lame."

"It's *awesome*," Kate repeated, staring her down. "I think I might do that with mine. We need a couple beer bottles to go with them."

Landon made a loud, unintelligible sound. "You can't copy me, man. My genius should only ever be appreciated, never duplicated."

"That's not genius," Rachel remarked. "That's just sick."

I carved a happy jack-o'-lantern face into my pumpkin. Despite my nightly extracurricular activities, I didn't really like scary things. The jack-o'-lantern smiled up at me with blank triangle eyes and a blocky-toothed grin. Though he was adorable, he was severely overshadowed by the spooky vampire face on Kate's. Even Rachel's was better. Both of their pumpkins could beat the crap out of mine. In fact, I think they *wanted* to.

Oh, well. I shrugged and pulled my happy jack-o'-lantern into my arms and set him on the front porch. Dark was beginning to settle, and within twenty minutes the streets would be filled with trick-or-treaters. My mom had strewn cotton spiderwebs across the porch and stuck plastic tombstones in the front lawn. She had even replaced the porch lights with black lights; beneath them my white zip-up hoodie glowed a toxic hue.

I headed back to the kitchen. Kate had pumpkin guts on her face, and Landon's fist was filled with even more of the gunk. Rachel was flattened against the wall on the far side, her expression terrified. Landon chucked the gob at Kate, but she squealed and spun away, and the guts smacked into the wall behind her.

"Landon!" I barked, jogging over to grab a handful of paper towels to mop up the mess.

"Sorry," he said in a not-so-convincing voice. "She started it."

Kate laughed. "Don't pin it on me! You're the one slinging that nasty stuff around."

"Where's Will, Ellie?" Rachel asked, daring to venture away from the wall.

"Who cares?" Landon interjected. "My pumpkin's puking his friggin' guts out." He made a grotesque sloshing face as he plunged his hands into the slimy mess. I grimaced.

"He'll be here when we get ready to leave," I explained.

Thanks to our wager, Will was coming with us to Josie's party, but until the time came, I assumed he was sitting on my roof keeping watch.

We cleaned up the last of the carving mess and placed the pumpkins out on the porch next to mine. Landon added the finishing touch of vomit to his jack-o'-lantern outside as planned.

Josie's party didn't start until nine, so we had a few hours to kill. Kate had an after party planned at her house, and I had an overnight bag packed to stay there. Chris and Evan arrived just after six. My mom mistook them for her first official trick-or-treaters of the night. They apologized for disappointing her, and we all went up to my room to watch a horror movie before getting into our costumes. I sat on my bed with Rachel and Kate, and the boys sat on the floor with their backs against my bed. We chose the original *Poltergeist*. Slasher movies were never my thing since they just made me sick. Ghost movies I could do.

When the movie ended, we had about an hour and a half to get ready. Kate and I curled each other's hair into big, bouncy updos and put on our costumes. She had lent me a pair of red stilettos that went with my nurse outfit perfectly. I pinned my little cap to my hair in case it decided to fly away. Despite Kate's plan to pin up Rachel's hair, we decided to leave her curls down her shoulders and back. The boys actually took longer to get ready than we did, but I guessed that was because they were wearing twice as much makeup. My glittery false eyelashes were brutally heavy on my lids, but I stuck it out and finished my face with some cherry red lipstick. Landon came back into my bedroom in full zombie getup, complete with gory prosthetics and tattered, bloody clothes. He was barely recognizable except for his gloriously highlighted hair. Evan came as a ghostbuster, and the state trooper with enormous aviator sunglasses and a bushy faux mustache turned out to be Chris. I eyed him, unable to prevent a smile from bursting through. "You weren't going for creative, were you?"

His expression exploded with shock. "Are you joking? I'm Mac!"

"Mac?"

"*Super Troopers*? Honestly, Ellie, you need to watch better movies instead of those lame Disney flicks." He slid the sunglasses down his nose and looked me up and down. "And don't talk to me about uncreative. You're a sexy nurse? As much as I appreciate that, you have to realize there are going to be fifty other girls there dressed just like you. Nobody else is going to be Mac."

I eyed him carefully. "Maybe that's for a reason."

Chris waved a finger at me. "Just you wait."

Evan slapped him hard on the back. "So where are the wings?"

Chris shot him a questioning sidelong look. "What are you talking about, man?"

"Well, you know," Evan said, visibly trying to hold in a laugh. "They'll be perfect for Halloween. Foot fairies need wings, right?"

Chris swore at him and shoved his shoulder hard enough to knock Evan off balance. Most of the soccer players didn't take foot fairy jokes very well. Chris and Landon were no exceptions.

As they wrestled around and bounced against my bed, I scowled at a mess of gory makeup and prosthetics scattered across my dresser. "You're all going to clean up this crap, right?"

"Of course," Landon assured me, and smiled brightly. He tugged on one of my hair-sprayed curls and released it, letting it bounce back into place.

Right then Will walked into my room wearing no costume except for his sword, strapped into a back scabbard over his T-shirt. The shirt also exposed the Enochian tattoos covering his arm. "Hey," he said, nodding to everyone. "Your mom let me in, Ellie."

I was elated to see him. "Hey! Where's your costume?" I poked at his chest. I noticed his eyes widening and his brow flickering as he took in my costume, and a twinge of triumph crossed my heart—*not* that I was wearing this outfit only to get his attention. That was just a bonus.

Chris stepped up to him, eyeing his arm. "That has got to be the *baddest* tattoo I have ever seen. You get that done in L.A. or something?"

"Italy," Will said.

"Nice. What are you supposed to be?"

"Pirate."

Chris scoffed. "Dude, your costume sucks. Sword's pretty sweet, though. No way that's plastic. Is that like a Final Fantasy replica or something? You get that on eBay?"

"Yeah," Will said. "Something like that."

Kate swayed her way up to him and leaned on Chris's shoulder. "What's the matter? Are you too cool for us?" she demanded sarcastically.

Will shrugged. "I don't really dress up for things."

"Oh, come on," I pleaded. "You have to wear something."

He threw up his hands defensively. "I don't think so."

"You're going to be the only lame person there," I warned him.

"I've got a Jason hockey mask in my trunk," Evan offered. "If you want it."

"No, thanks," Will said. "I'm not a costume guy."

"You are such a downer," I said, and picked my cell off my dresser to glance at the time. "It's after nine. We should probably get going by ten."

As I applied one last layer of lipstick, one of the boys bumped into me and I dropped the stick onto my white outfit. I swore when I saw the waxy red streak left behind on the neckline of my costume. "Landon!" I growled, and shoved his shoulder.

In the midst of stupid laughter, I caught a "Sorry, Ell!"

I huffed and stomped out of the room and down the hall toward the bathroom. My dad caught me as he was leaving his bedroom, and he gave me the once-over. Awkwardness settled over us both as he stopped, mouth agape, but nothing came out. He shut it and looked up at the ceiling as if he were thinking of what to say.

Embarrassed by the way he looked at me, I said, "Kate looks worse." That would have worked on my mom, or at least put a smile on her face, but since my dad rarely spoke more than two words to me a week, I wasn't sure what my next move would be.

His mouth scrunched and then flattened with indecision. "I shouldn't let you go out like that, should I?"

I crossed my arms over my chest. "Probably not."

"Well, you look like a—" He cut himself off abruptly.

I didn't want him to finish the thought anyway. "I'm just going to the bathroom."

"Cover yourself up some," he suggested, spitting out his words. "Put some pants on or something."

"Yeah, Dad. Sure thing."

His body locked up and his face twisted for a brief moment. I was about to ask him what was wrong when I heard footsteps behind me.

"Ellie," said Will's voice.

I turned around to smile at him. "What's up?"

"Just seeing if you needed help," he said. Will looked at my dad and held out a hand. "Hi. I'm Will, Ellie's friend."

My dad stared at Will, the corners of his mouth turning down, but he didn't shake Will's hand. Catching the hint, Will withdrew it and stole a glance at me. I knew my dad didn't like my guy friends much, but that was just beyond rude.

"Okay, well, I'll see you later, Dad." I brushed him off, and Will followed me into the bathroom to help me scrub the lipstick out of my dress.

"He didn't like you much," I said, rubbing a wet tissue into the red stain. Most of it had come out, but a remaining dull stripe looked like it would be permanent.

"He smelled like blood."

I choked back a laugh. "No shit, Sherlock. Yeah, my dad has blood *in* him. You say the weirdest things sometimes."

"No, I mean it was on his skin. I could smell it from your room and I thought you were hurt."

"Maybe he had a paper cut," I said, and looked up at him. "You shouldn't go around sniffing people. Really."

His lips tightened and his brow furrowed. It was kind of cute when he did that, to be honest.

"The men in my life are the strangest people on the planet," I grumbled, and proceeded to blow dry my dress. "At least I can tolerate you, out of all of them."

"You don't like your dad." It wasn't a question. I imagined my contempt was obvious to him.

"He's a piece of shit. You don't even understand."

He didn't say anything, but he probably understood a lot better than I gave him credit for. His hearing was as incredible as his sense of smell. He'd probably heard many of my fights with my dad. Something weighed my stomach down when I thought of Will overhearing my crying. It was one thing for him to know that the reapers scared me still, but there was no reason for me to be afraid of my dad. He'd never hurt me physically, but on the inside he'd repeatedly ripped me into pieces.

"Look," I said. "Just don't worry about it. It's not your problem."

The rest of the time in the bathroom went by in awkward silence. My dad wasn't a subject I wanted to talk about with Will or anyone. I avoided his gaze until we were back in my room.

We organized who was driving and cleaned up our costume messes. An hour later, we assembled downstairs in the foyer and piled into Kate's and Evan's cars. Will, Landon, and I rode with Kate to Josie Newport's house. We pulled through the iron gates, and Kate flashed an invitation to the man standing there. He let us through, and we passed the carriage house. As we wound up the wooded drive, we could hear—and *feel*—the powerful bass. I'd be damned if Josie hadn't hired a DJ.

The house itself was *sprawling*: high-peaked roofs, creamy stone, marble columns, and dark accents dazzling beneath ivory lights. We parked at the end of a never-ending line of cars and climbed out. I pulled my excruciat-ingly short dress as far down as possible as we strolled up to the front door. Behind me, Chris asked if I could handle my short skirt and then mumbled about issuing me a cita-tion for "sexy exposure" or something stupid like that. I ignored him.

The front steps were lined with jack-o'-lanterns, and plastic skeletons climbed the columns. A tall man in a suit answered the door and we walked inside. The grand entrance was dimly lit with multicolored lights dancing across the white marble floor. Kate led us through the mansion to a massive banquet hall lined with tall windows that offered sweeping views overlooking a lake. As soon as we stepped through the archway, I could see that half the school had already arrived. Strobe lights flashed in all directions from high above; the steady, heavy beat of music shook the floor and the walls; people in every costume imaginable danced as if it were their last night alive.

I had to hand it to Josie. She knew how to throw one hell of a party.

Kate grabbed my hand and we pushed our way into the writhing mass of waving hands, swinging hips, and stomping feet. We danced until Landon pulled Kate away. I danced by myself and with random partners for a few minutes until Evan and Rachel joined me. After a while I took a break, squeez-ing my way back to the front of the hall to the buffet table full of candy and hors d'oeuvres. I munched on cut strawberries, still dancing to the music. I felt a warm body behind me and smelled the warm scent I recognized as Will's. A flood of boldness swept through my chest and stomach and I closed my eyes. I stepped back into him, swinging my hips, trying to coax him into dancing with me, but he didn't. Instead, his hands ran down my arms, and he dipped his face over my shoulder until his cheek brushed mine.

"Having fun?"

I spun around and grabbed his hands, swaying from side to side with the beat. He didn't give in, but that didn't stop me from trying. "Dance with me."

He held my hands still and his green eyes pierced mine. "Sorry, I'm not a dancer."

I pulled my hands away and put them around his neck. "Six hundred years old and you never learned to dance? I think it's about time you lived a little."

"I know how to dance," he assured me with a handsome laugh. "Just not to *this* kind of music."

"It's easy. Just move with it." I placed his hands on my hips and tried to get him to follow my rhythm.

He pulled away, and he wrapped a hand under my chin and lifted it. The movement was slow, sensual, in rhythm with the music, his fingers sliding across my skin, and I felt electricity pass from his touch into me. I inhaled and closed my eyes at the intensity of it. Every single inch of me was coming alive. I didn't know if it was the adrenaline from the party that made me react so strongly or if it was something else. A stab of fire hit me when I felt his lips slide along my jaw to my ear, and I took a slow, agonized breath.

"Forgive me," he whispered.

I opened my eyes and he was gone. I spun around, looking for him everywhere, but he really was gone. Frustration boiled through me and spilled over. What was my problem? What did I expect from him?

I shook my head, trying to forget about him and enjoy myself, but something stirred in my gut that I didn't like. I stuffed my face with another strawberry and scowled at nobody in particular.

Kate swayed up to me by herself, laughing and singing along to the music. She grabbed both my hands and swiveled her hips with the beat. She turned around, leading me back into the crowd, and we danced for a while longer, but I couldn't get my mind off Will. I could still feel his touch on my face, even though only a dull tingle remained.

Dressed elaborately as Marie Antoinette—complete with a frilly thigh-length blue dress, a floral fan, high stockings and garters, and a white powdered wig—Josie found us and gave us both enormous hugs. "I'm so glad you came!" she shouted over the music, in that fleeting, oblivious way of hers.

"Amazing party as always!" Kate assured her, smiling.

I nodded. "Yes! The DJ is amazing!"

"Thanks!" she said, smoothing out her skirts and fluttering her pretty fan. "He works for MTV!"

Not surprising. She danced with us for a while, the music rocking through us as if the mansion were coming down on our heads, before she twirled away.

23

I TRIED TO RID MYSELF OF ANY DOUBT AND NEG-
ativity and enjoy the night. I only paused when a boy walked
up to Kate and me; he was wearing a white mask that concealed half his face like the Phantom of the Opera. The half
of his face I could see was breathtaking. I had never seen
any boy so beautiful. His pale gold hair was combed neatly
back with only a few escaping wisps, and he wore a black
tuxedo beneath a cape. Something about the exquisite fabric
of the tuxedo told me we hadn't gotten our costumes at the
same place.

Of course he must want to dance with Kate. I began to
step away from them, but the curve of his lips made me hesitate. He lowered his head to a very excited Kate, whose face
washed blank when he asked her, "May I cut in?"

She stepped aside and the boy took my hand, immediately

drawing me close to him. His presence wrapped around me, electric and inviting, and he spun me around the hall in a waltz that fit poorly with the music playing, but somehow he kept us in rhythm. Before I was aware of it, the music and commotion had sunk into a dull roar until I couldn't hear anything at all. I looked nowhere but up into his eyes, which were the most fiery opalescent hazel I had ever seen, practically inhuman. His dancing was like water, powerful and unyielding, yet fluid and smooth through every movement, like a river following its predetermined course. I let him lead me through the crowd in a state of shock and bliss twisted together, unable to perceive anything but his face. I wanted to take off his mask to reveal the beauty beneath. We danced until the end of the song, and still he held me to his chest, his mouth curving into a delicious smile.

"Come with me," he pleaded, and took my hand.

I nodded like an idiot and let him lead me across the hall, back toward the archway we had all entered through. The hideous feeling of Will's rejection washed away as the mystery guy led me off the dance floor. I was too eager to follow him, too eager to make myself feel worth something. For an instant I wished Will had seen me leave with this boy. Maybe a spark of jealousy would prompt him to make a move.

The Phantom boy stopped me on the other side of the wall and toyed with one of my curls as he studied my face with a look of both awe and amusement.

"You are a beautiful girl," he said in a slightly surprised voice, his face so close that he didn't need to speak up for me to hear him over the music.

"I like your mask," my mouth blabbed stupidly. I wanted to slap my lips off. I like your *mask*?

He laughed, his voice like velvet. "I'm glad you like it. What's your name?"

"Ellie," I answered, swooning. I leaned heavily against the wall to hold myself up.

"I'm Cadan," he replied.

"That's an unusual name," I noted absently.

"It's a very, very old one." The backs of his fingers traced along my bare collarbone. I shivered.

"Are you a friend of Josie's?" I asked, trying to concentrate on our conversation as he touched me. He made it next to impossible to accomplish that.

"No," he said, and looked up from my collarbone, his fiery opal eyes capturing mine.

As I stared into them, I could have sworn I saw golden flames flickering in the irises. I blinked and the flames vanished. "Do you go to our school?"

"No."

"Do you know a lot of people here?"

"Only one," he responded. "Your Will."

I blinked in confusion, suddenly sober. "My—?"

In that moment Will appeared beside Cadan, his fist flying and slamming into the boy's jaw. The Phantom mask sailed off and shattered on the floor as if it were made of porcelain.

Okay, that wasn't quite the move I had wanted Will to make a few seconds before.

"*Will!*" I screamed, grabbing his shoulder and yanking him back. "What the hell is the matter with you?"

He said nothing but only stared at Cadan. Will's eyes glowed bright green, and even in the dark hall I could see his power humming furiously around him. Cadan rose to his feet, cupping his jaw—*laughing.* I would have bet everything I owned that Will's punch should have crushed every bone in Cadan's face. How was he even *alive*?

Unless he wasn't human.

"What are you doing here?" Will demanded, his voice subzero cold, frightening even me.

"I only wanted to meet her," Cadan said. "I had to get a look at the girl who's been rustling everyone's feathers so much lately. She seems to be the object of Ragnuk's obsession, not to mention Bastian's. Can you blame me for my curiosity?"

Nausea clawed through my abdomen, and my body went stiff with fear. "Reaper?"

"He's one of Bastian's vir," Will growled, not looking at me.

Cadan leered knowingly at Will. He reached a hand out to me, but before I could react, Will's sword swung through the air, and the tip pricked the beautiful demonic vir's throat.

"Don't you dare touch her," Will warned, pressing the blade a fraction of a millimeter deeper. Blood peeked at the tip. I glanced around, praying no one would notice.

"She's a lovely thing," Cadan said, still as stone, his chin up, his eyes locked on Will's. "I see why you keep her so close. You wouldn't want anyone like me sweeping her off her feet, would you?"

"Leave!" Will demanded. "Or we'll take this outside and finish it."

Cadan licked his lips as if the prospect were delicious. "I can arrange that."

In my horror, my voice dropped to a harsh whisper. "I can't fight dressed like a sexy nurse!"

"My dear," Cadan said, his voice as sensuous as wine, "I don't intend to harm you. Your Guardian, here, is another story. We have unfinished business."

"We aren't carrying our quarrel into the world of humans," Will said. "It can wait."

I couldn't be sure if Cadan's face was disappointed or not. "Another time, then?" he asked.

"Agreed," Will snarled.

Suddenly Cadan vanished. Will stabbed forward in shock and anger, his blade punching through the wall. I felt warm lips on my neck and I screeched, wheeling away. Cadan grabbed me closer to him. As Will shot toward us, Cadan whispered into my ear, "We'll meet again soon."

Then he was gone again. This time for good.

Will cried out in rage and pounded his knuckles into the wall. A pair of girls came around the archway and stared at us for a brief moment before giggling and moving on.

I grabbed his arm. "Calm down! I can't believe you just punched a hole through Josie's wall!" I looked around us, my heart pounding. "We should walk away. . . ."

I led him away and down a quieter hall before turning back to face him. Despite my mild annoyance with him, his version of defending my honor was still sexy. With his angry face on, he looked amazingly gorgeous and just as dangerous.

"Will, who was that?" I asked, my senses returning to me, finally able to feel how unnerved I truly was.

"Cadan," he growled. "He's one of Bastian's thugs. I don't understand why he was here tonight. I'm surprised he would try to attack you."

I was doubtful. "I don't think he was looking to fight. He had plenty of chances. Don't you think he would have used the opportunity?"

"Don't think he isn't dangerous because he didn't kill you on sight." His voice was uneasy, worried. "You don't understand how destructive he can be."

I leaned back against the wall with a sharp pain in my stomach. I didn't feel threatened by Cadan at all, but I had to trust Will's word. He knew these creatures better than I did. He was one of them.

Will frowned and touched my arm gently. "You should get back to your party. Kate might be wondering where you are."

"I don't think I feel like partying anymore," I said.

A soft smile formed on his face. "How will you get home? You didn't drive here."

"Oh, right," I grumbled. "I guess I don't have a choice."

His apprehension seemed to wash away, and once again he became that familiar tower of security and comfort. He took my hand. "Come on."

I followed him back out into the hall, where Kate happened to hop in front of us, the sequins on her devil outfit making her glitter like a disco ball. One hand rested on her hip and the other held a Tootsie Pop propped in the inside of her cheek. She looked us both up and down.

"Where were *you* guys?" she asked with a suggestive flick of her eyebrows. "Makin' out, huh?"

I rolled my eyes, pulling away from Will self-consciously. "No," I grumbled. "Some guy was giving me a hard time." I thought it was wise to mention Cadan in case anyone had seen me with him.

"Not that hot guy, was it?" She frowned.

I nodded. "He wasn't as cool as he seemed."

"Creepers happen," Kate said with an indifferent shrug. "Well, it's midnight and they're about to judge the costume contest!" Full of enthusiasm now, she locked an arm around mine and danced her way into the middle of the hall, dragging me along with her. Will followed silently.

The DJ had turned the music down and his microphone up so everyone could hear him. Cheers rang out as he began to announce the winners. The scariest costume went not to Landon but to another zombie, resulting in a very pissed-off Landon. Chris actually won for funniest costume. I decided I'd have to watch *Super Troopers* now. The sexiest costume category was won by a girl dressed as Eve. Her much-too-tanned body was covered by a leaf over each breast and a very skimpy leaf bikini bottom. Unsurprisingly, the overall best costume honor went to Josie.

Kate leaned close to me and said, "She paid somebody off for that award."

I nodded in agreement.

When one A.M. rolled around, the party was cooling off. I was in a better mood, finally able to shake off the memory of Cadan. As we prepared to leave, we stood by our cars and discussed the next phase of the night's celebrations.

"Is the after party still at my house?" Kate asked excitedly.

"I'm down," Landon said.

Rachel was clinging heavily to Evan's arm, resting her head on his shoulder. Her face was flushed and she was missing her witch's hat. "I'm ready to just go home, actually."

"That's fine," Evan said. "I can take you home. I'm feeling a little tired too."

"I have *vodka*," Kate said, waggling her fingers, trying to convince them to join. "Shots, shots, *shots!*"

As Rachel started to get excited, Evan guided her to his car. "She doesn't need any more."

"See you guys later!" Rachel called. Her eyes were squeezed shut and her smile was outrageously huge. "I had so much fun!" Her face bulged suddenly and she dived around the back of the car and retched. Evan rushed to her side and pulled her hair over her shoulders. He rubbed her back gently until she was through, and they climbed into his car. My face scrunched when I smelled the puke.

"Ten bucks says they bang," Kate mused as they drove off.

I gaped at her in disgust. "She just threw up!"

Kate shrugged. "She can brush her teeth."

I frowned at her. "You couldn't be more blunt if you tried."

"Oh, I could," she said. "I could be *far* more blunt, but I don't want to damage your pretty little virgin ears."

I shoved her shoulder away as she laughed, and I turned to Will. "Are you coming with us?"

He looked down at me, his eyes a cool mint green. He seemed to have calmed down since Cadan left. "If you wish."

"I would feel better if you were close," I whispered. "Cadan freaked me out."

"Then of course," he said. "I'll follow you anywhere."

I felt instant relief when I knew Will would stay with me all night. Part of me was afraid Cadan or even Ragnuk would attack tonight. I'd give anything to keep that from happening when my friends were around, but that wasn't exactly something I could control.

24

WE FINISHED THE NIGHT OFF IN KATE'S BASEMENT by watching the original *Halloween* movie, but we just made fun of it the entire time, so it never got too gory for me. It was funny how many real horrors I faced every night, yet I still couldn't handle a stupid scary movie. Landon was sprawled across the sofa chair, and I sat on the couch with Kate and Chris while Will sat silently at my feet. The warmth of his body against my legs was comforting and I felt perfectly safe. I couldn't tell if he was enjoying the movie, but he sat still as a statue against me, his eyes on the TV.

I started to nod off, so I checked my cell. It was nearly three, and I knew I was going to crash any minute. I was pleased to see that everyone else seemed to be feeling the same way. Chris was already passed out with his head propped on the back of the sofa and his mouth gaping open as he snored. He still hadn't taken off his ridiculous mustache. Kate and Landon seemed to be in their own little world of giggles and clinking glasses. As soon as the movie finished, Kate wished us good night and left the den. Landon chose one of the two bedrooms, and Chris didn't seem like he'd be leaving the couch for a while. I left Will by the TV to go change in the unclaimed bedroom. With my overnight bag plopped on the bed, I unzipped it and pulled out my pajamas. I let my hair down and shook out the big curls.

I walked to the bathroom near the little kitchen to brush my teeth. As soon as I opened the door, I froze in my tracks. Kate and Landon leaped apart from each other and Kate yanked a towel off the rack to cover her bra. Landon bumped into the sink and knocked over a few things. Both their faces were twisted in shock. I looked from Kate to Landon to Kate's shirt lying on the floor.

"Oh, man," I said in a small voice. I promptly spun on my heels and headed back toward my room, letting the bathroom door shut behind me. I didn't need to brush my teeth *that* badly.

Looked like Landon was over me.

"Ellie, wait!" Kate called out in a hushed voice.

I stopped and turned back to her as she tugged her shirt over her head and raced down the hall toward me. Her expression was mortified. "Oh God, Ellie, I am so sorry. It just happened! Do you hate me? I swear we didn't do anything. We just made out."

"That's fine," I said honestly. "It's cool. I don't care. I'm not into Landon, remember?"

She slumped. "I know, but I didn't want it to get weird. I'm kind of drunk and I'm in a really good mood and he was just there and he's cuter than Chris. I don't know what I'm thinking."

Landon left the bathroom, said nothing, and disappeared into the bedroom he'd chosen, shutting the door behind him.

"Kate, it's cool," I assured her. "He's all yours."

"You sure?" She looked worried but happy, if that was even possible. Maybe she was faking the worried face.

"Definitely," I said with a firm nod. "Night." I turned briskly, without learning if she went into that room with Landon or back to her own bedroom. I didn't *want* to know.

I closed the door and sat on the bed. Well, that was a shocker. Maybe if Landon got preoccupied with Kate, he'd get over me for good. Then again, if they started going out, I could never hang out with them. I'd be like a third wheel. I certainly didn't want to watch them make out all the time. Oh God, *please* just let this be a fling.

A soft knock came at the door. "Come in," I said.

Will entered. "I'm going to go out and keep watch."

"Okay," I said. "Do you really think someone might attack the house?"

"It's always a possibility," he replied. "Good night." He smiled and turned to leave.

"Wait—Will?"

He turned back. "Yeah."

"Stay with me?" I asked. "Please? Just until I fall asleep."

"As you wish," he said. He stood motionlessly.

I climbed into the bed. The quilts were cool at first, but they warmed up quickly. Will walked over and sat down on the floor with his back against the bed. I inched closer to him so that I could lay my head down by his face. He still smelled wonderful despite having been at the party all night. I assumed I hadn't fared as well.

He let out a long, low breath and rested his head against the edge of the bed.

"Thank you," I whispered. "For staying."

"I will do anything you ask of me," he said.

I giggled. "Better not say that. I might ask you to do some pretty wild stuff."

"It's not like you haven't in the past."

I was intrigued enough to almost forget the thought of Landon and Kate hooking up on the other side of the wall. *Almost.* I had to think of something else before I lost my mind. "Distract me."

"What?"

"I'm desperate. Distract me."

"How?"

"What's the craziest thing I've ever asked you to do?"

He thought a moment. "This may not be the craziest, but once we chased a reaper and he jumped off a bridge. You asked me to go in after him while you ran downriver."

I laughed. "No way. I asked you to jump off a bridge?"

"We were pretty desperate for that one," he said.

"Will you tell me the story?"

"Because you asked, I will. It was in the eighteen eighties, Texas. A reaper had been terrorizing a small town. He had a taste for children."

My stomach churned. "That's awful."

He nodded. "The locals thought it was just coyotes dragging the kids off in the night, or the nearby Kiowa tribe stealing them for slaves or some other nonsense, but we knew better when we picked up the lead. The first night we arrived in town, you decided to use yourself as bait. I tried to talk you out of it, but you were determined to catch him before he hurt any more children. You dressed in a little girl's dress and waited at the edge of the town, pretending to play with a doll. It was one of the darkest nights I can remember. It was the dark of the moon and the town didn't have electricity yet, so we only had a handful of stars to see our way with."

As he spoke, I found myself picturing the scene in my mind, as if I were right there. Was I remembering? I fought harder to remember as he told me the story, and flashes of images streaked across my mind. I *knew* they had to be real.

"The reaper didn't take long to show himself and attack you. He got really close, and I remember being horribly scared for you, but you acted like he wasn't even there. I'd never seen you act so cool before. By the time he realized you were the Preliator, I was running from my hiding spot, swinging my sword. I didn't land a solid blow before he took off into the darkness. We gave chase, following him through the forest at the end of a field. He was a lupine reaper, so he was fast and more agile than we were. When he got to the river beyond the trees, he ran out onto the bridge and jumped. He let the river take him. I guess he thought he could lose us in the water. You yelled for me to jump in too, and you ran alongside the river in case he climbed out. I swam as fast as I could, and when I finally caught up to him, he fought back hard. He tore me open, but he was fighting so hard, he stopped paying attention to you, and that's when you jumped into the river. We got him that night."

"Wow" was all I could say.

"It was quite a night," he said. "You were amazing."

"Sounds like *you* were amazing."

He shook his head. "You've always astounded me. Your strength has kept me with you and it's why I follow you."

I smiled. "I wish I remembered."

"You will," he insisted. "I keep telling you that, because it's true. There are many things I wish you would never remember, but they all make you who you are. I've never known anyone else who's seen such unspeakable tragedy in their lives, and still you're more human than the entire rest of the world."

"You sound so sad," I said.

"I am." He didn't elaborate.

My fingers wove through his hair, and he leaned back into my hand, turning his face so that his eyes met mine. "Don't be. I'm sorry."

"There's nothing for you to apologize for," he said. "No matter how many times I tell you how sorry I am, it'll never make up for all the times I've failed you and let you die."

"Will . . ."

He looked fiercely into my eyes. "I meant it when I told you I've never broken a promise to you. You will survive Bastian, I swear it."

"I believe you."

He sat motionless and silent for some time. I laid my head back down and watched him. He seemed deeply lost in his thoughts, and it broke my heart to see him so tormented.

"I have a question about the Grigori," I said, struggling to think of something to take his mind off whatever was bothering him. "Didn't some of them have children with humans?"

He nodded. "The Grigori weren't truly wicked like the Fallen were when they rebelled against Heaven, but somehow being bound to Earth as punishment caused them to develop mortal desires and emotions. Instead of silently watching over the human world as they were supposed to, they slept with mortal women and fathered powerful half-human, half-angel creatures called the Nephilim."

"Could that be what I am?" I asked. "I'm mortal, but I use the power of angelfire."

"No," he said gently. "The Nephilim were monsters. They were born out of fallen spirit, and nothing good came from them. They were enormous and violent, more monster than the most frightening of reapers. God flooded the Earth to destroy them, and then He made the Grigori infertile so that no more abominations would be created. A handful of the Nephilim may have survived, but I've never seen one. It's not possible that you are one of them. You'd be ten feet tall and looking for a fight left and right."

"They sound nasty."

"They were," he said. "Nasty enough for God to flood the world to kill them all off. He's only ever done that once, and you know of all the horrible things out there now. He was pretty desperate."

I couldn't imagine monsters more terrible than the reapers I'd seen. It made me wonder what the Fallen were like and about the truth behind Lucifer, Sammael, and Lilith. "Why did Lucifer rebel? Why would he risk something like a war against Heaven?"

"I don't really think I'm qualified to answer that."

"But what do you think?" I asked. "I'm sure you have a theory."

He closed his eyes as I smoothed my hand over his hair again. "Love, I think."

"Love?" I gave a small laugh. "I thought Lucifer was evil. He can't love anything."

"He did," Will said, looking at me again. "He loved God very much, but an angel isn't supposed to feel love. God does, however, and he loves humans more than anything. An angel isn't supposed to feel jealousy, either, but Lucifer did. He was jealous of humans because God loves them more. And he rebelled. And lost."

"This sounds weird, but I kind of feel bad for him."

"Love is a beautiful but terrible thing," he said. "You have to be careful with it. It can destroy you. That is why the angels aren't supposed to feel emotion. They must be infallible and without doubt."

"Sounds like a rough gig. It must suck to have to be perfect."

He smiled. "Good thing we don't have to be."

I pulled the covers up to my chin and was quiet for a little while. His face was so close to mine that I could taste his breath. I wondered what it would be like to kiss him. "Thank you for coming with me tonight."

"Of course."

"And for staying with me. Thank you again."

"Anything for you, Ellie."

I smiled, but his selfless words broke my heart. He meant

that fully, and I trusted his oath. "I always feel better when you're close to me."

He studied my face for a few moments as his expression became more tranquil. "You should try to sleep."

I nodded. "Yeah. You'll be here when I wake?"

"I won't leave the room."

My eyes closed. "Thank you."

The vir erupted into flames as her head spun off her shoulders. Ashes settled around me, clinging to my hair and the thick folds of the skirts around my legs. I relinquished my swords, and when the angelfire died, the city street turned dark again. Will called my name as he finished off the other reaper, its body turning to stone and crumbling to the ground. The pain in my abdomen was mind numbing and my throat kept filling with blood. I choked on it and pulled my hand away from my belly to see how much damage the reaper had done when she'd stabbed me. The fabric was shredded and there was too much blood for me to even see my skin. I squeezed my eyes shut as another torrent of pain shot through me. I staggered dizzily on my feet as Will called my name again.

He touched my shoulder and I ground my teeth in pain. Every inch of my body hurt, and cold rushed through me, spreading from the wound in my belly.

"You were great," he said with a gentle smile as he

caught his breath. A gash on his neck was slowly closing. I reached up to touch it, to touch him, because I knew it would be my last chance. His smile faded as if he'd read my mind. "What's wrong?"

I bit my lip to keep from grimacing as something popped inside me, trying uselessly to heal. "I'm all right."

Will's eyes flashed brightly as he cupped my face with both hands, smoothing my hair back, examining me for damage. He knew. He hadn't found the wound yet, but he knew it was there. "You're hurt. Where? Please let me help you. Where is it?"

As his heart broke in front of me, tears slid down my cheeks and I pulled away, refusing to let him see. I didn't want it to be real for him. Not again. The sudden movement caused me to cry out and double over. Will screamed my name and fell over me, throwing his sword away and grasping me close to him as my knees hit the ground. Red drenched my dress and pooled around me, soaking the ground with darkness like a pit leading to Hell.

Will held me against his chest, cradling me gently. He pulled the torn bodice of my dress apart to examine the wound. I stared into his face as he saw the extent of the damage and clenched his eyes shut, sucking in his upper lip and setting his jaw tight. He took a deep breath and looked up into my face, tucking my tangled hair behind my ear and thumbing my cheek tenderly. He opened his mouth to say something but *closed it again. He wouldn't lie to me and tell me I'd be all right. He never lied to me. He leaned over me and pressed his forehead to mine, his body shuddering with a pain different from my own.*

"Will," I breathed. It hurt to speak and I could barely look at him, but I had to do both. For him. I studied his face, the jewel-like color of his eyes, the curve in his lips, memorizing every part of him. "I'm sorry."

He pulled back and shook his head. His thumb traced my bottom lip gently. "Don't be sorry for anything. Ever."

"I'll come back to you," I promised.

He nodded, tears budding in his own eyes. "I know. And I'll be waiting. I'll wait for you forever."

I woke with a death grip on the sheets. I released them and sat up, furiously trying to remember the nightmare I had just had. I touched my belly and was relieved to find it smooth and uninjured. It felt almost as if Will were still touching me, and it tingled where I remembered that he had. In my dream he'd thought I was going to die, but I wasn't sure if I did in the end.

Was it a memory or just a nightmare? I couldn't even tell the difference anymore.

In the real world, Will stood with his back to me, looking out the window. When the blankets rustled, he turned toward me. I blushed for no reason at all when I saw his face. The Will from my dream stared back at me with his beautiful, kind smile, and it took another moment for me to distinguish reality from my memory. He felt so far away, and he'd been so close to me moments before in my dream.

"How'd you sleep?" he asked. He leaned against the wall and folded his arms over his chest.

I stretched my arms wide. "I had a dream about you."

"I hope it wasn't an embarrassing one."

"No," I said. "But it wasn't a good dream, either."

His eyes fluttered to the side for a moment and he said nothing.

"Do you think it was a memory?" I asked.

"It could have been," he said. "What happened in it?"

I explained it to him: the battle with the reapers, and me lying in the street, but I left out the more intimate parts. He kept his expression blank and he nodded a couple of times. "Was it real?" I asked.

"Yes," he said. "It was in New York, just before the Civil War broke out. I'm happy your memory is coming back to you, but I wish you had remembered something else."

"Did I die?" I whispered.

His gaze was strong on mine and he said nothing. He didn't need to. His face told me the answer he didn't say aloud.

"At least you're remembering," he said softly. "We can be thankful for that."

"I am," I said, but I wasn't so sure. As much as I hungered

to learn more about my past, I was afraid of learning other things too—mostly about death and despair, and dark corners of the globe. I prayed that those memories wouldn't come back to me, because I felt in my bones that some things were too frightening to remember.

25

NOVEMBER WAS DULL. KATE AND LANDON NEVER mentioned the bathroom incident on Halloween, and there was no way I was going to ask. If they didn't want to talk about it, then it was fine with me. At least Landon seemed to be uninterested in me, finally, so I didn't have to worry about leading him on or hurting his feelings.

One night after a tough training session, I sat at a rickety desk in one of the old offices in our warehouse, scrambling through a pile of homework while Will sat serenely in a broken chair across from the desk. Trying not to flunk out of school while hunting reapers was becoming increasingly difficult. This wasn't the first time I'd had to bring my homework to our sparring sessions. We'd spar, I'd do a vocab sheet or something, and then we'd spar again. I was about to lose my mind.

"You know, if you're going to be looking over my shoulder, you might as well help me out with this," I grumbled. "I *am* telling everyone you're my tutor. Make yourself useful and tutor me."

"I'm being useful," he retorted. "I'm listening. And besides, I have no idea what any of this even means."

I huffed. "This isn't even advanced. I'm in the dumb-kid physics class."

"You're not dumb."

"I'm dumb at physics."

He blinked. "I don't know this stuff and I'm not dumb."

"Okay, well, we're both *uneducated* in physics," I said. "Happy?"

"But you're learning."

"Yeah, that's because I'm uneducated."

"That doesn't mean you're dumb."

I felt a powerful urge to smack him. The genuine look of confusion on his face prevented me from doing so, although I was still sorely tempted. Maybe if I just flicked him between the eyes or something . . .

"I'm sorry," he said, and stood. "I'm crowding you. I'll just wait outside."

"You don't have to go."

"No, I should. I won't be far." He left the office and me in silence.

As soon as he'd gone, I wanted him to come back. I found myself staring at his empty seat and feeling his absence. I had solved—or so I hoped—a handful more homework problems when I thought I heard music. It was very soft, but loud enough to make me wonder. Where was it coming from?

I got up and followed the sound through the dilapidated hallways, but as I crept through the failing light, the world faded away. *Not again.* I leaned against the wall, pressing myself into the peeling paint, feeling it scratch my skin— anything to keep my mind from falling away into a darker time. But as the world changed around me, my face tightened, squeezed until I couldn't move; but I didn't feel fear, only determination.

Something flashed in front of me, so blindingly bright I had to look away. The last reaper had gone up in flames. My skin and clothes were splattered with blood, but at least I wore men's trousers instead of the obnoxious thick skirts I was supposed to wear as a young woman among the humans. With no other enemies to face, I descended deeper into the castle, moving within the Grim, through winding stone halls lit only by my angelfire. My shining swords made excellent substitutes for torches.

I paused, questing out with my mind, and located a power nearby. It swelled and died and swelled again. But there was only one signature flaring, not many, so there couldn't be a fight. I followed the signature up a flight of stairs and through a doorway that was taller than most of the others I'd gone through in that place.

Stepping carefully into a large room, I held my swords ready. For a moment I thought I'd been wrong. There were three vir in the room, who all turned around to look at me and all recognized me instantly. They charged at me, wings, talons, and teeth gnashing and striking. I twisted and spun, ducking through the smoky flashes of power and the dizzying smell of brimstone. I dispatched them in seconds, my arms aching from swinging my swords. I looked around the room again to be sure I'd defeated them all.

Instead of meeting another battle, I found a fourth vir reaper in chains. His arms were held out and up, his wrists shackled to the wall. His power swelled and he yanked against the chains, but even from this distance, I could tell that the chains were made of silver and they weakened him. After he made another attempt at freedom, his strength waned and he went slack against his bindings.

I strolled up to him, my chest heaving from the fight as I tried to catch my breath. The imprisoned reaper would be no threat to me—as long as he remained bound.

As I neared him, he looked down at me, and I got a good look at his face for the first time. He was, for lack of a better word, beautiful. His hair was dark, rich like polished walnut wood, and his features were handsome, sharp, and predatory. His lips were sculpted like those of the marble statues in old Rome, and his eyes were bright crystalline green—the unmistakable inhuman eyes of a reaper. But *was he demonic? Or angelic?*

He stared down at my flaming swords and then into my face, gaping at me in shock and awe. This reaper was one I'd never come across before, and the surprise on his face proved it. He'd never seen me either, but he knew exactly who I was. He lifted his head in a valiant attempt to appear as if he weren't defeated and weak.

"I know what you are," he said in English. His voice was weak and strained, broken, but I recognized the Scottish accent. "If they'd taken my eyes, I'd still know what you are. Don't kill me."

"But I don't know what you are," I said, tilting my head up at him.

His fine white shirt was torn and bloodied, and his breeches had fared no better. He was dressed like a noble, and with his handsome face and clean hair tied back with a ribbon, it would have come as no surprise to me if he were an aristocrat. There were many reapers of hideous wealth taking up positions of power all over Europe.

His expression hardened. "I'm not what you think I am."

"No?" I asked, and sized him up. "You're a reaper and you've had the Hell beaten out of you. What did you do to deserve it?"

A smile curved in his lips. "The demonic don't like me much since I kill every one of them I find. They've finally caught up to me, as you can see."

I didn't find his remark amusing. "You're only what? A

century old? You don't have that kind of strength."

"Call it a gift."

I studied him for a moment. His eyes went bright as he attempted again to break his chains. "You've been caught, so you can't be that strong."

"I was ambushed," he said through a violent cough. "And you're one to talk. You are as well known for your own deaths as you are for your conquests."

His attitude was beginning to irritate me. "Must I remind you that you are at my mercy right now?"

"You don't destroy the angelic. Killing me would be to your discredit."

"I have no reason to believe you aren't demonic," I said. "What if you're a traitor to your master? You may have rebelled against him to stake out your own territory. For that, you would be punished severely. I understand the politics of your kind."

"I'm a traitor to no one," he growled. "I'm only doing my duty as the angelic should. If you don't believe me, then put your fire to my flesh. It won't harm me."

If he was truly demonic, then he was brave. But if he told the truth . . . I held his gaze for several heartbeats until I finally took up my sword, the silver blade swallowed in angelfire. I used the tip to part the collar of his shirt wider, exposing his bare chest. I looked up into his eyes. He stared firmly back without fear as the light from the angelfire danced off his features. Whoever he was, I admired him. I drew a line of blood down his chest with the blade as the fire licked at his skin, and his jaw tightened rock hard from pain. I stepped back to examine the wound. As he'd promised, the angelfire did no damage to him at all.

"Told you," he said with a dark grin. His wound closed, leaving only a trickle of blood behind.

"I can still leave you chained up."

"If you cut me down," he said, "I can help you. We're both hunting the demonic."

"I don't need your help."

"You don't want anyone to watch your back?"

"I can watch my own back."

"Sure you can." That beautiful grin widened. "Then turn around."

As soon as he said that, I felt a power flare behind me and I turned and swung my swords, removing the head of a reaper who'd lunged at me from behind. She went up in flames, and I turned back to the angelic reaper.

"See? I'm useful."

I glared at him. Then I took up my swords again and cut through his chains. He slumped to the ground and sagged against the wall, gasping from pain. "What's your name?" I asked.

"Just call me Will."

I stared down into his green eyes as he dragged himself to his feet. "I never want to see your face again, Will."

I turned my back to him and heard the music again. I shut my eyes, focusing hard on the gentle sound until it was all I heard.

When I opened my eyes again, I'd returned to the crumbling old warehouse. I breathed a sigh of relief. A veil of warmth fell over me as I realized I'd just remembered the first time I met Will. I smiled to myself, recalling how annoyed I was with his sharp tongue. Then I remembered he had introduced himself to me in September the exact same way he had when I met him five hundred years before: *"Just call me Will."*

I listened to the music again and followed it back out into the main warehouse storeroom. I pushed the heavy door open just a little, letting the soft music flood my ears and the hall behind me, and I peeked through.

Will sat in a chair against the wall with an acoustic guitar in his hands. I studied the way his hands moved quickly, fluid and precise like ripples on water, the muscles in his arms tight and defined. The way his head bobbed and his foot tapped the floor with the beat captivated me. I recognized the song, though I couldn't quite place it. But the name of the song didn't really matter. I was entranced. It was kind of sexy watching him play. Sexy and beautiful, like every other aspect of him.

As I listened and watched, I knew he was as perfectly aware of me as I was of him, though he kept his infallible rhythm. I knew he could sense every inch of my skin from across the floor, as I could his, feeling every thread of the powerful centuries-old bond we shared. In that moment my lips grew numb and something spun deliciously warm in my chest. In that precise moment I knew I was undeniably in love with him.

I took in a breath for courage and pushed the door open all the way so I could step through. I folded my arms across my chest as I eased toward him, smiling as if nothing had changed in me. He didn't stop playing as I approached, but he glanced up at me and grinned, turning my stomach to pudding. That knowing smile was the same smile he had given me the night I'd met him five hundred years before.

"I guess I'm lucky, then," I said, remembering what he'd told me about this side of him.

He never missed a chord. "I guess you are."

I said nothing more until he finished and I clapped for him. "What was that?"

"Journey," he said. "One of my favorites. 'Wheel in the Sky.'"

"It was really good. Where did you get the guitar?"

"I keep some of my things here. Most of my belongings are at Nathaniel's house."

I imagined what other things he might have kept over the years and longed to see them, just to know a little bit more about him. "Why don't you play more?" I asked.

He shrugged and set the guitar aside. "There are other things on my mind, I guess."

"Can you sing, too?"

He laughed and shook his head. "No. Singing is not one of my talents."

"That's too bad," I said, and chewed on my lip, mustering the bravery to tell him about my flashback. "Will, as I was leaving the office, I remembered something. It was the night I met you, when I cut you down from those chains all those centuries ago. You were a smartass even then."

"I don't deny it."

"How did you get captured like that?" I asked.

His gaze lingered on my face for some time. "I was hunting demonic reapers with Nathaniel. We got separated and I was cornered. They tortured and interrogated me to find out what I knew about the other angelic reapers, but I didn't know anything. I was playing vigilante with Nathaniel. We didn't know what we were doing back then. And then you came."

His expression softened as he gazed at me, the look in his eyes distant and longing. "You were like a warrior angel I'd seen in the stained glass of a cathedral. I knew who you were the moment I saw you, because I'd heard of you. Everyone had. And you freed me."

"But I told you to leave me alone," I said. "What made you try again?"

"That very night, an angel came to me," he confessed. "I don't know his name or why he appeared to me of all people, but he told me that your fate and mine were tied together.

He said that I needed to protect you, because you were the most sacred of all things. My destiny was to become your Guardian, in a long line of Guardians: I was chosen. He gave me my sword and the power to awaken you, so you could become the Preliator in each reincarnation. He gave me purpose, some sort of resolution in my immortality, a focus. *You* gave me purpose."

I smiled down at him, and he grinned right back. I was very thankful that he had became my Guardian. Remembering that flashback of ancient Egypt made me want never to know life without him ever again. I felt the losses of my previous Guardians, but I trusted no one more with my life than Will. Without him, I didn't think I could fulfill my mission of destroying the demonic reapers.

My phone rang, shattering the silence between us. "It's Nathaniel." I held the phone up to my ear.

"Ellie," Nathaniel said before I could speak. "Where are you guys?"

"The warehouse. What's up?"

"Don't leave. I'll meet you there." He hung up. The urgency in his voice got my pulse pounding. My eyes met Will's.

26

WE WAITED, TENSE WITH ANTICIPATION, FOR Nathaniel to arrive. When he finally drove into the alley and parked behind my car, he and Lauren, the psychic I had met the first time I'd met Nathaniel, climbed out and walked right past us and into the warehouse. Nathaniel waved a hand for us to follow him into the room where we kept the sarcophagus. As soon as I entered, I felt the frightening, familiar thrum emanating from the Enshi. Nathaniel and Lauren were standing by the sarcophagus.

"Nice to see you again, Ellie," Lauren said.

"You too," I replied with a smile. "What's up, Nathaniel?"

"I've figured out the language on the sarcophagus," he said.

Will perked up. "And?"

"The script is indeed an archaic cuneiform," Nathaniel

said excitedly. "But it's older than I thought. Older than Old Assyrian, older than even the Akkadian style."

I stared at the box, my head filling with thick clouds that prevented me from thinking straight. "How old is that?"

"Approximately five thousand years."

My eyes bulged. Will shifted uncomfortably next to me. I looked at him and his eyes met mine. "Jesus," I murmured.

"Nope," Nathaniel chirped. "Jesus isn't in here."

I blinked. "I wasn't . . ."

He grinned and winked at me. I assumed it was supposed to be another of his amazing jokes, but they just weren't funny to me. I gave a soft, uneasy laugh to humor him. He beamed proudly. I glanced at Will, who only shrugged and shook his head. He understood completely.

Nathaniel turned serious again. "What I mean is that the Enshi was locked up in this sarcophagus three thousand years before the birth of Christ."

"Does it say what the Enshi is?" Will asked.

Nathaniel half nodded, half shrugged. "Yes and no. It's all bad news, which is why I've brought Lauren here to help me determine what's inside."

"What kind of bad news?" I asked.

"Well, if you look closely at the sarcophagus," Nathaniel began, stroking the box tenderly, "you'll notice that it's beautifully decorated. The ancient Mesopotamians only buried very important people this way, so the body within is at the very least of great importance. That's the first bad news.

The second is—if you'd kindly look at this symbol here—the inscriptions tell me that our friend inside is a true soul reaper."

"In English, please?" I asked dully.

Nathaniel gave me a strange look. "That was English."

"In *American*, then," I said. "Nothing of what you say makes a lick of sense to me."

Will's shoulder brushed mine. "He means a being that can do whatever it wants with the souls instead of just sending them to Hell."

"No way," I said. "Like the Grim Reaper? Death himself?"

"That's what humans like to call it," Will said. "Is it possible that the Enshi is an angel, then? Of an archangel rank, perhaps?"

Nathaniel nodded. "Yes. Best-case scenario is that this is some kind of extrapowerful reaper who can send souls to Hell or Heaven. That's probably how the Grim Reaper legend began. The worst-case scenario is that our sleeping friend here actually *eats* the souls, meaning the soul is gone for good. No Hell. No Heaven."

"That's terrible," I said.

Will's expression grew dark. "And Ellie? Does that mean—?"

Nathaniel nodded. "Yeah, it does."

Will let out a long, painful breath edged with fear.

My heart sank. I searched both their faces. "What do

you mean? What does that mean for me? Will?"

He closed his eyes. "It means the Enshi can destroy your soul. If it does that, you're done. You won't pass on and you won't ever come back. You're gone."

I tried to keep my racing heart calm. "I won't come back?"

He gave a single shallow nod. "That's got to be why Bastian wants it so badly."

My mouth dried instantly. I would be gone? That would mean I'd never be reincarnated again. I'd never go to Heaven. I'd never see Will or Nathaniel or my mom and nana again. There was no way I could allow myself to just end like that. There was too much at stake, too much left for me to do, for me to just die and be gone. I didn't want to end.

"Then we need to kill this thing before it wakes up," I said breathlessly.

"We don't know how," Will urged. "I don't want to do anything that might make it wake up."

"Can't we just nuke it?" I asked. "Not like popcorn in a microwave, I mean like a *bomb*." I spread my hands wide and made a pathetic exploding sound. "A *big* one. You two seem like resourceful guys. I'm sure you could get one."

Nathaniel shook his head. "I don't have access to nuclear weapons, unfortunately."

"Oh, idea!" I chirped. "What if we chained it up good and tight and dropped it off in the middle of the ocean? All that pressure would crush the box, wouldn't it?"

Nathaniel shrugged and blinked. "That's actually not a bad idea. And I don't believe any nonmagical force could resurrect the Enshi."

"Where would we get a boat to do this?" Will asked.

"I can try to arrange that," Nathaniel said. "Now Ellie, there's something I need you to do. You can feel what's inside, right?"

I nodded, not sure I liked where this was heading.

"Lauren can feel it too. She is a clairsentient, meaning she's able to know things by touching objects and would be able to tell if there's a connection between you and the Enshi."

I looked at her and she nodded. "What good will that do?"

"I need to know what you're feeling," she said, "not just what I sense from the sarcophagus." Lauren stepped toward me and took my hand. She pulled me toward the box and motioned for me to lay my fingers on the lid. I jerked back, afraid.

"I thought I wasn't supposed to touch it," I said, looking anxiously at Will. His expression was calm but serious.

"Touching is okay," Lauren assured me. "I need to ignite a reaction, and whatever is inside likes you . . . a lot. So please, just touch it. It won't bite, I promise."

Her smile didn't help me feel better. Tentatively, I brushed the lid with my fingers and felt the instant response. The voice in my head grew louder for a moment, and I could have sworn I heard it gasp on contact. Electricity pumped through the stone into my skin, and I wanted to pull away, but Lauren grabbed my hand and held it still.

"What are you doing?" I asked when she didn't let me go. "I—"

I shut up when I saw Lauren's face. Her mouth gaped open and her eyes had rolled into the back of her head until only bright white orbs were visible. At that moment I tried to yank away, but her grip was as strong as a reaper's. Power leaked from the sarcophagus, oozed from it, and the energy crawled up my fingers through my arm and into Lauren. Her body jerked once and she released me. She staggered back, and I jumped away.

"What was that?" I demanded, putting a hand to my chest to quiet my racing heartbeat. Will protectively pulled me close to him and took my hand to make sure I was unharmed.

Lauren backed away, resting against a bent steel column, breathing heavily. Her eyes had returned to normal, but I could tell she was petrified. "This is bad," she whispered.

Will stepped forward and let my hand go. "How bad? What did you feel?"

"The Enshi," Lauren breathed. "I could hear it screaming in there, filling my head with these horrid shrieks. The Preliator's presence is driving it mad. Just that little touch sent it into a frenzy."

"A good frenzy?" I asked, hoping that it was perhaps afraid of me.

"No," she said, shaking her head slowly. "That wasn't

fear. It wants you. It *needs* you. It's screaming your name, and its power is huge—like a black void, a bottomless pit of death and despair. It's so dark in there, so dark and hungry. Nathaniel, I've never felt anything like this. You have to destroy it. You *can't* let the Enshi wake. You *can't* let Bastian get ahold of it."

My body shook with fear. Lauren's terror was plain to all of us. I could feel the Enshi in there, but not the way Lauren did.

"Do you know what we're dealing with?" Will asked, his voice dark.

"It's old," she said, her eyes frozen on the sarcophagus. "Older than Bastian, older than the Preliator, older than the sarcophagus it's trapped in. It's so old, it just feels empty. Like a black hole."

"Is it a real soul reaper?" I asked. "Is that true? Can it destroy my soul?"

"That's possible," she said. "Don't touch it anymore. I think Ellie's presence might be enough to wake it if she were around the sarcophagus for too long. Perhaps even a touch in the wrong place might do it."

Confusion spread over me. "But I thought you said touching was harmless."

Her eyes snapped to mine, her voice sharp and cold. "Don't touch it."

I nodded. No way was I going to argue with her.

"We need to get to the Caribbean," Nathaniel announced.

"I think if we ship out from Puerto Rico, we'll be able to sail pretty far out over the Puerto Rico Trench to the Milwaukee Deep. It's the deepest part of the Atlantic Ocean—almost as deep as Mount Everest is tall—and if dropping the sarcophagus overboard there doesn't crush it to oblivion, then at least there's no way anyone could dive in to retrieve it."

"Sounds like a good plan," Will agreed.

I raised my hand. "Uh, guys, I can't leave for a week in the Caribbean during school. How would I explain that to my parents?"

Will frowned. "You can't tell them it's a school trip or something?"

I laughed. "Yeah, and not give them any other information? There is a lot that goes into field trips. I don't think I could get away with them just signing a permission slip."

"Isn't Thanksgiving break coming up?" he offered.

Lightbulb. "Right. That would be perfect."

"Can we fly?" Nathaniel asked. "Fly down on Wednesday night and be back by Friday at the very latest? Shipping the sarcophagus will be expensive, but we don't have a choice otherwise. I'll have to get Ellie a fake ID, since she's underage. I'll make one for you too, Will. I think you'll need a seat on the plane to protect Ellie instead of traveling through the Grim. Fakes won't be that much trouble."

"I like this plan more," I said. "I can tell my parents I'm going up north to Kate's lake house for Thanksgiving."

"I won't be going," Lauren said. "I can't defend myself

and I don't want to be a liability."

"That is probably for the best," Nathaniel agreed.

Will nodded firmly. "Nathaniel, can you arrange it?"

Nathaniel nodded. "Yeah. I'll look into it immediately. We should get going, Lauren."

"I'm sorry I freaked you out, Ellie," Lauren said. "I needed to feel what you were feeling. You're a fearless girl."

"I don't know so much about that," I assured her with an uneasy laugh.

"Braver than I am." She smiled.

Nathaniel and Lauren left, and I listened to the car drive away.

"Are you okay?" Will asked, laying a gentle hand on my shoulder.

I nodded. "I'll live."

In truth, I was terrified. I didn't know how this was all going to work out, or *if* it was going to work out. I was pretty sure I could lie to my parents about the trip to Puerto Rico, so long as they didn't talk to Kate's parents. Kate would cover for me in case they questioned her. The lying part— that bothered me. It felt like everything that came out of my mouth was another lie to my parents.

"Yeah, but are you *okay*?" he repeated.

I looked up at him and met his gaze. "I'm scared out of my mind. That thing freaks me the hell out. Will, I don't want to just end like that. I don't want to never come back. I was just getting used to the idea that there really is a Heaven and angels. I don't want to lose my soul!"

"That thing will be gone soon," he assured me. "We'll dump it out in the middle of the ocean and it'll all be over."

"Not exactly," I said. "Even if we destroy the Enshi, we still have Bastian and his lackeys to deal with, including Ragnuk. I don't think I'm going to make it out of this alive."

He touched my cheek sweetly. "Hey, remember what I said? I promised I'd protect you from them. I'm not about to break a promise to you."

I smiled. "I know."

Suddenly the front door blasted open, and I spun around as it crashed to the ground. Something invisible slammed into the doorway, crushing the frame and the walls on either side.

My shock made me leap into the Grim, where I could see the dark, enormous form of Ragnuk widening the entrance with his body so that he could lumber through, as chunks of brick crumbled at his feet. He stared at me with his ravenous black eyes, and his tongue sagged over his jaws and dripped gobs of saliva onto the floor. He looked half insane with hatred and hunger.

Instinctively, I grabbed my winged necklace for comfort and stepped back toward Will, but I couldn't take my eyes off of Ragnuk.

"I have you now, Preliator!" the reaper roared, spitting

the curse at me as if the word itself were something disgusting. "I followed your filthy stench all the way here. This time you aren't getting away from me and we won't be interrupted. This is the end for you, and I'm taking the Enshi with me. It ends here tonight!"

27

A TREMOR OF FEAR RUSHED THROUGH ME, BUT I
stood my ground. He launched forward abruptly, but Will
was right there in front of me. As Ragnuk leaped up,
Will ducked and slammed his shoulder into the ursid's chest
with all his might and flipped him high over our heads.
Ragnuk crashed into the wall behind us, shattering more
bricks. He spun suddenly and drove his power straight into
Will's chest, propelling him back until he hit the far wall.
Will screamed and pulled weakly at his belly. My heart
sank. An iron pipe protruded from Will's abdomen, brutally
impaling him.

"Will!" I shrieked, and rushed to him.

Ragnuk turned toward me, slow as a serpent, with wicked
triumph on his blocky face. He vanished for a moment, and
I felt something powerful slam into my body and knock me

back into a column, cracking my back.

"*Ellie!*" Will roared from the other side of the room.

My eyes misted over and I slumped dazedly, and when I looked up, the reaper's dark face was inches from mine.

"Wake up, Sleeping Beauty," Ragnuk sneered, his hot breath blasting me.

I smashed my fist into his nose as hard as I could, and he flew from me, thrashing wildly. He scrambled back to his feet, shaking his head and thundering with rage. I ran to Will and slid to a stop as I reached him. He pulled his body forward along the pipe, desperate to free himself. I cupped his face with both my hands and pressed my forehead despairingly against his cheek. "I'll get you off this," I promised, breathless, my hands running the length of the reddened iron. "I'll help you!"

"Call your swords," he groaned. "Hurry."

I nodded and willed them into my surprisingly steady hands.

Will's eyes shot wide open. "Behind you!"

I spun around. Ragnuk bounded across the room, leaving me no time to react. He swiped at me and hooked a talon around my leg, pulling me off balance. I hit the floor, landing flat on my back. Ragnuk's teeth clamped down on my leg, and he threw me across the warehouse, knocking my swords from my grip. I crashed into a large wooden crate piled high with scrap metal and cardboard, cracking my wrist. I groaned as I lifted my broken wrist and looked for my weapons.

"Leave her alone!" Will thundered.

I looked up to see that he was still struggling to free himself from the pipe that impaled him. His hands were clamped around the end of it and he pulled himself forward with what little strength he had left, one inch at a time.

The reaper stepped toward me, his head low, his black eyes fixed on me with a hungry stare. "Get up, girl!"

I struggled to my feet in the debris, cradling my broken wrist, stumbling from the pain that rocketed up my arm. I could feel the tiny bones clicking and moving beneath my skin, snapping themselves back into place.

"So, here we are," he sneered. "Bastian doesn't even care whether you die now. Your death is no longer necessary, he says. Well, his orders mean nothing to me now. I'm still going to eat you alive."

"Ellie, don't listen to him!" Will shouted.

Ragnuk tossed his head at Will. "Your Guardian doesn't know when he has lost. Typical of a vir." The reaper thudded over to Will and looked him up and down. "You all think you're gods, storming around, barking orders. You're no better than the humans. You look just like them." He spat on the ground at Will's feet. "For the most part."

Ragnuk ran a talon down Will's cheek, drawing a red line of blood. The cut healed instantly. The claw was large enough to punch right through Will's skull, but the ursid reaper's movement was shockingly gentle. "You do a good job, Guardian. Looks like you've got her fooled into thinking you're human. She doesn't even remember what you're capable of, does she?"

Will didn't answer him. I didn't understand why Ragnuk didn't just kill Will. He had us both at his mercy at that moment, but he chose to taunt us instead of just finishing us off. It was like he was getting a high off his momentary power over us.

"You haven't told her anything, have you?" Ragnuk laughed. "You arrogant vir bastard. No attempt to jog her memory? Should I do the honors? Shall we remind her of the monster you truly are?" He smiled with his bear face and licked his fangs.

Will jerked away from him and swung a fist, but the reaper moved his head fluidly to the side, avoiding the strike effortlessly. Ragnuk grabbed the end of the pipe with his jaws and bent it upward. The metal creaked and groaned until it pointed at the ceiling at a ninety-degree angle. Will gasped for breath.

"Get out of *that*, Guardian," Ragnuk sneered, his voice dark and cruel.

"Will!" I cried in horror. I squeezed my fist and whimpered in pain.

Ragnuk smiled and stepped away from Will heavily, his talons clicking on the floor. He lumbered toward me but stopped halfway and turned to pace back and forth. He seemed conflicted somehow, probably deciding whether to kill me or to chew on me for a bit before I died.

"Why don't you show her your true self?" Ragnuk growled to Will. "You could escape that trap easily. I've seen you escape from worse. You're holding back, Guardian!"

I stared at Will in confusion. What was Ragnuk talking about? Will had told me he didn't shape-shift like Geir. My gut trembled. Had he lied to me? Was he about to transform right in front of me?

Will's arms strained with the excruciating effort of trying to free himself from the pipe. He didn't look up to Ragnuk when he spoke. He stared down at the pipe, his hair falling over his eyes. "I am not like you."

The ursid laughed, bellowing. "You are a reaper! I don't care if you're angelic or demonic or idiotic. You're not human, so stop pretending to be!" Spittle flecked his mouth as he yelled. "You have a hunger that can never be sated."

"I'm better than that," Will groaned.

"You are *not*!" Ragnuk roared. "You think you're not a monster, but you are. Show her, Guardian. Show the girl!"

"I'm not a monster!" As Will dragged his body toward the end of the pipe, his power detonated, slamming the ground and wall behind him. He grabbed the pipe with both hands and bent it until the metal was straight. I watched in horror as Will slid forward and he dropped to the ground, leaving the pipe stained dark and a gaping hole in his abdomen. He collapsed to the ground on all fours, spilling red. He coughed and moaned as he struggled weakly to his feet and faced Ragnuk. "But I am not human either."

Will staggered to the side, leaning against the gore-covered pipe as the hole in his gut closed over. When he turned back to me with anguished eyes, his belly was smooth, but his shirt was shredded. He ripped the pipe clean out of the wall, yanking a chunk of the wall with it.

Ragnuk snarled, curling his lips back and exposing his massive fangs. The ursid pounded Will's back to the wall, his jaws gaping wide, ready to snap. Will swung the pipe up with both hands, striking Ragnuk in the mouth. The ursid chomped savagely, lashing his head back and forth, gagging and snarling. Will yanked the bar out of Ragnuk's mouth and jammed it through the ursid's neck. Ragnuk roared and thrashed, ramming his skull into Will's temple with a sickening crack. Will hit the ground hard and didn't move.

I tested my grip again and found my hand now fully healed, and I bolted forward, grabbing one of my swords on the way as I ran to help Will. Ragnuk's paw struck my chest and slammed me to the floor, knocking the breath right out of me. As I lay there gasping, his other front paw stomped on my arm holding the sword, pinning my blade. I yanked, but the lack of oxygen had weakened me. I stared up into the reaper's inky black eyes.

"This is the end for you," he hissed. Blood from the bar impaling his neck leaked onto my shirt.

"No, it's not," I snarled.

He smiled cruelly. "Oh, I think it is. Once again, your Guardian is down and you are alone. I know you remember the last time you and I were alone. I'd like to *relish* the moment, savor it, if you don't mind."

I glared up into his empty eyes. My fear for Will's safety consumed me, and that fear spun into hate and rage. "That was then. This is now."

My power swelled into a swirling orb in my palm, the heat of it blasting both of us. Ragnuk's eyes widened. I let it erupt point blank into his face, the white-hot light swallowing his entire upper body. He shrieked and reeled back, shaking his head violently, blinded by the light of my power. I rolled away from him and swept up my second sword.

Ragnuk backed away, fighting against the glaring light. When it settled, I gaped at the damage I had done to him. Half his face had burned away, revealing sinewy muscle, sagging chunks of flesh, and gleaming white bone. His massive fangs were exposed completely on the right side, and the charred bones of his jaws clicked grotesquely. His right eye was missing from the dark, bony socket, and his remaining eye was shut tight from pain. He breathed heavily, wheezing, staggering on his feet. I watched in horror as his face tried to heal itself; the flesh bubbled and spread slowly, uselessly. He needed to feed.

The reaper stared at me with his one bloodshot eye, a new hate and hunger boiling within him. My pulse pounded faster.

"Now, look what you've gone and done," he spat with

his half-skeletal face. "How did you burn me? It burns like angelfire!"

I held my ground, my own fury matching his. The corners of my vision pulsed, darkening, and I fought to stay focused. My power was building steadily, swelling past my limit of control. I was slipping again, but I didn't fight it. All I yearned for now was to dig my hands through Ragnuk's entrails, to smell the sizzle of angelfire on his hide.

"You don't stand a chance, girl," he snarled. "You reek of humanity. I can smell your soul through your skin. It makes you weak."

"My humanity makes me strong!" I shouted, the truth in my words resonating deep within my heart. "It gives me passion so I can keep on fighting, and my friends and family give me something worth fighting for!"

"And if you didn't have those swords?" He laughed, spittle and blood flying from his maw. "You and your weapons. You're helpless without them. You'd be nothing without them. My weapons are part of me. Tooth, claw, and bone." He dug his nails into the floor and licked the charred remains of his black lips. "You're *helpless*, Preliator, and you always will be."

Something swelled deep within me, something angry, desperate, and dark. It flowed at my feet like fog, flickering with snaps of electricity. I crouched, feeling the energy pulsing from me and out through space. The floor throbbed as if it had a heartbeat, hammering inside my head in time with my own pulse, drowning my senses in the hypnotic rhythm. I forced my eyes up to meet the reaper's angry stare.

I snarled, binding my power to me, feeling it pounding against my will. "I am not helpless!" I shrieked, releasing my power full force. The concrete floor sank beneath me and I with it, the white light swallowing Ragnuk whole. He roared and leaped high into the air before coming down on me. He landed with an earth-shattering thud and lashed a paw at me, but my arm shot up, deflecting his strike. I swung the sword in my other hand up, but his teeth clamped down on the flaming blade, wrenched it from my grip, and threw it aside. I jammed my fist into his soft throat and his jaws crunched shut.

I stared into Ragnuk's eyes and felt myself slipping away again, into the darkness deep within me. Deep down inside I knew that if I lost control, I could hurt Will. But as soon as the thought had passed, so did my sense. Crouching low to the floor, I gathered my power as I had done moments before, my swords back in hand. I ground my teeth tightly as the energy collected inside me, swallowing me in white light, pressing outward on every inch of me.

"You can't do it, girl!" Ragnuk thundered, the white of his one remaining eye flashing like a crazed animal's.

I felt the floor creak and groan, throbbing under strength that couldn't have belonged to me. With a hoarse cry I forced my power into the floor, crushing the concrete with the might of a tidal wave. The floor rolled in waves, rising and falling like water, before it sank deeper into a massive crater. The building ached and moaned as dust shook free.

"It's not going to happen!" The reaper's voice was distant and muffled.

I sent another shockwave rocketing in a circle around me, and it exploded into the walls and columns like a bomb. The windows shattered and sprayed countless glittering glass shards all around me. Steel crunched and screeched, and the ceiling sagged heavily. Debris crashed to the floor. My hair blazed around my face like a wildfire. Someone far away seemed to be screaming, and I realized after a moment that it was me.

Again. The columns closest to me and the beams above crashed to the floor, ripping out giant hunks of the ceiling. As a beam collapsed beside Ragnuk, I could see fear finally resonate across his scorched face. He roared and launched himself at me, talons outstretched.

My power rocked the building once more, and the ceiling plummeted down on top of Ragnuk. I squeezed my eyes shut and braced myself to share his fate.

But it never came. Warm hands wrapped around me, cradling me close to an even warmer body. I felt a strange rushing feeling, and then it was gone a moment later. The air was now cold and I was on my feet again. As my eyes focused, I found myself in the middle of the street looking back at the ruined warehouse. My vision pulsed, and I was unsure whether or not what I saw was actually real. Half the building had collapsed to the ground and was nothing but an undefined pile of wood, brick, and metal.

I searched for Ragnuk in case he had survived. All seemed quiet until I heard a rustling amid the debris, and the fury inside me swelled once again to the surface and spilled over. I climbed over the pile of debris and found Ragnuk crushed beneath a section of the ceiling. Blood seeped from his mouth. His bones were flattened beneath the rubble—all but his half-exposed skull and a single foreleg. The claws of his free paw raked the rubble weakly, as if he were trying to climb his way to freedom, but his efforts were useless. I stepped up to him, both my swords in hand, the blades scraping the chunks of concrete beneath me. The reaper's wet, black eye rolled up to meet mine, swiveling so much that a stripe of reddening white showed around the rim.

"Are you . . . ? You're going to . . . finish me now?" Ragnuk strained, his jawbone creaking in its joints, the visible muscle shredded, his talons clawing desperate streaks into the concrete. The burned flesh on his face still bubbled and strained, trying to heal. It amazed me that he could even speak, let alone breathe.

I said nothing as I stared down at him coldly. I couldn't make sense enough to reply. All I could perceive was how much anger I felt toward the beast who was now at my mercy. For so long I had feared him, but now that he was helpless at my feet, I felt nothing but satisfaction and a burning need for destruction.

"Who . . . is the monster . . . now?" He laughed, a pathetic, wheezing laugh, as my blades erupted with angelfire. The white light flickered on our faces beneath the black night sky.

"You . . . don't have the *spine*!" he hissed with morbid, sadistic amusement.

Unfortunately for him, it was mercy that I lacked, not a spine. I raised my swords high overhead. He stopped laughing when I had finished hacking off his head.

28

SOMEONE SPOKE BEHIND ME AND I SPUN AROUND, swinging my sword high as I let out a terrible cry. Bloodlust blurred my vision as my attacker struck my arm, blocking my sword strike. I kicked my foot into his chest, and he fell back with a grunt. My sword slashed again, this time ripping flesh, and I swung again, but he grabbed my wrist and squeezed until I dropped the sword from pain. I threw my newly freed fist and struck his jaw. He groaned and staggered to the side. I lunged for his throat, but the heel of his palm struck my chest, knocking the wind out of me. I collapsed forward, breathless, into my attacker's arms.

"Ellie."

My heart seemed to stop as my knees hit the ground and he fell with me. His voice shook my soul and woke me, and his firm hands on my shoulders kept me from falling. His scent filled my head and I clung to him, horrified at myself for what I had done—what I had done to *him*.

I opened my eyes and stood, looking down into Will's face as he stared up at me, looking brokenhearted. I bit down on the inside of my cheek as I touched the deep cut I had made in his arm.

"I hurt you," I said, my voice cracking. "You got me out of there and I hurt you."

Will's face remained pained. "I'm all right."

The wound vanished. My hand slid up his shoulder and neck to cup his cheek. "I am so sorry. I shouldn't have let it get this far."

"It doesn't matter. What's done is done."

I buried my face in my hands, Ragnuk's final words echoing in my head. "All these nightmares, hallucinations . . . I'm becoming a monster!"

Will stood, and his presence wrapped around me. "You're not becoming a monster."

"How do you know? How are you so sure that I'm not going to become something that isn't me?"

"Because I know you," he said, lifting my chin and looking into my eyes. "I know you better than I know anyone else. After all these centuries and every life you've led, you've always held on to who you are."

Shaking my head, I fought back a sob. "I can't take it when I feel like someone else. I get so angry, so violent, and I know this isn't who I am. What if I can't control it? What if I hurt you even more next time? I couldn't tell you from my enemy. I mean, look at what I did!" I threw my arm out toward the wreckage of the warehouse. "I'm as demonic as the creatures I fight."

"You aren't demonic and you aren't a monster," he said, his voice firmer. "Even when your power threatens to control you, it has never succeeded. Things have happened, yes, but you're still *you*. You've got to trust me, Ellie."

"But I'm so afraid of myself and what I'm capable of. And now I'm going to lose my soul forever. I don't want to die and I don't want to become nothing."

"I won't let that happen to you. I'll make sure you survive!"

"I don't want to survive, Will, I want to *live*!" I cried.

He froze then, staring at me as what I'd just confessed to him sunk in.

"I want to live," I repeated. "I want to be myself and go to school, to college, to parties, to the movies, bowling, football games. I want to roll around in the snow in my bathing suit and then jump into a hot tub. I want to pick out prom dresses with my mom and I want to road trip with Kate this summer. I want to grow up. I want to get married and maybe have a baby someday. I don't want to spend every day afraid of what might jump out at me from the shadows. I don't want to hide because horrible things are hunting me. I don't want to die and come back and not remember your face, Will. I don't want to spend another lifetime not knowing who you are!"

He pulled me close and wrapped his arms around me. I pressed my face against his warm chest and finally allowed myself to cry.

"It'll be all right," Will whispered into my hair, taking in a long, tortured breath. His hands spilled over my shoulders and my back, holding me tightly to him. My fingers curled around his shirt just to hold him closer.

With a deep breath, I peeked past him and saw my car sitting unharmed in the alley on the side of the warehouse that hadn't collapsed, covered in a thick layer of dirt. The sarcophagus sat just beyond the Audi and was equally unharmed. Will had somehow gotten himself and the sarcophagus out of harm's way just in time. Just in time before I let a building fall down on top of him.

I didn't know how long he held me there before I stepped away. It could have been hours, but I wouldn't have noticed. "What did Ragnuk mean when he wanted you to show your true self?" A part of me didn't want to know the answer, but another part ached for it.

He didn't respond at first and his hands rubbed my shoulders gently. His cheek burrowed into my hair. "He believed I'm something I'm not," he said. "I've tried very hard not to be the kind of dark they are. The demonic reapers hate my kind for that, and they hate me even more for protecting you."

I leaned into him. I understood what it felt like to be something frightening and try to maintain some shred of humanity. Will fought the same kind of darkness that threatened to destroy who I really was, the darkness that threatened to destroy *him* and take him away from me. We both waged internal wars against the monsters inside us. It made us dangerous to everyone around us, and to each other. I'd been so busy worrying about fighting the scary side of me that I'd forgotten he was doing the same. He was always thinking of me and what I needed, and I never thought about what *he* needed.

"What's wrong, Ellie? Tell me how I can fix this."

My breath trembled as I drew it in and I pressed my face deeper into his chest. "I thought he had killed you."

He exhaled and kissed my hair.

"I thought I was going to lose you," I confessed, biting back a sob that threatened to break free.

Will pulled away so that our eyes met. The centuries we had spent together were filling my heart with so much emotion that I felt it was about to burst. I didn't remember any of it, but I knew it all in my soul.

"You'll never lose me," he said gently, and wiped the tears from my cheeks. "I'll always be here."

I wrapped my arms around his back and held him as tightly as I could, afraid he'd drift away.

He dropped his head to mine, his body so close to mine I could hardly stand it. "If we're separated—if I lose you—I'll find you," he breathed, his cheek touching mine gently, lighting tiny fireworks on my skin.

Fresh, relentless, warm tears rolled down my cheeks. His promise melted through me, and my heart ached for everything that I wanted and couldn't have. In the end, he was all I had. Through each lifetime, every last thing that I came to know and love in the world changed or vanished completely except for him. He was the only thing permanent in all of forever.

Then he kissed me, slowly and gently. It was just a light brush of his lips on mine, but I stiffened, surprised and unsure of how to react. He pulled away, only just, holding my gaze with his, his lips almost touching mine, as if waiting for me. I tilted my chin up and parted my mouth until his returned, kissing me again, long and leisurely. He seemed too careful, as if he expected me to be frightened. I forced myself to relax and I lifted a tentative hand to stroke his cheek and I kissed him back. His fingers trailed up my spine and brushed across my bare throat before threading tenderly through my hair, his thumb tracing along my cheek. When I didn't pull away, he deepened his kiss with a hunger, fervently, as if it were our last, even though it was our first. He finally broke free, but he didn't pull away. He touched his forehead to mine and closed his eyes.

"I'm sorry," he whispered.

My hands wound around his neck. My nails traced the contours of his back and shoulders, and I felt his muscles lock where I touched him. I breathed in his scent, trying to take all of him in. For a moment I forgot about the beast that might destroy my soul, and the only thing I feared was losing *this* and never seeing his face again. If I died before I had to fight the Enshi, I didn't want to forget his face or his voice or what it felt like when he touched me. I couldn't let myself forget him again. "Don't be," I said, my hands sliding up into his hair.

"I shouldn't have done that," he breathed, pushing a lock of my hair behind my shoulders.

"There's nothing to regret," I replied urgently.

He pulled away until he was no longer touching me at all, and I craved for him to come back. I fought everything in me to not reach for him.

His expression was terribly vulnerable and pained; he seemed to be trying desperately not to break. "You have to understand how difficult this is for me," he said finally. "I've been devoted to you for so long. I've done my best to serve you and keep you safe. And this—how I feel—is going against too many of the rules. I know it's wrong, and I know it's stupid, but I don't really care."

I studied his face for several moments, watching for the intensity of his eyes to give me a sign. "Whose rules are they?"

"The angel who made me your Guardian," he said. "I think he was an archangel. He told me I was to protect you and nothing more. I'm not supposed to feel what I feel."

"What exactly . . . do you feel?" I asked carefully. "What do you mean?"

He closed his eyes and looked away. "I'm so confused."

We didn't speak for some time but only stood there next to the collapsed warehouse. Finally he turned away from me.

"We should get out of here," he suggested. "Someone is bound to have heard the building fall."

I nodded. "What do we do about the sarcophagus?"

He thought for a moment. "I can carry it a little ways from here. Give Nathaniel a call. Tell him to bring a truck. We have to relocate, but I just don't know where to."

"Where do you want me to go?"

"Drive to the first stop sign and turn right. Follow that road all the way to the dead end. I'll meet you there."

I gave him a perplexed look. "You sure know your way around here."

"I had to study the location and its surroundings, including all roads, intersections, and buildings in the area." He smiled when he noticed my quizzical expression. "Better safe than sorry."

"Right."

There was an awkward pause before either of us moved. I could still feel his mouth on mine as I stood there with nothing to say. Finally, I got into my car and drove exactly where he told me to. I wasn't sure if I was surprised he was right about the dead end or not. I parked there and turned my car off and called Nathaniel, telling him where to meet us. Not even a second after I hung up, Will appeared out of nowhere, dropping the sarcophagus in the glare of my headlights. I got out to meet him as the wails of sirens echoed in the distance, most likely responding to calls about the warehouse's recent demise.

"Nathaniel should be here shortly," I said.

"Good."

He didn't say anything else. It annoyed me a little that I couldn't tell what he was thinking. He seemed to be avoiding the topic of what had happened between us minutes before, but then again, I hadn't brought it up either. I was torn over whether or not to bring it up at all. I wanted to ask him about it, since I felt so empty inside for some reason. I wanted— scratch that, I *needed*—to know how he felt about me. Then I wondered, had we been *together* before? Had he kissed me before in my past lives?

"What are you thinking about?" he asked with a soft voice, interrupting my thoughts, for which I was thankful.

"Wouldn't you like to know," I said glumly.

He walked up to me and leaned back against my car, crossing his arms over his chest. "Yes, I would. You twist up your face funny when you're deep in thought."

"Thanks for the observation." I narrowed my eyes. "What do you *think* I'm thinking about?"

His jaw clenched for just a fraction of a second before the

tension washed away. "I have a good idea."

"Are we just going to pretend it didn't happen?" I asked.

He sucked in his top lip. "I don't think that would be wise."

"Well, you're on a roll." I studied his expression meticulously. He gave nothing of his thoughts away.

"I didn't plan on it, if that's what you're wondering." He seemed honest.

"Have you ever kissed me before?"

"Do you mean before you were Ellie?"

Whatever that meant. "Yeah."

"No."

I wanted to ask him if he had ever wanted to, but I decided on a different question. "So what does this mean?"

"I don't understand."

I sighed. "What does it mean between you and me?"

He didn't answer right away. Neither of us spoke for a few moments, and the longer the silence lingered, the more nauseated I felt. My body tensed.

"I care about you very deeply," he said. "I just don't think—"

At that moment a large white van pulled up and stopped in front of us. Nathaniel and Lauren hopped out. I scowled. Will had gotten lucky . . . for now. I had a lot more questions to ask him once we were in private again.

"Are you guys okay?" Nathaniel asked, his voice trembling.

"I'm *really* hungry," Will said dramatically.

Nathaniel laughed. "I can imagine. Ellie, are you unharmed?"

I shrugged. "I've healed. Ragnuk is dead. That's all that's important."

Lauren watched me with a strange mix of emotions flickering across her face. I couldn't decide what she was feeling. It was almost as if she understood exactly how shaken I was—by more than just Ragnuk. Briefly, I wondered how far her psychic talents extended.

"We'll take the sarcophagus to my house," Nathaniel offered. "I think it will be safely hidden there until we can leave for Puerto Rico."

"They won't track you there?" I asked skeptically. "Ragnuk tracked us to the warehouse."

"If Bastian's vir were around, we'd already be dead and they'd have the Enshi," he said. "They won't sit around in the shadows and stalk us. What they want is right here."

I felt that was the cue to get the hell out. "So then the sarcophagus *shouldn't* be right here."

Will nodded. "Let's get going. It's suicide hanging around."

Will and I followed the van in my car. He didn't say anything, and neither did I. The van pulled onto a quiet street with houses spaced far apart. We followed it up a long wooded driveway to a beautiful house overlooking a lake. Nathaniel opened the doors of a three-car garage, and Will jumped out of the van to help him unload the sarcophagus.

"Is this your house, Nathaniel?" I asked, admiring the view of the lake.

"Yes," Nathaniel said, and closed the garage door. I remembered Will had said he lived here, and I imagined him sitting in his room, playing the guitar. I couldn't stop myself from glancing at him and feeling a rush of warmth at the memory of our kiss. For a moment it was hard to breathe.

"You'd better have food," Will said with a grin.

Lauren laughed, laying a hand on his shoulder. "Check the kitchen."

He jogged inside the house.

"Don't clean out the pantry, though!" she called after him. "Or the fridge! Please don't make me go grocery shopping twice in one week."

"I'll make sure," Nathaniel offered, and followed Will inside.

"So do you live with Nathaniel too?" I asked Lauren as we went in the house.

She shook her head. "No, I just make sure these boys eat right and take care of themselves. I have a condo near campus. My parents are helping me rent it while I'm in school."

"Are you a professional psychic? Do you do readings and stuff?"

She laughed. "Oh, no. I'm a nursing student."

I imagined she'd make a very kind nurse someday. "How do you know Nathaniel?"

She smiled sweetly. "Reapers don't like it when you can see them. Nathaniel saved my life. I owe a lot to him, and I care about him deeply."

Before I could ask her what had happened, she took my hand and led me into the kitchen, where Will was making a sandwich. Nathaniel was scolding him about destroying yet another shirt.

"I'll be right back," Lauren said.

I stared at Will as he devoured his sandwich. "You weren't kidding about needing to eat, were you?"

He shook his head and wolfed down another bite. "Nope."

Lauren returned and held out a clean red T-shirt. "Put this on," she said. "You look disgusting."

He laughed and took it from her hand without setting his sandwich on the counter. "Thanks, Lauren."

She folded her arms over her chest. "Be grateful that I'm so generous. I almost brought you down a pink one."

Will laughed. "Must be one of Nathaniel's. I don't own a pink shirt."

Nathaniel rolled his eyes. "What makes you think *I* do?"

Lauren lifted a finger. "Behave. You, finish that sandwich."

Will grinned through his last bite, pulled on the shirt, and went to make a second sandwich. I stepped up to help him, and when his eye caught mine, I smiled warmly at him. He touched my arm tenderly, letting his hand slide down my skin. Another hot rush went through me, and I fought the urge to lean into him.

"I'll stay here and guard the Enshi and Lauren," Nathaniel said. "I'll have our flight itinerary tomorrow. We'll probably have to ship the sarcophagus on a separate cargo plane."

"Right," I agreed.

"I'll be in touch." Nathaniel smiled.

29

WILL AND I DIDN'T SAY MUCH ON THE WAY HOME. I
got out of my car and he vanished, I presumed to the roof.
The first thing I did when I got inside, after rushing up to
my room, was call Kate. A shower could wait.

"Kate?" I asked when she answered.

"Hey," she responded quickly. "What's up?"

I braced myself. "I need you to do an enormous favor for
me on an epic, life-changing scale."

"Uh-oh."

"Are you going up north for Thanksgiving?"

"Yeah, why?"

"I'm going with you."

She paused. "You . . . are?"

"Not really. I need you to cover for me." I winced.

"For . . . ?"

"If my parents ask you about where I am, or just *any-thing*, please, please can you tell them that we're up north until Friday?"

She paused. "Why? Where are you *really* going to be?"

I knew what I had to say to get her to vouch for me. "I'm going to be with Will."

"Oh my *God*!" she squealed. "I knew it."

I pulled my cell away from my ear as she freaked out.

"Are you going away on some romantic getaway?" She was far too excited. "I *knew* he was your boyfriend. Ellie Marie, I can't believe you lied to me, you hooker!"

"I'm really sorry, Kate," I said honestly. "I just didn't want it getting back to my parents. He's older, you know, and they'd freak. Especially if they knew I was going out of town with him. So if my parents happen to not believe me for whatever reason, can you please cover for me?"

She snorted something incomprehensible. "Uh, yeah. You're my girl. I'd lie for you anytime."

I let out a long sigh of relief and a short, uncomfortable laugh. "Thanks a lot."

"You had better tell me *everything*!" she chirped. Her voice suddenly grew low and serious. "Do you think you guys will . . . you know?"

My eyes bulged. "Probably not."

"Five bucks says you do."

"*What?* You're putting wagers on my virginity?" Actually, I wasn't that shocked. "You're going to Hell, you know."

"I wouldn't doubt it."

"It's nice that you've accepted your fate so graciously."

"Come *on*," she groaned. "I assume by now you've finally kissed him since he's your boyfriend, and you're a total loser for not telling me, but whatever. You're going to be alone with him for three days doing God only knows what—okay, hopefully God doesn't really know *what.* . . ."

I rolled my eyes. "Yeah, well, *you* never told me everything."

She didn't answer right away. "I don't know what you're talking about."

I laughed. "Oh, yeah, you do. You and Landon?"

"Ellie, I swear nothing happened."

"Don't get me wrong," I insisted. "It's cool with me if you guys are . . . together."

"I didn't sleep with him," she said. "Nothing happened. We just kissed, that's all. I was too drunk to know what I was doing."

"Do you like him?" I tried not to sound too curious, in case she got the impression I hoped she'd say no.

"I'm not really sure," she confessed. "Kind of. Maybe. I don't know. I'm really happy nothing happened on Halloween, though. If I'm glad nothing happened, then it has to mean I'm not into him, right?"

I smiled even if she couldn't see me. "If you admitted it, I think you'd feel better."

She laughed. "There's nothing to admit, trust me."

I took a step back and bumped into a warm body and yelped. I turned to see Will standing there, frowning down at me.

"Ell?" Kate asked. "You okay?"

"Yeah, I thought I saw a spider." I shook my fist at Will and scowled. "A big, *really* ugly one. Sorry."

"Understandable," she said. "I'll see you in school tomorrow, okay?"

"Okay, bye!" I glared up at Will, fearing what he might have heard of my phone conversation. "Why the ninja stealth? Is it really necessary?"

"I thought you knew I was in here," he said. The apologetic, defensive look in his green eyes made me forget how irritated I was.

"It's okay. Just try to be a little more noisy next time."

He laughed softly. "I don't think I could make a lot of noise if I tried. You should be a little more perceptive."

I narrowed my eyes. "You're a boy. You're all noisy when it gets down to it. You'll figure it out. What are you doing in here, anyway?"

"I wanted to see how you're doing."

"Ha!" I shouted, immediately clamping my hand over my mouth, embarrassed by how loud I had just been. I lowered my voice to a harsh whisper. "You're a liar. You got bored sitting up there on my roof all alone. Admit it."

He frowned. He looked shockingly vulnerable at that moment. "I've never lied to you."

Regret grew in my throat. "I'm sorry. I shouldn't have said that."

"Don't worry about it." He gave me a sideways look. "Are you going to take a shower?"

I flushed scarlet and gave a nervous laugh. "What's that supposed to mean?"

"Just reading your mind."

I narrowed my eyes. "Don't scare me and say that. I just might believe you."

He laughed. "I know you well enough to know that a shower is your highest priority right now."

I huffed at him for being right as usual, and I grabbed my robe off its hook and walked to the bathroom, where I took an obscenely long shower. The hot water ran over me, washing away the dirt, dust, and dried blood. I wished the water would wash away the ache in my heart, but it only soothed my aching muscles. For now, that would have to do. I leaned my head against the glass shower door and closed my eyes, lost in thought. Ragnuk's half-burned-away face haunted me in the darkness behind my eyelids, flashing gnarled flesh and white bone. I tried to will the image away, but that was useless.

I knew I had to get past him. There were scarier things to worry about now, like losing my soul forever. And the Apocalypse.

I finished, dried off, dressed in my robe, and blow-dried my hair before heading back to my room. Will was sitting on the end of my bed, leaning forward with his hands folded together. I self-consciously pulled my robe a little tighter and flashed a small smile. "You okay?"

His gaze met mine. "Isn't that my line?" he asked, his voice weak and tired.

"Usually." I plopped down next to him. "I guess it's my turn now."

He didn't immediately respond. We sat in silence for some time. I didn't feel confident enough to say anything at all. So I waited.

"What's ahead is going to be difficult," he said gently. "Not simply this week but in the coming weeks. If we don't destroy the Enshi off Puerto Rico, then I'm not sure what will happen. We can't fail."

I made a slow nod. "It's our only option, unless we blow it up."

He shrugged. "I don't know how effective that would be. If it's an angel, then I have no idea how to kill it. If it's at the bottom of the ocean, at least nothing else can get to it to wake it up. Nothing can survive thirty thousand feet below the ocean's surface. Nothing is absolutely indestructible."

"What if Bastian intercepts?" I asked.

His voice grew dark. "Then we'll have to fight him. I want to avoid him until the Enshi is at the bottom of that trench. We can't risk running into him or Geir and the others before then. We *can't*." The desperation in that last word sent a spark of fear through me.

I didn't want to think of the possible results of something like that happening. We had to get it out of the city—out of the *state*—as soon as possible. Will wasn't the only one who didn't want to fight Bastian's vir. I knew I wasn't ready. They'd mop the floor with me, and I knew only the half of it. I'd seen none of what Ivar could do and only a little bit of Geir's power. We'd been lucky when we'd gotten away. I couldn't even fathom what the rest of them were truly capable of.

I grabbed my pajamas from a wad of clothing on the floor and went into my closet to change. When I came back out, Will hadn't moved. The furious concentration in his expression had furrowed his brow and tightened his lips. He stared at the floor.

"Did you eat enough at Nathaniel's?" I asked him, lifting his hair away from his eyes.

He didn't answer.

"Guess not. I know you needed to eat after the fight tonight."

"I really don't want to eat right now."

I smiled. "Don't move." I went to the kitchen and explored my fridge. I was lucky to find a half-empty two-liter bottle of root beer in there, and a carton of vanilla ice cream in the freezer. I made a float, smiling fondly to myself as I stuck a spoon and straw into the glass and I took the sugary concoction upstairs.

Will still hadn't moved.

I stopped in front of him and held out the float. He looked

up at me, his eyes flashing, and he grinned.

"Ellie . . ."

"You aren't going to pass up a fabulous root beer float, are you?" I winked playfully.

He gave a gentle laugh and took the glass. I sat down on the bed beside him and watched him eat.

"Since I made it," I said, "I get a sip and a bite."

That beautiful smile widened. "Agreed."

He gave me the spoon, and I took a bite of ice cream and then sipped a gulp of root beer to wash it down. "Mmm, that had better be the best damn root beer float you've ever had."

"It is, trust me." He watched me for a moment before he took the straw back and stirred. "However, it's even better when the ice cream melts. Just a little trick for you."

He stirred until most of the ice cream was dissolved and the root beer had turned a milky brown color, like hot cocoa. "Try it now."

He held the straw still while I took another sip. The root beer was softened with creamy vanilla and the carbonation was almost all gone. The result might have been the most delicious thing I'd ever tasted.

"It's amazing," I said, and took another sip.

"Told you."

We shared the last of it and I set the empty, frothy glass on a coaster on my nightstand. My heart pounded as I turned around to him, feeling the heat of his eyes on my back.

"Thank you," he said. "I feel a lot better."

"You couldn't fool me." I eased up to him, and my heart sank when the worried expression returned to his face. "Will, do you regret it all? The fighting? Killing the demonic reaper?"

"I don't regret it, no."

"But it bothers you," I said. "That's why you wear the crucifix your mother gave you. And because you miss her."

He looked up at me and his brow softened. "I guess you can read people better than I thought."

I smiled warmly at him and smoothed my hand over his hair. "Only you. Hard as you try, you can never fool me."

"I suppose not."

My smile faded. "You know there are higher powers and Heaven and Hell out there, but you don't seem very religious."

"I think religion is based on faith," he said. "I don't need faith to know what I deal with every day. I know that there is a God and that Lucifer challenges Him. I know that there are the Fallen and there are angels who fight them. I know that there are creatures who drag innocent human souls to Hell to prepare for the Apocalypse and that I was designed to fight those creatures. Faith has nothing to do with my existence, but yes. You're right. I don't like killing, but I have to do it because it's my duty. Protecting human souls is the duty of any angelic reaper. Protecting you is my duty. I'm a soldier in a war, and the only difference between our war and the ones between humans is that this fight has been going on since time began and it's not likely to be over any time soon."

"Why would your mother give you a crucifix if reapers aren't very religious?"

He did that lip thing again, and my stomach flipped. "My mother was very devout in her belief that what we're doing is the right thing. She fought hard against the demonic, and I think wearing a cross made her feel closer to the archangels she served and to God. We get very lonely sometimes, and we lose track of our goals after so many centuries of fighting. I think it kept her grounded."

"Does it keep you grounded too?"

"*You* keep me grounded," he said. "And this crucifix reminds me that there are bigger things happening out there than just you and me. That there is a world beyond protecting you, even though you're all I really know. You asked me if I regretted any of it, and the answer, truthfully, is yes. The only thing I ever regret is failing you, letting you die."

I continued to stroke his hair and said nothing. To be honest, I didn't really know what to say.

"And yes," he continued, "I do miss my mother."

"Do you think she's watching over you in Heaven?"

He tensed and didn't answer me right away. "Reapers don't have an afterlife. Heaven and Hell are for human souls. When a reaper dies, that's it. So, no. My mother is gone."

My heart kicked in my chest and sadness blanketed me like heavy, freezing cold snow as the blood drained from my face. I'd always felt a small comfort knowing that when

I died, my soul would be safe. Nothing frightened me more than the possibility of the Enshi destroying my soul so that after my death, I would disappear. And here, this entire time, for Will's entire life, he knew that if he were ever killed, he would end the same way I would if my soul were eaten. My Guardians before him had all died for me and ended their existences. Will had known all along that his ultimate sacrifice for me would only bring him eternal nothingness, and despite knowing this, he still risked his life for me every night, every battle. If he died protecting me, fighting for me, he'd give up everything. There'd be no Heaven for him to rest and find peace in. All he would ever know was war and death and loss and sadness.

How could I be so selfish? Why would I let him risk so much for me? My thoughts made me angry at myself, for caring for no one but myself.

But he was there. Day and night he was there for me, risking his very existence to protect me from a war that claimed my life over and over again. He never faltered, never wavered, never feared for his own safety. He was beaten, stabbed, abused, and tortured again and again, and yet he still stuck by me, ignoring the possibility that he would die for me one day. It wasn't right. I didn't deserve everything he sacrificed for me. I wasn't worth so high a price.

I wrapped a hand around his face and turned his gaze to mine as I folded my legs underneath me. Kneeling, I smoothed my hand over his rough cheek and into his hair.

I leaned forward and kissed his lips softly just to feel that much closer to him. His kiss tasted like vanilla and sugar, warm and delicious against my lips. The ache in my heart reminded me of how much I loved him and I pressed my lips to his more desperately, as if I were afraid that he might vanish right there next to me. I bit back a tear that might have been happy or sad—I wasn't even sure myself—and pulled away.

"You're amazing" was all I could say to him.

His gaze fell. "I'm not even close." He leaned toward me, resting his forehead against my shoulder, and his hand slid up my arm. He held me close to him and pressed his lips to my arm, brushing his nose across my skin as I ran my fingers through his hair. I bit on my lip to stop the tears.

I lifted his face, and his eyes opened up into mine. I couldn't help the smile that formed when I could tell that I'd embarrassed him. "Yes, you are. You need to relax. Don't worry about anything for once."

His troubled look began to fade. "I don't mean to."

"Let me help you," I offered. I walked around my bed and climbed in, reaching for his hand. He let me take it and I pulled him toward me. "Lie down with me. Sleep for a little while. You don't need to sit up in the freezing cold on my roof. You owe that to yourself. Forget about everything else. You're always so worried about taking care of me. Let me take care of you for once."

He lay on his side, the mattress sinking beneath his weight all too intimately, and he slid an arm tentatively around my belly. I didn't say anything as we lay there, and I fell asleep feeling his warm, sugar-sweetened breath on the bend of my neck.

30

❦

NATHANIEL HAD ARRANGED A FLIGHT FOR US AND
air freight for the sarcophagus to Puerto Rico via Miami. My
parents bought the story about my spending the holiday with
Kate's family at their lake house up north, since I had done
it a hundred times before, and everything was falling into
place. Despite Nathaniel's preference for working behind the
scenes instead of fighting on the front lines, he would be
coming along as backup. I hadn't seen him in action yet, but
I was intrigued. He didn't fight with the traditional blades
Will and I were used to. Nathaniel had a thing for guns.

He managed to have the box containing the sarcophagus
classfied as an archaeological artifact, and we had no trouble
shipping it on a cargo plane. Nathaniel, rightfully afraid of
leaving the Enshi on its own, concealed his presence from the
airport staff by staying within the Grim and managed to sneak

onto the flight unseen—invisibility proved to be a handy reaper trick. He would stay with the sarcophagus until we arrived in the Caribbean. Thankfully we didn't have to check our swords along with Nathaniel's guns. That would have been fun to explain.

We arrived in Miami after ten on Wednesday night and after a layover we boarded another plane to San Juan. I was definitely feeling the exhaustion when we finally got to our little motel at almost four in the morning. We got a room in the motel instead of one of the glamorous hotels I would have preferred, but Will said it was for our safety and that of the locals that we would stay in a small building with an easy exit in case Bastian got wind of our location. The motel was off a narrow street and only a couple blocks from the airport. It was a little run-down, and the pavement outside had tufts of weeds sticking out of cracks. When Nathaniel's cargo plane arrived in San Juan, he rented a large truck to carry the sarcophagus and parked behind the motel. He'd be watching the truck like a hawk until dawn in case of attack.

Will let me sleep in until eleven in the morning, which was heaven after the rough week and late night. After my shower in the darling little bathroom, I was anticipating with excitement getting outside and seeing what the city really looked like. I peeked my head out of the bathroom while I blow-dried my hair and spotted Will standing over his suitcase and pulling off his shirt. I felt my face fill with heat

when I saw him shirtless, and I almost looked away. *Almost.*
He shrugged on a new tee, and the muscles in his abdomen
constricted as he smoothed out the cotton.

"Is Nathaniel still out with the truck?" I asked.

He turned around and eased over to me. "No," he answered.
"He took a taxi to the marina to get a boat. I thought we'd get
lunch when he gets back. Sound good?"

I smiled wide. "Definitely. Is he coming with us?"

"No, he's staying with the truck. We can't leave the box
alone." He sounded genuinely disappointed. "I brought him
food before he left, though. We both need to eat a lot before
tonight, just in case."

"You mean you already ate?"

"Some." His tone was so nonchalant, as if everyone ate
before they went out to a restaurant.

"And you're going to eat *more*?"

"Yeah," he said. "I told you I didn't want you seeing how
much I really have to eat. It would give you nightmares, I
assure you."

I rolled my eyes. "Oh, thank you for protecting me from
the painful truths of how much guys *really* eat when girls
aren't looking."

He smiled down at me. "You should take me more seriously."

"You should take yourself *less* seriously," I retorted,
standing my ground as he leaned in to me.

He laughed. "Are you finished in the bathroom yet?"

"Makeup."

"Hurry."

I didn't. I took my sweet time applying liner and mascara over rosy pink shadow. The day was sunny, and I was in a freakishly good mood. I tried not to think about later in the day, when we'd be sailing out to drop the Enshi off the edge of the world.

"Are you serious?" I heard Will shout from back in the room. I poked my head out. "There's nobody else?" He paused. "All right, fine." Will shut my phone and ran an angry hand through his hair.

"What's up?" I asked, sliding balm over my lips.

"Nathaniel found a fishing boat for us to rent," he replied, his voice annoyed. "The problem is that it won't be available until after five. No one else would let us take their boat out far enough. What are you *doing* in there? You're taking forever."

"Makeup!" I repeated, scowling. I put an unneeded extra layer of lip balm on just to annoy him.

"Aren't you concerned about how late we have to leave?"

"Well, five isn't bad," I offered. "Sunset isn't until, what? Seven?"

He frowned at me. "We have to sail almost eighty miles out to get to the Milwaukee Deep."

I shrugged. "So? What's that? An hour?"

"Ellie, we aren't driving a car. This is a really big, old

deep-sea trawler. We'll be very lucky if it tops out at fifteen knots."

"I don't know what that means!"

"It's about seventeen miles an hour."

I didn't attempt to calculate since I couldn't even count the toes on my feet without getting confused. "Will that get us there by six?"

"No, it's most likely going to take us over four and a half hours."

My jaw dropped. "We're going to be out there after dark?"

He let out a long breath. "That's what it's looking like."

"Can't we wait until tomorrow?" I asked hopefully.

He shook his head. "Our plane leaves at nine in the morning and we can't risk spending another day here."

"Great."

"I know."

I huffed. It would be okay, I told myself repeatedly. There was no way the demonic vir could know we were in Puerto Rico. We were safe. "Let's not worry about it. We'll be fine."

He gave me a quizzical look. "Since when did you become Miss Optimistic?"

"Since I got this hungry, so let's go."

Will called a cab to take us into Old San Juan. I was absolutely enchanted. The streets were ablaze in a rainbow of colors; every building was bright and unique in its own way. Arched windows gave onto wrought-iron balconies lined with planters full of fragrant flowers spilling over the edges. Every doorway was unique, ornately decorated and protected by beautiful iron grillwork. I'd have to revisit again one day when I wasn't expecting to meet certain doom at sundown.

We stopped at a little café and ate on the stone patio. Though it had a name I could never pronounce, I ordered a colorful salad with all sorts of surprises folded into the greens. Will ordered some kind of chicken stew with rice and beans. It smelled *amazing*, and I stole a few bites of it despite his protests. For a little while, to my surprise, I felt normal again. I liked the feeling. I enjoyed pretending to be a normal girl on vacation with a normal—although gorgeous—guy in a beautiful town.

When we finished eating, we didn't immediately take a cab back to the motel. Will insisted I have a good day. He seemed excessively concerned about whether I was enjoying myself, which didn't put me at ease at all—instead, I suspected that Will thought this might be my last day. We walked through Old San Juan, making our way through the crowds that surrounded street musicians and artists, gazing up at the spectacular sights. We walked along a crowded beach and took a tour of Castillo San Cristóbal before heading back.

When we pulled up to the motel, Nathaniel was sitting in a chair outside the door. He stood when we climbed out of the cab and Will paid the driver.

Nathaniel smiled. "Have a good day?"

"Yeah," I said with a grin. "It was nice." I tried to treasure how I felt at that moment, because I knew the feeling wasn't going to last.

We piled into the truck with the sarcophagus and the duffel bag full of Nathaniel's weapons in back and drove to the Port of San Juan on the other side of town. I sat between Will and Nathaniel and stared silently out the windshield, trying not to think about the worst thing that could happen that night. We drove past a seemingly endless line of cruise ships and ferries to the fishing boat docks. These vessels were much smaller than the big tourist ships, but they still towered over me. The distinct smells of salt water, fish, metal, and nylon nets assaulted my nose all at once. Ropes and wires were strung everywhere, and crewmen dodged among them fluidly, going about their chores. We stopped at a huge deep-sea trawler with the name *Elsa* stamped in faded letters on the bow. A stout, greasy, balding man jogged heavily down the loading dock to greet us.

"*Hola,*" he said, nodding to us, his beady eyes lingering on me.

"*Hola,* José," Nathaniel replied. "Sorry we're a little late."

"All okay," José bellowed. "You already paid me, so I don't care if you show." He laughed, his belly bouncing, and he swiped the back of his hand across his filthy, sweaty brow.

Nathaniel forced a smile. It was obvious that he didn't like our new friend. "We'll take the *Elsa* off your hands now."

José's laughter boomed even louder. "There is no way

you will able to captain my ship with one other guy and a teenage girl and still have it back in this port in one piece. And I don't care how much you pay me, my crew doesn't leave the ship."

Frustration crinkled Nathaniel's face. "That's not necessary. We'll be perfectly fine."

"Not a chance," José said, his voice more serious this time. "Me and my crew come with you."

"Nathaniel," Will said in a careful voice, "we don't have a choice."

Nathaniel closed his eyes in annoyance. "Fine, but remember what I'm paying you for. That includes not asking questions."

José laughed once again. "I know this. Transport wherever you want. No questions."

"Thank you. Let's load so we can get there as quickly as possible."

José shrugged. "This is a hundred-foot trawler and it isn't very fast. It would take a miracle to make it to the Deep before dark. No promises."

"We'll take what we can get," Will interjected. He and Nathaniel went back to the truck and pulled out the large black duffel bags containing the arsenal.

"You can put those in the cabin, if you'd like," José called.

They did just that before heading back to unload the sarcophagus. When they lugged the large wooden box off the truck, the *Elsa*'s crew watched them suspiciously. I prayed they wouldn't get too curious.

José wasn't immune to curiosity either. "What you got in there? And why do you want to take it out over the Deep? You dumping it over?"

Nathaniel glared briefly at him. "No questions, remember?"

The captain nodded in disappointment. "Can't be too heavy, if you're swinging it around like that. And if it isn't heavy, then it isn't important."

I wanted to laugh.

"This needs to go below," Will said as they walked past. José pointed the way.

I followed Will and Nathaniel past the cabin and down belowdecks and into the large, stuffy hold, which smelled strongly of fish. Water thumped against the boat's steel sides, making echoes that bounced around the cavernous room. They set the box down and shoved it up against a wall. A heavy padlock kept the lid locked tightly.

"Do you think it'll be okay?" I asked.

"Yeah," Will answered. "It's much safer down here than up on deck."

"If we're attacked, then it won't matter."

He dipped his head and flashed me a silly grin. "We won't be attacked."

José's voice called from somewhere above. "*Amigos*, we're casting off soon."

We went back up to the main deck, staying out of the

crew's way. They lifted and stowed the gangplank, and we finally set off. The gritty trawler rumbled out of port and into the open sea. I peered over the edge of the railing into the dark water, watching the waves. I wandered around the perimeter of the boat to explore. When José appeared around a corner, I stopped.

He walked up to me smelling of fish and cigarette smoke. I failed to keep my nose from wrinkling at his unpleasant stench. "So what are you kids planning on doing once you get over the Deep? You're not going swimming, are you? You some kind of thrill seekers? Where are your parents?"

I shook my head, my pulse building. "I thought you weren't supposed to ask questions."

He shrugged. "I don't mean any harm. You don't want to go into that water, little girl. There are sharks bigger than the *Elsa* swimming down there. Like monsters from a nightmare."

"I don't plan on going into the water," I assured him. In truth, it wasn't sharks that gave me nightmares.

"You going fishing?" he probed. "Why not board one of those fancy fishing boats to do it? Why do you pay an old fool like me for a few hours on this old trawler?"

"I don't exactly know why," I said, and turned away to walk briskly back toward the bow, hoping he wouldn't follow me.

"You had better not be doing anything illegal!" José called behind me. "I hope you don't have bodies in that box, and you better not be CIA!"

I rounded the front of the cabin to get away from him, found Will, and stuck close to him for the rest of the voyage. He seemed to sense that the crew was weirding me out, and his protectiveness turned on full force. If anyone got too friendly with me, I could probably beat the crap out of them myself, since I was used to fighting much bigger monsters than a bunch of smelly dudes, but I let Will do his thing. He seemed happiest when he got to play bodyguard.

After an hour on the ship, I began to get bored. I leaned on the railing next to Will as the wind whipped my hair around like a tornado. My natural waves were beginning to rear their ugly heads, and I hadn't remembered to bring a hair tie to tame them. Annoyed, I tucked my hair behind my ears, but the locks didn't stay under control.

I looked over the edge and my eyes went wide when I saw dolphins, at least a half dozen of them, dipping in and out of the water, their shimmering gray backs vanishing and reappearing through the waves. I couldn't help the squeal that escaped me.

"Dolphins!" I cried, pointing at them for Will to see. He peered apathetically over my shoulder and said nothing. "They're following us. It must be good luck or something, right?"

I heard an ugly snort behind me. I turned to see José walking by. "Don't get too excited," he grumbled, scowling down at the dolphins. "They're hoping we find shrimp for them to steal. Greedy bastards. *Carroñeros!*" He angrily slapped the side of the boat, and I was glad when the loud resulting thump didn't spook them. When José was out of earshot, Will leaned toward me.

"Don't let him bother you," he said.

"He's just creepy." The captain left a bad taste in my mouth. I couldn't wait until we got rid of the Enshi and got the hell back to San Juan. And then *home.*

"You used to think *I* was creepy," Will said. He grinned.

I held his eyes challengingly. "Used to?"

His grin widened. "You don't mind me so much now."

I huffed. "Don't get your hopes up."

Nathaniel appeared around the cabin, glowering. "These men are really awful."

"Why?" I asked.

He shook his head. "They like to *talk*—and we'll just leave it at that."

I had an idea of what he meant by that. I suddenly felt cold and damp and wished I'd brought a hoodie to wear on board. Or even a trash bag.

"Shall we go below?" Nathaniel offered, seeing me shiver.

Will and I agreed, and we all went into the kitchen belowdecks. The room was painted a dull white, with only steel appliances, rust, and something black growing on the walls as accents. The room smelled of mold. I wrinkled my nose disapprovingly. Will sat down at the wobbly kitchen table and I joined him. Nathaniel pulled out a grimy pack of cards from his jeans pocket and laid them on the table as he plopped down on a chair.

"Where'd you get those?" I asked, happy that we had something to do during the trip.

"The first mate gave them to me," he explained, pulling the yellowing cards out and shuffling them. "What shall we play?"

"Poker," I answered.

"No chips."

I raised a finger. "*Imaginary* chips."

He laughed. "All right, then. You in, Will?"

Will nodded and smiled. "Deal me in."

We played a few hands, and Nathaniel kept trying to bet with more imaginary money than he had, which got annoying. Will was pretty good and had a disturbingly effective poker face, but I still destroyed them both. I got bored after a few games and left to go above. Will followed me.

On the main deck some of the crew sat at a small table, two of them smoking fat cigars. I smiled pleasantly when I walked by them and made my way to the stern. When I saw the sun dipping below the horizon, I uselessly willed the ship to go faster. A giant wake streamed behind the boat, and swirling strips of white water danced on the dark surface of the sea. The water was no longer the bright sapphire of the Puerto Rican coastline but a murky blue-black with no end I could see. The Caribbean twilight sun cast fiery golden light on the clouds above as it set. I caught myself searching the horizon for the silhouettes of winged monsters. I had a horrible vision of reapers swooping down us, like the Wicked Witch of the West's army of flying monkeys, tearing us to pieces and taking off with the sarcophagus.

Will stepped up close behind me and laid his hands on the rail on either side of mine, resting his chin on my shoulder. "We'll be fine," he assured me. "This is the scariest part of the night, but we'll make it through." His cheek touched mine inadvertently and my gut did a little flip. I stood frozen like a statue, afraid to move. "Relax," he said, and kissed the back of my neck. His warm touch sent a shiver through my body and I didn't pay much attention to what he said next. "Nothing is going to happen. We're almost there, and we're going to shove that damn box off the ship and it'll be crushed to nothing before it even hits the bottom of the ocean."

I smiled and let out a breath, trying to loosen up. I turned around to face Will, who kept his arms wrapped around me, but his body stiffened. I leaned back against the railing.

"You always say the right things, don't you?" I grinned playfully up at him.

The wind blew through his hair. "I like happy Ellie more than sad Ellie."

"It's going to take more than that to make me happy."

He flashed me a mischievous grin and relaxed. He dipped his head low, but his lips stopped a few inches from mine. "Then what will it take?"

I struggled to breathe and speak at the same time,

staring at his mouth. "You've got a good imagination. I think you could come up with something."

"May I?" he whispered.

I nodded stupidly, unable to articulate a *yes*. His lips brushed mine, lighting tiny firecrackers on my skin. His hands settled on my waist, and he pulled me a little closer to his body.

I heard a scream and Will spun around, releasing me. A second scream tore through my skull. Will threw an arm out to shield me, and I stepped up close behind him.

A body flew through the air and landed on the deck in front of us. When he slid to a stop, I recognized him as one of the crewmen. He was bleeding horrifically from his chest. He sputtered and reached up for me, his eyes wild and bloodshot. My body froze with fear as I watched the man die. I heard another shriek.

We were under attack.

31

MY BREATHING WAS SHALLOW AND RAPID. THE screams grew louder and they multiplied, filling my head. I heard laughter, high and lilting, maniacal, like a clown on crack. I was suddenly lightheaded, and nausea overcame me. I pressed against Will's back, feeling faint.

"Ellie," Will said firmly as he turned to me. "Do you hear me? We need to get our weapons and fight. We aren't at the trench yet."

I said nothing but stared ahead into the blinding glare cast by the ship's lights, which reflected off the mist that was rising from the seas with nightfall. Beyond was darkness and more screams. I heard the *pop-pop* of gunfire and saw white flashes like firecrackers on the other side of the cabin.

Will jumped in front of me and grabbed both my shoulders, his green eyes brightening fiercely. "Snap out of it,

Ellie! If you stay here, you will die and so will everyone else. You can't let everyone die!"

"I need my swords," I said weakly.

"There's my girl," he said, and touched my cheek.

I called my swords. The fading light caught the Enochian etchings running the length of both blades. I took a deep breath and closed my eyes. I believed in myself. I had faith in my power.

We ducked low and darted in through the cabin door. Will lugged the hard gun case out of the duffel bag and flipped it open. Inside were two pistols and a shotgun, along with a lot of ammunition.

"I've never shot a gun before," I said shakily.

"Don't worry," he assured me. "They're not for you." He loaded up and stuck the pistols in his jeans and held the shotgun in one hand.

"But guns won't kill a reaper," I said.

"You shoot enough bullets to destroy the head. It will turn into stone once it's dead."

I gave a slow, understanding nod. "Where's Nathaniel?" I asked, my voice steadying.

Will shook his head and stood up with me. "I have no idea. Probably fighting. He needs these. Are you with me?"

I nodded.

"I need you, Ellie."

"I'm with you."

He studied my face for another few excruciating moments,

his expression hard. "Let's go. People are dying."

I followed him back out of the cabin and up onto the main deck. The cries were chaotic and shrill, flooding my ears. The first thing I saw when I emerged was Nathaniel standing with his back to me, and above him Ivar. Her massive wings spread high and wide, her pale eyes bright like twin full moons embedded deep in her skull. Her power surged around her, whipping her ashen hair wildly about. She backhanded Nathaniel's face, and he crashed to the ground.

"Nathaniel!" Will bellowed and threw the shotgun.

Nathaniel grabbed it, spun around, pumped the shotgun once, and blasted Ivar square in the chest, knocking her back a few steps. She righted herself and stared down at the hole in her rib cage. She looked back up to him and snarled, baring fangs, and the wound closed back up.

"You ruined my dress," she hissed, and stomped toward him.

He pumped the shotgun again, blowing a hole through her shoulder as she jerked her head out of the slug's path, which thumped her body to the side, but she kept coming.

Something *thunk*ed above me, and my head snapped up to see the madly grinning, shark-toothed face of Geir leaning over the roof of the cabin. His wings spread like a canopy over me, and he leaped off the roof and landed between me and Will.

"Thought you could run, eh, Preliator?" he asked, licking

his lips with a devilish hunger. His mouth grinned wider than biology should have allowed.

A rush of courage went through me, and I ran at him, swinging my swords, but he vanished from my sight for a heartbeat. Something pounded into my back and I hit the floor. I flipped over and saw that Geir's hands had transformed into monster claws again. He reached down for me and grabbed me around the throat. His other hand yanked my swords away, and lightning fast, he wrenched me high over his head and slammed me into the cabin wall. He held me too high for my toes to touch the floor, and his claws tightened around my throat. He pressed me harder into the wall until I could barely breathe.

"Where is the Enshi?" he snarled.

When I didn't answer him, he yanked me forward and then slammed me deeper into the wall, the metal crunching. I cried out as pain shot up and down my body.

"Where is the sarcophagus?" he screamed into my face, his yellow eyes blazing. He roared and threw me. I hit the floor hard and slid until I struck the gunwhale. Geir's clawed hand snatched my ankle and dragged me back toward him. He flipped me onto my back, held both my wrists over my head with one hand, and crouched over me, digging his talons into my cheek and throat with his other hand.

A crewman swung a steel rod at Geir, but the reaper slashed with his talons and ripped the poor man's chest wide open. "As I was saying," the reaper said, flicking the points of his needle teeth with his pale tongue. "Even if we have to tear this tin can apart bolt by bolt, we're still going to kill you all."

I wrenched an arm free and punched Geir in the face. He released me and doubled over, hissing obscenities at me. I twisted away from him, but a hand grabbed a fistful of my hair and jerked my head back. I stared into the beautiful, ghostly face of Ivar.

"I've had about enough of you," she growled, her hair flowing around us wildly in the misty ocean wind.

My fear spun into anger and I threw a fist at her, but she grabbed me by the throat, flipped me over her head, and chucked me upside down like a rag doll into the ship's smokestack. The metal clanged and crunched upon impact, and I slid to the deck headfirst, crumpling into a heap. I looked up to see Ivar launching herself toward me, wings spread wide, hands outstretched to grab me, and I saw one of my swords lying between us.

I leaped for it, grabbed the helve with both hands, and swung high. Ivar hissed and dived to the left, but my blade sliced through her wing. She shrieked and lost control, spiraling into the rail. I jumped to my feet as she recovered, and as I raised my sword high and slashed down, her hands caught both my wrists and we were locked in a battle of brute strength.

Ivar snarled like an animal up at me, her corpse blue lips curling back and flashing viper fangs. Her wings spread wide, and I swore as I watched the damaged wing regenerate to perfection. Her power erupted in my face and sent me flying through the air. I landed on my back hard enough to crack the steel surface of the deck beneath me.

"Ellie!" Will cried when he saw me hit the ground. He was battling against Geir, and I lost track of both of them through the hysteria.

"Where is Nathaniel?" I yelled as I climbed to my feet. My fear for his life made me forget about the pain in my back.

Ivar's too-large pale eyes glowed bright white until her pupils nearly vanished, and a cruel smile spread across her lips. "You don't have to worry about him any longer," she sneered as she took a step toward us, her wings wide and blocking out the light. The movement of her wings and swirling wind stirred the hem of her dress at her ankles, and I could see that she was barefoot. "You killed Ragnuk, and I thank you for ridding us of that annoyance. However, I must confess I didn't think you had it in you."

"It's your mistake that you keep underestimating me," I shot back, my grip on my sword tightening. I searched the deck for the other and spotted it lying against the cabin door.

Ivar scoffed. "Don't presume too much, child. Bastian seems to think very highly of you, though. In fact, he even wants to meet you."

"Excuse my lack of enthusiasm," I growled. "The feeling is not mutual."

Ivar pouted. "He'll be so disappointed."

"Bite me," I snapped.

Her lips curved into a sensual, eloquent smile. "I can do that."

She lunged at me, but I twisted around, bolting for my sword by the cabin door. In two long strides I was there, grabbing the hilt with my free hand and lighting it with angelfire as I turned around. Ivar slammed into me and sent us both crashing through the wooden cabin door, splinters flying everywhere. I smashed into a wooden table and Ivar landed on top of me. I shoved a helve into her throat as she gnashed at my face, snapping and snarling like a wolf. Her fingers grabbed at me, pulling at my shirt and hair, her claws slashing away at my skin. My power slammed into her, launching her into the ceiling and filling the cabin with bright white light. Her body crushed the fiberglass; the glossy surface crumbled into chunks and the flaky insides fell like snow, covering Ivar with powder. She flapped her wings and settled gracefully down to the floor. The room was entirely too small for her wings to be spread as wide as they were.

She grabbed hold of my shoulders, swung me into a strung-up fishing net, and then smashed me into a set of shelves. Clutter rained down on me, and I fought my way to the surface, clawing free of the net. Ivar's fingers curled around my shirt and lifted me until I was eye level with her.

"I'm going to enjoy killing you," she sneered. "And when you come back, I'll enjoy killing you again. If the Enshi doesn't eat your soul, I'll gladly eat your heart."

Instead of replying, I stabbed her in the gut with a Khopesh. Her eyes bulged and she dropped me. I pulled the flaming sword out and slashed, but she caught my wrist before my blade could catch her skin, and she hissed, pulling her lips back viciously.

"Wrong move." Her flesh healed shut with only an ugly marbled scar left behind. She lashed her black power at me, striking me across the chest like a whip, and I staggered back. I shook off the blow and saw her lunge for me through the smoky remains of her attack. My own power detonated in a deafening explosion of white and collided with her. It blew her through the cabin, and she crashed through the wall and flew back out on the other side of the deck in a storm of fiberglass and steel.

Ivar hit the deck and climbed shakily to her feet as I stepped through the wreckage of the cabin. Instead of coming for me again, she snapped her eyes to the side, and my gaze followed hers. Will stood there with his hands at his sides.

"William!" she sneered, her voice ringing out over the crashing waves. "So good of you to join us!"

Will said nothing and threw his arms up and fired Nathaniel's two pistols into Ivar's body. Bullets ripped through her chest, spraying blood like confetti, forcing her back. She jerked and screeched as he unloaded both clips into her. When the guns clacked empty, Will dropped the clips, reloaded effortlessly, and began firing again.

A hand fell on my shoulder and I swung a sword. Nathaniel caught my arm. "Hey, it's me."

I breathed a sigh of relief and hugged him. "I thought you were dead."

He shook his head when I let him go. "I'm fine. Are you okay?"

"Yeah." I looked beyond him for Will and spotted him fighting Ivar hand to hand now. Her dress was riddled with bloody holes, but she appeared unharmed. "Where's Geir?" I asked Nathaniel frantically, grabbing his shoulder.

"He must be below."

We rushed past Ivar and Will, and I said a silent prayer for him to be alive the next time I saw him. Nathaniel kicked open the door to the hold. It swung wide and we descended into the dim, greenish-blue light. The dank odor of the room filled my nose, and I heard a faint, raspy whimper from somewhere within the darkness. I strained my eyes and spotted the untouched sarcophagus. But who else was down there?

Nathaniel threw a hand over my chest and I froze. A dark shape rose, and a head swiveled toward us, revealing the shark-mouthed face of Geir, his teeth stained red, his yellow eyes mad like a wild animal's. The light coming in through the door cast a sickly glow across his pale skin and mud-colored wings. Held tightly to the reaper's chest was José, gaping unseeingly at the ceiling, his complexion ashen. A chunk of his throat had been torn out, but the massive wound wasn't leaking nearly as much blood as it should have been. Geir had drunk it all.

"Your Guardian injured me greatly," Geir rasped, glistening blood dribbling from his lips and down his chin. "I needed to feed in order to heal and finish you off, Preliator. I'm much stronger now that I've had a snack."

Overwhelming revulsion made me stagger back on my heels, nearly collapsing to the floor. Geir tossed José's body to the side, but with so much force that the poor man flew twenty feet and crashed into the wall. Geir turned to face us squarely, and I could see that his clothing was shredded and soaked dark with his own blood. The only satisfaction I had was the knowledge that Will had done that to him.

Nathaniel raised the shotgun, but Geir was there in an instant. His monster hands yanked the shotgun away from Nathaniel and chucked it at the wall hard enough to snap the barrel off the stock. He grabbed Nathaniel by the throat and hurled him at the same wall. Faster than my eyes could see, Geir was on top of Nathaniel, throwing punch after punch. Nathaniel ducked, and then Geir's fist plunged through the steel wall of the hull. He pulled it back in and water burst through. The metal had flayed Geir's hands to ribbons, and his blood cascaded into the salt water pouring inside, but the reaper's skin healed quickly. Water rushed into the hold with a thundering noise. The ship was going to sink.

A wave of fury washed over me, crashing heavily. I was

tired of it all. The monster in front of me had slaughtered innocent people only because he could. He'd hurt me, terrified me, hurt Will, who had tried to defend me, killed humans who had tried to defend me when they couldn't even defend themselves. All of this would be over. I'd end it tonight.

"Ellie!"

Will's voice came from behind me. I glanced over my shoulder, not ready for him to interfere. He could sense what raged through me, but I wouldn't let him stop me this time. I could control my power. I could control myself. There was no madness coursing through me this time but only fury in its purest, darkest form. My power spiraled around me, pushing the water at my feet away.

"No." I threw my power at Will and it hit him like a wall, preventing him from coming any closer.

He threw his shoulder into the barrier, but I didn't give him another inch. His eyes, bright in the gloom, met mine, but his gaze was firm, as if he could read my mind and knew it was no use trying to bring me back from the edge. Even if he wanted to stop me, calm me down, it would be impossible. At that moment, as my power pounded on the inside of every last inch of my skin, desperate for release, I was very aware of how much damage I could do to him and everything else on that ship.

"Get the sarcophagus!" Nathaniel roared as he fought off the demonic vir. "Throw it over before Ivar takes off with it!"

Will's gaze left mine at last and he nodded. He bolted to

the wooden box containing the sarcophagus, sweeping it up over his head effortlessly. He ran back up the stairs.

"*No!*" Geir shrieked. He darted away from Nathaniel, but I caught him with my sword in his belly before he escaped. He snarled at me, sharp teeth bared, and grabbed my throat, squeezing hard. His other hand clenched my wrist and pulled my sword from his body as flames of angelfire lapped up his chest. Time slowed, and everything around me blurred except for Geir. He swiped his talons at my face, but I jumped back and swung my swords. The flames slashed through the darkness, casting twisted flashes of light and shadows across our faces. My blades sliced across his belly, but not deeply enough to kill him. I kicked him in the chest as hard as I could and he soared backward, smacking into the far wall.

"Nathaniel!" I shouted.

He turned to me, eyes wild.

"Go help Will! I'll keep Geir busy."

His mouth dropped. "But—?"

"*Go!*"

He obeyed, disappearing from the hold. I spun back to face the reaper, who grinned at me as his belly wounds closed up and scarred within seconds.

"Now it's just you and me, baby," he sneered, his eyes cold yet blinding like sunlight.

I stepped back on my heel, summoning my power. The trawler shivered and groaned.

Geir launched himself toward me, and as I raised my sword, he vanished right in front of me. I swung, slicing through air, and he reappeared to my right. I slashed my other sword at him but met only his disembodied laughter echoing through the hold as his form disappeared into the darkness.

"You're going to die down here, little girl," his voice sneered.

My eyes searched around me, and my heart pounded with fear. If I couldn't see him, then how could I fight him? I let the fury wrap around me, drowning out every distraction, every creak and whine of the ship, the rushing of water, everything but the heartbeat of my enemy stalking me from somewhere in the blackness. I felt none of the uncontrollable bloodlust that had consumed me during my final battle against Ragnuk; instead, my mind was now disturbingly clear as I ached to release my power. Now it obeyed *me*, not the other way around.

I felt energy flicker behind me and I spun like a tornado, swinging the flaming Khopesh up. The blade cut through Geir's throat. He staggered back, spilling blood, gurgling and clutching at the wound. When his skin didn't burst into flames, I knew my strike hadn't been enough to kill him. With a cry, I stabbed my other sword up and under his rib cage, destroying his heart. He collapsed forward onto me, drenching me in his blood. I shoved him off of me, disgusted, and ripped my sword back out. I felt the hook on the back of the blade catch on his rib cage, and things inside ripped and crunched as I wrenched the Khopesh free.

Geir staggered toward me, his face twisting in horror and agony. One hand fell away from his throat and grasped at his torn chest. A dark, brackish flood spread from his wounds, and flames erupted over every inch of him, licking over his body and drowning him in light. His claws swung at me, engulfed in angelfire, until they crumbled into ashes. In moments the rest of his body burned up, his flapping wings vanishing last, until nothing remained of the reaper but ashes drifting in the water rising to my ankles.

I froze. Something heavy settled on me, like a great power, but not my own. It weighed down on me like a thick blanket of snow and just as cold, with an immense strength that seemed to slow down all my senses and even time itself. I turned my head to look behind me, fearful of what I might see, and my body followed my gaze.

A silhouette shaped like a man stood in the hold's entrance at the bottom of the stairs. His black form was etched in the light from the deck, and feathered wings spread wide as if he'd just landed. He stepped closer to me, the light billowing around him so that I could at last see his face. He didn't appear much older than me or Will.

His white wings folded into his back and vanished. His power rolled from him like a storm, but he felt like a black hole, sucking in every last bit of oxygen, so I was left feeling dizzy and ill.

"Hello, Ellie," the reaper said, his voice smooth and cool as chilled butter. "I am Bastian."

32

I STARED HELPLESSLY AT BASTIAN'S HAUNTING face. His smoky black power pulled at mine, like fingers combing through my hair and brushing my face as gently as a flutter of eyelashes. His eyes were the brightest, most unnatural blue I had ever seen, a toxic cerulean. He seemed so familiar to me, as if I had met him before, but I couldn't recall when or where. Even his energy, at a level deep below what I felt on the surface, seemed familiar.

"Red is a good color on you," he said at last.

Bile rose in my throat. I was drenched in Geir's blood. The dirty, salty smell revolted me. I held my breath, desperate to keep from retching in front of Bastian. "Where's Ivar? Where are my friends?"

"Ivar is destroying the angelic vir on the upper decks. They're lost to you now."

No! I wanted to scream, but no words escaped my lips. I cried out and rushed forward, swinging my blade, but a blinding wall of black power hit me all over and launched me back through the air. I crashed into the far wall and climbed to my feet with my arms and legs aching. Bastian's power had bruised my skin and torn the cloth of my shirt, but the pain and wounds vanished in seconds.

"I'm not here to kill you," he said.

I glared. "No? Well, I'm still going to kick your ass."

He watched me, his eyes examining me so thoroughly, I felt like an animal on exhibit at a zoo. "How charming. I am so pleased to finally meet you."

"We've never met before?" I asked, surprised. Then why did I feel certain that I knew him? Surely I'd met him in a past life. His face . . . He was so familiar.

"No, my dear," he said, his voice soft, but I heard him perfectly over the noise of water rushing into the hold, swallowing my shoes.

"So you thought you'd swing by with your buddies and kill us all?" My fingers clenched my sword tighter.

"I'm here for the sarcophagus and that is all. If I kill you now, then all this would have been for nothing."

"Where's Cadan?" I asked. "He decide to sit this one out?"

Something dark flickered in Bastian's smile. "He and I don't quite share the same sympathies."

I studied his face, trying to find any emotion to read, but

he revealed nothing. "Just fight me already!"

His form blurred, and he appeared suddenly right in front of my face. His voice was a whisper, seething with malice. *"I know what you are."*

"What?" I asked without thinking.

Bastian drifted away from me, spreading his white feathered wings wide. "Your very presence breaks all the rules."

My body locked up until I felt like I was about to break. "What are you talking about?" I asked through clenched teeth.

"You hide among the humans you love, and in doing so, you gamble with their lives."

My temper flared. "I'm not gambling with their lives!"

His smile darkened to pitch-black. "Don't be angry. Selfishness is only a side effect of living in this mortal world. It's very human, don't you think?"

"Humans have taught me compassion," I said. "The best parts of me exist because I was taught to love and to be kind. What can you say? That you've killed and tormented only creatures weaker than you?"

That smile faded. "For one so very ancient, you certainly are naïve. Do you think you're better than me? You know even less about me than you do about yourself. Little girl, you are barely any different from me."

And he vanished, blurring from sight. I stared at the space he had just occupied. Was he lying? Did he really know what I was? Fear lapped at my legs in the form of swelling, ice-cold seawater. I shook my head, steadied my nerves, and splashed up to the main deck. I swung around the cabin and spotted Nathaniel just as he hurled the sarcophagus over the side of the boat. My heart leaped for joy—but crashed right back down again when I saw Ivar dive into the ocean after it.

A shadow passed over my head, and I spun around, preparing for attack. Will landed. Spreading out from his back was a pair of ivory wings—*wings!* I staggered away from him in shock. The feathers glistened in the moonlight, pearlescent. They were absolutely beautiful. He looked like an angel towering over me, and his electric green eyes met mine for a brief, terrible moment. He folded his wings above his back and spread them wide again before shakily returning them to his body. I couldn't move, couldn't breathe. All I could do was stare at him as he collapsed to the deck, holding a hand over his chest. When I saw darkness spreading over his shirt, I knew he was badly hurt.

"Will!" I screamed, running to his side in terror. He doubled over and his wings stretched over us, cloaking us in shadow. When I reached for him, he pulled away from me, his face showing more than just his physical pain. I wanted to hit him hard for keeping the fact that he had *wings* from me, but as soon as I saw them, I remembered them as if I'd seen them only yesterday.

He pulled his face away from my hands and shivered. "Don't—"

"Let me see," I said.

His wings shook and shuddered. "I don't want—"

I laid my hand over his and pulled it away from the wound. "Let. Me. See."

He closed his eyes in agony and allowed me to move his hand. It was worse than I thought. Blood leaked from a wound in his chest. I panicked and rolled up his shirt. He grimaced and let out a choked swear. My lips went numb when I got a good look at the extent of his injuries. A hole bigger than my fist had been punched right through the center of his chest. I forced my eyes away when nausea boiled in my gut. He gasped and gagged as if he couldn't breathe.

"My lungs—," he sputtered.

I looked at him frantically, touching his face. "I don't know what to do. I don't know how to help you!"

He grabbed my hand and clenched it tight. "Can't breathe—just wait—"

The glow in his eyes dimmed, and my worst fear whispered in the back of my mind. Was this one of those wounds too severe to heal? "You can't die," I told him. "I can't do this without you!"

"Just wait—," he repeated, closing his eyes and grimacing.

The hole in his chest began to fill in, and his skin started to cover it over. His breathing became less ragged and his hold on my hand loosened. "I said . . . to just wait. . . ."

My smile widened, and relief overwhelmed me. I had completely forgotten about the sarcophagus. I smoothed Will's shirt back down and took a deep breath. "You're okay," I sighed, elated.

"Of course I am," he said in a weak voice. "But I didn't want you to see me like this. I didn't want you to see them— not before you remembered."

There was no time for any questions. Another shadow loomed over us, and I craned my neck back to see Bastian perched on top of the cabin, silently watching Will and me with a blank expression. I heard a great splash behind me as I helped Will to his feet. His wings vanished, and we turned around. Ivar surfaced without the sarcophagus, her soaking-wet hair matted and stringy but one arm hanging limply at an odd angle. I looked more closely, and as Ivar dropped her head back and screeched in fury, I saw why her arm looked so strange. Her shoulder blade was exposed, her arm ripped from its socket, her body torn wide open, and her collarbone stabbing out in plain sight. She held her uninjured hand wrapped across her chest and pulled her ripped-off shoulder back to her body. The muscles and veins strung back together, weaving in and out, pushing out dead flesh and sealing up what was left until she was perfectly healed. Her throat was a deep red, as if someone had grabbed hold of it savagely in order to tear her arm off, but that injury too was fading.

I stared in horror. My eyes found Will, whose hands were covered in blood. An icy-cold feeling rushed through my body. Had *he* done that?

"Surrender, Preliator!" Bastian called from the top of the cabin.

I looked back up, and he stepped off the edge, landing light as a feather on the deck, his wings folding into his back. "You've lost, Bastian!" I shouted. "Geir is dead and the Enshi is at the bottom of the ocean!"

Bastian ignored me and looked at Will. A cruel and subtle smile spread across his face. "So good to see you again, William. I see you're pleased to be reunited with your charge, though it appears to me things have changed between you."

Will stared back, his gaze dark and defiant.

Ivar stepped forward, her face twisted with wrath, but Bastian's power lashed her across the chest. She staggered back, her wings shivering around her in pain and not because of her ice-cold, drenched clothes.

"Leave them," Bastian warned.

Ivar snarled and bared her teeth. "But why?"

"If you kill her now, she will just return. We must wait. Be patient." Bastian's cerulean eyes met mine. "Have no doubt, Preliator, this isn't the end, not yet. The Enshi will awaken and consume your soul."

Ivar's head cocked to one side like a bird's, her soaked, pale hair pouring over her shoulders. "Have you ever watched a soul die?" she asked. "Just wait until you feel your own soul dying."

I stared back at her boldly, but my bravado began to waver when I considered what the Enshi might be able to accomplish.

From the corner of my eye, I caught a flash of silver-gray wings. I staggered and backed into Will as another vir descended to the deck.

Cadan. His opal eyes were on fire as he looked from Bastian to me and back again. His leathery wings gave a shake and folded to his back but didn't disappear.

"A little late, aren't you?" Bastian asked calmly.

Cadan straightened and brushed off the front of his shirt. "Better late than never."

Bastian vanished and reappeared directly in front of Cadan and grabbed hold of his chin. "The repercussions of your . . . act of defiance will be great," he hissed very close to Cadan's face. "I would feel nothing if I killed you."

Their gazes locked until Bastian shoved him away and strode up to Ivar. She stared at Cadan with a strange, hardened expression. Bastian's blinding white feathered wings spread wide, and he took off into the air and vanished. Cadan looked away from Ivar as if her gaze hurt him, his pale-gold hair whipping in the air, his fists clenched tightly. Ivar stretched her wings to take flight and follow Bastian.

"The sarcophagus," Cadan began as he started toward me. "Where is it?"

The next instant Will's sword sliced through the air between us and halted, poised right between Cadan's eyes. Will was exhausted and breathless, but he'd never give up fighting. "One more step and I turn your face into a doughnut."

Cadan stared wide-eyed down the blade. "Pretty sure that sword would turn my face into two pieces, if you want to get technical."

"Only one way to find out."

"Will!" I shouted, grabbing his free arm. "We don't have time for this. Cadan, the sarcophagus is gone. There's no way you can—"

"Good," he said abruptly. "Bastian can't let that thing out."

"What do you care?" I demanded. "You work for him, though it sounds like you might get fired."

He let out a surprising laugh. "If only. Things are a little more complicated than that."

"Save the speech," I said coldly. "The ship is sinking, and we need to get the hell off it."

"I love it when you get assertive," he said with an edge to his voice.

I rolled my eyes, and Will shoved his sword a little closer to Cadan's brow. "Are you done?"

He gave a curt nod. "Quite."

Will withdrew his sword, but he didn't step away from

me. He touched my arm. "We have to go."

"Yeah," I agreed.

"So, the sarcophagus," Cadan said. "It's gone?"

"Nathaniel threw it over," Will said, his voice laced with ice. "Now go."

Cadan stared at him for a long moment before spreading his wings wide. "Then this journey wasn't for nothing." He beat his wings and flew off into the black sky.

Exhaustion consumed me suddenly, and I looked around me, dazedly, at the human corpses—all that was left of the *Elsa*'s crew—littering the deck. The sarcophagus was gone, I was emotionally and physically depleted, and now we were stranded on a sinking ship.

Nathaniel rushed by me. "We need to get the lifeboat down. The ship's going under!"

"Did we make it to the Deep?" Will cried out.

"Close enough!" Nathaniel yelled frantically. "There's no way the sarcophagus could've survived, but we've got to get out of here or we're going down with it!"

Will scrambled for our swords and disappeared into the cabin.

"Gabriel."

The voice was a whisper in my mind, creeping through my veins, through every part of my insides. I felt my winged necklace grow hot and I gaped down at it, pulling it away from my bare skin.

"Will?" I asked. "Is that you?"

"Gabriel," the gentle voice in my head whispered again. *"Close your eyes."*

That was definitely not Will.

The world grew bright very quickly, so bright that all I could do was obey, or else—I knew from deep within—my eyes would burn up in their sockets if I didn't. I threw my hands over my face as the black night lit up as bright as day. I shivered, my eyes squeezed shut as the temperature dropped, and energy rolled across the deck—pure power unlike anything I'd ever felt before. I fell to my knees beneath its onslaught.

"Ellie!" Will's voice called from somewhere around me.

The brightness dimmed enough for me to open my eyes. Ethereal golden-white light beamed out from all around a silhouetted form, like sunlight peeking out from behind clouds. Had Bastian returned? My pulse pounded through my skull as I tried to find my balance, and I stared up in wonder at the thing above me.

A figure came into view: the ghostly shape of a man surrounded by creamy white wings covered in a fine layer of fiery gold, as if the feathers were the color of dawn on a field of newly fallen snow. His head was crowned by close-cropped golden curls, and over his billowing, blinding white robes he wore armor made of gleaming gold. The weight of his power bore down on me like the summer sun, the glory too pure and divine to be real. My lips grew numb, and I couldn't stop myself from weeping.

"Gabriel," the creature said again, his voice smooth as fine wine. "You must not let the wicked seize the Beast. Lucifer must not gain control. There is no price too great to pay to prevent that."

It took me ages to get my voice to work. "Who are you speaking to?"

His beautiful, determined face watched me for moment. He gave a slow nod toward me. "To you."

I shook my head in confusion. "That's not my name. I'm Ellie."

"You are Gabriel," he said. "The left hand and power of God. The Preliator."

I stared up at him. His wings did not move but remained spread wide in all their luminous glory as he floated above me. The revelation of what the mysterious creature said to me hit me like a flood. I couldn't breathe. Couldn't move. I didn't want to believe him, but I knew. . . . Something deep inside me stirred, something bright, something frightening.

He was no reaper. He was an archangel. Like me.

"Who are you?" I asked him at last.

"I am Michael, and I am here to guide you, Gabriel, my sister."

Heaviness settled on me, and I felt my body sag—this frail human body that didn't belong to me. I found myself resenting it, longing for something different, something truly mine and without limitations.

Michael came forward, his wings folding back, and he

reached out a phantom hand to mine. I stared into his face and could almost see right through him. His body was like a sheer veil hung over a summer dawn, his skin glowing from a source of light unseen. I laid my hand on his and felt the magnetic pull between us. On contact, I felt the tremors of electricity; he seemed to be made of pure energy instead of flesh. He helped me stand without touching me. Somehow I felt my body pull forward onto my feet.

"You have work to do, Gabriel. The wicked will retrieve the Beast from the belly of the sea, and you must be there to prevent the awakening. All will be lost if you fail. The Second War is nigh."

"The Beast is the Enshi, isn't it?"

Michael nodded. "Guardian," he boomed, and looked to my right.

I followed his gaze to find Will standing there, gaping at us both in disbelief.

"Guardian," Michael said again.

Finally Will tore his eyes away from mine to stare at the archangel.

"I gave you my sword so that you could protect my sister," Michael said, his face hard as stone. "Nothing more. She is not yours. You belong to her."

Will opened his mouth but said nothing. His eyes shone even brighter than Michael in all his glory.

"Michael!" I called and the archangel turned toward me again. "If you're supposed to guide me, then why don't you speak to me anymore? A long time ago you used to give me orders, tell me where to go. Why did you stop helping me? Did I do something wrong?"

"You've forgotten how to listen."

I rose to my feet, unsure if I fully understood what he said. "Are you the one who keeps sending me here? Every time I die, are you the one who brings me back?"

"You are reborn by your own power," he said. "Our prophets foresaw the coming of the Beast, and you remained in Heaven to train and gain strength for the trials ahead."

"Why do I feel this way?" I asked. "Why do I feel so much anger in battle? How can I be Gabriel if I feel so evil?"

His expression was kind, his sympathy infinite. "The divine were never meant to be mortal, my sister. The emotions you're feeling now are something you were never meant to feel. You have not fallen from grace, for your grace is with you always. You must stay strong, vigilant, and do not forget yourself, or you will never understand your power. Humans are amazing creations, but their ability to hate is as great as their ability to love. Let your humanity become a strength, not a weakness."

"If I spent all that time in Heaven training, then why am I not stronger than before? Why am I not laying waste all my enemies? I will fail if I'm not strong enough!"

His glory wrapped around me in a veil of light and warmth. "God has faith in you. Do not lose your faith in Him."

He vanished, and I was momentarily blinded by the

sudden absence of light. When I could see again, Will's gaze met mine, his eyes wide with disbelief. He reached for me and touched my hair, his gaze falling over every inch of my face. And he fell to his knees before me.

"What have I done?" He closed his eyes and bent his head.

"Will," I pleaded. "Don't—"

"I've touched you in ways I shouldn't have, and I've wanted you—"

"Will." I knelt in front of him and lifted his chin with my hand. His eyes were red and raw. "Hey. It's me, Ellie. I'm still me!"

"But I—"

"Hey! I need you. Don't freak out on me."

"What have I—?"

"Will! I'm Ellie, not some archangel. Not God's left hand, or whatever Michael called me. I'm just me and you're just you."

"How can I ignore this?" His voice cracked with pain as he stared at me, his face full of sadness. "What I've done and felt for you is forbidden. You are—"

"Please, Will," I begged, cutting him off. "I need to figure this out. Please, for me? I'm not really ready to deal with this."

He squeezed his eyes shut again and took a long, labored breath. His jaw clenched tight as he drew himself together again, but he said nothing.

I turned to see Nathaniel, who stared at us, the same

shock flooding his face. "We've got to go."

My head spun suddenly, and I collapsed from exhaustion. Will scooped me into his arms before I hit the floor. I curled into him, giving in, and suddenly all I wanted to do was sleep. Our duffel lay at his feet, much fuller than before. Nathaniel got the lifeboat ready, its stark yellow practically glowing in the moonlight, and he threw the duffel down into its belly. Will carried me down and settled us both gently in the little boat. Nathaniel revved the motor, and as we sped away, I peeked back, shivering from the ocean chill and my wet clothes, watching the *Elsa* sink farther into the Caribbean. Will reached for the duffel and pulled out a heavy, smelly blanket and wrapped it over us. Warmth and exhaustion melted over me as I leaned into him, barely feeling the wind rushing over my head and the sea mist settling on me. I imagined the ocean pressure crushing the Enshi to bits despite Michael's warning until, finally, I fell asleep.

33

WHEN I WOKE, DAWN WAS BREAKING OVER THE horizon and we were pulling into a little lagoon lined with small, colorful homes. Nathaniel stopped the boat at a dock, swung the duffel around his back, and climbed out. Will lifted me, still wrapped in my dusty quilt cocoon, and carried me out of the lifeboat.

A man I couldn't see spoke Spanish from somewhere nearby, and I heard Nathaniel answer him fluently. I peeked out and saw the man who had spoken. He was looking at us strangely, his eyes flickering from us to the lifeboat parked at his dock. He said something else, and that seemed to be the end of it.

Nathaniel leaned close to Will and said, "I told him he could keep the boat if he kept his mouth shut."

I loosened my hands a little from around Will's neck and

let them slip down to my chest as he cradled me. My eyelids weighed a thousand pounds again, and soon I was asleep once more.

I woke again in the bed at the motel, and within moments of my opening my eyes, Will was leaning close to me. I pulled the quilt tighter and leaned toward his warmth.

"Do you want to take a shower?" he asked, brushing the hair from my face.

"No." My voice cracked pitifully. I didn't want to bring up what had happened on the ship after Bastian had left, because I was worried that it hadn't been a dream. But even if it had really happened, what would it mean? It wasn't even conceivable. How could I be an angel?

"We have to leave in an hour for the airport. Nathaniel is returning the truck before we check out."

I examined my blood-caked skin and clothes and decided a shower was a good idea after all. I sat up slowly, zombie-like, and staggered to the bathroom. I shut the door behind me and undressed, turned on the hot water, and climbed in, pulling the curtain shut. The water washed down my body, smearing blood, dirt, and unidentifiable grime. I smelled like fish and blood. My legs gave out, and I slid down the shower wall until I sat at the bottom of the tub and the water poured over my head. I cried.

I heard a knock at the door.

A few moments later, Will called gently, "Ellie?"

I said nothing.

"Do you need anything?"

I was glad he hadn't asked if I was all right. If he had, I might have been too strongly tempted to rip out his tongue.

I heard his back slide down the door and the soft thump as he sat down. "I know how you're feeling," he said.

I stared at the rust-colored water streaking into the drain as the shower splattered me like hot rain.

"We've both felt this a million times before," he continued. "The helplessness, the desolation, the feeling—the *knowing*—that the end is coming. We'll get through this."

"Bastian is still going to come for me," I said at last, my voice empty and dry. "He won't give up."

"Ellie," he said, his voice firmer, "we didn't lose. Yeah, we got pretty banged up, but we won. The Enshi is at the bottom of the ocean. It would take a miracle to keep that thing intact, let alone retrieve it. As far as we know, they wouldn't even know how to open the sarcophagus and awaken it. It's destroyed and it'll never awaken."

"But Michael said that Bastian would get it back."

He was quiet for a moment. "He must be wrong. If he's not, then we will stop Bastian before he awakens the Enshi."

Will's words gave me little hope. Bastian didn't have the Enshi, and we still had a long way to go. Was whatever lay sealed inside that sarcophagus really capable of destroying my soul? I didn't want to die, but I was more afraid of not even passing on. How did Will and Nathaniel deal with knowing they would just end after death? If the Enshi got hold of me, what would it be like to have my soul eaten?

"Ellie?"

I stood up and finished washing my hair. When I stepped out and dried off, I wrapped the towel around me. I opened the door to see Will sitting on the other side, turning his head to look up at me. He stood and faced me, his gaze lingering on the damp cotton towel tucked tightly around me.

"I'm not finished fighting," I said shakily. "I don't want that monster to destroy my soul or anyone else's. I can't let Michael down. No price is too great to pay to prevent that."

Will smiled, and the hope that filled his eyes made the glimmer inside me a little stronger. "It'll be all right," he said.

He edged closer to me, and my back touched the cold wall. Though I no longer felt embarrassment around him, I did tremble the closer he got to me. I wasn't simply attracted to him the way I had been a month before. I was in love with him now, and when he was this close, the thought of him touching my bare skin stirred more than just emotions within me. When his hand touched my arm, a tremor ran through me and I sank deeper into the wall just to hold myself up. I forced out the memory of Michael's warning. I did belong to Will. I loved him and I was his.

"I'll protect you," he said softly into my cheek. "I won't let anything happen to you."

I wanted to believe him and I tried. The horrible image of Ivar's half-torn shoulder flashed across my mind, and I looked away.

"What is it?" His face was full of pain suddenly as he sensed my apprehension in that strange way our centuries-old bond allowed.

I spoke slowly, carefully choosing my words, watching his face for a reaction. "I saw Ivar's shoulder. Did you do that?"

His eyes held mine for a moment, the pause lasting painfully long. He chewed his upper lip and let his forehead rest against the wall next to me before he answered. "Yes."

"You almost ripped her entire arm off. How are we supposed to be things that fight for good if we can be just as terrible as the monsters we fight?"

He closed his eyes and took a breath. "A reaper's power is great. It doesn't matter who we serve, the angels or the Fallen. But it's the way we choose to use it that makes the impact. I serve *you*, my angel, my Gabriel, my Ellie. You're stronger than I am. What I've seen you do is beyond anything I could have imagined."

My heart sank. "Don't tell me that."

"You *will* remember."

"I already scare the hell out of myself," I confessed. "I don't want to scare you, too."

He smiled but just a little. "I'm used to it."

"*I'm* not exactly used to it." An invisible weight pressed on my shoulders, making me tired.

"But we know what you are now, and things will be different. You're Gabriel, bound in human form, the archangel of revelation, mercy, resurrection, and death. There's nothing you can't do."

His words ignited fear in me. I wasn't ready to fully understand what I was, or how to accept it, or what would happen once I did.

"I'm going to take a shower before we go," he said. "In the meantime, think of plenty of imaginary stories to entertain your parents about your up-north adventures with Kate."

I forced my own smile. "Definitely."

I pulled on jeans and a tank top, discarding my towel on the floor. I lay back down on the bed on my side, tucked my knees to my chest, and stared at the wall. I tried my best not to think about the night before, but I felt horrible for the poor crew of the *Elsa*. Because of our task, because of me, they were all dead. José's blank face stared back at me when I closed my eyes. A flash of a different vision—one of my own body clutched in Geir's monster hands—struck me, sending shivers all the way down to my bare toes. Will had promised me that my full strength would return along with my memory, but I was afraid that it would come all at once, traumatizing me, damaging me. In that last battle, I'd been able to control the other side of myself that my power had created. But if that was only a fraction of what I was capable of, then it was possible that I wouldn't be able to control all of it. I wasn't sure I could handle the truth about my past and what I was meant for. It seemed far too simple: kill some reapers, die, live again, kill some reapers, die—lather, rinse, repeat. . . .

What if that wasn't *it*? What if there was something more? What if I really was an angel—Gabriel, the archangel, God's left hand?

What Mr. Meyer had said to me the last day I saw him echoed through my mind: *"Life is going to test you in ways it never has before. Don't let your future change the good person that you are or make you forget who you are."*

The bathroom door opened and Will stepped out, clad only in jeans. As he brushed past me, I caught his clean scent and sat up, my half-wet hair in tangles. He rummaged through his bag for a dark chocolate tee that brought out the green in his eyes and shrugged it down over his lean torso. The idea that it was forbidden for me to touch him the way I wanted to and for him to touch me was absurd. It was impossible not to want to explore every last inch of him. He sat down on the edge of the bed to tug on a pair of socks, then his shoes. He turned his head to look at me as he slipped the chain of his crucifix over his head and tucked it into his shirt.

I crawled forward and knelt beside him on the bed. I wasn't anything close to the infallible, perfect vision of the angel Will had told me about. I felt like a girl sitting next to a boy who I cared for more than anything else. Just a silly girl who liked shopping and eating ice cream. This whole thing was too beyond me, too out of my control. A few months before, I hadn't even been sure that God existed, but now people were talking about Him as if He and I were old pals. How do archangels behave? Would I have to stop swearing? Stop watching horror movies? What else would I have to give up, if I had to give up anything at all? I kind of lied a lot. That wasn't angelic in the least. Was it possible for me to go on with my life as normal knowing what—*who*—I was? I didn't want to feel different. I didn't want anyone to treat me as if I were different. I wanted Will to look at me the same way he always had. I didn't want him to look at me as if I were more of a freak of nature than I already was. I couldn't handle it, damn it, and I sure as hell wasn't going to stop saying *damn* and *hell*.

"You about packed?" Will's breath was cool and minty from his toothpaste. The dampness of his hair brought out its maple shine, and it was tousled wildly from vigorous drying with a towel.

"Yeah," I said. "I didn't bring much. This wasn't exactly a vacation, so . . ." I trailed off.

He smiled crookedly. "Sorry about that. Maybe one day."

"Are you promising me a real vacation someday?" Hope fluttered through me, giving my words a lilt.

"Maybe," he said with an edge to his voice.

"With horses?"

"Maybe."

He wrapped a hand around my cheek, stroking the corner

of my lips with his thumb as softly as if a feather were brushing against them. My pulse quickened, and something fluttered through my chest.

"I told you I wouldn't let them kill you," he whispered. Then his eyes changed suddenly and he took his hand back, turning away from me.

I frowned, climbing off the bed to walk over to the dresser, and I turned around to face him. My fingernails tapped impatiently on the cheap wood. My confusion over how Will felt about me had distracted me from the horrors of the night before and what was to come. I couldn't help thinking that it was actually Bastian who had prevented my death—but, of course, only so he could kill me later. He had had the perfect chance to finish me off in the hold of that ship, but he hadn't even tried. I knew Bastian was actually trying to figure out a way to get the Enshi back, awaken it, and destroy my soul so I could never be reborn again. I couldn't let that happen.

"What's wrong?" Will asked.

The question was funny since there was absolutely nothing wrong with me. I should have asked what was wrong with *him*. "Do you think Bastian will find more thugs to do his dirty work, since we killed most of them off?"

He nodded. "I would imagine that as word gets out among the demonic reapers of what Bastian is trying to accomplish, more will flock to him. There's no telling what sort of monsters he will find."

"I'm afraid of Bastian," I confessed. "But I'm prepared to fight him."

He stood up from the bed and walked toward me. "I know you are." He slid a tentative hand around my waist, but he didn't pull me closer, or hold me tightly. His hand was just—agonizingly—there. I wanted to wrap my hands around his neck and pull him down to kiss me, but I could see the fight in his gaze, feel it in the rigidity of his body. Was he afraid to touch me?

The front door swung open—Will and I sprang apart—and Nathaniel appeared, looking more tired than I had ever seen him. Dark circles rimmed his lower eyelids, and his face was white as a ghost. I wondered if he had eaten anything since his injuries the night before. "I've checked us out and the cab's here. Time to go."

He gave us a nod before leaving the room again. When he shut the door, I realized I hadn't breathed since he'd opened it.

"We should get going," Will said.

As he stepped around me, I held a hand to his chest. "Will. Was that really Michael back on the ship? Was what he said to you true?"

His gaze fluttered away for a moment. "That was the angel who came to me centuries ago. The one who told me to protect you."

"You recognized him?"

He nodded. "Being mortal for so long must have made you

forget. You're drifting further away from who you really are."

"Do you believe that?"

He stepped away from me and ran a hand through his hair.

"Please don't let that be a yes." I groaned.

"We should get out to the taxi."

"So that's it, then? You're just going to shut me out and treat me like a leper after what you found out about me?"

"That's not what this is about."

"It's not?" I snapped in challenge. "You look at me and I know you want to touch me, but you hold back. How does knowing what I am change things?"

"Michael gave me a warning. I don't know how to explain it to you."

"That's because you can't. I accepted what you are when you told me. Why can't you do the same for me?" The color of his eyes flashed, and I could tell he was getting angry, but it felt like he was angry with himself and not me.

"Ellie, it's not about what I want and think. You are an archangel."

"Do I look anything like Michael?" I asked. "Look at me. No wings, no glow, no anything." I took both his hands and set them on my hips. "This body is human, Will, solid and warm, and I know you can feel that." I squeezed his hands when he tried to withdraw. I stepped up close to him and tilted my head back as our bodies touched. "I'm just a girl with a few weird things about me, but all you can see is a girl—the same girl you've known for centuries. The same girl you fight for. The same girl you've kissed. I'm no different. In another world I may be who Michael said I am, but right now, right here, with you, I'm just Ellie. I don't care what he said to you—I just care about right now."

He gazed down at me, his lips parted as if he wanted to say something, but he remained silent. Then he took his hands away and stepped back, his gaze falling away.

"You're acting like a dumbass," I said.

He stopped and stared at me, and ran his hand through his hair. He seemed shocked. I almost laughed. I'd give him something to be really shocked about.

In a single long stride, I swept up to him, stretched to the tips of my toes, cupped his face with both of my hands, and kissed him fiercely. He stiffened at first, and as soon as he melted into me and his fingers wrapped around my waist and tugged at the band of my jeans, I let him go and continued past him, refusing to look back.

I'd let him think about that for a little while.

34

LAUREN MET US AT THE DETROIT METRO AIRPORT.
She seemed especially overjoyed that Nathaniel had made
it home in one piece. She dropped Will and me off at my
house on her way home. Will wished me luck before disappearing to my roof, and I went inside to face my parents.
My mom was cheerful and eager to hear my stories from
the trip. Of course, I fed her sugarcoated lies with a cherry
on top. I accomplished this more easily than I'd thought I
would, but telling my parents the truth would have gotten
me locked up in a psych ward. It was all just too terrible and
strange—I was doing them a favor by keeping them in the
dark. I prayed my parents would never find out how much
I'd lied to them in the past couple of months, but in my heart
I knew that I had bigger things to worry about in my life

than household rules and curfews.

I called Kate to thank her for covering for me and, consequently, had to explain to her many times over that nothing had happened . . . at least not what she *thought* had happened, anyway. I'd have to do this all over again when I saw her in class on Monday.

I felt too restless to change into my pajamas and go to sleep. Instead, I tugged on a sweater over a pair of jeans, climbed out my window, and scaled the roof to where Will was sitting. He watched the sky serenely, his arms folded over his knees. He peeked over at me as I crawled up to sit beside him.

"So—is this what you do when you're sitting up here by yourself?" I asked, playfully nudging his shoulder. "Stare at nothing?"

"Among other things," he answered. "I don't usually think this much. Keeping a lookout keeps me preoccupied."

I studied his face for clues, but his gaze was soft and without worry. "What are you thinking about?"

"Too much."

A chilly breeze rushed through my hair. "Care to elaborate?"

He took in a slow breath. "I don't know how to handle this."

"We both learned a lot about each other last night. What do you say we just call it even?"

He almost smiled, but he caught himself. "I suppose that's true."

"Why didn't you tell me you had wings?"

"I was afraid of scaring you," he confessed.

I frowned. "You know, for someone who believes in me so much, you really have no faith in me at all."

"That's not what I've meant to make you feel," he said. "I guess I'm a walking contradiction. I'm not perfect."

"You told me that you're my servant, yet you decide what I ought to know. You can't control me like that, Will."

"I don't want to control you, Ellie. I just want to do the right thing and what's best for you."

"How would you know what's best for me?" I asked sharply. "You're not me. You have no right to make decisions for me."

"Ellie—"

"Why couldn't you have been up front with me in the beginning? I'm a big girl. I can handle it."

"Right." He almost laughed. "Tell you everything the first day: 'So, my name's Will. You don't remember me, but we've known each other for five hundred years. You hunt monsters and I'm one of them, but I'm also your friend. Oh, I can fly, too.'"

"Will," I said sadly. "Okay, you have a point, but you should have told me these things a little sooner. I shouldn't have had to find out the way I did. It was like a slap in the face. That shocked me way more than it would have if you had just been more honest."

"You're right," he said. "I'm sorry. No more secrets."

"Swear?"

"I swear."

I smiled and stood. "Show me. Show them to me."

He watched me curiously. He knew what I meant. "Why?"

"I want to see them."

He climbed to his feet. "As you wish." He took off his shirt and his wings appeared, spreading wide, their ivory pearlescence shimmering in the moonlight. I reached out to touch them and he shied away, almost as if in embarrassment. A feather fell and drifted away in the breeze.

"What's wrong?" I asked. "Don't be silly. I'm not going to yank on them."

He smiled weakly and looked away from my face. "I know. I just . . . I hate them. I don't want to be anything like Bastian and the others. I try so hard to distance myself from the rest of my kind, but these wings remind me that I'm a monster."

Sadness washed over me. I couldn't stand seeing that he hated himself so much. "You're not a monster. You are an angel, not me. My guardian angel."

His eyes lifted to meet mine and he said nothing. I held a hand out to touch one wing, and the softness of the feathers startled me. I'd felt bird wings before; Kate had had a parrot up until a couple of years before, but its feathers had been stiff and slick and there was a funny, oily smell to them. Will's were soft and delicate, and the scent brought memories of a warm, golden dawn to my mind. I ran my fingers down the length of the feathers, and the wing quivered beneath my touch.

"I missed them," I said softly. "They're so beautiful."

"Do you remember them now?" His voice was barely more than a fragile breath.

"Yes." My gaze returned to his, and he smiled ever so slightly. I wanted to do nothing more than curl up in his arms. "This is why I don't think I'm an angel. If I were, shouldn't I have wings like Michael?"

"You're a mortal angel," he suggested. "You can't shape-shift like a reaper. Your body isn't an angel's body either, but you have their power. Do you remember how ghostlike Michael was, as if he were only half here, as if he couldn't completely enter the mortal world? Maybe that's also why you're reborn into a human body. Your true form—your arch-angel form—can't exist here."

"Perhaps," I said. I was a mortal angel. Was there a way for me to become who I really was? My true form? Will once had told me that a powerful relic could help angels and the Fallen come to the mortal plane, but what if something like that wasn't really lost to the world? If the Grigori were out there somewhere, the keepers of angelic magic and the gates between worlds, they might know of a relic that could restore my true form. What if things more terrible than the reapers, wicked or divine, could walk the earth among us, like the extinct Nephilim?

"Will, why do you keep so much from me?" I ran my hand down his arm, tracing the beautiful tattoos with my fingertips. I had a clear memory of myself inking his skin centuries before in a warm candlelit room, whispering a prayer in a language long lost to me, and it brought a smile to my face.

"Because I'm an idiot," he confessed. "I was wrong to judge you. I didn't think you were strong enough to take in everything at once, but that was stupid. You have more strength in you than I've ever seen in anyone, and I don't mean how hard you can hit. I mean the strength you have to keep doing this without giving up. You might want to, some days, but you never do."

"What about you?" I asked. "You stay by my side day and night and take the hardest hits of them all. Why, Will? Why have you stayed with me all these centuries? You watch me die again and again, yet you never leave. You keep trying to save me, even though you know I'm doomed. All because some angel told you to? Come on. No more secrets, you said. Tell me."

He didn't answer me, but his chest rose and fell with quicker breaths.

"Why would you do it?" I asked earnestly. "Why would you risk nothingness after death for me? You can't go to

Heaven, and you'll never know peace because of that. You'll only ever live this awful, wretched life of fighting. You could have so much more."

"That's not true," he said. "I don't need to go there to find peace. I've found peace with *you*, Ellie, in between the fighting and the years when you aren't with me. You've brought me peace."

His words made my heart spin, and I fought hard not to cry. I watched his face carefully before I spoke. "Why did you kiss me?"

His expression froze in place, as if he were determined not to reveal anything in his expression. "I thought all that would have been obvious."

"That wasn't a straight answer." His eyes flickered away and back to mine indecisively. "Is it supposed to be something I have to remember on my own?"

He studied my face intensely, his gaze locked on mine instead of looking away again. "No."

"Then why—?"

"I hate . . . ," he started, his shaking voice trailing off. "I hate when you die. It destroys me. I know I have no right to be so upset, because I'm not the one losing my life, but it breaks me apart inside. I'm not very good with words, and I don't know how to explain to you how I feel. I get lonely when you aren't with me. I miss you. And every time you die, a little piece of me dies with you."

I wasn't sure what to say to him. I couldn't imagine that

I was a source of comfort to him as he was to me. I could see his hands trembling, and he stood so tensely that I thought he might shatter at any moment. I stroked the back of his neck with my hand as I tried to soothe him.

"I wish I could do better," he confessed. "I wish I could save you, but I can't."

"You've saved me countless times," I said. "You saved me on the ship just last night."

"But I've failed you too," he said urgently. "I've watched you fall so many times and been unable to do anything to save you. I don't know how many more times I can watch you die, Ellie." His gaze fell away. "Forgive me. I shouldn't be saying this to you."

"No," I said, shaking my head. "I'm sorry I make you believe that you can't tell me how you feel. That's not how I want it to be between us. Please, just be honest with me?"

He leaned forward, touching his cheek to mine, making me completely forget whatever I had just said. I closed my eyes and leaned into him as his skin brushed mine and his hand touched my waist. His other hand cupped my cheek and his thumb stroked my lips. His wings lifted high over both of us, shielding us from the cold air.

"When Ragnuk killed you, I looked for you everywhere," he said into my cheek. "But you didn't come back. For decades I looked for you, terrified the angels were punishing me for letting you die alone. I thought that you'd never come back to me—that I'd lost you forever."

The backs of his fingers traced down my arm delicately, as if I were made of glass. His lips softly pressed just below my ear, warming my neck. "And when you came back, when I saw you for the first time in so very long . . . I'd never been so happy in my life."

"I'll always come back to you," I promised as a warm flood rushed through me.

"I love you, Ellie," he breathed, his words lighting my skin on fire, and something inside me disintegrated, leaving a rushing feeling behind. "God, I've always loved you."

I turned my face into his, desperate to meet his eyes, and when I did, centuries' worth of memories of his face flashed across my mind, and of everything he had sacrificed for me, of all his blood that had been shed, of all the torment he had endured for me. His expression was so stoic, so hardened, but his eyes told me everything. They always gave him away.

"Will," I said, unable to form any other words on my lips but his name.

His smile was small and delicate, and his shoulders eased as if a weight had been lifted from them. He leaned further into me, his strong embrace engulfing me. My heartbeat quickened and thrummed stronger. "All this time," he breathed. "I've always loved you and never said a thing."

He kissed me hard and folded his arm around the small of my back, pulling me even more closely in to him. I wrapped my own arms around his shoulders and felt his other hand on my waist. I drew a nail down his biceps and the muscle trembled reflexively beneath my touch. He broke away and his lips grazed my jaw. I shivered and pulled him closer to me.

"Don't forget that I'll *always* love you," he whispered against my lips, rubbing the tip of his nose to mine. "Don't forget."

I nodded and reached again for his lips, needing them more than I needed air to breathe. He kissed me again, deeper this time, luxuriously slow. His hands moved up from my back and slid through my hair to cradle my head.

He ended the kiss, folded his wings back, and rested his forehead against mine. Emotion flooded through me and I said nothing, finally understanding what he had just said to me. I knew in that instant that he was saying good-bye to his love for me. He pulled away, and his fingertips trailed along my arm, as if to make the moment last just a little longer.

As he stepped away from me, his eyes were still that striking emerald, and I prayed the color would never fade. It took everything I had not to run to him and hold him close to me, to feel any part of him, to stare at him in wonder. I didn't know what to do—didn't know if I should have said something back.

"But my love for you is wrong," he whispered. "I can't have you. Not this way."

Something invisible stabbed me in the gut. "Are you really doing this?"

"You're a holy being. I can't touch you. I can be with you

every day as your Guardian because it's my duty, but I can't touch you the way I ache to. This isn't what Michael intended when he asked me to protect you. It's dangerous for us both if we get too close."

I shook my head and fought back tears, unable to say anything.

"Other Guardians have died fulfilling their duty to you long before I came along," he said, touching my cheek, my hair. "I will die for you one day."

"Don't say that," I begged. "Will, I'm in love with you. You're the only one who understands what I go through every day, the only one I can share this world with. You're my best friend, and I can't take it if you're going to shut me out like this."

He closed his eyes, squeezing them tight. His hands balled into fists and his wings gave a shudder. I felt like I was dying inside.

"You can't love me," he said, his voice pained. "And I can't love you either. You're not mine to love."

"I *am* yours—"

"Ellie—"

"No!" I shouted, tears stinging my eyes. "You can't get this close to me and then push me away."

"I have to." His wings unfolded, moonlight gleaming off their feathers, and he jumped in the air. As I stared up at him, he flew away and disappeared into the woods behind my house, letting me know how different we truly were with that last image of him.

Anger rushed through me. I wanted to follow him and smack him harder than I'd ever hit anything before in my life. But I was too tired and too emotional to do anything. And I didn't want to fall off my roof. I stared straight after him and let out a long breath, so my next word had no trace of rage. "Coward."

35

ON TUESDAY MY MOM CALLED ME INTO HER OFFICE
as soon as I walked in the door after school. I prepared for a
lecture over a progress report one of my teachers might have
sent home, but something in her face when I entered told me
she was way more pissed than she should have been over a
bad grade.

"Come sit down, Ellie," she said coolly. Her calm voice was
too wrong coming from such an angry face. It petrified me.

I sat down in the chair across from her desk. I was pretty
sure I was about to die. "What's up, Mom?"

"You'll never guess who I ran into while I was grocery
shopping today."

Names spun through my head, but I tried to make it look
like I wasn't thinking too hard. My body locked up with fear.

"Kate's mom," she said. "How could you do it, Ellie?

How could you lie like that?"

"I . . ." I didn't know what to say. To save the world? To save my soul? I had to do what I had to do, but I could never explain it to her. She could never understand.

She folded her arms over her chest. "That was one hell of an extravagant lie. And getting poor Kate to lie *for* you? Not to mention you made a fool out of me when I thanked her mom for taking you up north with them. It was very embarrassing when she had no idea what I was talking about."

It was almost impossible to get my lips moving enough to form words. "I'm sorry."

"Yeah, I don't think that cuts it, Ellie," she said with a dark edge to her voice. "Where'd you actually go? Were you with a boy? Landon?"

I closed my eyes tiredly. "No. I was with Will."

She didn't respond at first. "That boy in college? Your tutor?"

I felt so heavy in my seat, so heavy I just wanted to lie down. "Yes."

My mom stood and leaned over the desk. "You're *seventeen*! What were you thinking? I don't even know how to react to this. I honestly don't know what to say to you."

"I'm so sorry," I said, even though I knew she didn't want to hear it. "There's just a lot going on in my life right now and I don't really know how to deal with it all. I've made a lot of mistakes."

"Come to *me*," she said. "It's my job to help you when you

need it. Most of the things you're going through right now I've survived. School, boys, friends, mean girls. You tell me that you're fine and that I should trust you, but how can I when you've lied to me like this, Elisabeth? I can't be your mother if you won't let me into your life."

I stayed silent, knowing that anything I could say wouldn't justify how much I'd hurt my mom. She might never have had to deal with fighting soul-eating monsters, but I was facing all those other things too in one way or another.

She collapsed back into her chair and pressed a hand to her forehead. "Are you two intimate? Did you sleep with him?"

"No, Mom," I said. "No, we didn't, I swear. But would it be so terrible if we had?"

When her eyes met mine, the moment was intense and I refused to look away first. "I know you're at the age where you're going to start experimenting and there's nothing I can say or do to prevent it. Just, please, for the love of God, when you do, be safe."

"I will."

"You're grounded," she said exhaustedly. "I don't want you going anywhere with Will. I can't prevent you from seeing him, because I think it's wrong to try to control you and prevent you from finding your own way through life. But you have to understand that he is, technically, an adult, Ellie. If you're going to be seeing him, it'll be under my roof and under my supervision."

I wanted to protest, but I knew how lenient her restrictions were. She could have banned me from seeing him altogether and she had every right to. I wasn't a bad kid. I wasn't wild. I wasn't into drugs; nor was I promiscuous. I just had a terrible responsibility and I didn't know how to balance that with a normal life. I didn't know if that was even possible.

My mom dropped her hand and looked at me finally. "I'm not going to tell your father that you lied, because, frankly, I'm quite sure he'd kill you. You need to be punished, not murdered, so we'll handle this, you and I. No parties, no Movie Night, no car, no phone, no hanging out with your friends for a month. *At least.* I'm taking your keys, and I'll be driving you anywhere you absolutely have to go. As soon as school is out, you're to be inside this house until you leave for class the next morning. God, I don't know what's with you lately. The drinking, the lying, the poor grades . . . How do you expect to get into Michigan State with grades like that? And I want to talk to Will. I want to get to know him if he's your first serious boyfriend. You have to clue me in on your life, Ellie. Help me out here."

I nodded slowly, clutching the winged pendant around my neck for courage. I wished I could tell her everything, and I wanted to cry because I couldn't. Bastian's words burned through my heart. Was I really gambling with my family's and friends' lives by keeping them so close to me? Were they targets? Did I put them in danger? Could I give them up if I had to? I'd completely forgotten that my mom and I could really talk. Considering how many times I'd almost lost my life in the last few months, I wanted to feel close to her again. I didn't want anything to happen to her because of me. "I love you, Mom."

"I love you too, baby," she said. "I really do. I want you to be okay. The rest of your choices are up to you. I hope to God you make the right ones."

"This probably won't make you feel any better," I began, "but—I'm in love with him. I am." It felt right saying it, knowing that I'd felt this way for centuries but had been too much of a damn fool to see it.

She stared at me for what seemed like hours. "Does he love you back?"

"Yes," I said without hesitation, and held my mom's gaze confidently. "I don't expect you to understand how far he's gone to demonstrate it, but I promise you there's no limit to what he'd do for me—he's shown that again and again. I know I've made some terrible mistakes and hidden things from you, but this is something you have to really trust me on. It's the only thing I'm sure about in the mess my life has turned into."

Her gaze fell to my winged necklace between my fingers. "Is he the one who gave you that?"

"Yes."

She stared at the pendent for too long before she spoke. "If you say you're in love with him, then I believe you. Please understand, however, that at your age very few loves ever last. You don't know if he'll just decide to leave you one day. Keep that in mind, okay?"

I maintained an iron resolve, because I knew in my bones Will wasn't that type of guy. If he had stuck by my side for five hundred years, risked his life and his soul for me, then it would take a lot for him to just walk away. He was my Guardian, my guardian angel.

When the first snow fell a few nights later just before midnight, I sat on the roof of an office building with Will by my side. I conceded that I'd lose fun nights with my friends as part of my punishment, but hunting was something I couldn't give up. I pulled the neck of my sweater higher to my chin when the chill of winter bit at my skin. Not even the Grim could keep the freezing temperature away.

"I hate snow," I grumbled. "It's so pretty, but why does it have to be *cold*?"

Will laughed softly. "It's a necessary evil."

I frowned. "So where is our *un*necessary evil?" I asked, referring to the reaper we had been following.

His eyes scanned the dimly lit and nearly empty parking lot below us. Grayish orange streetlamps dotted the lot in a grid, but they revealed no monster.

"This is where he killed last night. He should be here again."

Reapers were truly creatures of habit. Will was no exception, although his habits were: fight reapers, drive me crazy, sit on my roof, eat when I'm not looking, fight reapers, drive me crazy . . .

A man dressed in a black pea coat exited the building, jangling his keys as he walked to his vehicle. He whistled a tune, happy to be heading home after working so late. As if on cue, a dark shape the size of a minivan lumbered out of the darkness. The man was completely oblivious to the reaper's hidden presence.

Will and I hopped off the building, landing two stories below with little more than the bend of our knees. I eased toward the man and stood between him and the gigantic ursid reaper. The monster's black eyes found me, and he licked his lips. When he noticed that I was staring right at him, he tilted his head curiously as if he didn't know me. That was a shocker.

The businessman noticed me. He dropped his keys in a fright. "What the—?"

"Just drive home," I said coolly. I tightened my grip on my swords.

The man's gaze fell to my blades and his mouth opened dumbly at the same time.

I glared at him. "Get. In. Your. Car."

He scrambled, ducking for his keys and darting to the driver's-side door, muttering something under his breath that sounded a lot like "Crazy . . ."

As he drove away, the reaper growled. He stepped toward me, his talons scraping the delicate layer of snow on the pavement. Flakes stuck on his muzzle and caught the tips of the thick, inky black hair on his back. The reaper backed away from me in a circle, creeping toward the darkness he thought would conceal his body. Since I had scared off his intended victim, he must have decided I'd make a tasty replacement. Idiot.

He launched himself at me, springing a dozen feet in the air, claws outstretched. I blurred by him, igniting my swords with angelfire, as he landed on the cold pavement. I twisted and plunged a sword into his ribcage. The flames died as I released the helve and jumped back. He roared, rocking my brain, and staggered on his feet until he collapsed, wheezing painfully. He looked shocked that I had seen him coming.

He curled his back and used his mouth to yank my blade out from his side. He spat it out and growled. He vanished for a heartbeat, and I stepped back on my heel, waiting for him to reappear. His face flashed in front of mine, and I shoved my hand onto his muzzle, grabbing his nose as his jaws gnashed at my head. I forced him back as he thrashed his head, and I lifted my remaining sword and thrust upward. The ursid twisted to one side and my sword plunged into his shoulder instead of his neck. He wrenched his muzzle out of my grip and roared furiously into my face. I yanked my sword back and kicked him in the chest, sending him flying. He hit the pavement and slid in the fine layer of snow until he came to a stop and climbed to his feet. He gave his shaggy coat a shake, sending snowflakes falling to the ground.

I summoned my power, and it swallowed me in white light. The ground thrummed beneath my feet and my power rolled through the air, melting the snowflakes before they hit the pavement. The streetlamp behind me let out a low, metallic groan, creaked, and bent to one side, shaking free a dusting of glittering white flakes. My skin felt as if it were stretching as more energy leaked from me in controlled waves.

The reaper hissed and turned his face away from the bright light, baring his massive canines. He lifted his dark gaze to mine. "You're no vir. How do you have such power? Who are you?"

I stepped up to him, my power swirling around me, and I straightened my other sword, poising the flaming blade at his skull. I stared intensely at him, my gaze colder than the winter air. "I'm the Preliator."

Acknowledgments

Mom, you're more amazing than you'll ever know. I would be lost without you. Dad, Tara, and Ashley, I love you guys. Danielle, Mike, Janet, and Tom Pulliam for being a wonderful second family and always giving me a home away from home. My agent, Elizabeth Jote, for being the first person to love this book and really believe in how far it could go. Thank you for helping me make my lifelong dream come true and for working your butt off to make me a better writer. My editor, Sarah Shumway, for your faith and patience, and for knowing just what to do every time. A special thank-you to Katherine Tegen and the rest of the Katherine Tegen Books crew for all your support and hard work. Thank you to my horseback riding trainers, Kim Carey, Sheila Tobaczka, Melissa Hirt, Nancy Whitehead, and Julia Houle, who have taught me discipline, patience, and above all to love what I do and have fun doing it. Leah Clifford, a.k.a. "the other reaper girl." What can I say? You kept me sane through the summer of 2009 and beyond. Thank you for being such an amazing friend and all-around badass. Kody Keplinger, you rock. Write Nights, good music, stupid jokes, cute boys . . . I am so glad I randomly asked you one day if you liked chicken pot pies. Even though you said no (and I forgive you), it was one of the best questions I ever asked. Sarah J. Maas, Amy Lukavics, and Kaitlin Ward for being great friends and such talented writers. Love you guys. Eleanor Boyall and Robert Truppe, you were my incredible first beta readers. This book would still be a first draft without your guidance. I'll carry what I learned from both of you forever. My friends in Purgatory on AbsoluteWrite, thank you for many hours of great laughs and for your support. My English teachers throughout middle school and high school for reading my weird stories always encouraging me. Everyone on deviantART and PI who supported my writing and art. I've made some awesome friends. Another special thank-you to Yue Wang, who created such brilliant artwork for this book. Your talent astounds me. This is a long shot, but here's a shout-out to the girls of BTRS and PTSRS, wherever in the world you are, especially Alyssa and Becka. I miss staying up past five A.M. writing with you. If by some twist of fate you happen to pick this book up and recognize those acronyms and your names, look me up. Lisa, Mattie, and Teagen, you're the most amazing group of girls I've ever known. The boys of the Sigma Kappa chapter of ΔKE, thank you for a million wild times and for being (mostly) good to Smiles. Kyle, you're my greatest inspiration. I love you. PS: I'm not sorry that I whomped your ass at MarioKart the day we met. PPS: I think I officially just got the last word.

Angelfire

The Angels of Heaven, Hell, and Earth

Archangel
The seven archangels are the most powerful and highest order of angel in Heaven. They are closest to God and perform the most important tasks, such as being the commander of Heaven's army, the messenger, and the healer, and ferrying souls to their final destinations. Their names are Michael, Gabriel, Uriel, Raphael, Zerachiel, Raguel, and Remiel.

Soldier Angel
The soldier angels perform various minor tasks but are mostly trained as warriors in Heaven's army to protect it from demonic threats.

Grigori Angel
The Grigori are angels who joined Lucifer during the First War. After Lucifer's defeat, God believed that some of them were not truly wicked and could be rehabilitated. Instead of being damned and joining the Fallen, the Grigori were bound to Earth to guard and watch over the humans they became so jealous of in the first place. One day, they may be allowed to return to Heaven, and they cling to that hope.

The Grigori have four Cardinal lords, the elemental Watchers, who rule over the quadrant points of Earth. Their names are Formalhaut, Regulus, Aldebaran, and Antares, representing the North (winter), South (summer), East (spring), and West (autumn). They are the keepers of angelic magic and medicine, and they represent the spirit of their quadrant's element.

Fallen Angel

After Lucifer's defeat in his war against Heaven, the most wicked of his allies were damned and exiled to Hell where they became the Fallen. Lilith, Lucifer's Right Hand, became queen and lover of the then-archangel Samael. When Samael fell, he joined Lucifer as his Left Hand.

The Reapers of Earth

The reapers are descended from angels, both Fallen and Grigori. The maternal side of a reaper's lineage is typically dominant, so if a reaper's father is angelic and its mother is demonic, then the offspring will typically be demonic.

The demonic typically reside in the dimension parallel to the mortal plane called the Grim. All reapers, the Preliator, and some psychics have the ability to move easily from the mortal world and into the Grim. While in the Grim, they are invisible to anyone in the mortal world, but it is not true the other way around. Those in the mortal world who are sensitive to the Grim may hear and/or sense reapers within the Grim, but will not be able to see the creatures unless they cross over.

Angelic Reapers

Angelic reapers are descendants of the offspring of Grigori angels. They serve the archangels in Heaven and fight against the demonic reapers alongside the Preliator. Some of them choose to undertake difficult tasks, such as protecting divine relics, and are fully committed to their duties.

Types of Angelic Reapers

Angelic Vir reapers, because they are not borne from the wicked or the damned, are not created in monstrous forms like the demonic reapers. The angelic Vir resemble the angels they are descended from and have shape-shifting abilities, such as being able to grow wings.

5

Demonic Reapers

Demonic reapers are descendants of the offspring of Fallen angels. The function of the demonic reapers is to collect souls by killing and devouring human beings and taking control over the victim's soul. These harvested souls are then sent to Hell where they rebuild Lucifer's army of the damned with the intention of unleashing it upon Earth and Heaven, igniting the Second War and possibly the end of the world.

Types of Demonic Reapers

Vir

The most powerful of demonic reapers. Their bodies have the ability to shape-shift and appear human if they desire. They can grow wings, talons, horns, and other inhuman aspects, which also can be used as weapons.

Nycterid

An elusive and powerful species. They are the largest type of reaper and are very dinosauric and hairless in appearance. They have long necks and skeletal apelike faces with snouts filled with jagged teeth. Their forelimbs are gigantic membranous wings with claws on the thumb joints. The hind legs are powerful and clawed, and their tails are long, lightly furred, and very adept at bashing and thrashing. They are blind and rely on their other senses in battle.

Ursid

The bearlike Ursids are aggressive and rely more on brute strength than speed. Their bodies are the size of pickup trucks, their heads are blocky and bulky, and their saber teeth and claws are strong enough to tear through metal.

Lupine
The wolflike Lupines are speedy and as large as the average sedan. They have thick fur and gnarled teeth. They often take care of minor tasks for more powerful reapers.

Leonine
The Leonine reapers are rare and resemble maned, saber-toothed leopards. They move lightning fast and rely on razor-sharp teeth and claws in battle.

Other Creatures and Artifacts

Creatures

Nephilim

A Nephil is the unnatural offspring of a Grigori male and a human female. These creatures were so gigantic in size and violent in nature that God was forced to flood the Earth to wipe them out. They are believed to be extinct.

Psychics

Some humans have supernatural abilities that allow them to enter the Grim and see reapers, have the gift of foresight, and sense energies. Some psychics will choose to ally with the angelic reapers and fight with them. Demonic reapers will usually kill any psychic they come across, and some even specialize in hunting psychics.

Artifacts

The Grimoire

The Grimoire is an ancient book written by and belonging to the Grigori lord Antares. The book contains every angelic spell and ritual in existence, including the secrets of divine medicine.

Relics

Relics are powerful items with a connection to either the divine or the damned. They have a variety of uses during spells, and some have the ability to give corporeal form to an angel or a Fallen in the mortal realm.

Tattoos

Ink infused in magic can be tattooed onto skin to cast a spell on the wearer. If the proper angelic symbols are used, the tattoos can protect, give power to, or even enslave the wearer by binding his or her power.

A Prequel Scene to

Angelfire

From Will's Point of View:
"Perish Song"

THE LAST TIME I HELD HER IN MY ARMS WAS THE
last time she died.

I feared for her, more afraid for her life than my own,
because she was all that mattered. I could be replaced—
would be replaced—but she was most precious in all the
world. She was the only one who could save it.

I shut my eyes tight and clenched my jaw, determined
not to make a cry of pain. That would only encourage them.
It would take a lot of damage to kill me, but that wasn't their
goal. Reapers were patient, for they had eternity to do whatever they desired, and many loved to spill blood just to watch
it run.

One of them grabbed a fistful of my hair and yanked me

upright so that his yellow eyes could drive into mine. His mouth slid wide to show multiple rows of jagged needle teeth.

"For a moment I thought you had passed out," Geir said as he crouched in front of me. "That would have been disappointing."

If the chains weren't so tight around my arms, I'd have punched his face so hard those shark teeth would have shot out the back of his head. I jerked against the metal to its limits, but halted brutally with Geir's throat just out of reach. I was too weakened to break free of the chains and of the angelic spell cast into the pentagram drawn on the ground around me. My body would heal and then they would begin again, tearing me up until I was near death only to let me heal so they could start all over. I didn't know how long I'd been in this barn. I didn't know if it was night or day. And I didn't know if she was still alive.

I had to return to her. The reaper struck my face and blood ran over my eyes. I had to return to her.

He stopped after some time, releasing me roughly, but I was so numb from agony that it made little difference whether he was torturing me or not. The closer I was to death, the less it hurt. My chest heaved painfully in order to breathe. One of my lungs had collapsed and its desperation to heal was even more excruciating than the initial blow that had damaged it. When my eyes were shut, I saw her face. When I opened them, blinking through blood, I saw Geir's face. Ivar stood behind him, talking to Cadan. He wrapped a hand around her cheek tenderly for a moment before leaving the barn with her. Their show of affection for one another was alien, so untrue to their natures. They were incapable of love. They didn't even know the meaning of the word.

My teeth ground together as my heartbeat quickened with rage. Bastian had returned. He appeared from the Grim with a flash of black hair and shadows of power that made my skin crawl. I shivered and sank deeper on my knees, my knuckles dragging to the dirt floor. Geir moved aside as Bastian approached, the lesser reaper bowing out submissively.

Bastian's icy indigo gaze met mine with satisfied amusement. "Hello, William. Did you miss me?"

"What took you so long?" I asked hoarsely, looking up into his face. "Geir hits like a bitch."

The yellow-eyed reaper hissed and moved to strike me.

"Enough," Bastian said in a low, calm voice. He didn't need to shout for his thugs to obey. Often, one look was more than enough to send them cowering.

It was painful straining to see Bastian's face above me, waiting for him to start torturing me again.

"I'm impressed you haven't lost your spirit, William," he said. "By now I thought you'd be begging for death, but I have to admit I'm pleased. I have a gift for you. He should be here soon."

My mind raced as my pulse pounded in my head. I needed to eat in order to heal and escape and return to her. Hunger made my brain numb, but I couldn't resort to what they would do to heal. I wasn't one of them.

I sensed the arrival of another reaper and a moment later, Ragnuk appeared through the barn door, his enormous bear-like shape silhouetted in the dim light. He was the largest Ursid reaper I had ever known—and one of the oldest. He lumbered in awkwardly, as if one leg was lame.

When I saw the small form he carried in his jaws, my soul died.

Her. His teeth clamped down on her body, puncturing her skin. Her clothes were drenched with dried blood, some of it still running. Her eyes were closed. I could see her, but I couldn't feel her. She wasn't there inside that body anymore. She was dead.

Ragnuk brought her closer, and underneath all of that blood I could smell her perfume. Her scent, the same scent of skin and jasmine I had known for centuries. She always smelled like jasmine. The torn up trousers and shirt hanging off her made her seem even smaller and more fragile. Her hair, like cherries and dark chocolate, was matted and thickly tangled with dried cruor.

He dropped her limp form to the ground in front of me and I couldn't breathe. I couldn't even scream. I could only stare at her. It felt like a sledgehammer pounded into my chest over and over each time my heart took a beat.

I had promised her I would protect her and I had let her die alone. She was all that mattered to me, all that I loved, and I had failed her again. Not again. My lips formed the shape of those two words, but my voice wouldn't work.

Not again.

"Want a bite?" Ragnuk sneered. I didn't look up at him, but I felt his triumphant black eyes on me. "She tastes like candy."

I didn't respond. The hammering in my chest dragged me more heavily to the floor and my mouth opened to let out a silent scream as my eyes squeezed shut and my head hung low.

"What's the matter, Guardian?" Geir rasped close to my ear. "Does seeing your beloved's corpse finally shut your big mouth up?"

She would come back. She would come back. I repeated that over and over in my head, desperate to drown out the reapers' words.

With a furious roar I summoned all the power I had left in me and let it explode, the flash of smoky shadows drowning my vision for a moment. I raised my fist over my head and brought it down, slamming it into the dirt floor with all of my strength. The earth roiled and groaned, and a crack rocketed through the pentagram, shattering it, uplifting rock and soil and spreading to the farthest edge of the barn. The walls shivered and wheezed and dust from the rafters above clouded the air. Wood cracked apart and metal equipment whined. I heaved against my chains, my power unbound at last, and the metal snapped like brittle bones.

I swung the loose chain through the air and it wrapped

around Geir's throat. I yanked, dragging him down to me, and my fist pounded into his temple and the other side of his face smashed into the dirt. I didn't stop to admire the blood oozing from his mouth as he lay at my feet. I called my sword into my hand and swept it up, but Ragnuk ducked to the side as I surged past him. My attack on Geir destroyed any chance to truly surprise Ragnuk. The blade sliced deep through the Ursid reaper's neck, shoulder, and side, grinding across his ribcage and spraying blood. The strike wasn't lethal, but the tremendous roar shattering my ears assured me that it had hurt him like hell. Already wounded from his earlier battle, Ragnuk staggered and hit the ground as I rushed toward Bastian with my sword high.

He vanished from my sight and reappeared directly in front of my face, his bright eyes drilling into mine. His palm slammed into my chest with a blast of his power and the force sent me soaring backward through the air. My body crashed through the barn wall and I landed on the grass outside with a rush of excruciating pain as all the air expelled from my lungs. Wood and other debris settled on and around me.

I lay there for just a moment, blinking my mind back into the present until I could breathe again. My sword was still in my hand and I sat up and looked around. Bastian was climbing through the hole my body had made high up in the barn's wall and then he dropped to the ground, his white wings high over his head. He straightened and those wings vanished back into himself and he stepped toward me. I scrambled to my feet, my body aching to fight him, to tear him apart the way *she* had been torn apart, but my mind was screaming at me to run. I wasn't strong enough to kill Bastian, and if I were to stay, he would destroy me. If I died here tonight, I wouldn't be able to protect her when she returned. Perhaps another Guardian would do a better job than I, but I didn't trust any of them. It had to be me. I loved her. I had to be here when she returned, and I had to protect her better than I ever had before. I wouldn't let her die again.

I forced back my instinct to fight and avenge her death, and I took my first step back, away from Bastian. Then I relinquished my sword and turned, compelling my body to move faster than I'd ever run in my life, to get away from the reapers, to escape, to ensure that I would survive until her return.

She would come back, and I would find her. I would be waiting. I would wait forever.

A first look at

Wings of the Wicked

I HIT THE FREEZING PAVEMENT ON MY BACK, AND the air rushed from my lungs. I lay there for only a few moments, but long enough for a few snowflakes to settle on my face. The pain in my back shot in waves down to my toes and back up through my skull. That thick, musty smell of reaper fur and brimstone smothered me as the ursid reaper's throaty growl shook the ground and rattled my ears. I wondered why she hadn't tried to bite my face off already—she was certainly close enough to do it. I opened one eye to see that she had stopped to watch my Guardian, Will, who was battling her companion a few yards down the alley.

Dragging myself to my feet, I looked up to see the reaper turn back toward me, hate spilling over her ugly face.

I tightened my grip on both my sickle-shaped Khopesh swords, and they burst into angelfire, the bright white flames licking up the blades. The light danced across the reaper's features, the sharp highlights and shadows making her appear even more like the Hellspawn that she was.

"It's going to hurt so bad when I pay you back for that," I promised, my voice ragged with pain.

"I think not." Her black lips pulled back, revealing saber canines as long as my forearm. She snapped her jaws and laughed, grinding her talons into the pavement. "I'm shocked you're back on your feet after that one, Preliator," she sneered.

I didn't know how the reapers made that purring growl sound whenever they said my title aloud, but it never failed to make the hair on the back of my neck stand up. I took a deep breath, shaking off the malice in her voice. "Don't get too excited. I've been hit harder than that by things a lot worse than you."

The reaper's lips curved into a grotesque smile, baring as much of her giant teeth as possible. She rolled her shoulders like a cat, crouching on her haunches, ready to spring. I stepped back on my heel, my gaze locked on her empty black shark eyes.

She launched herself into the air, claws spread wide. I dropped to the ground, spun on the slick pavement, and swung my sickle-shaped blades with precision through the air—and through flesh. The reaper's body turned into a fireball before it hit the ground, and her burning head helicoptered through the air over me. In moments, nothing was left of her but ashes.

I took a deep breath and rose just in time to see Will plunge his sword into the side of the second reaper's chest. He pulled his blade back out and the reaper fell dead, its skin hardening to stone instead of bursting into flames, which was something only my angelfire caused.

Will came to me, trying to catch his breath, and he thumbed my cheek and lifted my chin. I'd gotten used to him inspecting me for injuries. His touch was businesslike at first, but when he was satisfied that I hadn't been hurt too badly, his hands became softer. "Are you okay?"

I nodded and let my angelfire die. "Yeah. She hit me with just about everything she had and I landed pretty hard, but nothing broke. Doesn't it seem like more and more of them are traveling in packs these days?"

His lips tightened for a moment, hardness crossing over his handsome features. "It does. You shouldn't have let her get such a good hit."

I rolled my eyes. "Yeah, sure thing there, Batman. I'll bring a bazooka next time. Screw these swords. Can we call it a night?" My entire body ached like I'd been hit by a van—a van-sized reaper, to be exact.

Before he could answer, something landed just behind him, shaking the earth beneath us. Will spun around and stood over me like a shield. A creature—a reaper even bigger than an ursid, covered in dark leathery skin—had landed in the street. The skin of its face stretched tight over jutting bone, and its long, gnarled snout was filled with jagged, yellowed teeth. Its eyes were sickly, pale, glazed-over orbs staring unfocused right through us, and wide ears topped its skull. Instead of true arms, bones were stretched into gigantic, membranous wings like a bat's, with foot-long, hooked claws that gouged the pavement for support. Its hind legs were thick with muscle, and it had a long, lizardlike spiked tail that swayed back and forth like that of a cat whose eyes had spied a bird within reach—only this reaper's eyes saw nothing.

My lips quivered and I took a frightened step back. "What the hell is that?"

"Nycterid" was all Will said as his hand tightened around his sword. "That's Orek, one of the oldest and strongest of them."

And then two more landed behind the first. My stomach leaped into my throat as I gaped in horror up at the towering monsters. There was no way we could fight all three of them at once. I wasn't even sure I could fight *one* of them.

"Step aside, Guardian," Orek rumbled in a deep voice, his long jaws snapping, forked tongue flicking as he spoke human words. His glossy pale eyes stared unseeingly and made what felt like worms crawl through my stomach.

Will straightened and said nothing.

"So be it." Orek craned his long neck toward one of his companions. "Take her, Jabur."

In a flash, Orek lurched forward and slammed a wing

into Will, sending him soaring through the air. The nycterid chugged toward Will and snapped his jaws like a crocodile. Will pounded his fists into Orek's head as the jaws crunched air, questing for soft flesh. Orek's tail swung around and smashed into Will's body, sending him flying again across the alley and into the wall of the nearest building, crushing brick. He hit the ground with a low groan, and Orek descended on him.

I bolted forward to help Will, but something massive slammed into me before I could react, knocking my swords out of my hands and to the ground. The other nycterid, Jabur, grabbed me with the talons of his hind limbs. His gigantic wings spread, and he took off with me in his clutches.

"Will!" I screamed, wildly reaching for him. I beat and clawed at the reaper's leathery skin, but he ignored me as we flew up and away. Panic sent shock waves through my body as I twisted and flailed, desperate to get away. The alley was disappearing far below me.

Will broke free from Orek, tearing away from claws and gnashing teeth, and he dived beneath beating wings.

"Ellie!" He ran down the street, his ivory wings spreading from his back, and he jumped into the air after me, sword in hand. He was lighter and faster than the nycterid, and when he reached us, he swung his sword, but Jabur's other foot collided with Will's chest, sending him careening downward. The wind rushed violently into my face like an arctic hurricane, and I struggled to see where Will had fallen, my heart pounding in my ears. I cried his name again, but I couldn't catch sight of him. Jabur lurched suddenly, dropping several feet in the air, and my stomach jerked into my throat before we steadied again. I twisted my head to see Will's wings stretched out above Jabur. The nycterid swung his body left and right, trying to shake Will off. Jabur's long snout crunched his crooked teeth together, and he made a dragonlike hiss.

The nycterid jerked into a barrel roll, and Will slid free. He dropped through the air until he was beneath us. His wings beat hard and he flew up ahead of Jabur. He slashed his sword down with a furious cry, slicing the blade through Jabur's neck. The reaper's head fell away and vanished. The rest of his body slowed its flight as it hardened into rock.

And then I fell, still trapped in the clutches of the stone reaper. I plummeted much faster than we'd risen, the immense weight of the giant reaper's stone body hurling us both like a rocket. I screamed until I was nearly deaf from the sound of my own voice and the wind rushing into my face. I beat at the rock leg, trying to break free, and I saw Will diving past me like a falcon. He swung his body, and then he was in front of me, his sword gone and his hands freed.

"Get me out of here!" I shrieked, tugging my trapped body uselessly.

Will pounded his fist over and over again on the stone limb. I stared past him at the rapidly approaching street below. The limb cracked at last, and Will threw it into the air and kicked the body away from me. His arms wrapped around me, but we didn't stop falling. He swore as he beat his wings, futilely trying to catch us in the air, but we were falling too fast. I held back a scream of terror as we plunged toward the earth. At the last moment, Will flipped us in mid-air so that he was below me and I stared into the blinding green blaze of his eyes.

Then we hit—Will's back cracked pavement beneath us as I buried my face in his chest. We lay frozen, clinging to each other, his arms still tight around me as if he thought I'd keep falling if he let me go. At last I lifted my head and looked into his face, my body shaking violently. His eyes were closed and he was breathing haggardly, his chest rising and falling dramatically under my body. His wings were splayed flat out on the ground, but they looked unharmed. The falling sensation still sickened my gut as I looked around in disbelief and found the smashed remains of the nycterid littering the area around us.

"Are you okay?" Will asked up at me, his warm breath on my cheek.

I nodded, taking long, slow breaths to put myself back together, my hands still clutching him. I needed my head in the game, but I didn't want to let go of Will.

I climbed off him weakly, my legs trembling on solid ground, and I looked around for my fallen swords. I picked them up, and the angelfire sparked once again. The two remaining nycterids loomed over us. My body screamed at me, begging me to run, but I had to stay and fight.

Orek took a step toward me, dipping his head and curling his lips back into a freakish smile. The talons on his wings grabbed at the pavement, hooking into cracks. "We were not supposed to lose one of our own."

"Sorry, but I always leave a body count," I said, tightening my grip on my swords.

Orek laughed, sending splinters of ice through me.

A form dropped between us and I stepped back on my heel. It was one of the vir reapers, like Will. This one's back was to me, and his sparrow brown wings folded behind him. Another reaper descended—a girl—and she landed facing me. Her wings, the feathers dark silver like pencil lead, spread wide and gave a shudder. Blue-black hair fell around her shoulders, and she stared at me with a hardened gaze. I didn't think I'd ever seen anyone so terrifyingly beautiful. She looked from Will to me and back again.

For a moment, I felt like I was still plunging through the air. *More* of them? Had half of the demonic reapers in Detroit been sent to kill me tonight?

The girl's eyes brightened to an iridescent blue-violet, and she held out her hands. I sucked in a sickened gasp as her fingernails all lengthened into horrible foot-long talons made of pale bone. If I had to fight her, I'd have to chop off her hands before things got too serious.

"What is this?" Orek hissed, backing away. "You called for reinforcements?"

26

Weren't the new reapers demonic? I took a step toward Will, just to feel his comforting presence.

"We didn't anticipate this," Orek's remaining companion growled in a strangely feminine voice.

Orek snarled. "Come, Eki. We'll return when we have a greater advantage."

The two nycterids spread their massive wings and took to the air like a pair of misplaced dinosaurs. But I couldn't breathe a sigh of relief that they were gone. I raised my swords to the mysterious newcomers, prepared to keep fighting.